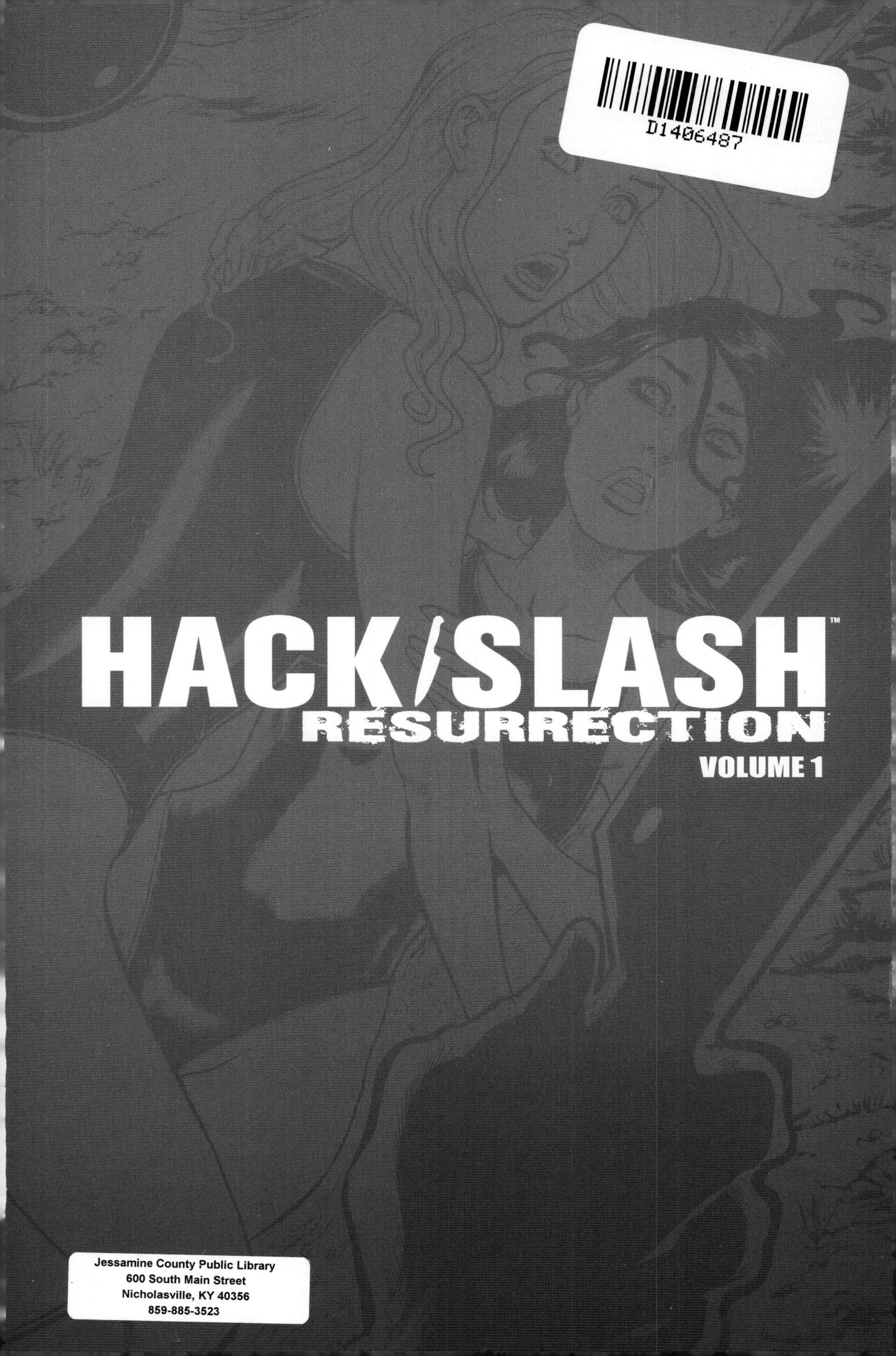

HACK/SLASH

RESURRECTION

VOLUME 1

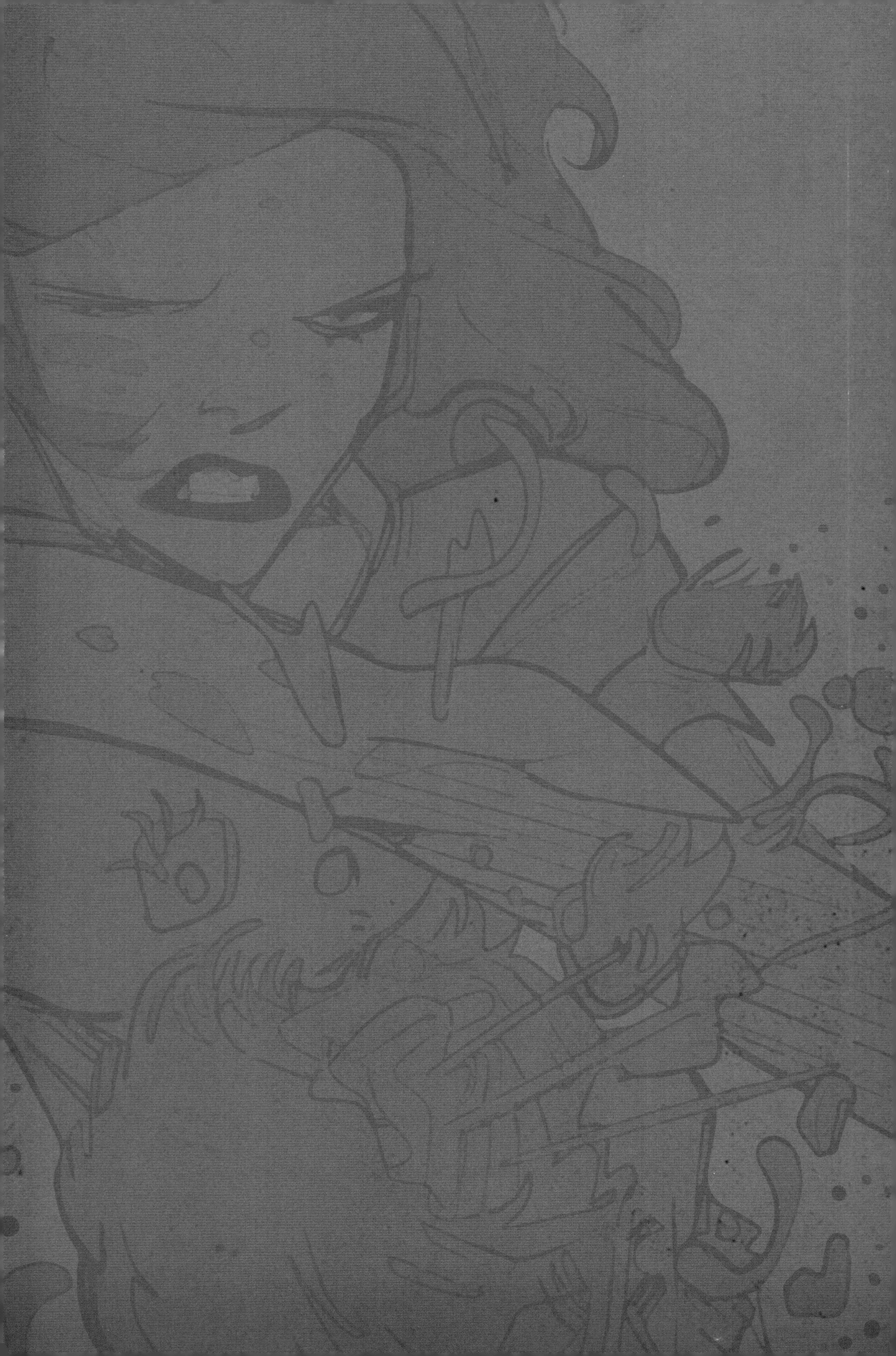

A TIM SEELEY / STEFANO CASELLI PRODUCTION

Written by **TINI HOWARD**

Art by **CELOR**

Colors by **K. MICHAEL RUSSELL**

Lettering by **CRANK!**

Production by **RYAN BREWER**

Edits by **TIM SEELEY**

IMAGE COMICS, INC.

Robert Kirkman: Chief Operating Officer • Erik Larsen: Chief Financial Officer • Todd McFarlane: President • Marc Silvestri: Chief Executive Officer • Jim Valentino: Vice President • Eric Stephenson: Publisher / Chief Creative Officer • Corey Hart: Director of Sales • Jeff Boison: Director of Publishing Planning & Book Trade Sales • Chris Ross: Director of Digital Sales • Jeff Stang: Director of Specialty Sales • Kat Salazar: Director of PR & Marketing • Drew Gill: Art Director • Heather Doornink: Production Director • Nicole Lapalme: Controller

IMAGECOMICS.COM

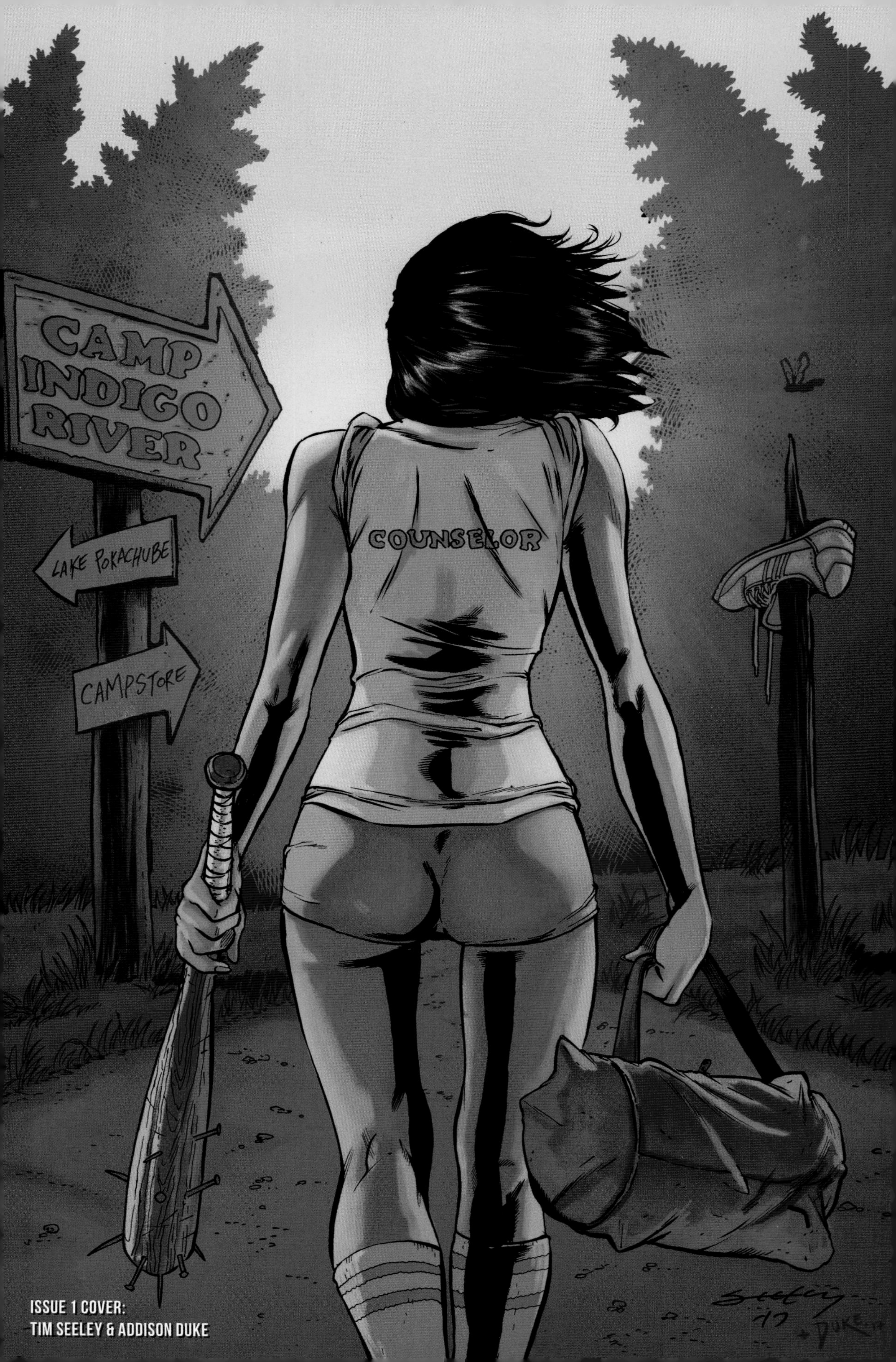
CAMP INDIGO RIVER
LAKE POKACHUBE
CAMPSTORE
COUNSELOR

ISSUE 1 COVER:
TIM SEELEY & ADDISON DUKE

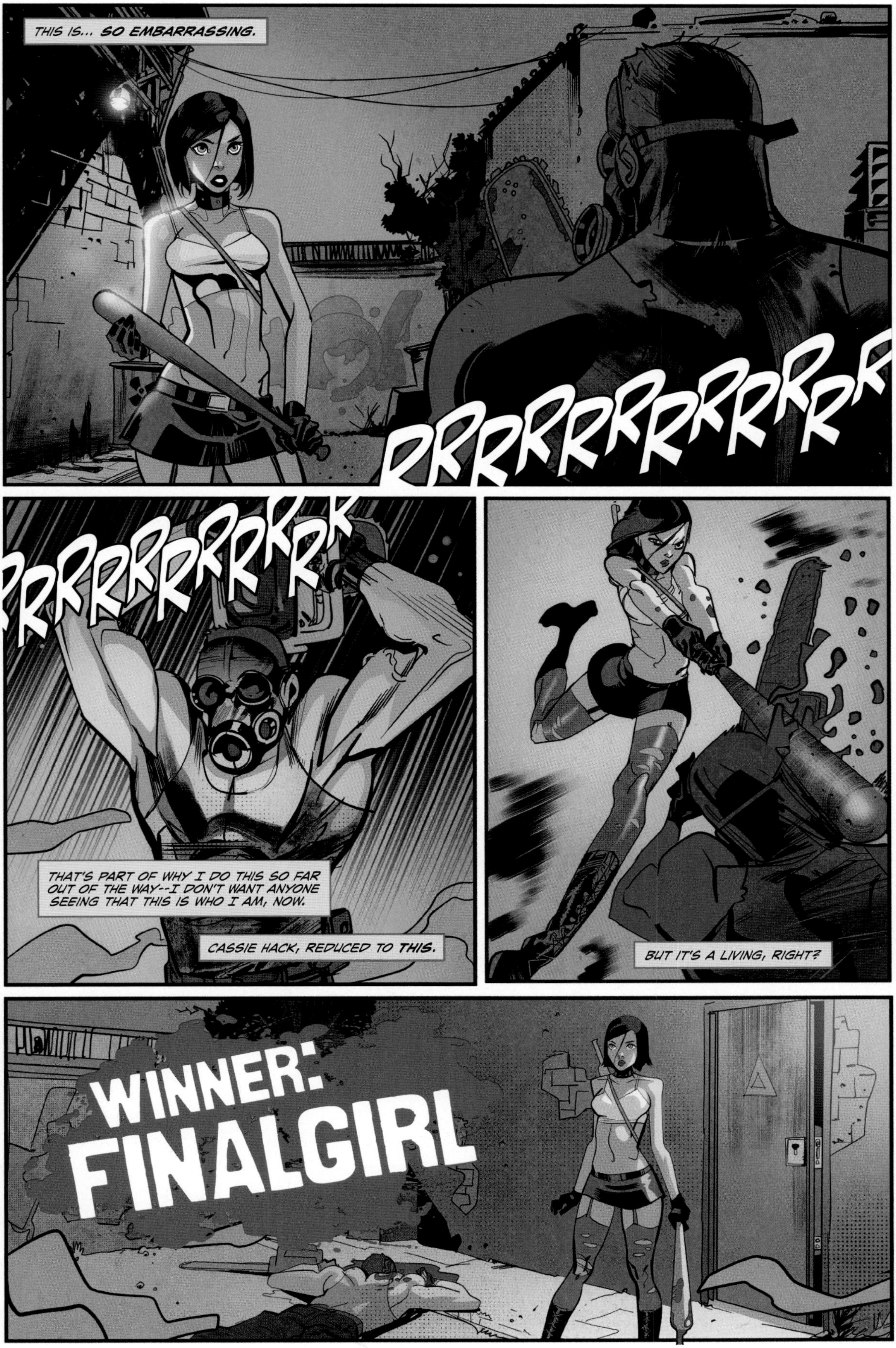
THIS IS... SO EMBARRASSING.
RRRRRRRRRRRRRR
RRRRRRRRRRRRRK
THAT'S PART OF WHY I DO THIS SO FAR OUT OF THE WAY--I DON'T WANT ANYONE SEEING THAT THIS IS WHO I AM, NOW.
CASSIE HACK, REDUCED TO THIS.
BUT IT'S A LIVING, RIGHT?
WINNER: FINALGIRL

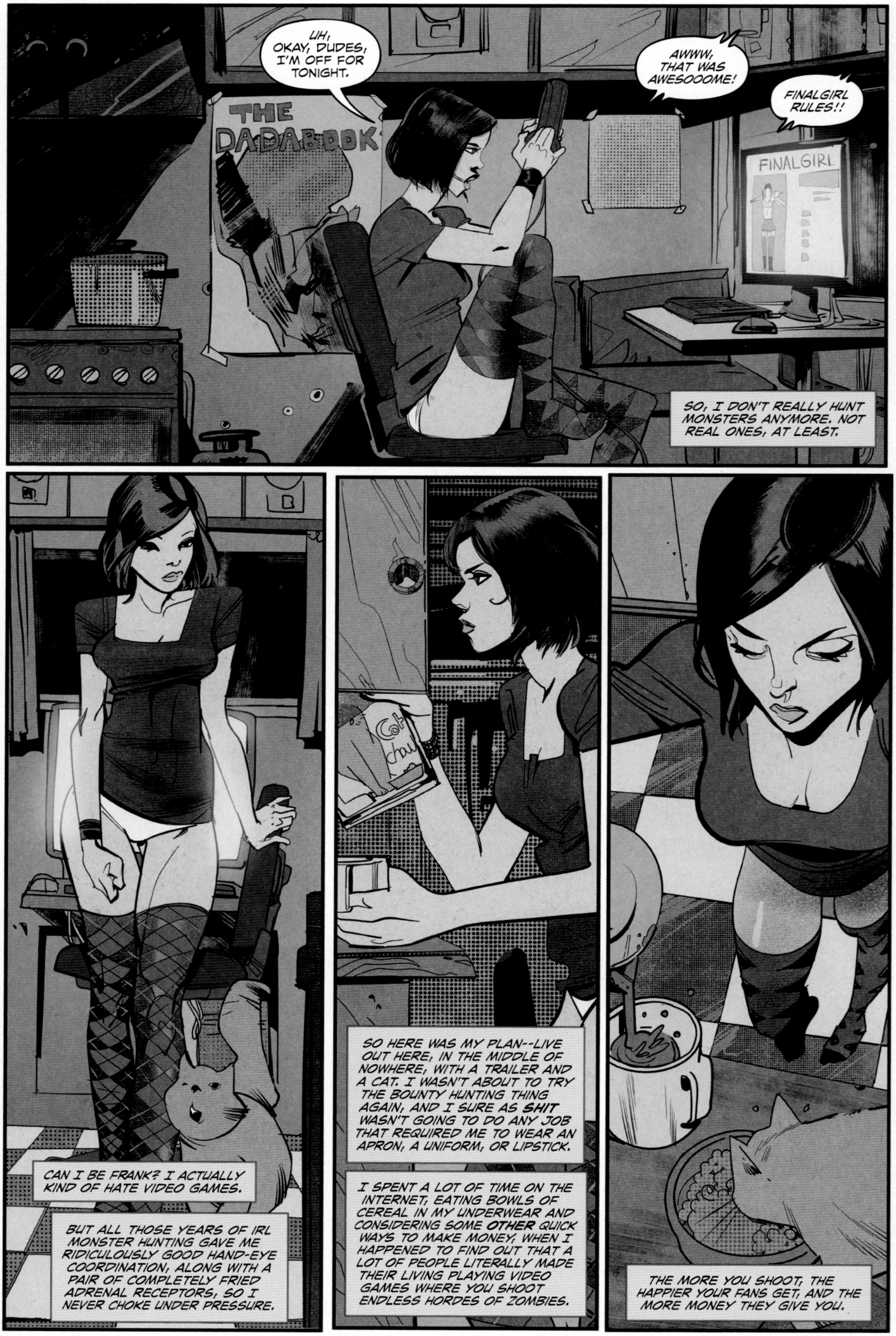
UH, OKAY, DUDES, I'M OFF FOR TONIGHT.
THE DADABOOK
AWWW, THAT WAS AWESOOOME!
FINALGIRL RULES!!
FINALGIRL
SO, I DON'T REALLY HUNT MONSTERS ANYMORE. NOT REAL ONES, AT LEAST.
CAN I BE FRANK? I ACTUALLY KIND OF HATE VIDEO GAMES.
BUT ALL THOSE YEARS OF IRL MONSTER HUNTING GAVE ME RIDICULOUSLY GOOD HAND-EYE COORDINATION, ALONG WITH A PAIR OF COMPLETELY FRIED ADRENAL RECEPTORS, SO I NEVER CHOKE UNDER PRESSURE.
SO HERE WAS MY PLAN--LIVE OUT HERE, IN THE MIDDLE OF NOWHERE, WITH A TRAILER AND A CAT. I WASN'T ABOUT TO TRY THE BOUNTY HUNTING THING AGAIN, AND I SURE AS SHIT WASN'T GOING TO DO ANY JOB THAT REQUIRED ME TO WEAR AN APRON, A UNIFORM, OR LIPSTICK.
I SPENT A LOT OF TIME ON THE INTERNET, EATING BOWLS OF CEREAL IN MY UNDERWEAR AND CONSIDERING SOME OTHER QUICK WAYS TO MAKE MONEY, WHEN I HAPPENED TO FIND OUT THAT A LOT OF PEOPLE LITERALLY MADE THEIR LIVING PLAYING VIDEO GAMES WHERE YOU SHOOT ENDLESS HORDES OF ZOMBIES.
THE MORE YOU SHOOT, THE HAPPIER YOUR FANS GET, AND THE MORE MONEY THEY GIVE YOU.

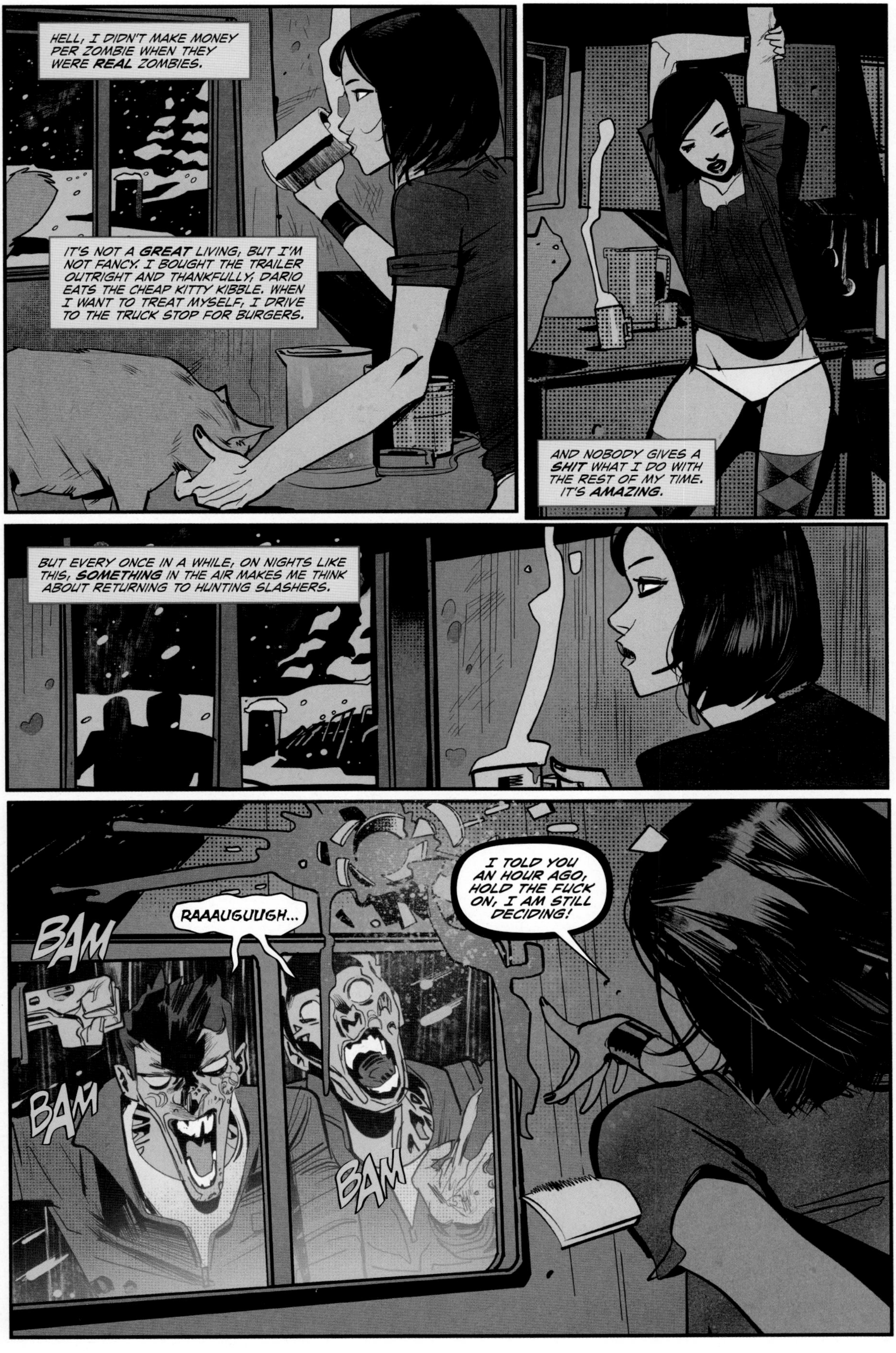
HELL, I DIDN'T MAKE MONEY PER ZOMBIE WHEN THEY WERE REAL ZOMBIES.
IT'S NOT A GREAT LIVING, BUT I'M NOT FANCY. I BOUGHT THE TRAILER OUTRIGHT AND THANKFULLY, DARIO EATS THE CHEAP KITTY KIBBLE. WHEN I WANT TO TREAT MYSELF, I DRIVE TO THE TRUCK STOP FOR BURGERS.
AND NOBODY GIVES A SHIT WHAT I DO WITH THE REST OF MY TIME. IT'S AMAZING.
BUT EVERY ONCE IN A WHILE, ON NIGHTS LIKE THIS, SOMETHING IN THE AIR MAKES ME THINK ABOUT RETURNING TO HUNTING SLASHERS.
BAM
RAAAUGUUGH...
I TOLD YOU AN HOUR AGO, HOLD THE FUCK ON, I AM STILL DECIDING!
BAM
BAM

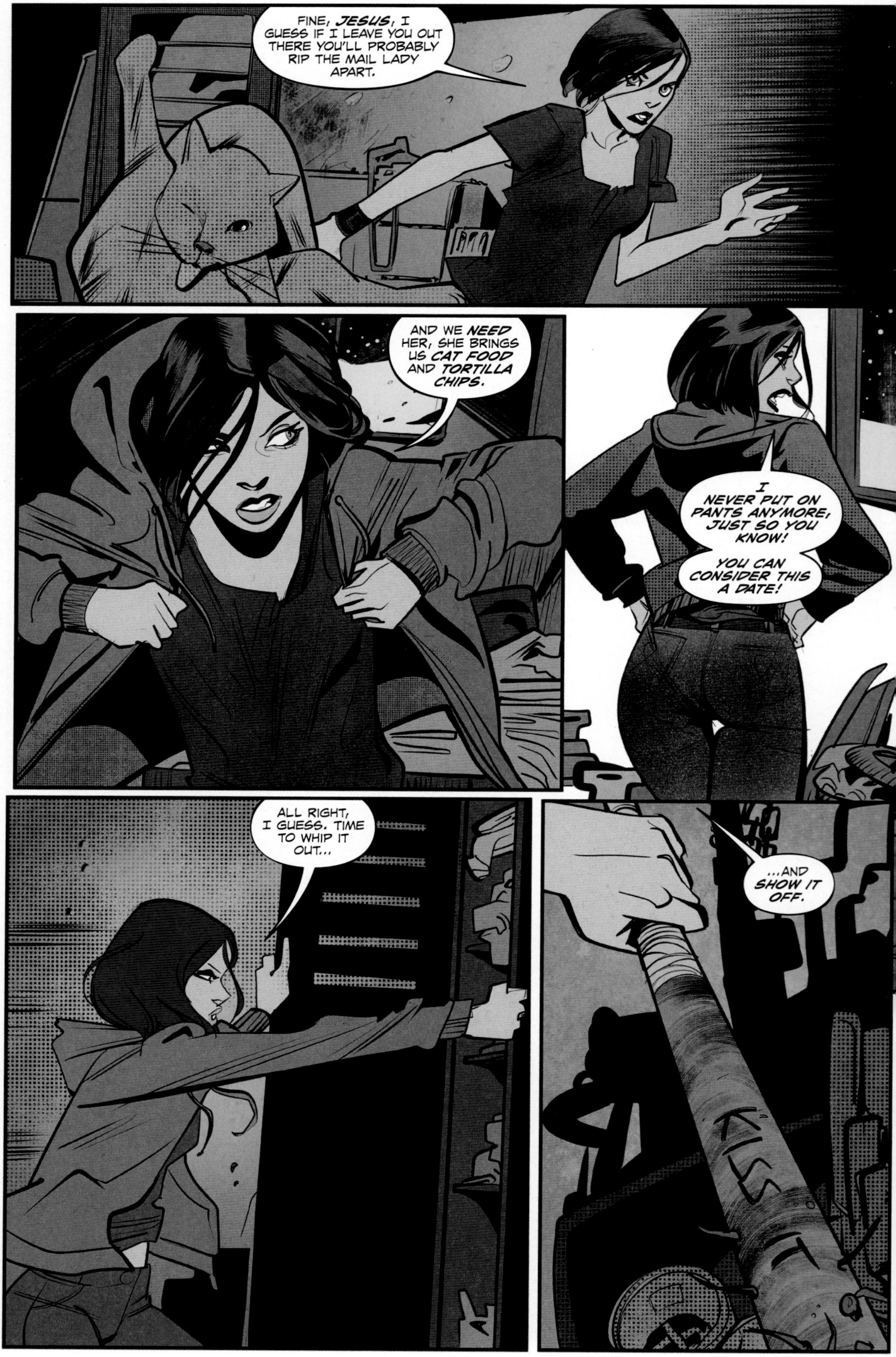
FINE, *JESUS*, I GUESS IF I LEAVE YOU OUT THERE YOU'LL PROBABLY RIP THE MAIL LADY APART.
AND WE *NEED* HER, SHE BRINGS US *CAT FOOD* AND *TORTILLA CHIPS*.
I NEVER PUT ON PANTS ANYMORE, JUST SO YOU KNOW!
YOU CAN CONSIDER THIS A DATE!
ALL RIGHT, I GUESS. TIME TO WHIP IT OUT...
...AND *SHOW IT OFF*.

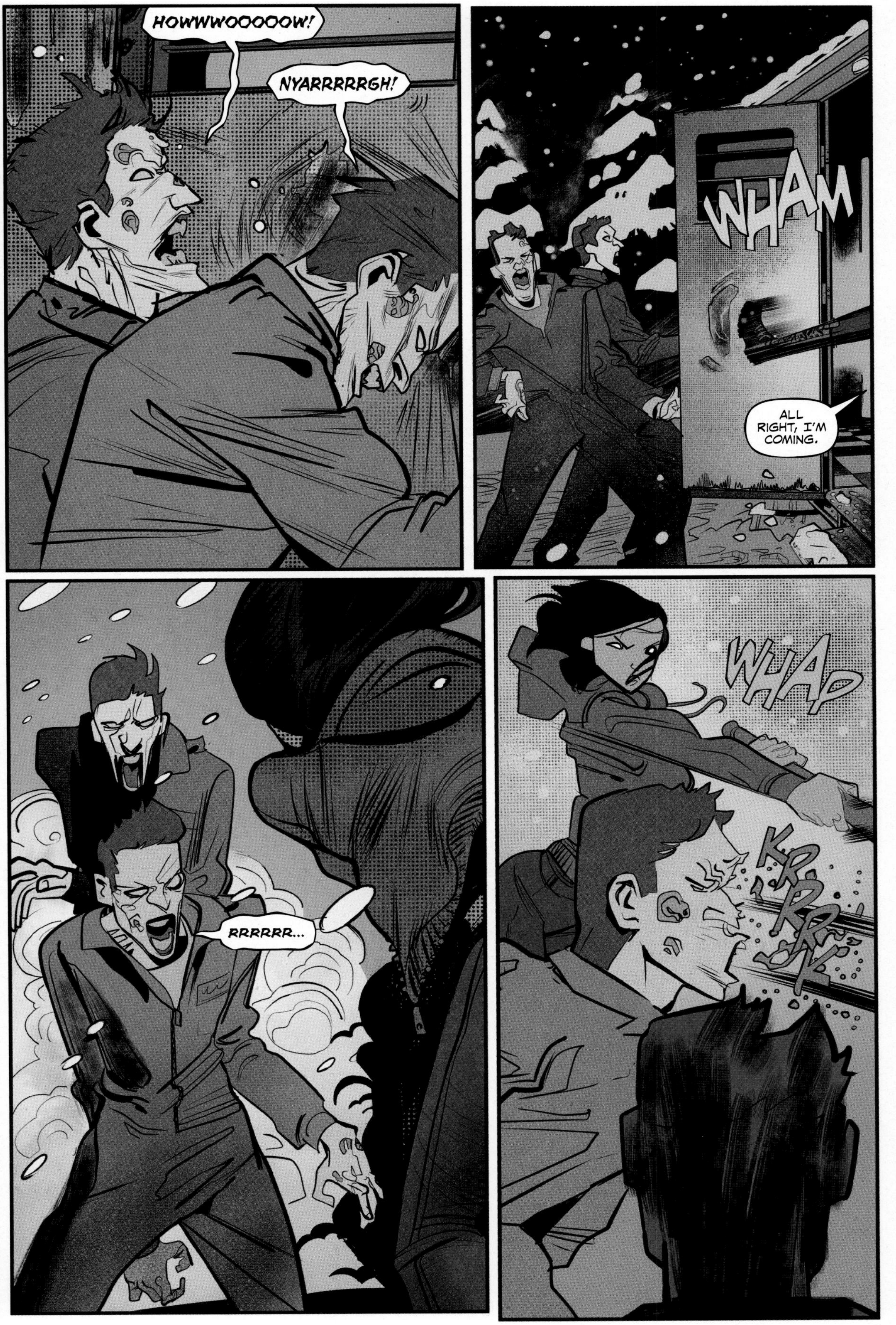
HOWWWOOOOOW!
NYARRRRRGH!
WHAM
ALL RIGHT, I'M COMING.
RRRRRR...
WHAP
KRRRK

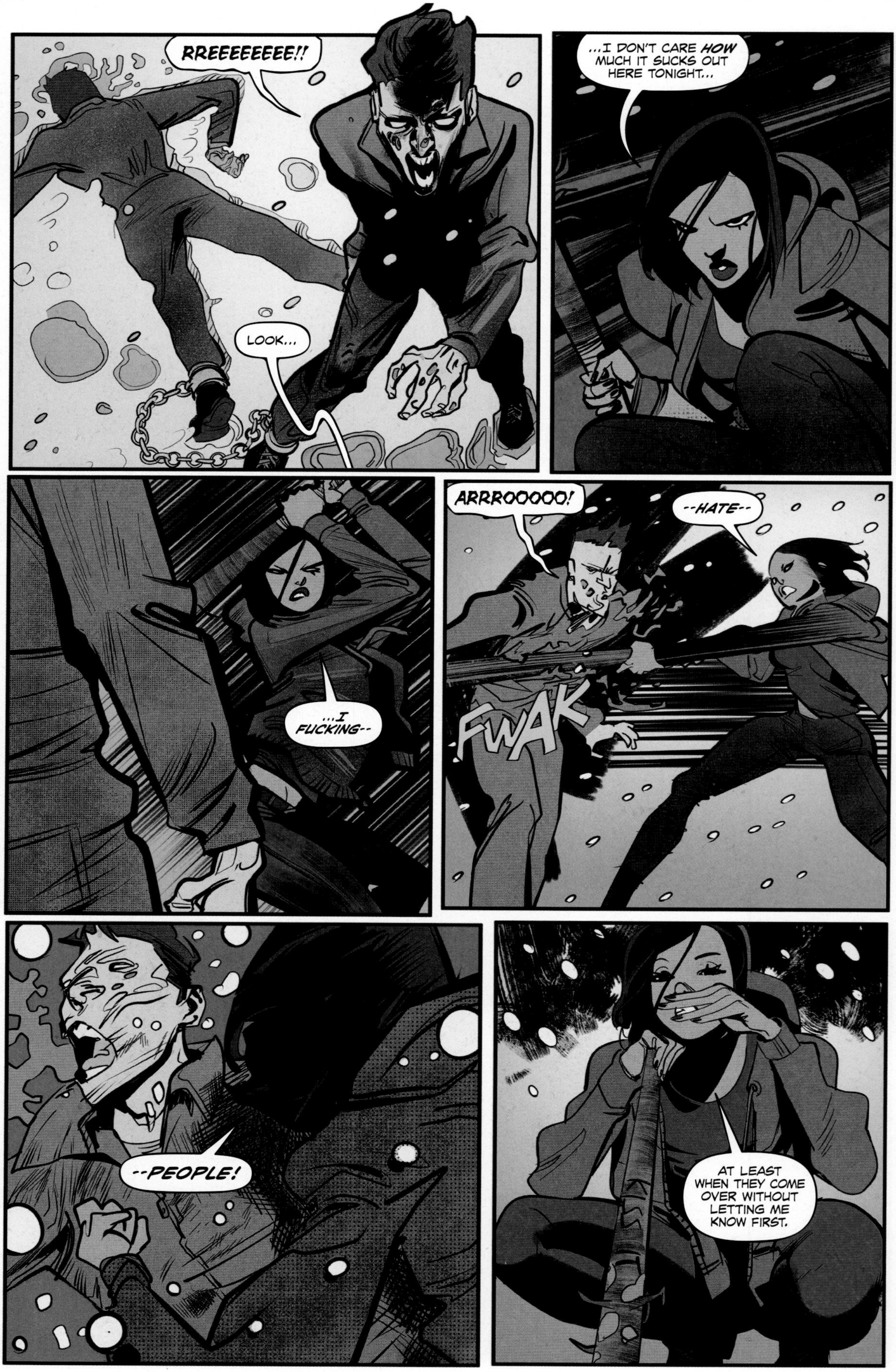
RREEEEEEEE!!
LOOK...
...I DON'T CARE HOW MUCH IT SUCKS OUT HERE TONIGHT...
...I FUCKING--
ARRROOOOO!
--HATE--
FWAK
--PEOPLE!
AT LEAST WHEN THEY COME OVER WITHOUT LETTING ME KNOW FIRST.

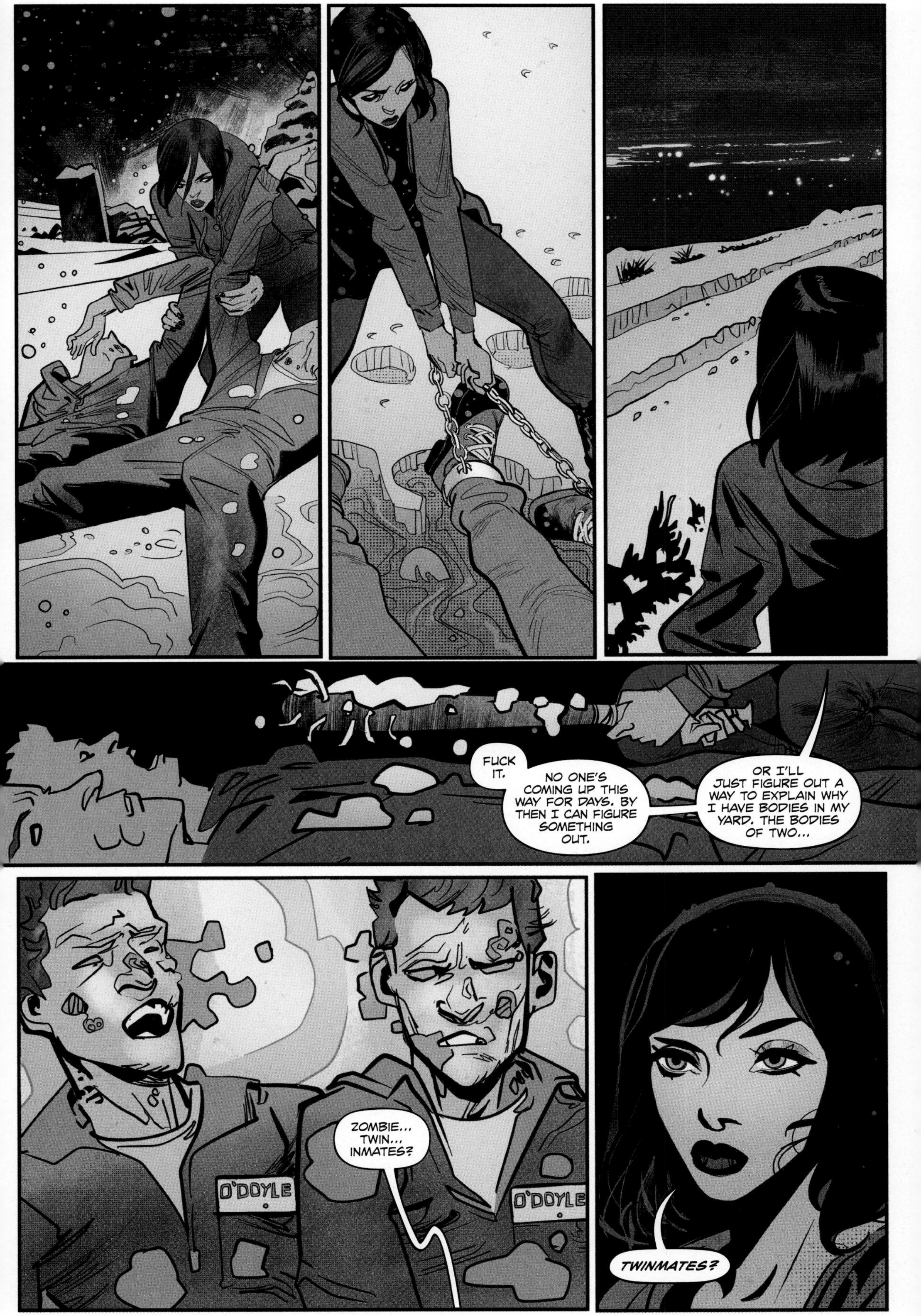
FUCK IT.
NO ONE'S COMING UP THIS WAY FOR DAYS. BY THEN I CAN FIGURE SOMETHING OUT.
OR I'LL JUST FIGURE OUT A WAY TO EXPLAIN WHY I HAVE BODIES IN MY YARD. THE BODIES OF TWO...
O'DOYLE
O'DOYLE
ZOMBIE... TWIN... INMATES?
TWINMATES?

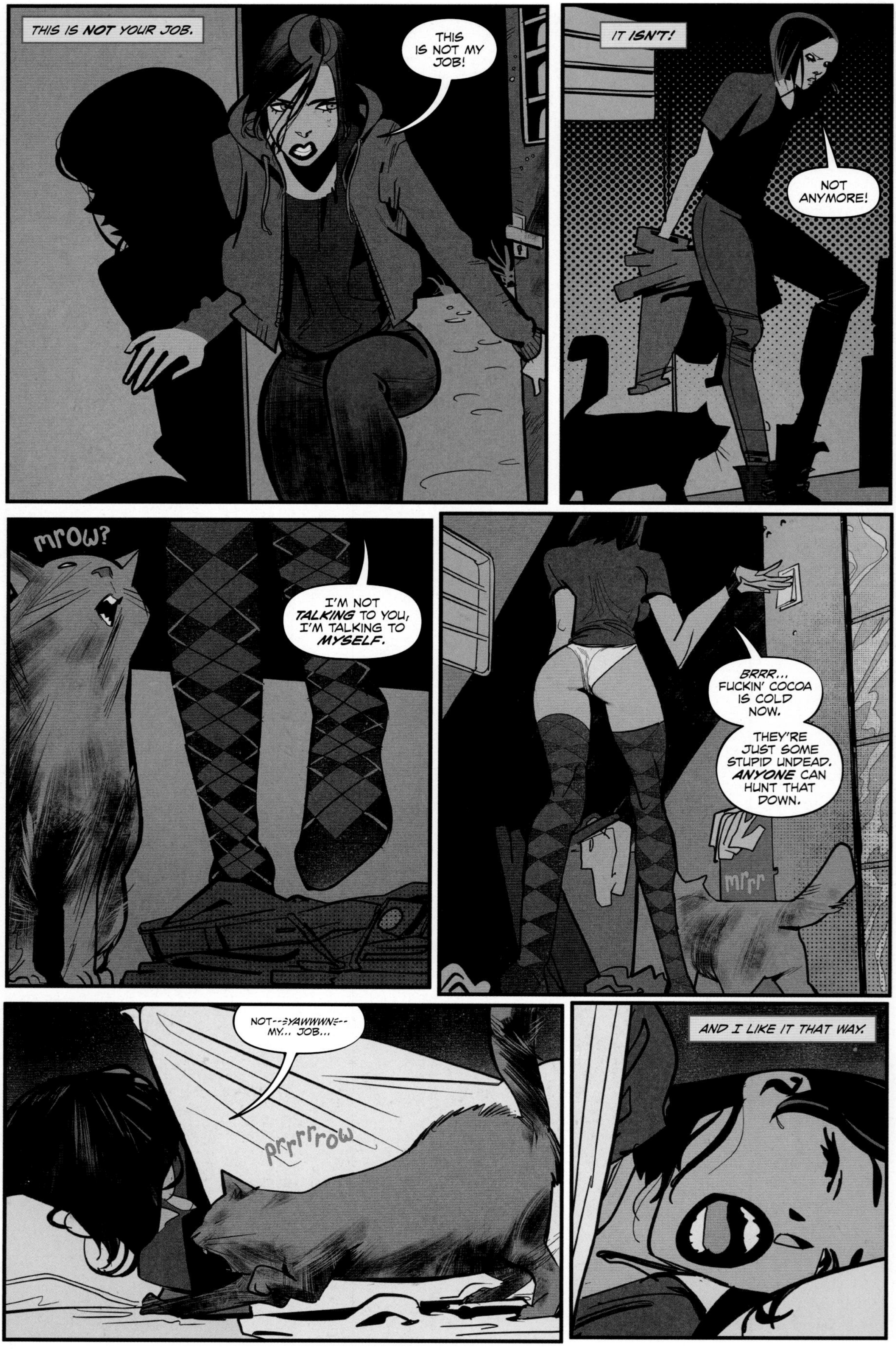
THIS IS NOT YOUR JOB.
THIS IS NOT MY JOB!
IT ISN'T!
NOT ANYMORE!
mrow?
I'M NOT TALKING TO YOU, I'M TALKING TO MYSELF.
BRRR... FUCKIN' COCOA IS COLD NOW.
THEY'RE JUST SOME STUPID UNDEAD. ANYONE CAN HUNT THAT DOWN.
mrrr
NOT--YAWWWN--MY... JOB...
prrrrow
AND I LIKE IT THAT WAY.

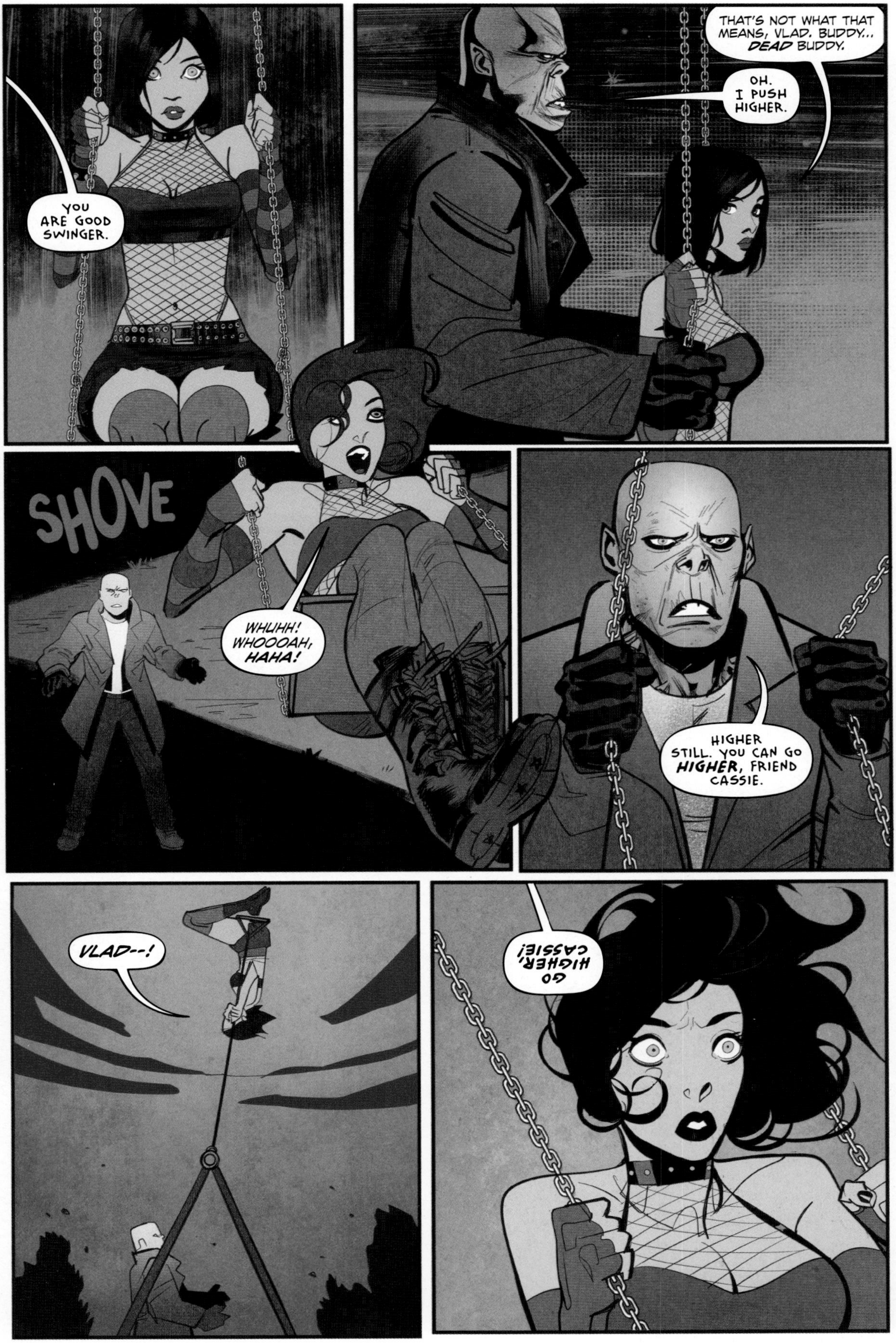
YOU ARE GOOD SWINGER.
THAT'S NOT WHAT THAT MEANS, VLAD. BUDDY... **DEAD** BUDDY.
OH. I PUSH HIGHER.
SHOVE
WHUHH! WHOOOAH, **HAHA!**
HIGHER STILL. YOU CAN GO **HIGHER**, FRIEND CASSIE.
VLAD--!
GO HIGHER, CASSIE!

OH NO.

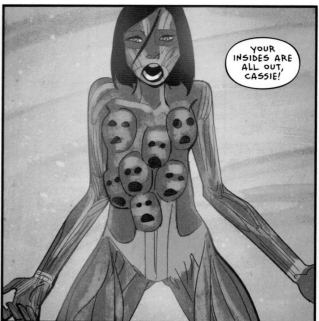

YOUR INSIDES ARE ALL OUT, CASSIE!

OO!

OOVEEDYAME SAY!

I CAN'T... UNDERSTAND YOU! ARE YOU TALKING... BACKWARDS?!

OOVIDYAME SAY POZDAY, FRIEND!

OOVIDYAME SAY POZDAY!

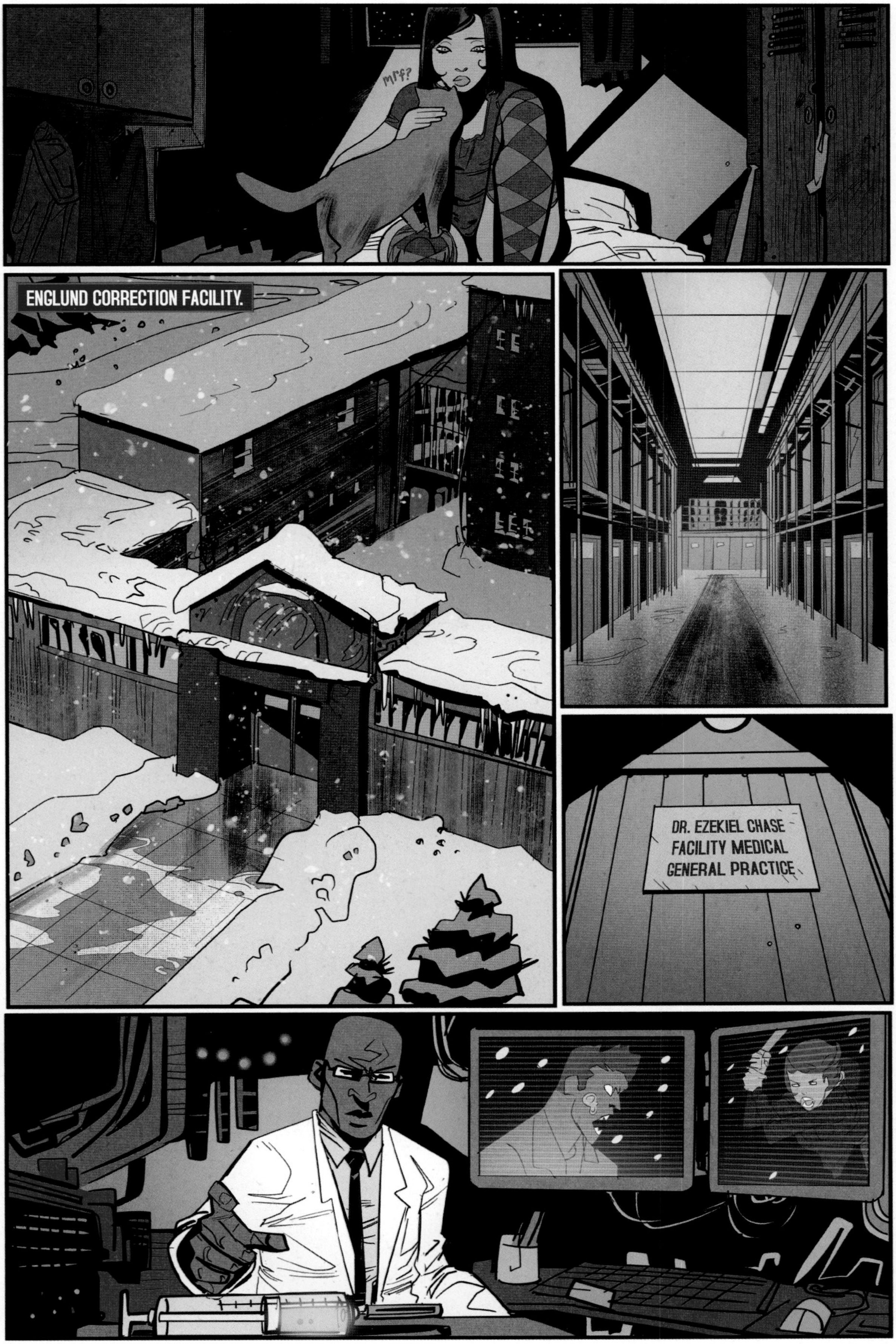
mrf?
ENGLUND CORRECTION FACILITY.
DR. EZEKIEL CHASE
FACILITY MEDICAL
GENERAL PRACTICE

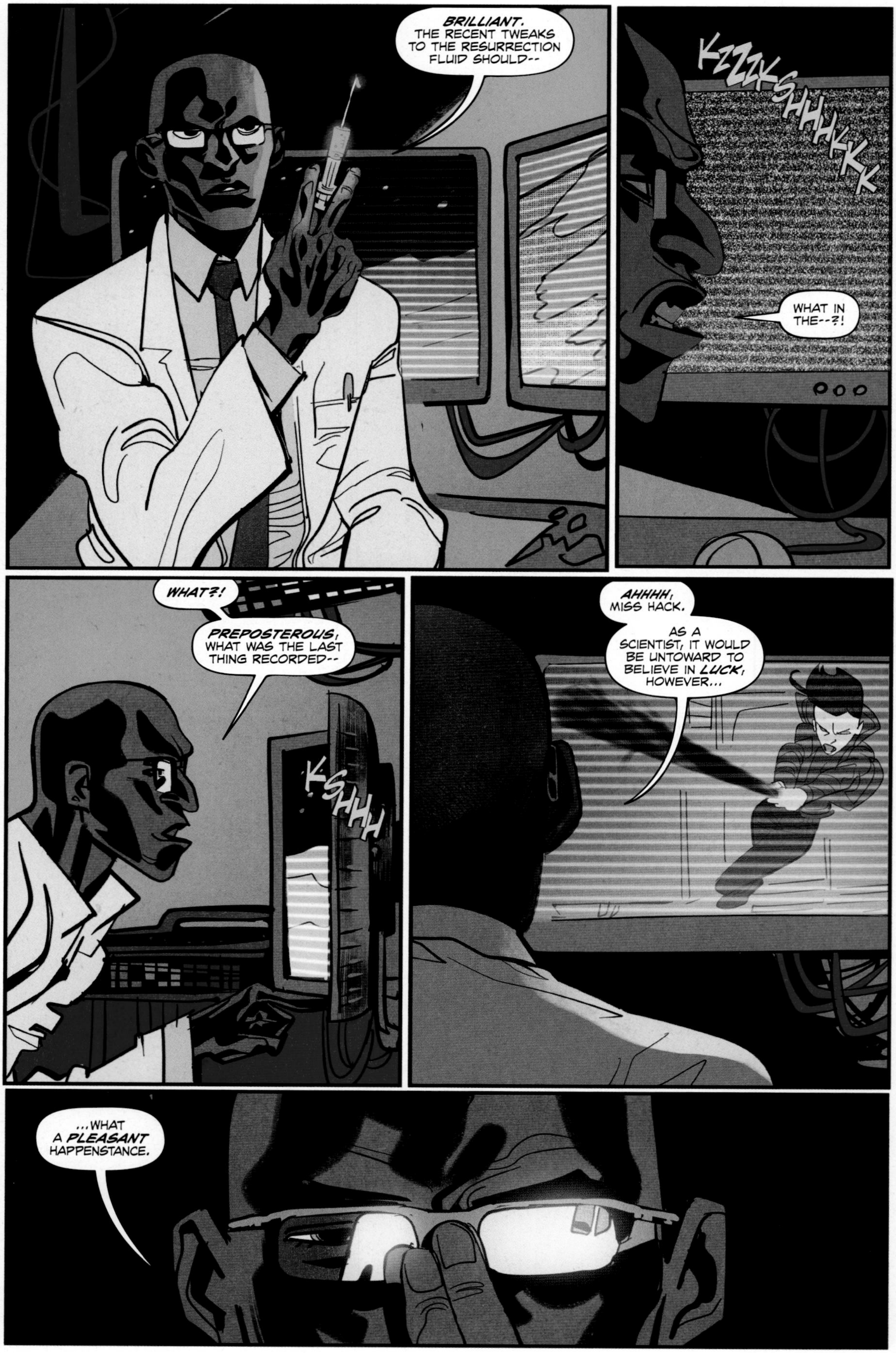
BRILLIANT. THE RECENT TWEAKS TO THE RESURRECTION FLUID SHOULD--
KZZZKSHHHKKK
WHAT IN THE--?!
WHAT?!
PREPOSTEROUS, WHAT WAS THE LAST THING RECORDED--
KSHHH
AHHHH, MISS HACK.
AS A SCIENTIST, IT WOULD BE UNTOWARD TO BELIEVE IN LUCK, HOWEVER...
...WHAT A PLEASANT HAPPENSTANCE.

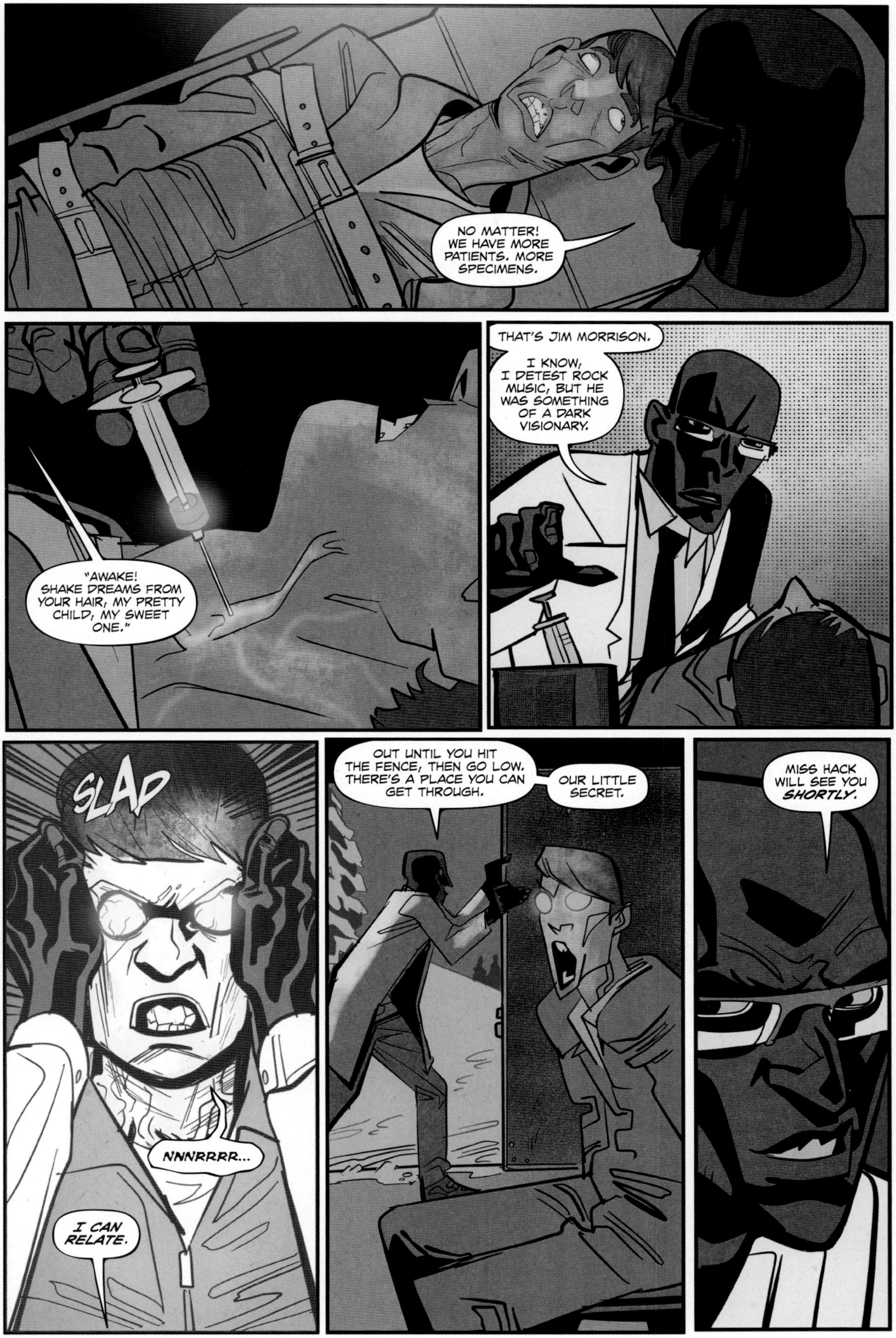
NO MATTER! WE HAVE MORE PATIENTS. MORE SPECIMENS.
"AWAKE! SHAKE DREAMS FROM YOUR HAIR, MY PRETTY CHILD, MY SWEET ONE."
THAT'S JIM MORRISON.
I KNOW, I DETEST ROCK MUSIC, BUT HE WAS SOMETHING OF A DARK VISIONARY.
SLAP
NNNRRRR...
I CAN RELATE.
OUT UNTIL YOU HIT THE FENCE, THEN GO LOW. THERE'S A PLACE YOU CAN GET THROUGH.
OUR LITTLE SECRET.
MISS HACK WILL SEE YOU SHORTLY.

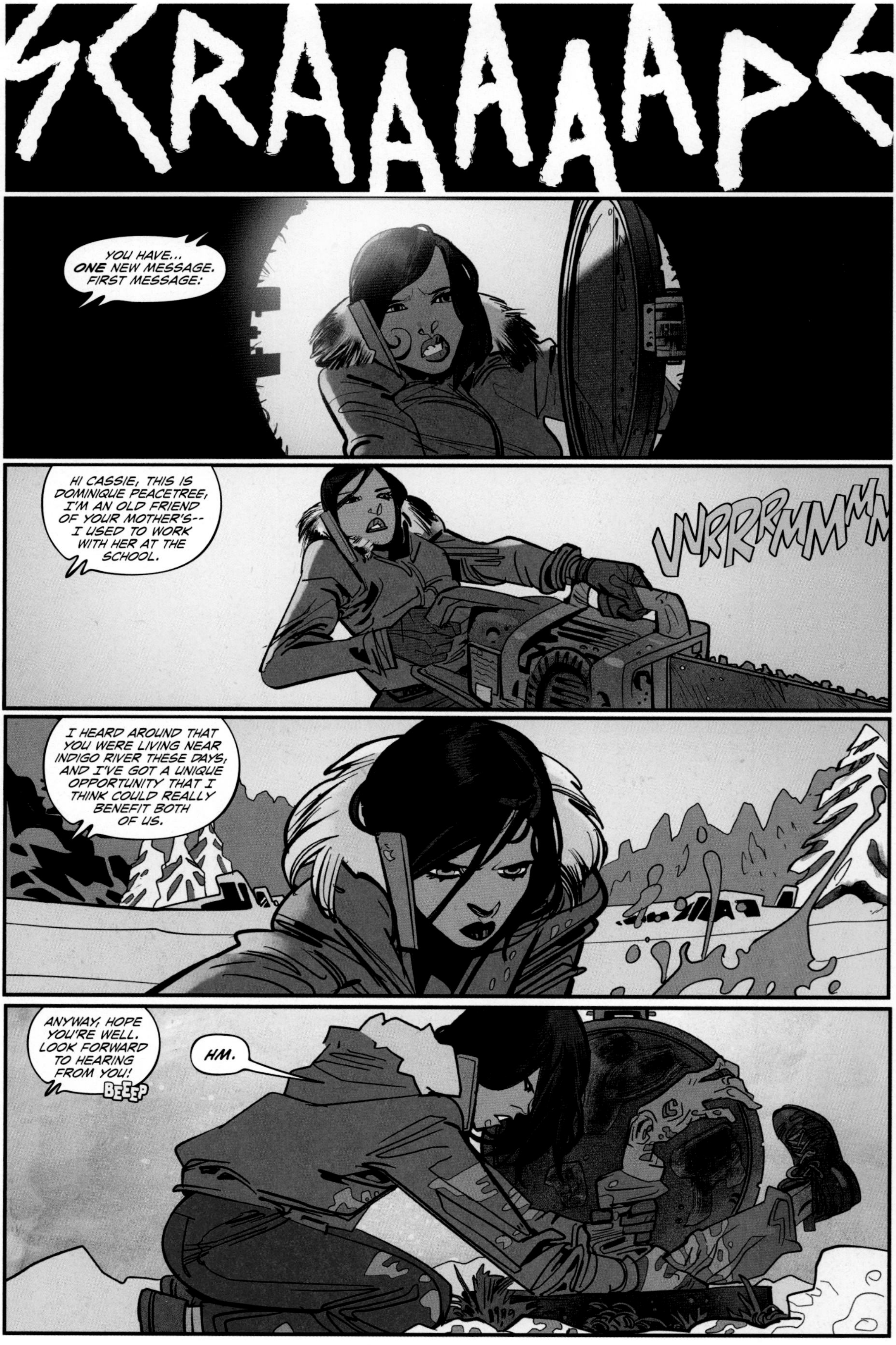
SKRAAAAAPE
YOU HAVE... ONE NEW MESSAGE. FIRST MESSAGE:
HI CASSIE, THIS IS DOMINIQUE PEACETREE, I'M AN OLD FRIEND OF YOUR MOTHER'S-- I USED TO WORK WITH HER AT THE SCHOOL.
VVRRRMMMMM
I HEARD AROUND THAT YOU WERE LIVING NEAR INDIGO RIVER THESE DAYS, AND I'VE GOT A UNIQUE OPPORTUNITY THAT I THINK COULD REALLY BENEFIT BOTH OF US.
ANYWAY, HOPE YOU'RE WELL. LOOK FORWARD TO HEARING FROM YOU!
BEEEP
HM.

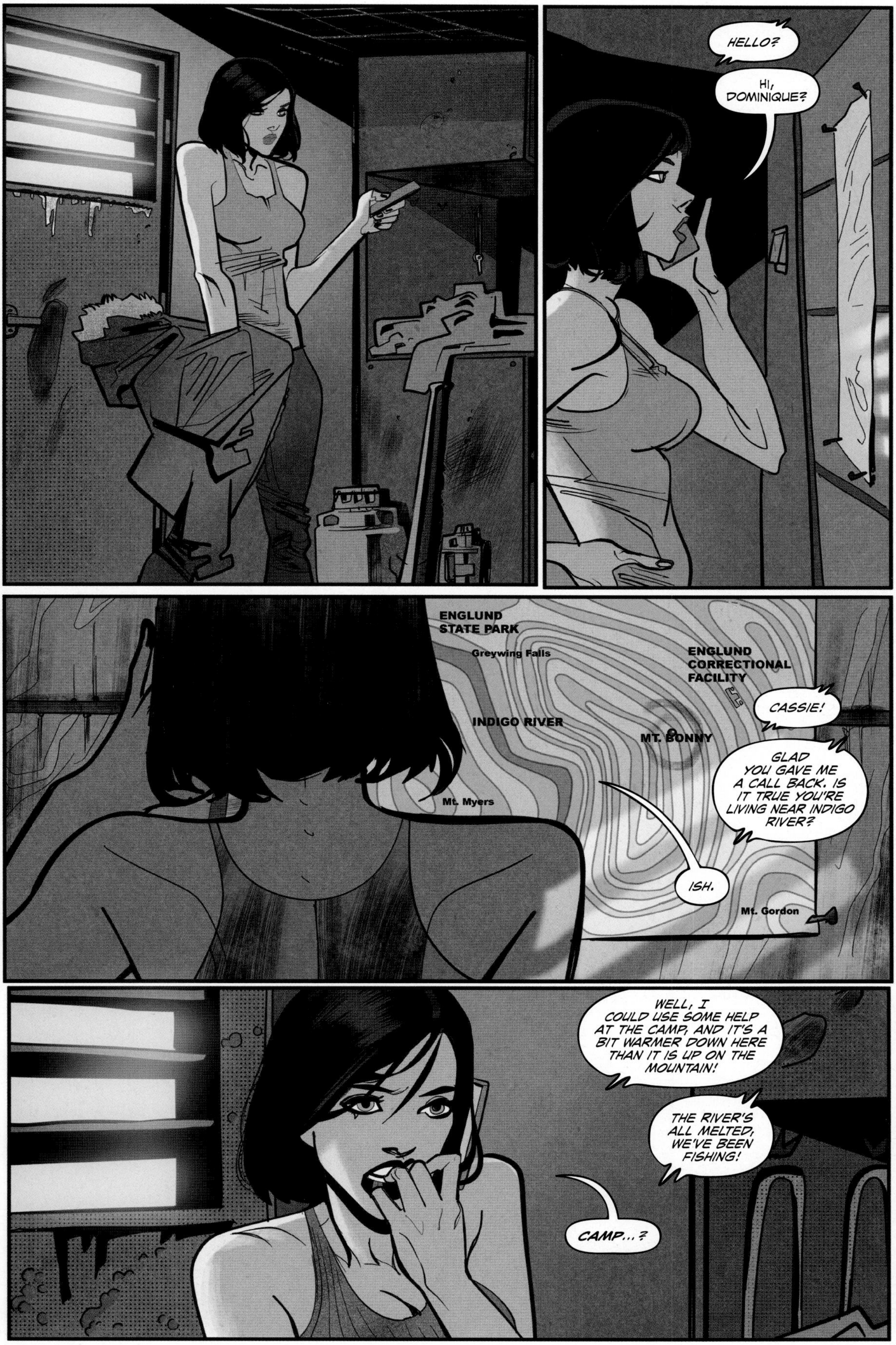
HELLO?
HI, DOMINIQUE?
ENGLUND STATE PARK
Greywing Falls
ENGLUND CORRECTIONAL FACILITY
INDIGO RIVER
MT. BONNY
Mt. Myers
Mt. Gordon
CASSIE!
GLAD YOU GAVE ME A CALL BACK. IS IT TRUE YOU'RE LIVING NEAR INDIGO RIVER?
ISH.
WELL, I COULD USE SOME HELP AT THE CAMP, AND IT'S A BIT WARMER DOWN HERE THAN IT IS UP ON THE MOUNTAIN!
THE RIVER'S ALL MELTED, WE'VE BEEN FISHING!
CAMP...?

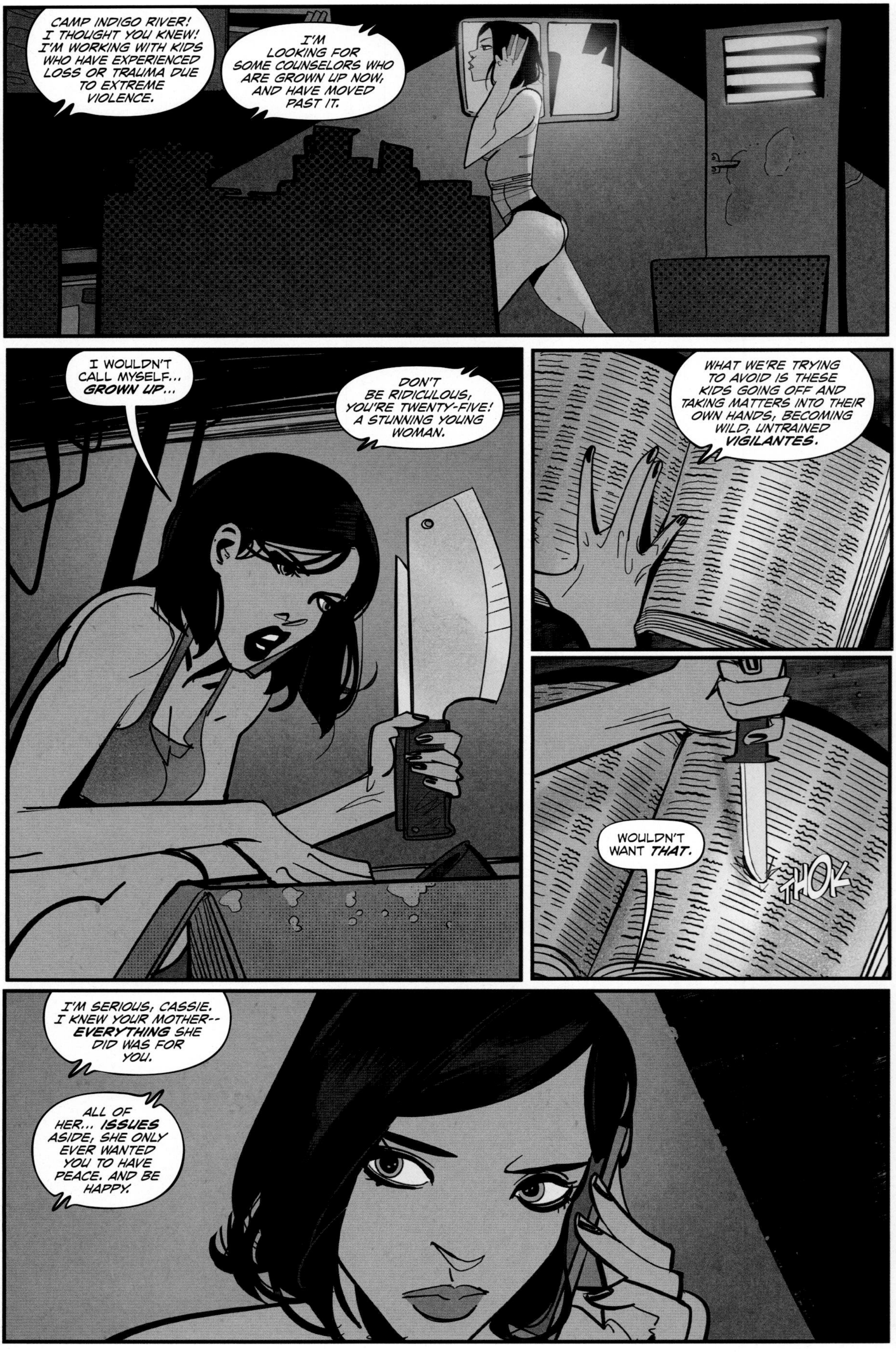
CAMP INDIGO RIVER! I THOUGHT YOU KNEW! I'M WORKING WITH KIDS WHO HAVE EXPERIENCED LOSS OR TRAUMA DUE TO EXTREME VIOLENCE.
I'M LOOKING FOR SOME COUNSELORS WHO ARE GROWN UP NOW, AND HAVE MOVED PAST IT.
I WOULDN'T CALL MYSELF... GROWN UP...
DON'T BE RIDICULOUS, YOU'RE TWENTY-FIVE! A STUNNING YOUNG WOMAN.
WHAT WE'RE TRYING TO AVOID IS THESE KIDS GOING OFF AND TAKING MATTERS INTO THEIR OWN HANDS, BECOMING WILD, UNTRAINED VIGILANTES.
WOULDN'T WANT THAT.
THOK
I'M SERIOUS, CASSIE. I KNEW YOUR MOTHER-- EVERYTHING SHE DID WAS FOR YOU.
ALL OF HER... ISSUES ASIDE, SHE ONLY EVER WANTED YOU TO HAVE PEACE. AND BE HAPPY.

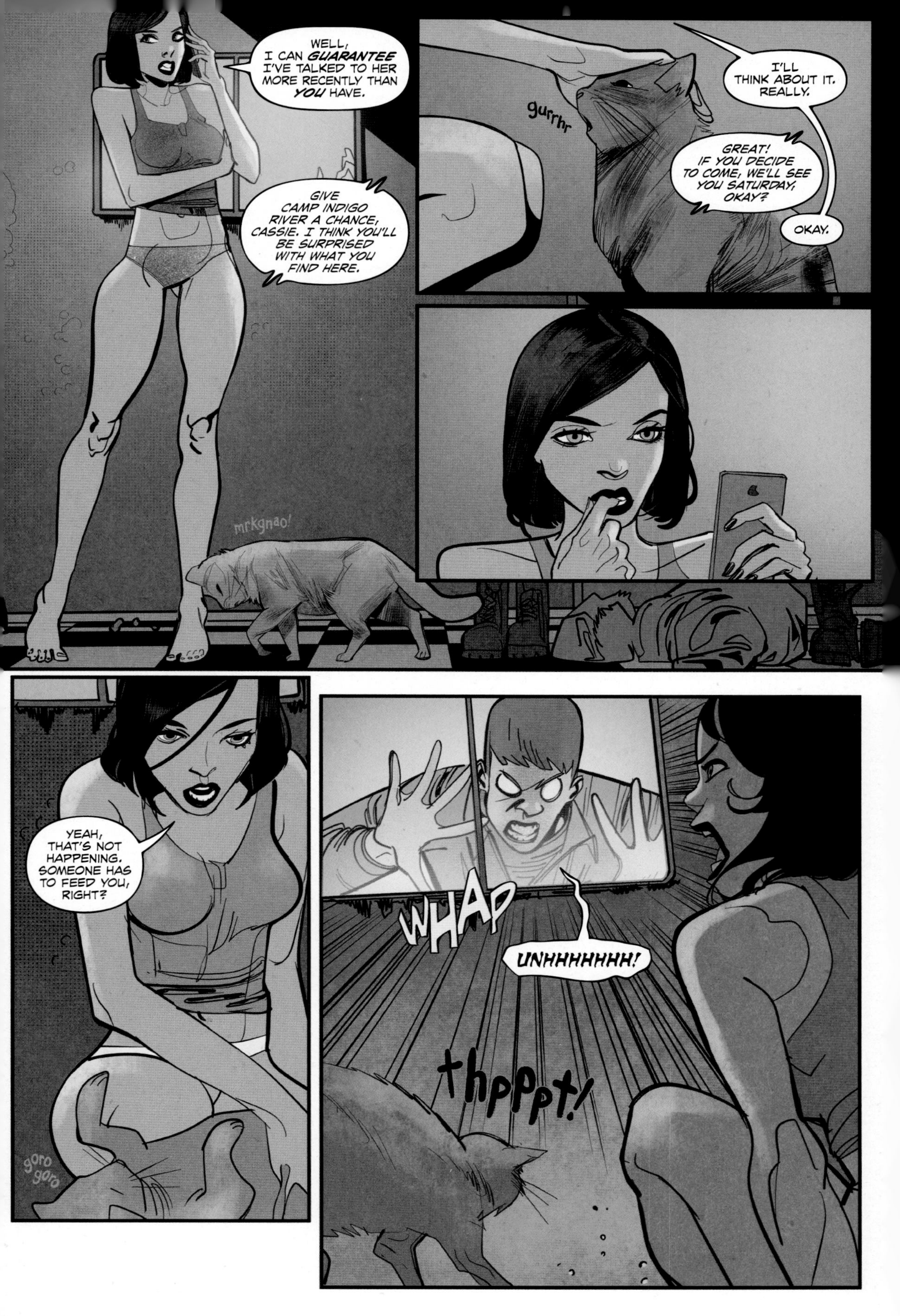

WELL, I CAN GUARANTEE I'VE TALKED TO HER MORE RECENTLY THAN YOU HAVE.
GIVE CAMP INDIGO RIVER A CHANCE, CASSIE. I THINK YOU'LL BE SURPRISED WITH WHAT YOU FIND HERE.
mrkgnao!
gurrhr
I'LL THINK ABOUT IT. REALLY.
GREAT! IF YOU DECIDE TO COME, WE'LL SEE YOU SATURDAY, OKAY?
OKAY.
YEAH, THAT'S NOT HAPPENING. SOMEONE HAS TO FEED YOU, RIGHT?
goro goro
WHAP
UNHHHHHHH!
thpppt!

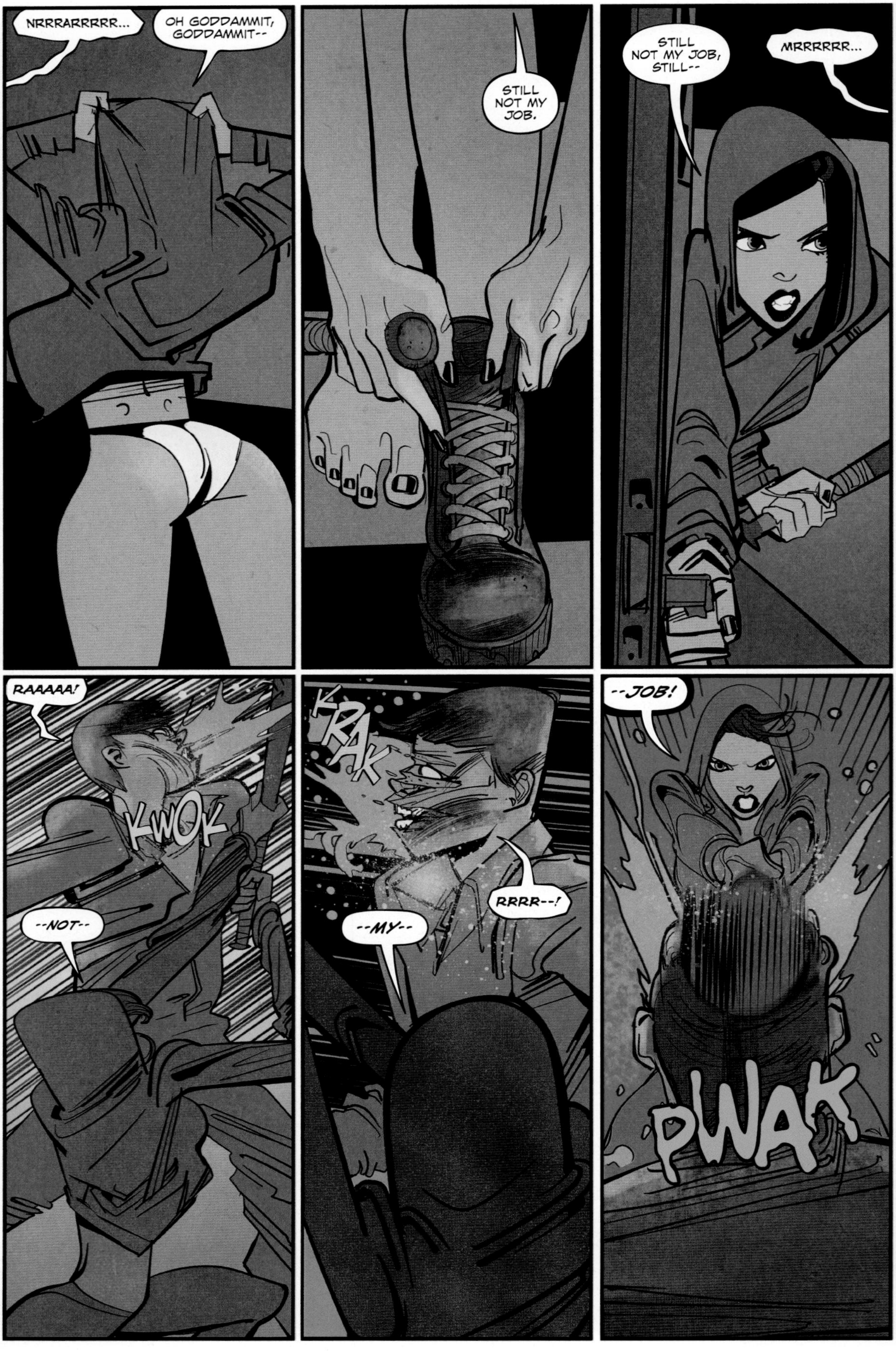
NRRRARRRRR...
OH GODDAMMIT, GODDAMMIT--
STILL NOT MY JOB.
STILL NOT MY JOB, STILL--
MRRRRRR...
RAAAAA!
KWOK
--NOT--
KRAK
RRRR--!
--MY--
--JOB!
PWAK

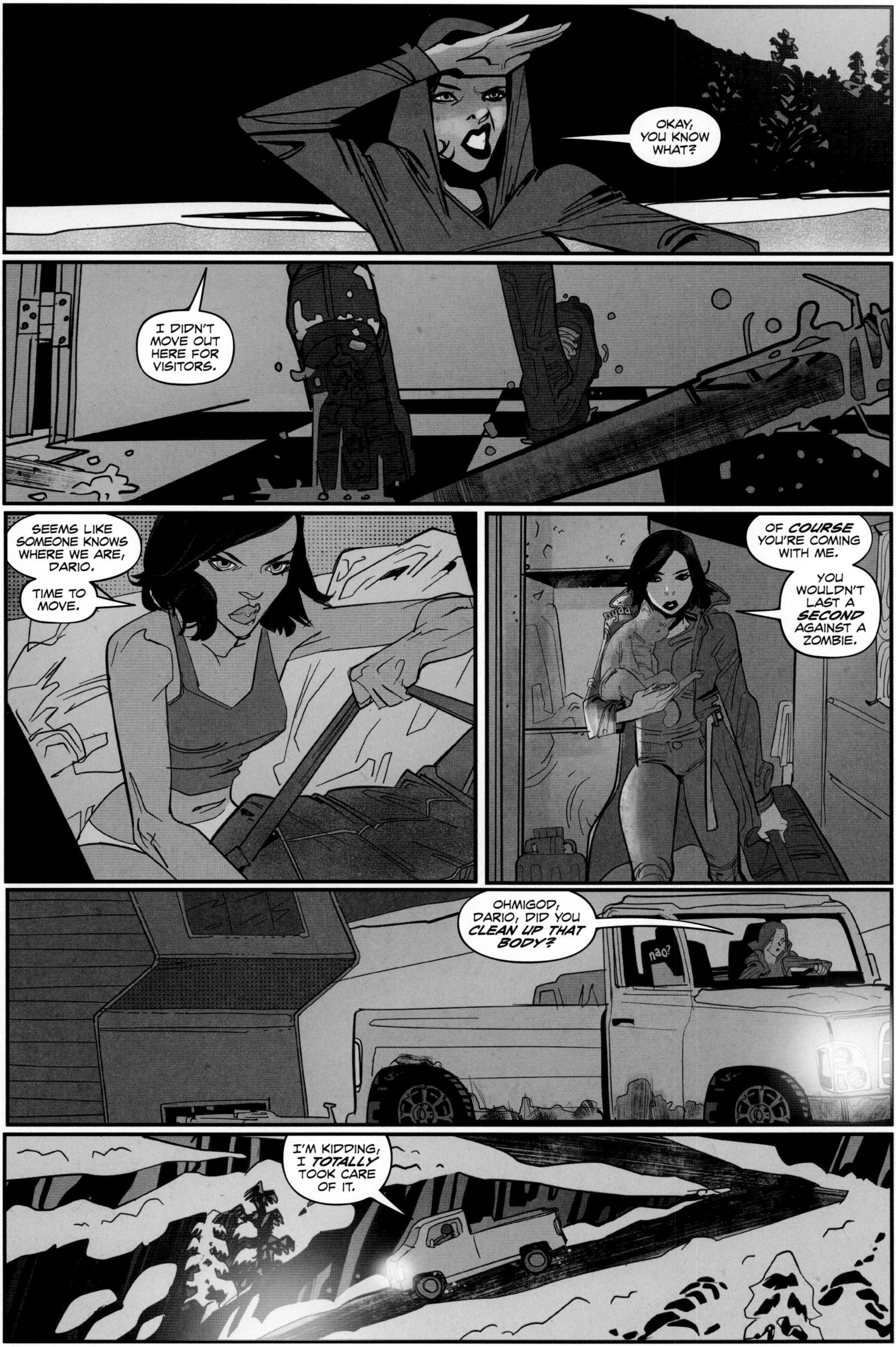
OKAY, YOU KNOW WHAT?
I DIDN'T MOVE OUT HERE FOR VISITORS.
SEEMS LIKE SOMEONE KNOWS WHERE WE ARE, DARIO.
TIME TO MOVE.
OF COURSE YOU'RE COMING WITH ME.
YOU WOULDN'T LAST A SECOND AGAINST A ZOMBIE.
nyaa
OHMIGOD, DARIO, DID YOU CLEAN UP THAT BODY?
nao?
I'M KIDDING, I TOTALLY TOOK CARE OF IT.

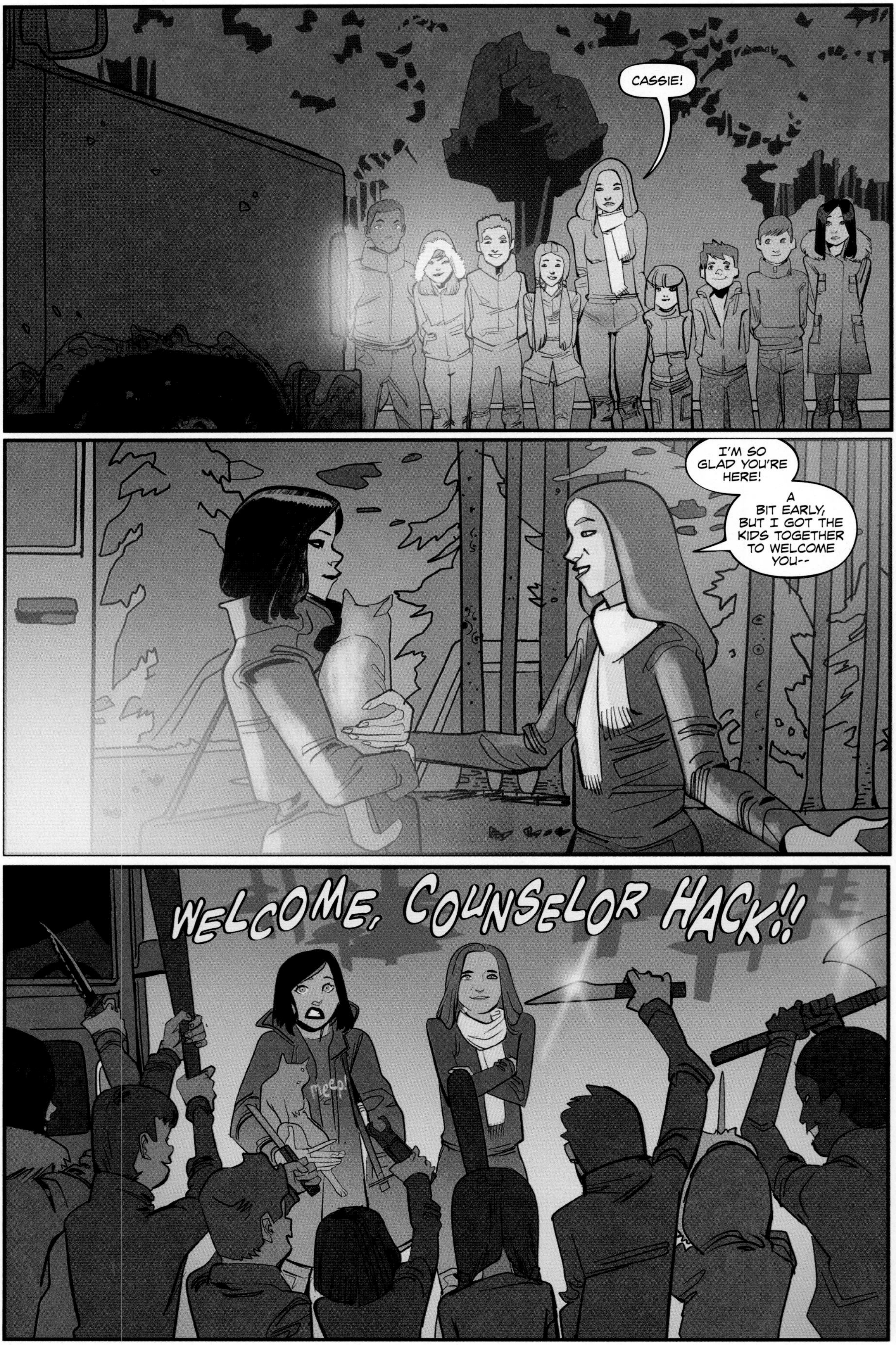
CASSIE!
I'M SO GLAD YOU'RE HERE!
A BIT EARLY, BUT I GOT THE KIDS TOGETHER TO WELCOME YOU--
WELCOME, COUNSELOR HACK!!
MEEP!

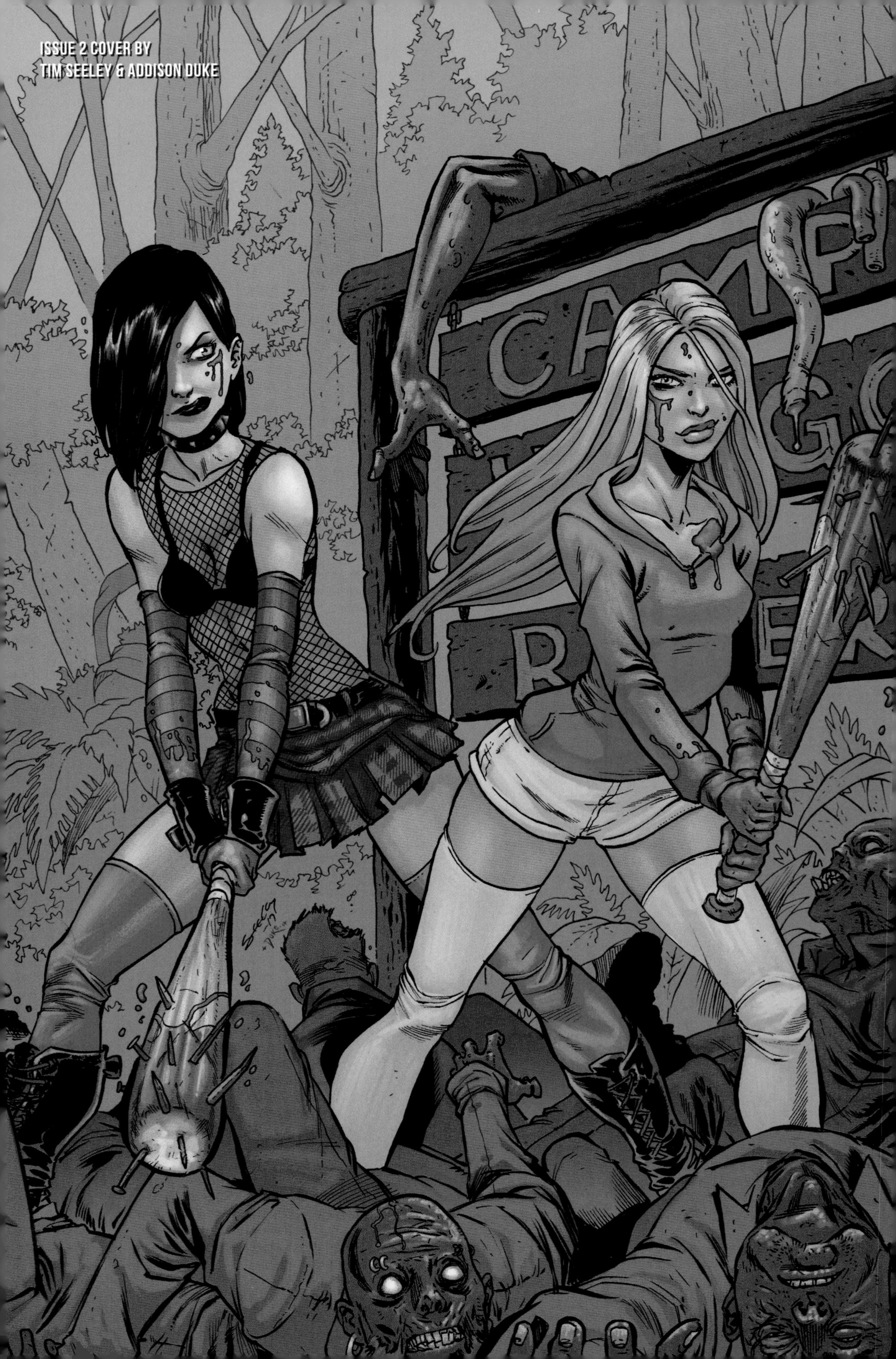

ISSUE 2 COVER BY
TIM SEELEY & ADDISON DUKE

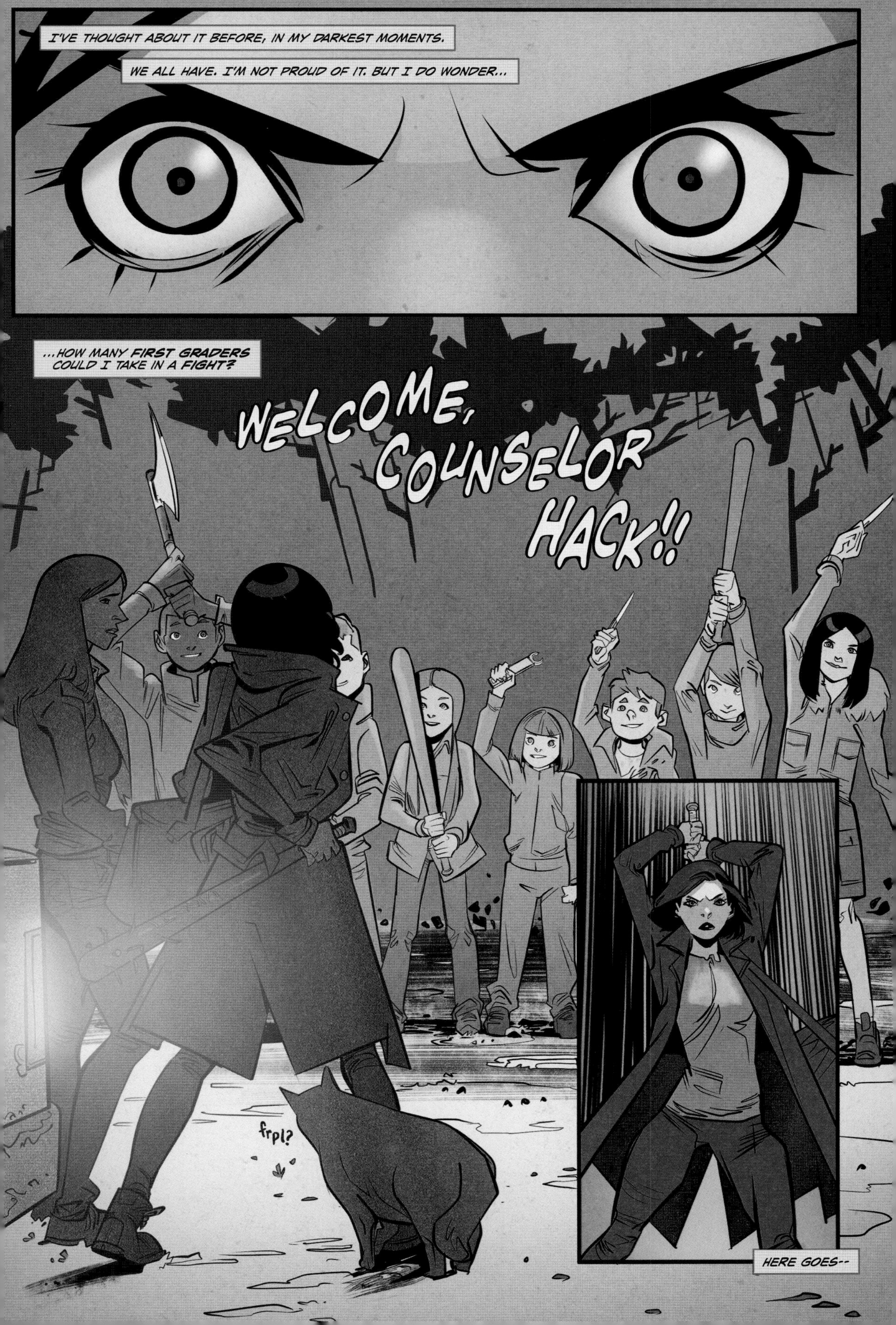
I'VE THOUGHT ABOUT IT BEFORE, IN MY DARKEST MOMENTS.
WE ALL HAVE. I'M NOT PROUD OF IT. BUT I DO WONDER...
...HOW MANY FIRST GRADERS COULD I TAKE IN A FIGHT?
WELCOME, COUNSELOR HACK!!
frpl?
HERE GOES--

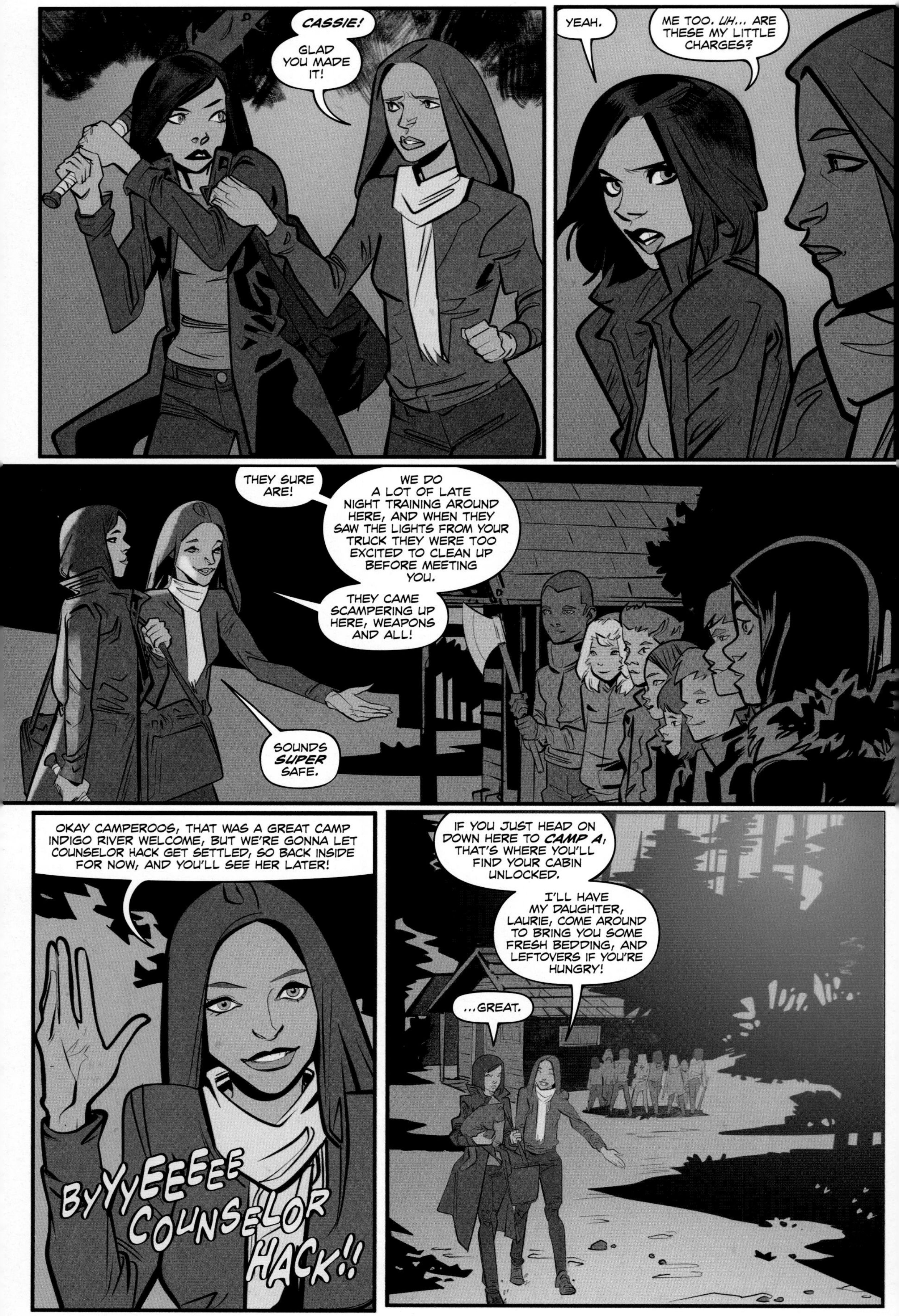
CASSIE!
GLAD YOU MADE IT!
YEAH.
ME TOO. UH... ARE THESE MY LITTLE CHARGES?
THEY SURE ARE!
WE DO A LOT OF LATE NIGHT TRAINING AROUND HERE, AND WHEN THEY SAW THE LIGHTS FROM YOUR TRUCK THEY WERE TOO EXCITED TO CLEAN UP BEFORE MEETING YOU.
THEY CAME SCAMPERING UP HERE, WEAPONS AND ALL!
SOUNDS SUPER SAFE.
OKAY CAMPEROOS, THAT WAS A GREAT CAMP INDIGO RIVER WELCOME, BUT WE'RE GONNA LET COUNSELOR HACK GET SETTLED, SO BACK INSIDE FOR NOW, AND YOU'LL SEE HER LATER!
BYYYEEEEE COUNSELOR HACK!!
IF YOU JUST HEAD ON DOWN HERE TO CAMP A, THAT'S WHERE YOU'LL FIND YOUR CABIN UNLOCKED.
I'LL HAVE MY DAUGHTER, LAURIE, COME AROUND TO BRING YOU SOME FRESH BEDDING, AND LEFTOVERS IF YOU'RE HUNGRY!
...GREAT.

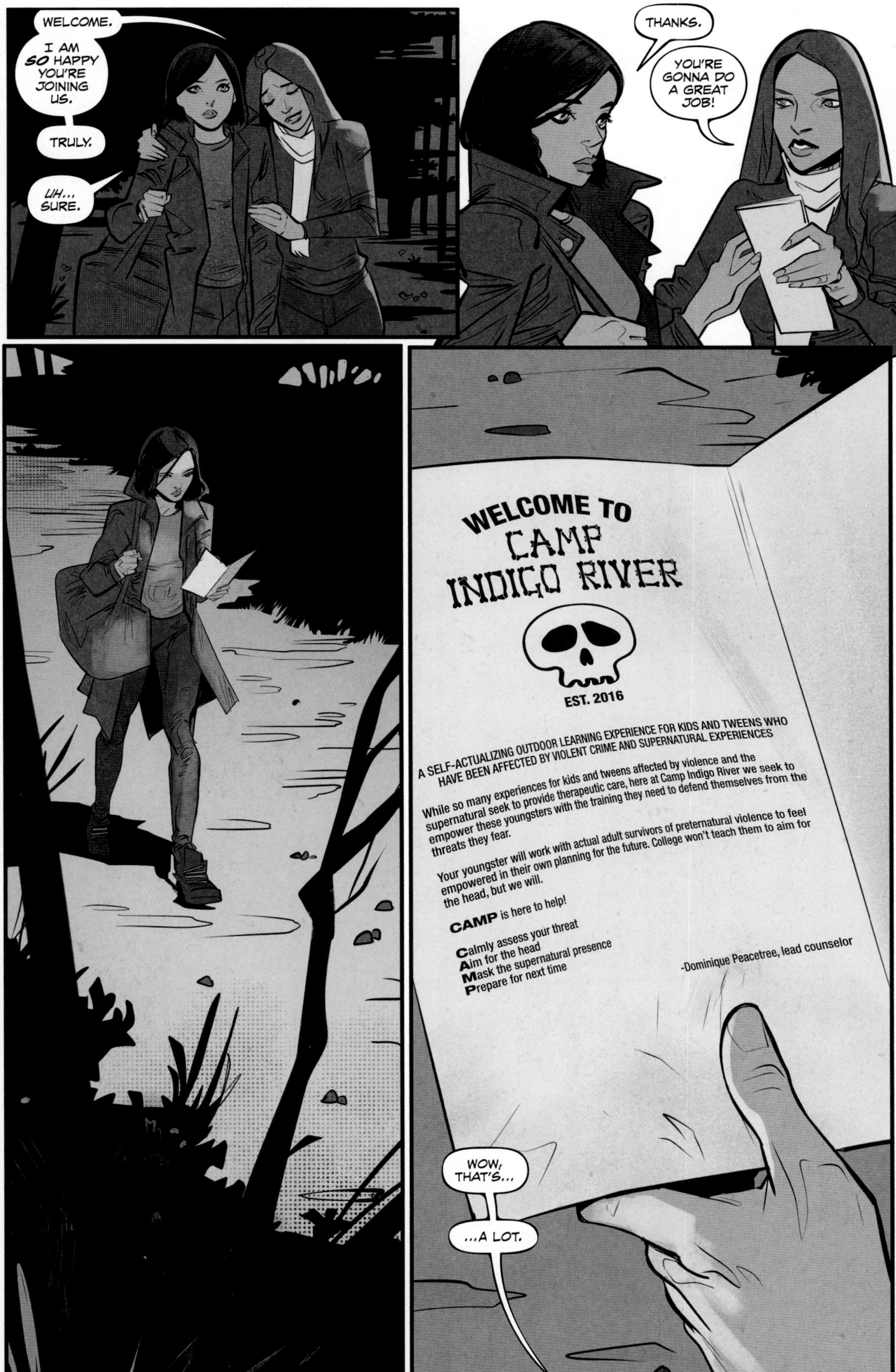
WELCOME.
I AM SO HAPPY YOU'RE JOINING US.
TRULY.
UH... SURE.
THANKS.
YOU'RE GONNA DO A GREAT JOB!
WELCOME TO CAMP INDIGO RIVER
EST. 2016
A SELF-ACTUALIZING OUTDOOR LEARNING EXPERIENCE FOR KIDS AND TWEENS WHO HAVE BEEN AFFECTED BY VIOLENT CRIME AND SUPERNATURAL EXPERIENCES
While so many experiences for kids and tweens affected by violence and the supernatural seek to provide therapeutic care, here at Camp Indigo River we seek to empower these youngsters with the training they need to defend themselves from the threats they fear.
Your youngster will work with actual adult survivors of preternatural violence to feel empowered in their own planning for the future. College won't teach them to aim for the head, but we will.
CAMP is here to help!
Calmly assess your threat
Aim for the head
Mask the supernatural presence
Prepare for next time
-Dominique Peacetree, lead counselor
WOW, THAT'S...
...A LOT.

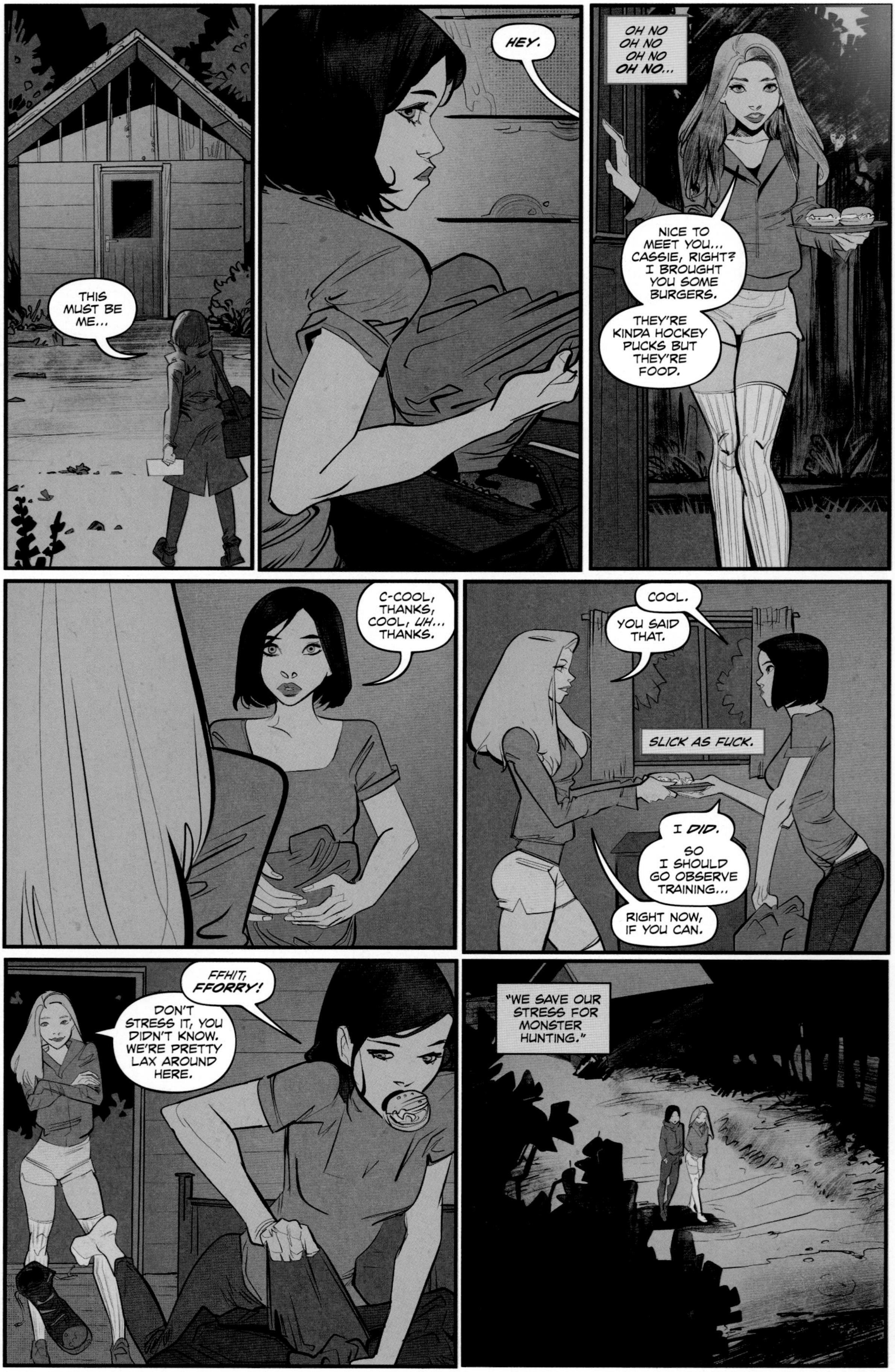
THIS MUST BE ME...
HEY.
OH NO
OH NO
OH NO
OH NO...
NICE TO MEET YOU... CASSIE, RIGHT? I BROUGHT YOU SOME BURGERS.
THEY'RE KINDA HOCKEY PUCKS BUT THEY'RE FOOD.
C-COOL, THANKS, COOL, UH... THANKS.
COOL.
YOU SAID THAT.
SLICK AS FUCK.
I DID.
SO I SHOULD GO OBSERVE TRAINING...
RIGHT NOW, IF YOU CAN.
FFHIT, FFORRY!
DON'T STRESS IT, YOU DIDN'T KNOW. WE'RE PRETTY LAX AROUND HERE.
"WE SAVE OUR STRESS FOR MONSTER HUNTING."

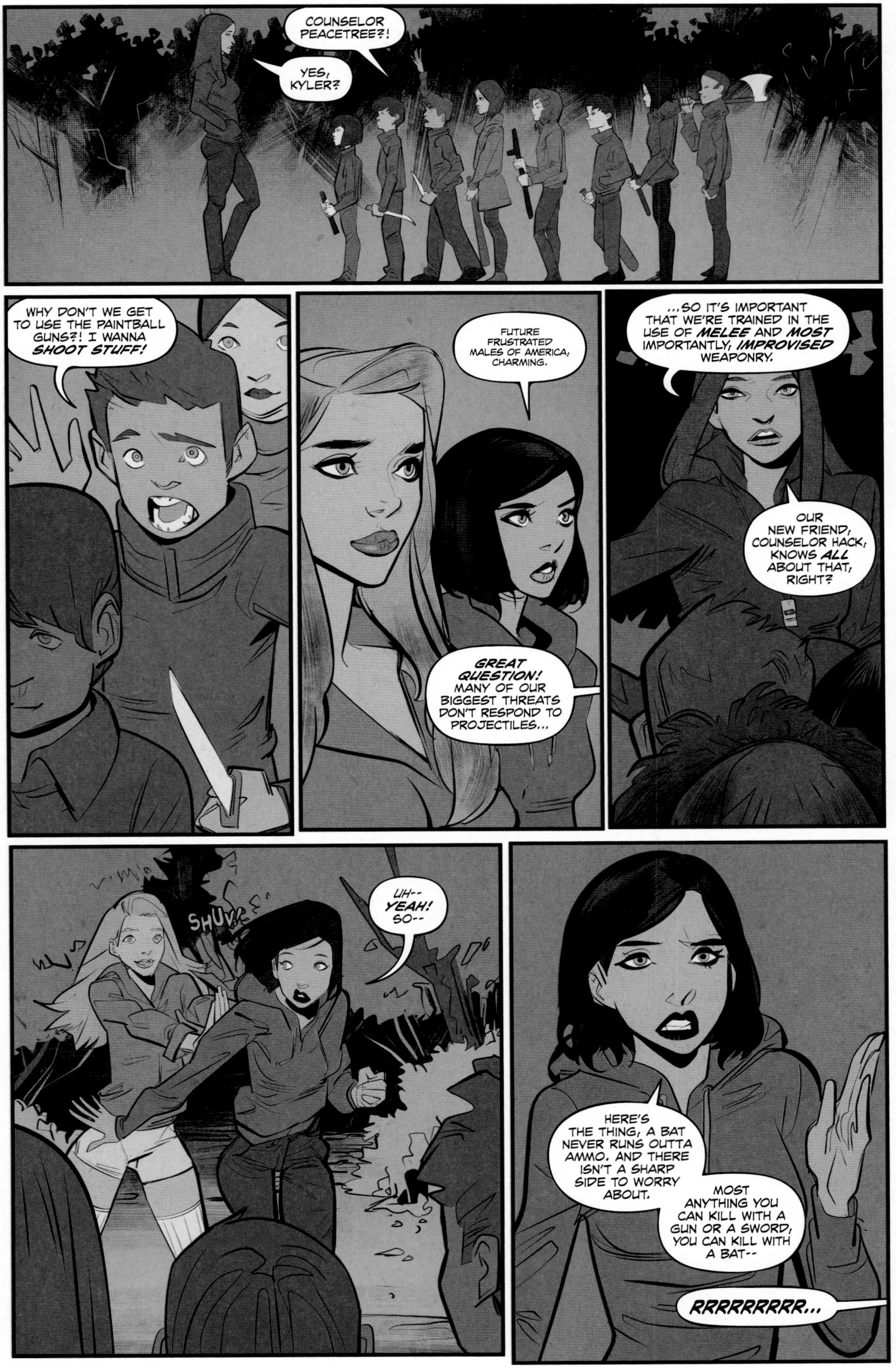
COUNSELOR PEACETREE?!
YES, KYLER?
WHY DON'T WE GET TO USE THE PAINTBALL GUNS?! I WANNA SHOOT STUFF!
FUTURE FRUSTRATED MALES OF AMERICA, CHARMING.
GREAT QUESTION! MANY OF OUR BIGGEST THREATS DON'T RESPOND TO PROJECTILES...
...SO IT'S IMPORTANT THAT WE'RE TRAINED IN THE USE OF MELEE AND MOST IMPORTANTLY, IMPROVISED WEAPONRY.
OUR NEW FRIEND, COUNSELOR HACK, KNOWS ALL ABOUT THAT, RIGHT?
SHUV!
UH-- YEAH! SO--
HERE'S THE THING, A BAT NEVER RUNS OUTTA AMMO. AND THERE ISN'T A SHARP SIDE TO WORRY ABOUT.
MOST ANYTHING YOU CAN KILL WITH A GUN OR A SWORD, YOU CAN KILL WITH A BAT--
RRRRRRRRR...

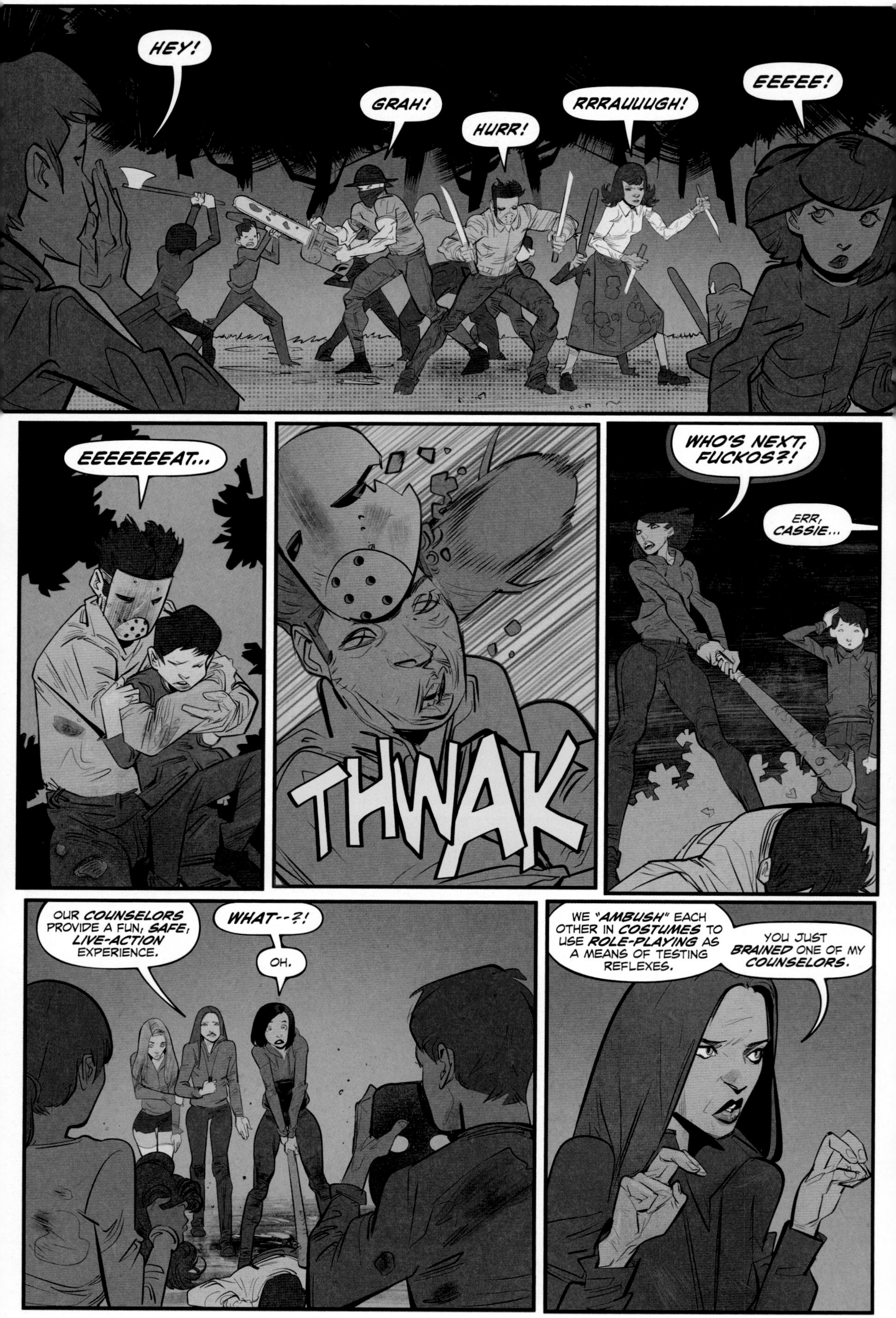
HEY!
GRAH!
HURR!
RRRAUUUGH!
EEEEE!
EEEEEEEAT...
THWAK
WHO'S NEXT, FUCKOS?!
ERR, CASSIE...
OUR COUNSELORS PROVIDE A FUN, SAFE, LIVE-ACTION EXPERIENCE.
WHAT--?!
OH.
WE "AMBUSH" EACH OTHER IN COSTUMES TO USE ROLE-PLAYING AS A MEANS OF TESTING REFLEXES.
YOU JUST BRAINED ONE OF MY COUNSELORS.

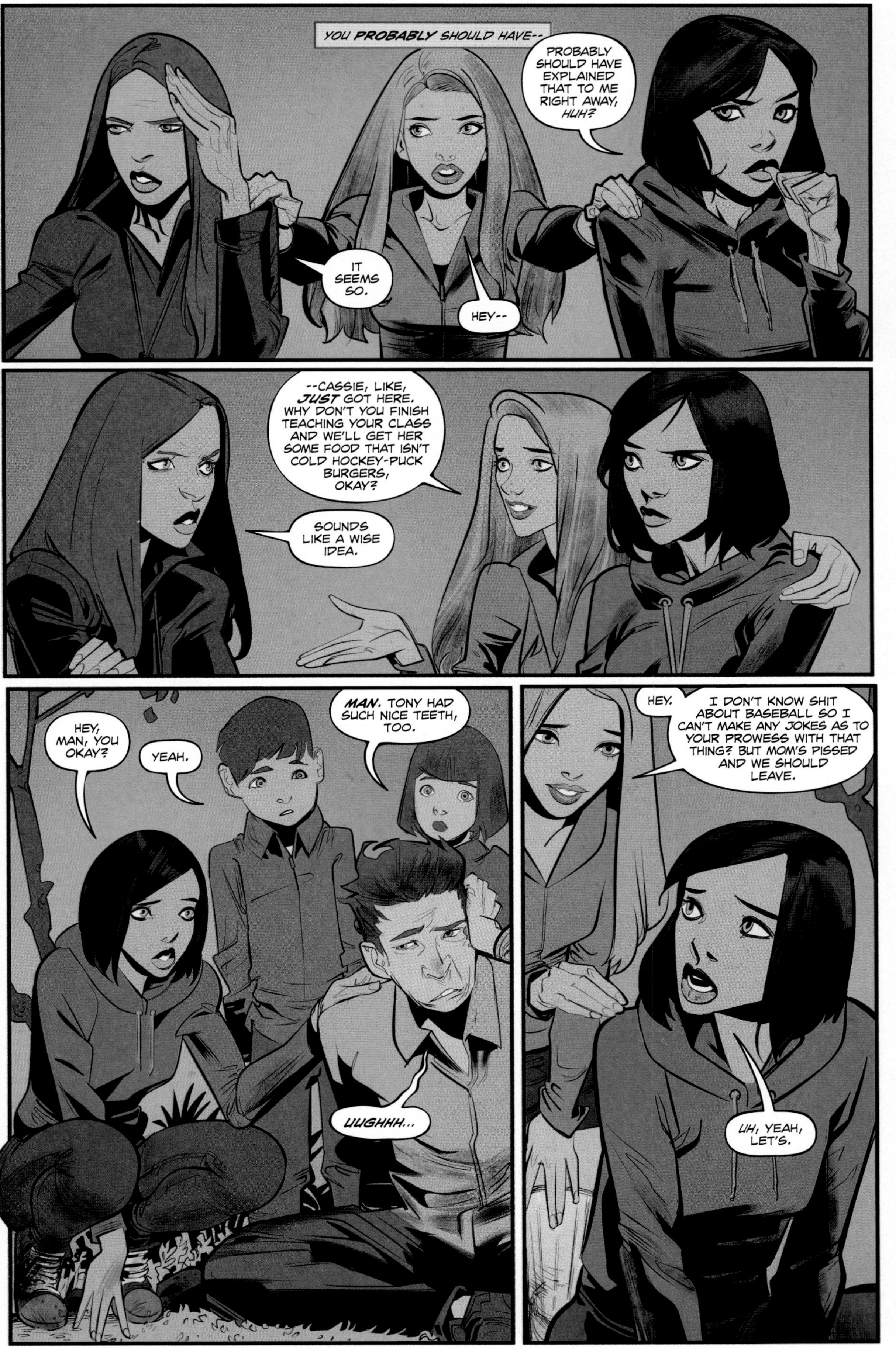
YOU PROBABLY SHOULD HAVE--
PROBABLY SHOULD HAVE EXPLAINED THAT TO ME RIGHT AWAY, HUH?
IT SEEMS SO.
HEY--
--CASSIE, LIKE, JUST GOT HERE. WHY DON'T YOU FINISH TEACHING YOUR CLASS AND WE'LL GET HER SOME FOOD THAT ISN'T COLD HOCKEY-PUCK BURGERS, OKAY?
SOUNDS LIKE A WISE IDEA.
HEY, MAN, YOU OKAY?
YEAH.
MAN. TONY HAD SUCH NICE TEETH, TOO.
UUGHHH...
HEY.
I DON'T KNOW SHIT ABOUT BASEBALL SO I CAN'T MAKE ANY JOKES AS TO YOUR PROWESS WITH THAT THING? BUT MOM'S PISSED AND WE SHOULD LEAVE.
UH, YEAH, LET'S.

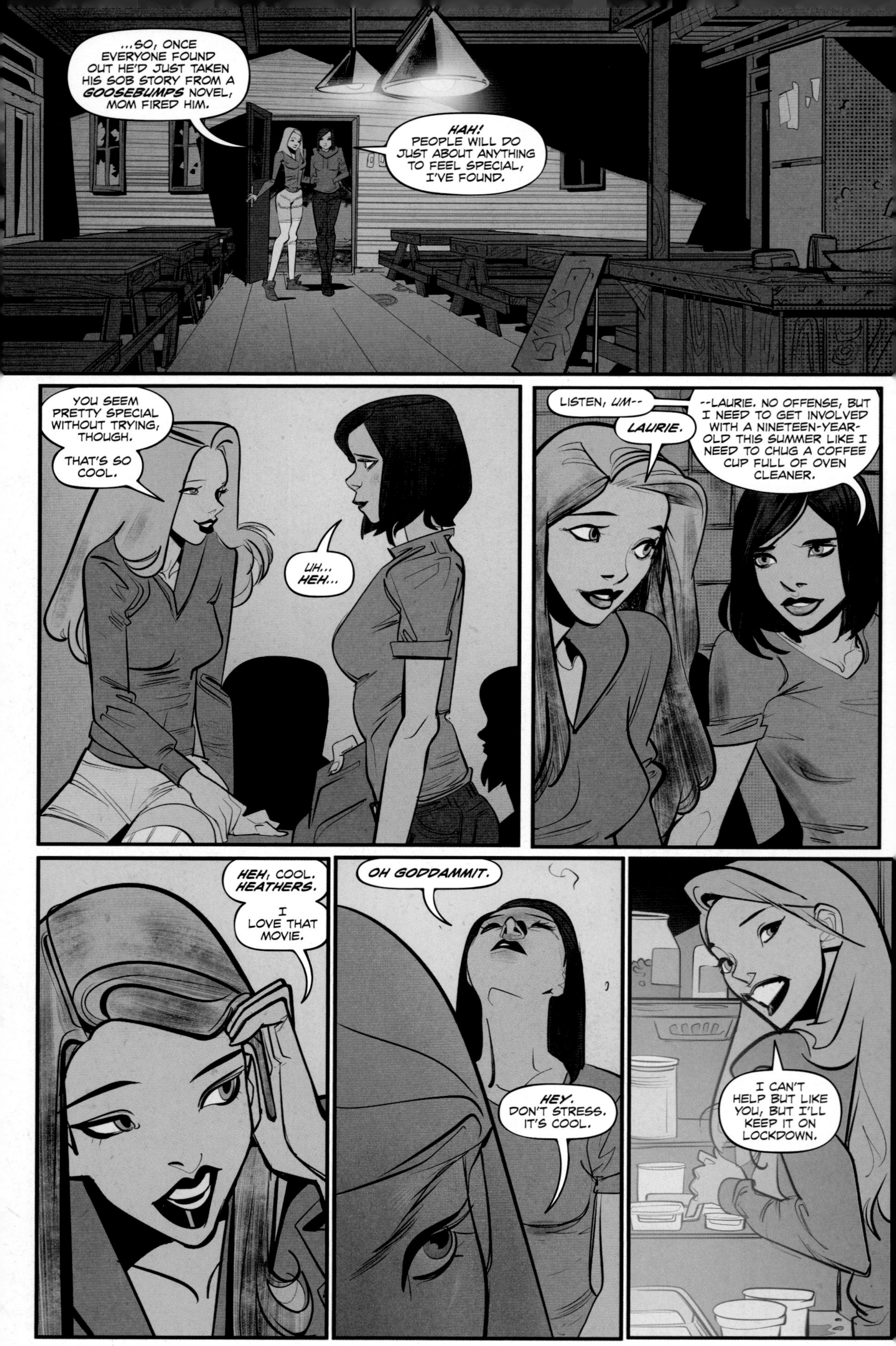
...SO, ONCE EVERYONE FOUND OUT HE'D JUST TAKEN HIS SOB STORY FROM A *GOOSEBUMPS* NOVEL, MOM FIRED HIM.
HAH! PEOPLE WILL DO JUST ABOUT ANYTHING TO FEEL SPECIAL, I'VE FOUND.
YOU SEEM PRETTY SPECIAL WITHOUT TRYING, THOUGH.
THAT'S SO COOL.
UH... HEH...
LISTEN, *UM--*
LAURIE.
--LAURIE. NO OFFENSE, BUT I NEED TO GET INVOLVED WITH A NINETEEN-YEAR-OLD THIS SUMMER LIKE I NEED TO CHUG A COFFEE CUP FULL OF OVEN CLEANER.
HEH, COOL. *HEATHERS.*
I LOVE THAT MOVIE.
OH GODDAMMIT.
HEY. DON'T STRESS. IT'S COOL.
I CAN'T HELP BUT LIKE YOU, BUT I'LL KEEP IT ON LOCKDOWN.

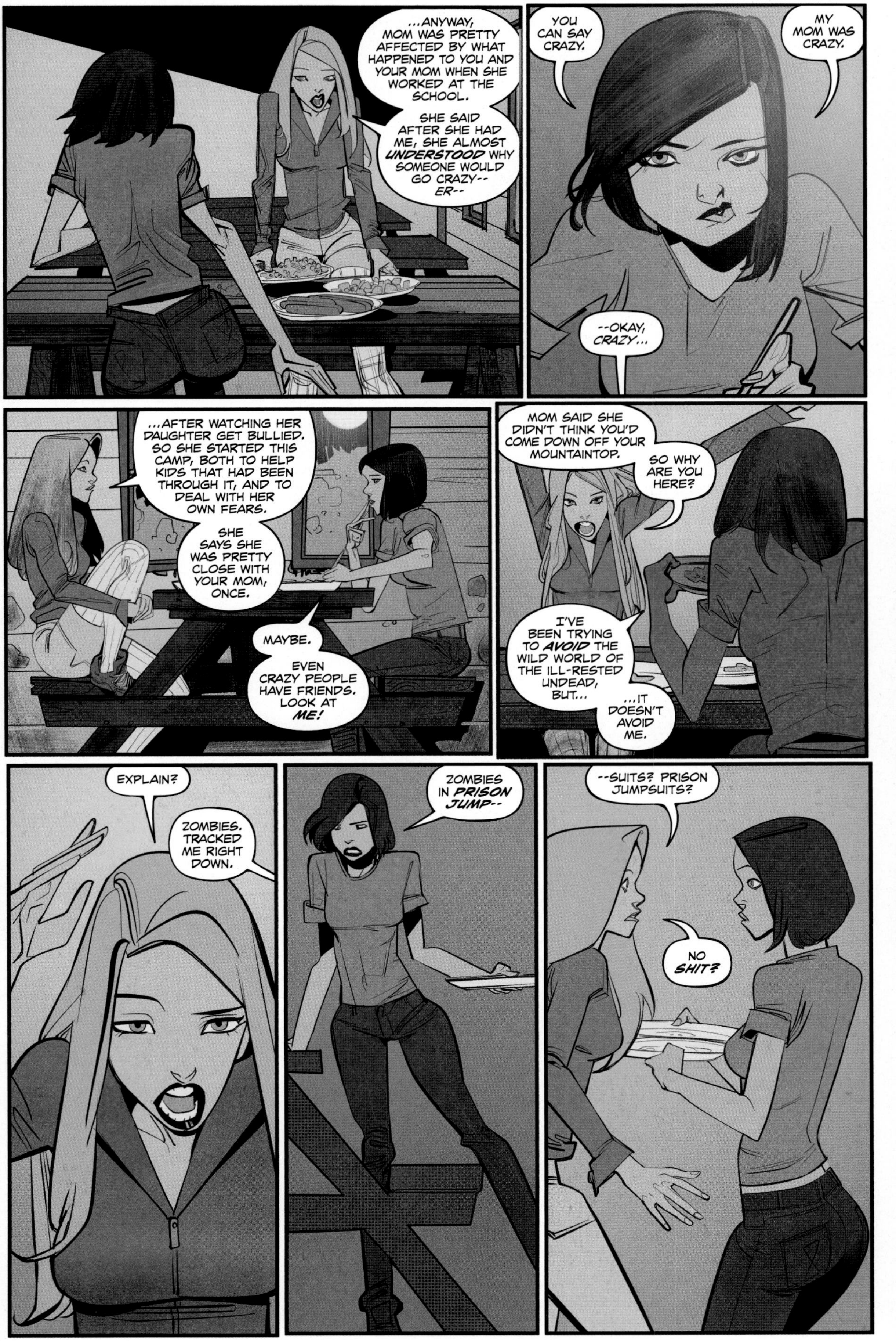

...ANYWAY, MOM WAS PRETTY AFFECTED BY WHAT HAPPENED TO YOU AND YOUR MOM WHEN SHE WORKED AT THE SCHOOL.
SHE SAID AFTER SHE HAD ME, SHE ALMOST UNDERSTOOD WHY SOMEONE WOULD GO CRAZY-- ER--
YOU CAN SAY CRAZY.
MY MOM WAS CRAZY.
--OKAY, CRAZY...
...AFTER WATCHING HER DAUGHTER GET BULLIED. SO SHE STARTED THIS CAMP, BOTH TO HELP KIDS THAT HAD BEEN THROUGH IT, AND TO DEAL WITH HER OWN FEARS.
SHE SAYS SHE WAS PRETTY CLOSE WITH YOUR MOM, ONCE.
MAYBE.
EVEN CRAZY PEOPLE HAVE FRIENDS. LOOK AT ME!
MOM SAID SHE DIDN'T THINK YOU'D COME DOWN OFF YOUR MOUNTAINTOP.
SO WHY ARE YOU HERE?
I'VE BEEN TRYING TO AVOID THE WILD WORLD OF THE ILL-RESTED UNDEAD, BUT...
...IT DOESN'T AVOID ME.
EXPLAIN?
ZOMBIES. TRACKED ME RIGHT DOWN.
ZOMBIES IN PRISON JUMP--
--SUITS? PRISON JUMPSUITS?
NO SHIT?

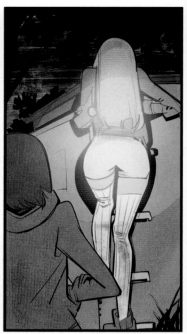

OH *SHIT*.

WHEN DID THESE GUYS ARRIVE?

LAST WEEKEND.

SOME OF THE *GENTLER* KIDS THOUGHT THEY WERE COUNSELORS DRESSED UP AND JUST RAN FROM THEM, CAME AND GOT ME. TOOK ME A MINUTE, BUT I REALIZED THEY WERE THE REAL DEAL.

YOU TOOK THESE GUYS OUT?

ON YOUR OWN?

YEAH. FIRE AXE, RIGHT AT THE NECK.

YOU *LIKE?*

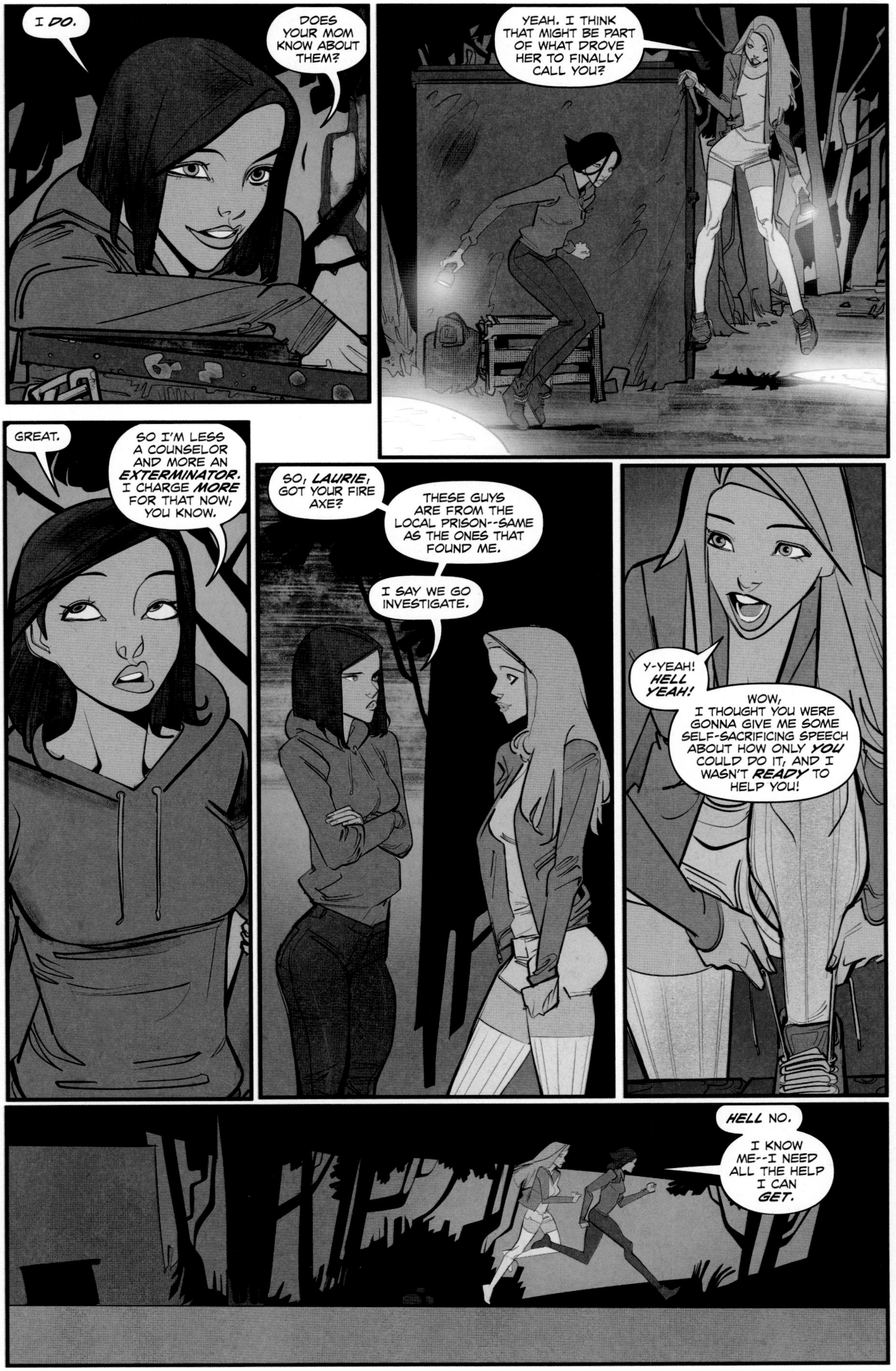
I DO.
DOES YOUR MOM KNOW ABOUT THEM?
YEAH. I THINK THAT MIGHT BE PART OF WHAT DROVE HER TO FINALLY CALL YOU?
GREAT.
SO I'M LESS A COUNSELOR AND MORE AN EXTERMINATOR. I CHARGE MORE FOR THAT NOW, YOU KNOW.
SO, LAURIE, GOT YOUR FIRE AXE?
THESE GUYS ARE FROM THE LOCAL PRISON--SAME AS THE ONES THAT FOUND ME.
I SAY WE GO INVESTIGATE.
Y-YEAH! HELL YEAH!
WOW, I THOUGHT YOU WERE GONNA GIVE ME SOME SELF-SACRIFICING SPEECH ABOUT HOW ONLY YOU COULD DO IT, AND I WASN'T READY TO HELP YOU!
HELL NO.
I KNOW ME--I NEED ALL THE HELP I CAN GET.

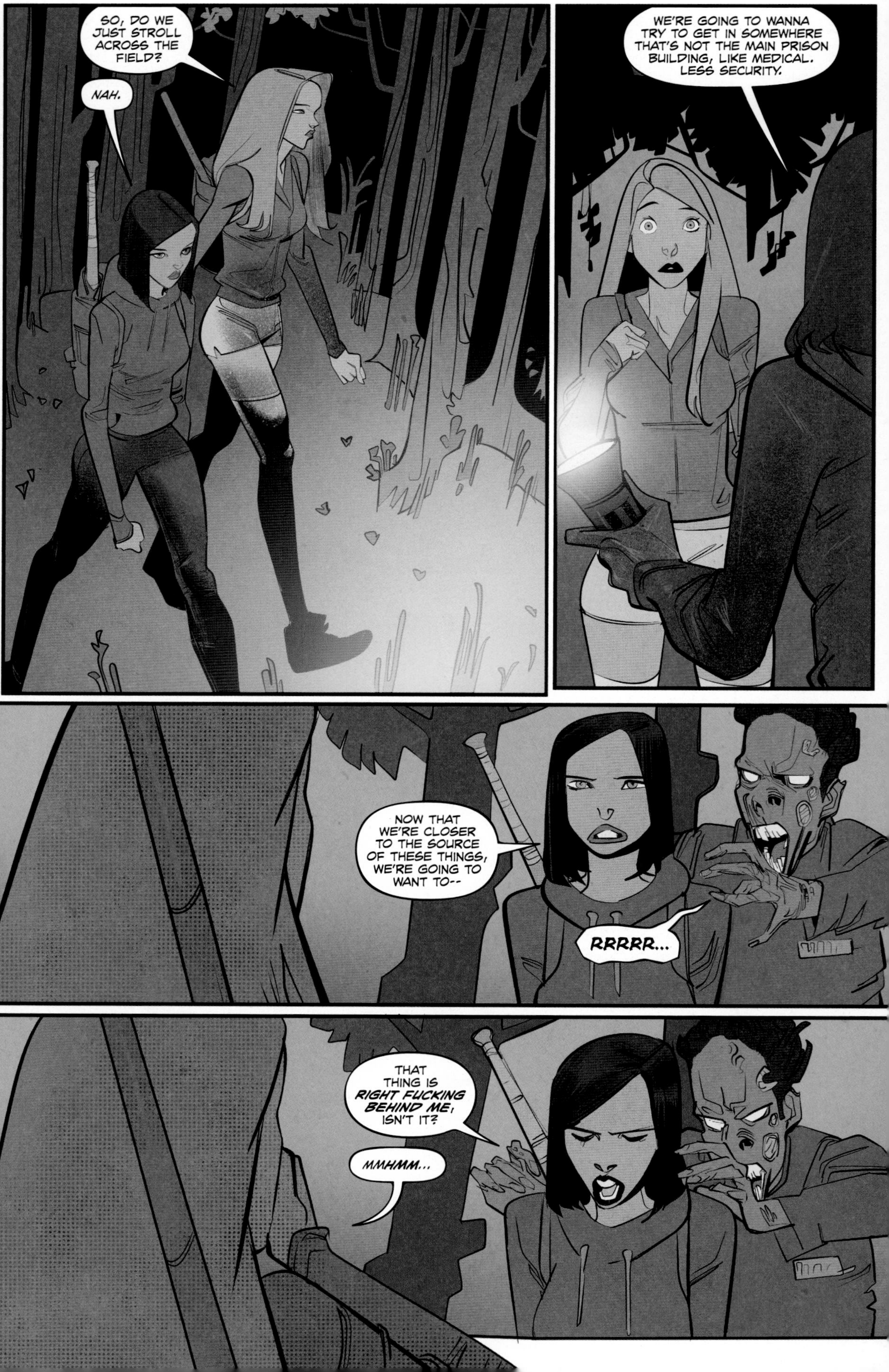
SO, DO WE JUST STROLL ACROSS THE FIELD?
NAH.
WE'RE GOING TO WANNA TRY TO GET IN SOMEWHERE THAT'S NOT THE MAIN PRISON BUILDING, LIKE MEDICAL. LESS SECURITY.
NOW THAT WE'RE CLOSER TO THE SOURCE OF THESE THINGS, WE'RE GOING TO WANT TO--
RRRRR...
THAT THING IS RIGHT FUCKING BEHIND ME, ISN'T IT?
MMHMM...

RRRAAAAA--

THUNK

SSSH

KRRAK

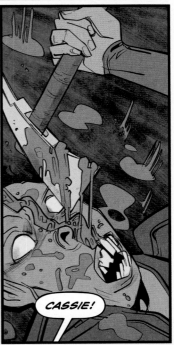

CASSIE!

MAYBE I *SHOULD* HAVE GIVEN HER THE WHOLE SELF-SACRIFICING SPEECH, HONESTLY.

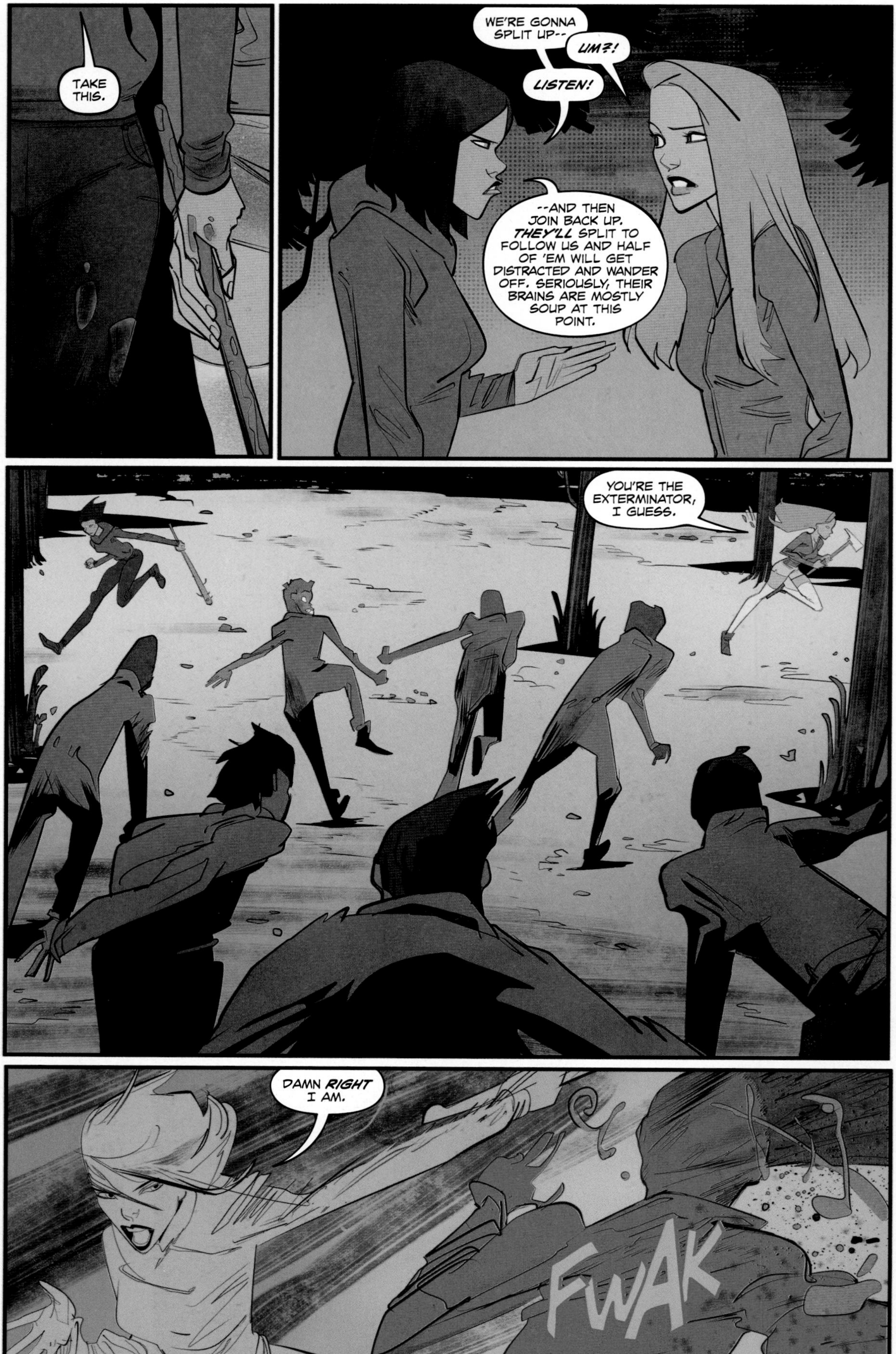
TAKE THIS.
WE'RE GONNA SPLIT UP--
UM?!
LISTEN!
--AND THEN JOIN BACK UP. THEY'LL SPLIT TO FOLLOW US AND HALF OF 'EM WILL GET DISTRACTED AND WANDER OFF. SERIOUSLY, THEIR BRAINS ARE MOSTLY SOUP AT THIS POINT.
YOU'RE THE EXTERMINATOR, I GUESS.
DAMN RIGHT I AM.
FWAK

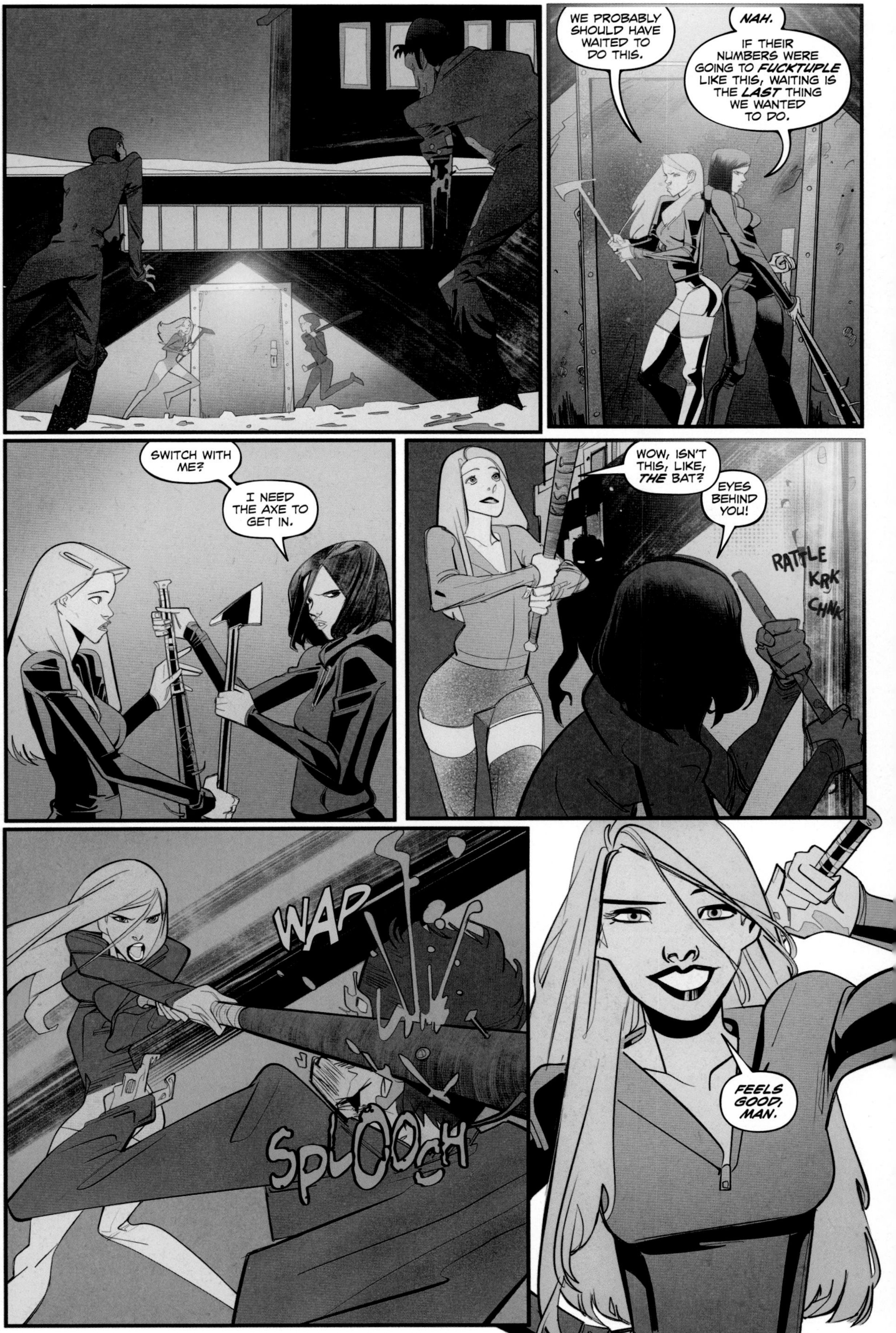

WE PROBABLY SHOULD HAVE WAITED TO DO THIS.
NAH.
IF THEIR NUMBERS WERE GOING TO FUCKTUPLE LIKE THIS, WAITING IS THE LAST THING WE WANTED TO DO.
SWITCH WITH ME?
I NEED THE AXE TO GET IN.
WOW, ISN'T THIS, LIKE, THE BAT?
EYES BEHIND YOU!
RATTLE
KRK
CHNK
WAP
SPLOOSH
FEELS GOOD, MAN.

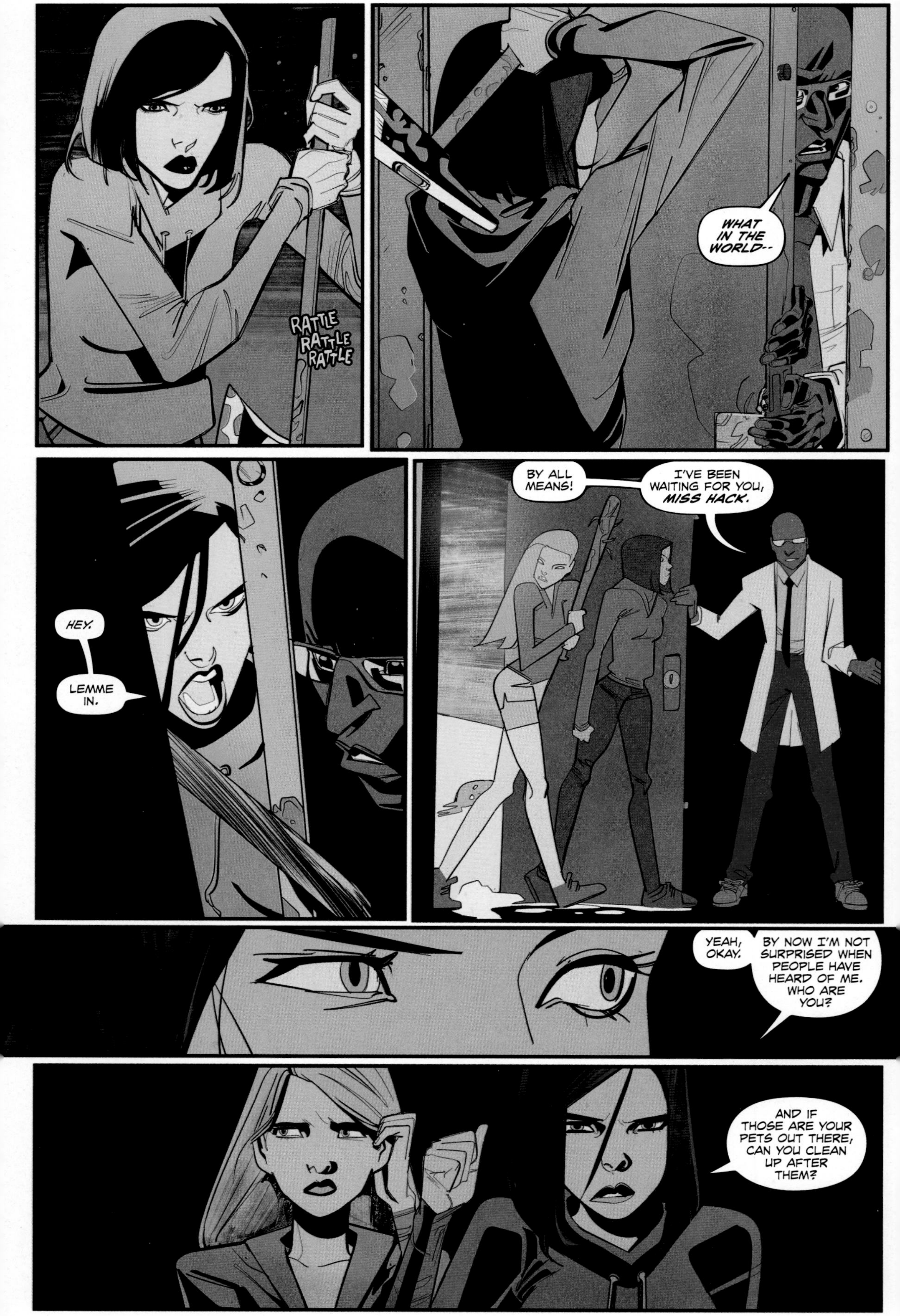
RATTLE
RATTLE
RATTLE
WHAT IN THE WORLD--
HEY.
LEMME IN.
BY ALL MEANS!
I'VE BEEN WAITING FOR YOU, MISS HACK.
YEAH, OKAY.
BY NOW I'M NOT SURPRISED WHEN PEOPLE HAVE HEARD OF ME. WHO ARE YOU?
AND IF THOSE ARE YOUR PETS OUT THERE, CAN YOU CLEAN UP AFTER THEM?

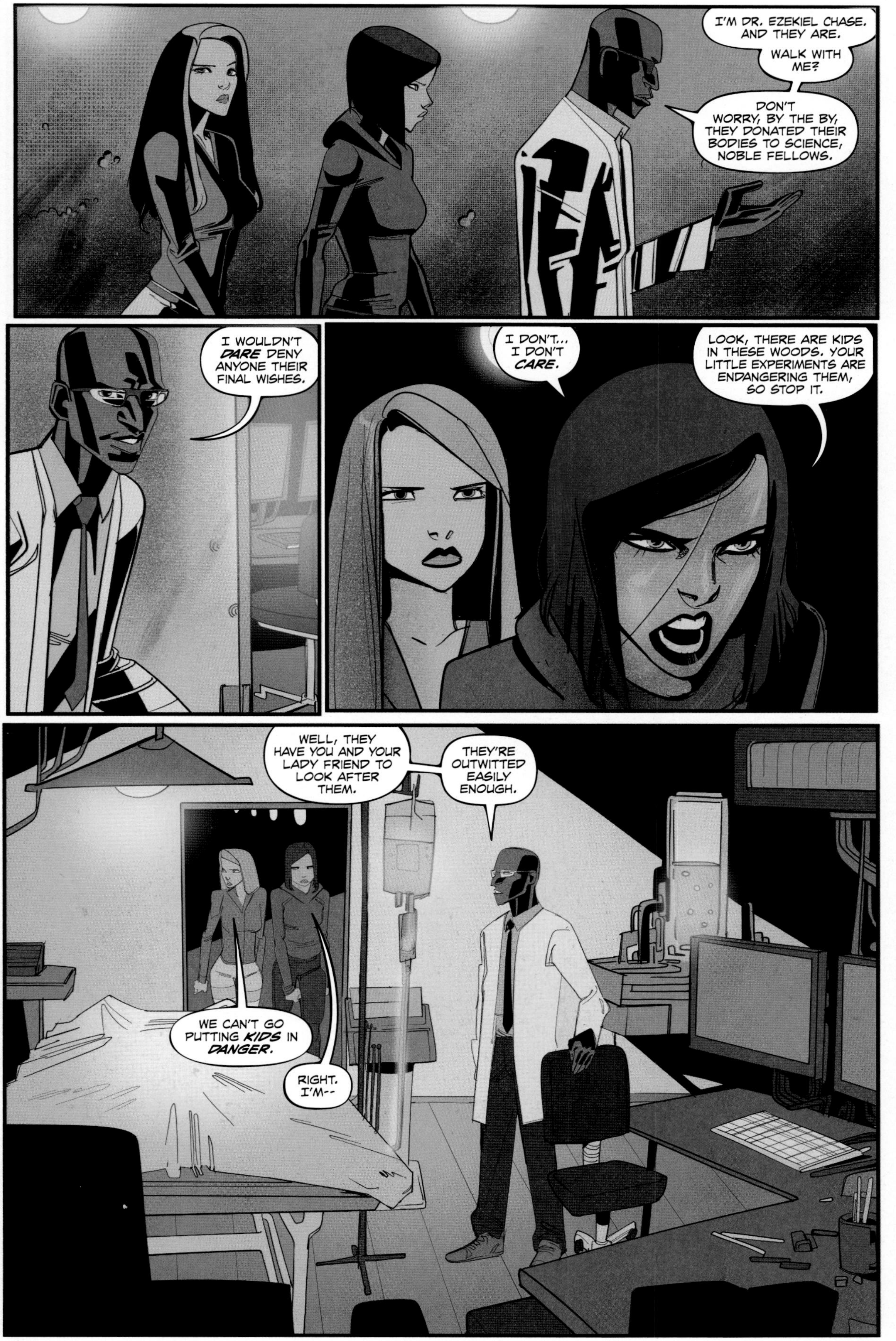
I'M DR. EZEKIEL CHASE. AND THEY ARE.
WALK WITH ME?
DON'T WORRY, BY THE BY, THEY DONATED THEIR BODIES TO SCIENCE, NOBLE FELLOWS.
I WOULDN'T *DARE* DENY ANYONE THEIR FINAL WISHES.
I DON'T... I DON'T *CARE*.
LOOK, THERE ARE KIDS IN THESE WOODS. YOUR LITTLE EXPERIMENTS ARE ENDANGERING THEM, SO STOP IT.
WELL, THEY HAVE YOU AND YOUR LADY FRIEND TO LOOK AFTER THEM.
THEY'RE OUTWITTED EASILY ENOUGH.
WE CAN'T GO PUTTING *KIDS* IN *DANGER*.
RIGHT. I'M--

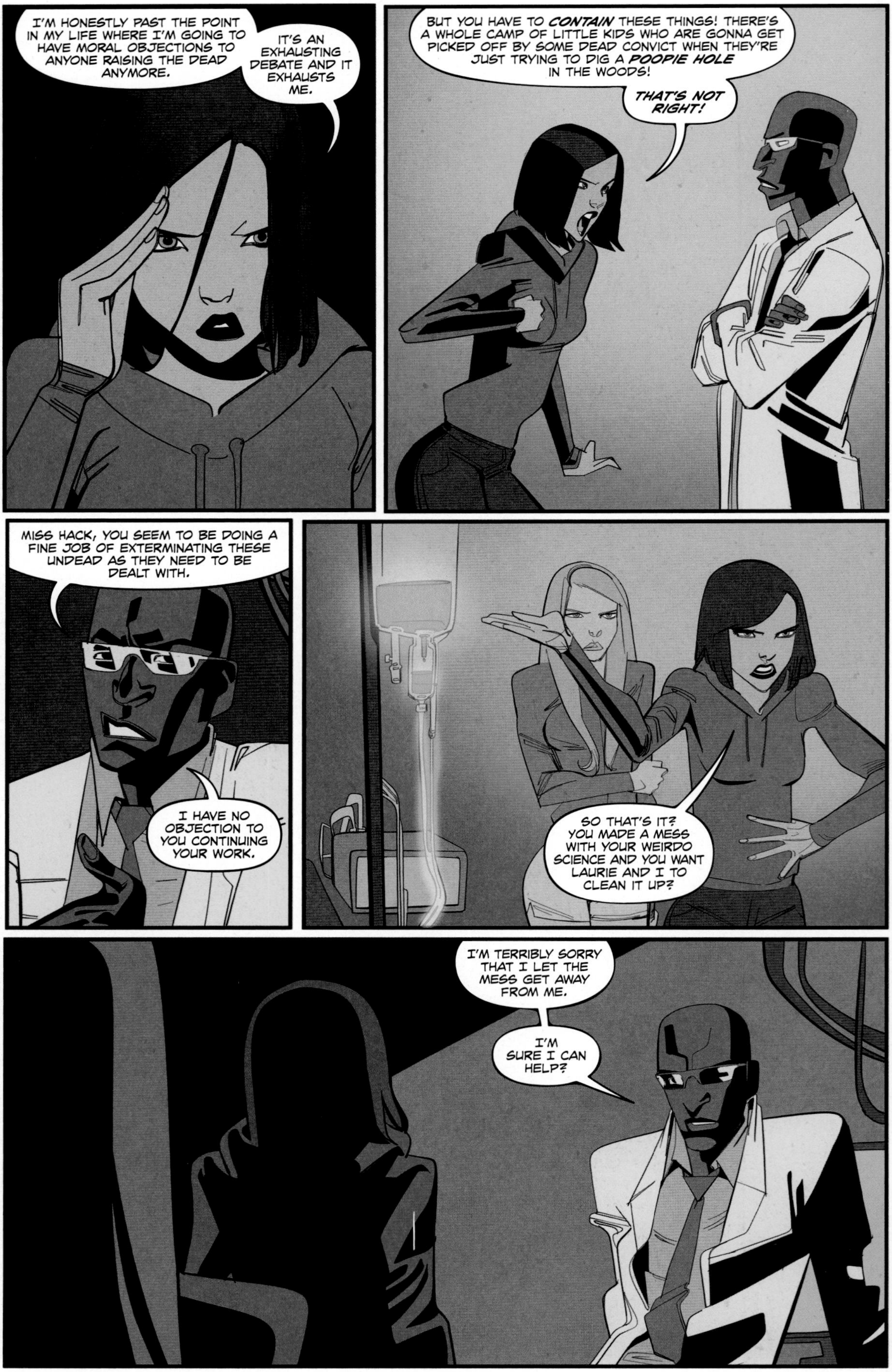
I'M HONESTLY PAST THE POINT IN MY LIFE WHERE I'M GOING TO HAVE MORAL OBJECTIONS TO ANYONE RAISING THE DEAD ANYMORE.
IT'S AN EXHAUSTING DEBATE AND IT EXHAUSTS ME.
BUT YOU HAVE TO CONTAIN THESE THINGS! THERE'S A WHOLE CAMP OF LITTLE KIDS WHO ARE GONNA GET PICKED OFF BY SOME DEAD CONVICT WHEN THEY'RE JUST TRYING TO DIG A POOPIE HOLE IN THE WOODS!
THAT'S NOT RIGHT!
MISS HACK, YOU SEEM TO BE DOING A FINE JOB OF EXTERMINATING THESE UNDEAD AS THEY NEED TO BE DEALT WITH.
I HAVE NO OBJECTION TO YOU CONTINUING YOUR WORK.
SO THAT'S IT? YOU MADE A MESS WITH YOUR WEIRDO SCIENCE AND YOU WANT LAURIE AND I TO CLEAN IT UP?
I'M TERRIBLY SORRY THAT I LET THE MESS GET AWAY FROM ME.
I'M SURE I CAN HELP?

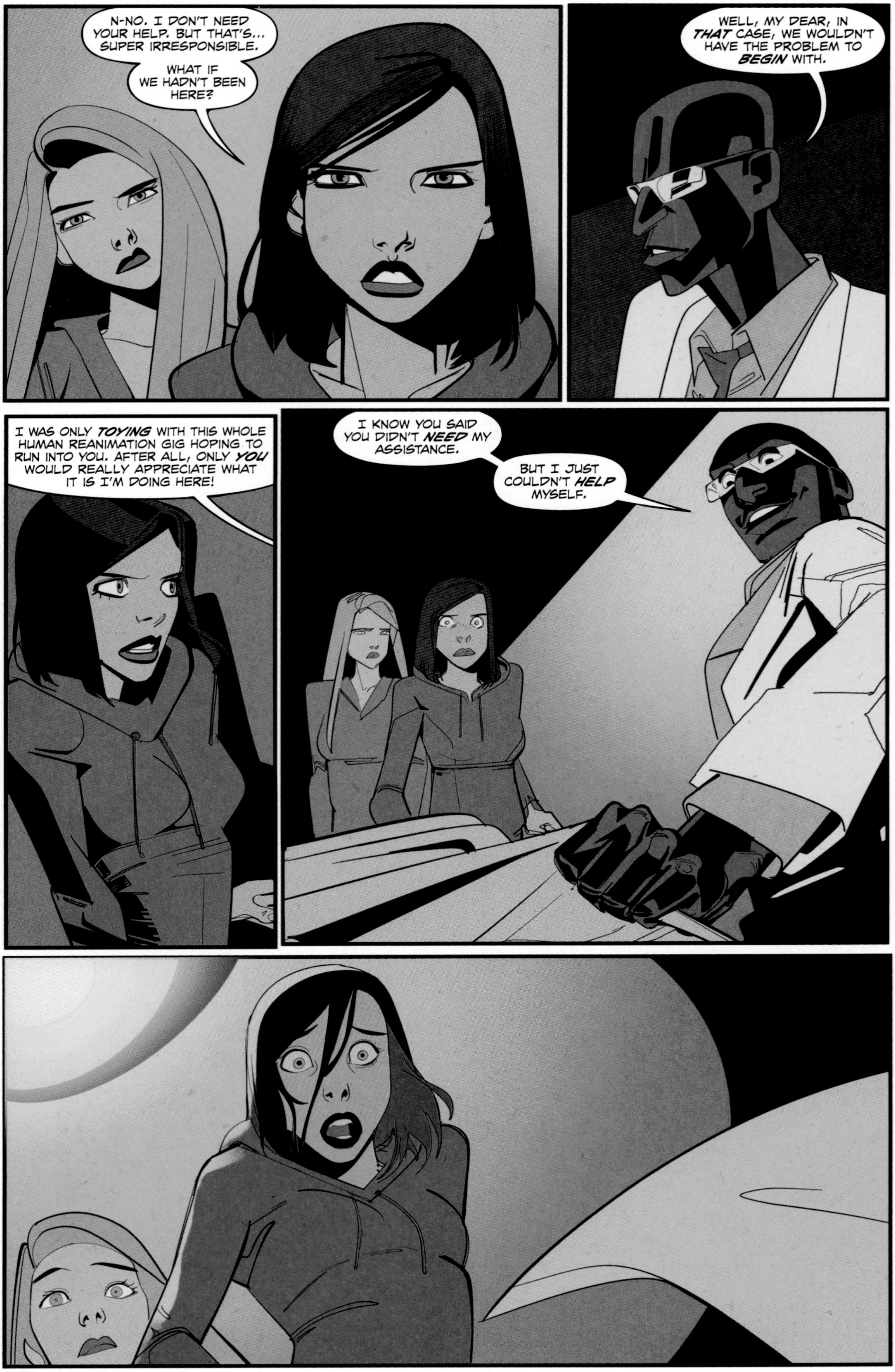
N-NO. I DON'T NEED YOUR HELP. BUT THAT'S... SUPER IRRESPONSIBLE.
WHAT IF WE HADN'T BEEN HERE?
WELL, MY DEAR, IN *THAT* CASE, WE WOULDN'T HAVE THE PROBLEM TO *BEGIN* WITH.
I WAS ONLY *TOYING* WITH THIS WHOLE HUMAN REANIMATION GIG HOPING TO RUN INTO YOU. AFTER ALL, ONLY *YOU* WOULD REALLY APPRECIATE WHAT IT IS I'M DOING HERE!
I KNOW YOU SAID YOU DIDN'T *NEED* MY ASSISTANCE.
BUT I JUST COULDN'T *HELP* MYSELF.

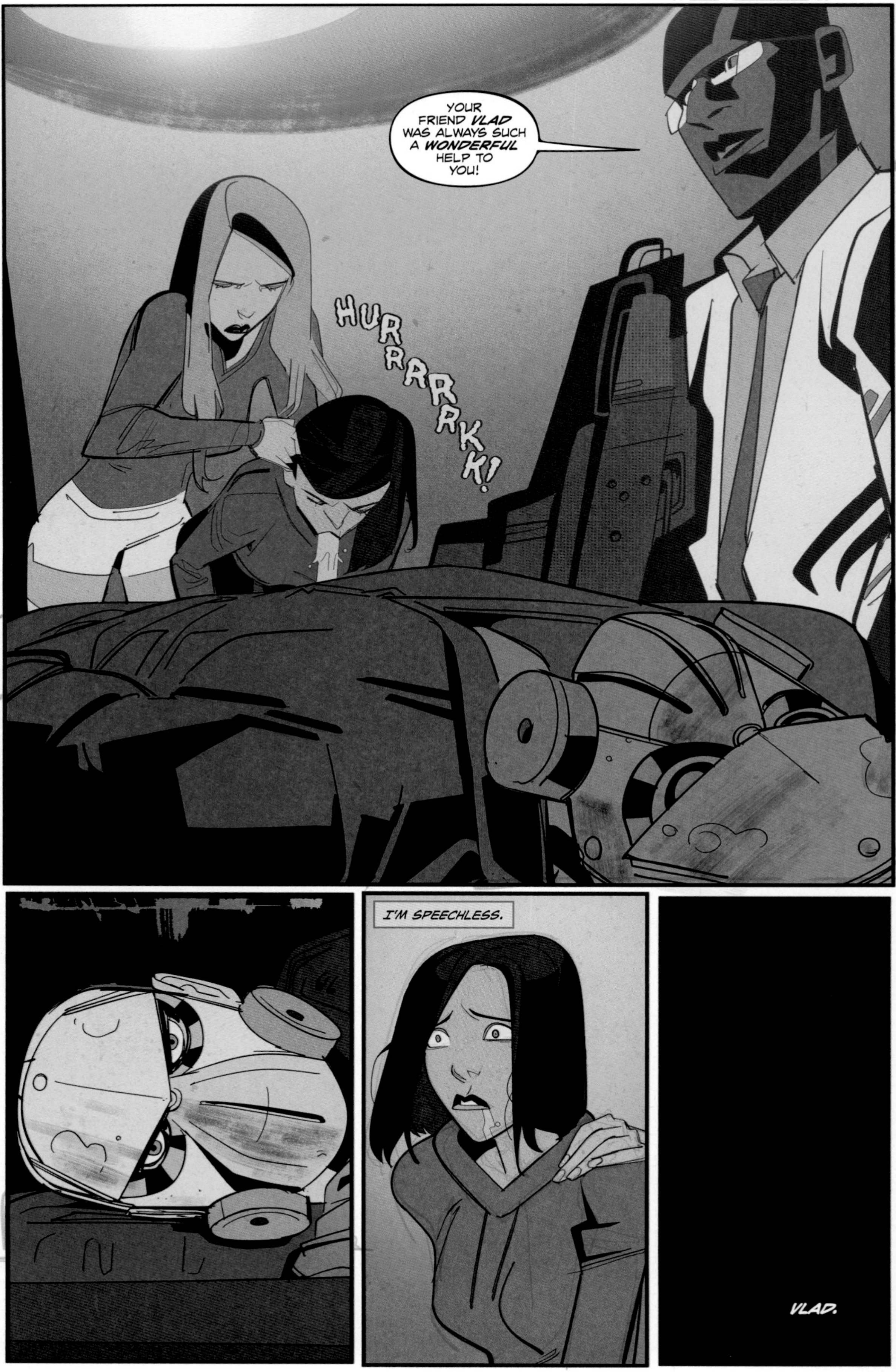
YOUR FRIEND VLAD WAS ALWAYS SUCH A WONDERFUL HELP TO YOU!
HURRRRRKK!
I'M SPEECHLESS.
VLAD.

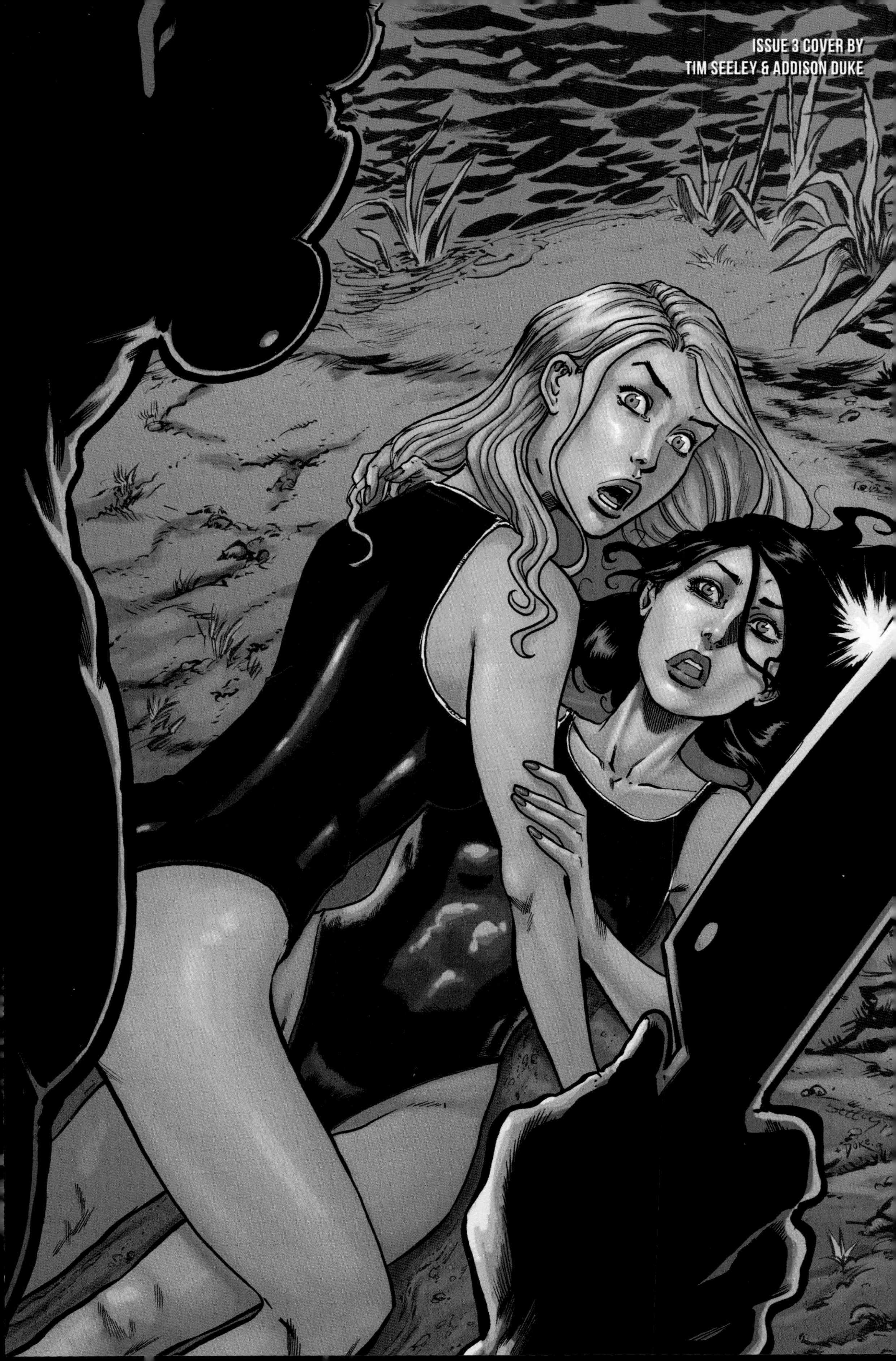
ISSUE 3 COVER BY
TIM SEELEY & ADDISON DUKE

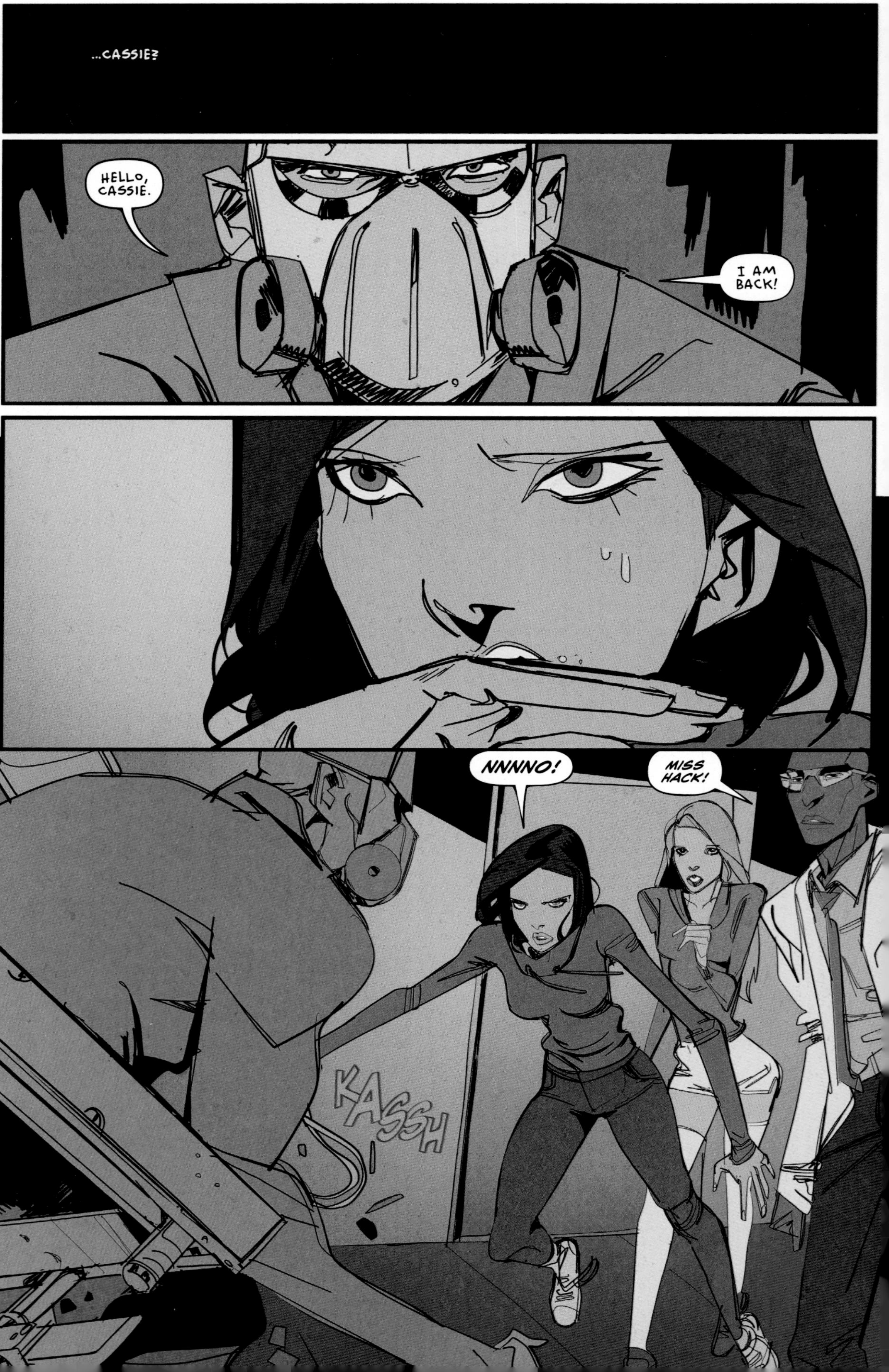
...CASSIE?
HELLO, CASSIE.
I AM BACK!
NNNNO!
MISS HACK!
KASSH

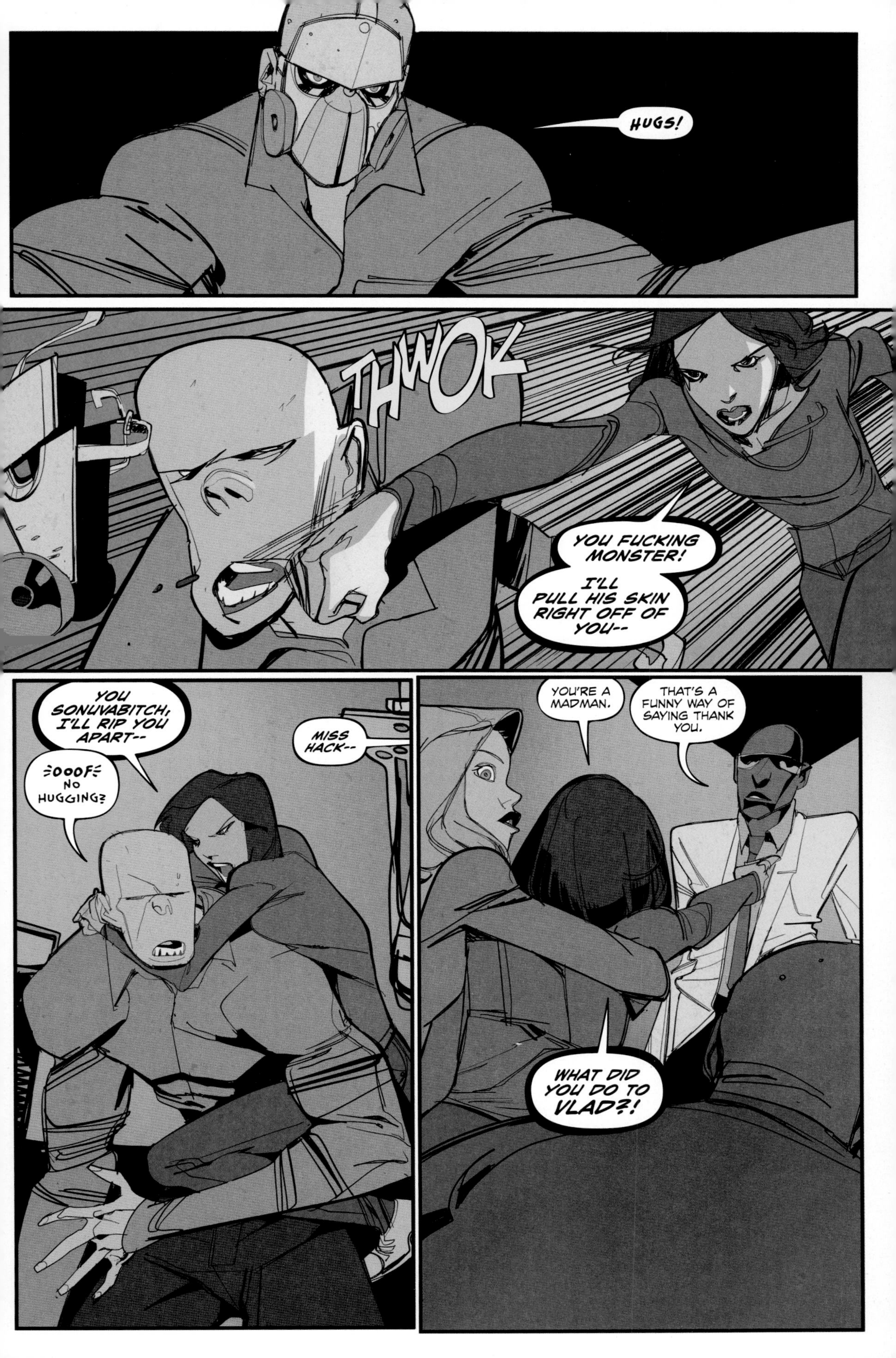
HUGS!
THWOK
YOU FUCKING MONSTER!
I'LL PULL HIS SKIN RIGHT OFF OF YOU--
YOU SONUVABITCH, I'LL RIP YOU APART--
MISS HACK--
OOOF NO HUGGING?
YOU'RE A MADMAN.
THAT'S A FUNNY WAY OF SAYING THANK YOU.
WHAT DID YOU DO TO VLAD?!

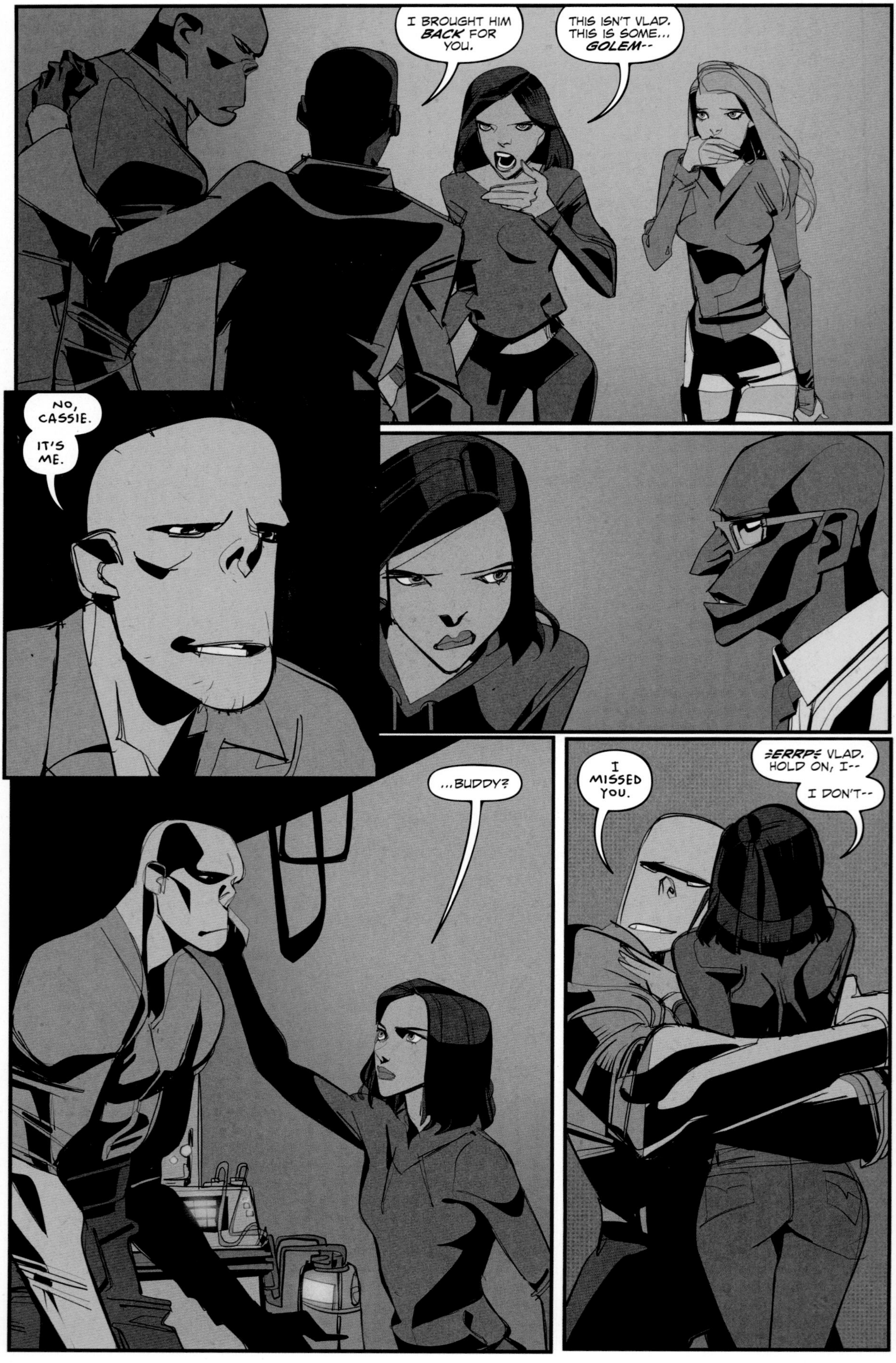
I BROUGHT HIM BACK FOR YOU.
THIS ISN'T VLAD. THIS IS SOME... GOLEM--
NO, CASSIE.
IT'S ME.
...BUDDY?
I MISSED YOU.
ERRP VLAD. HOLD ON, I--
I DON'T--

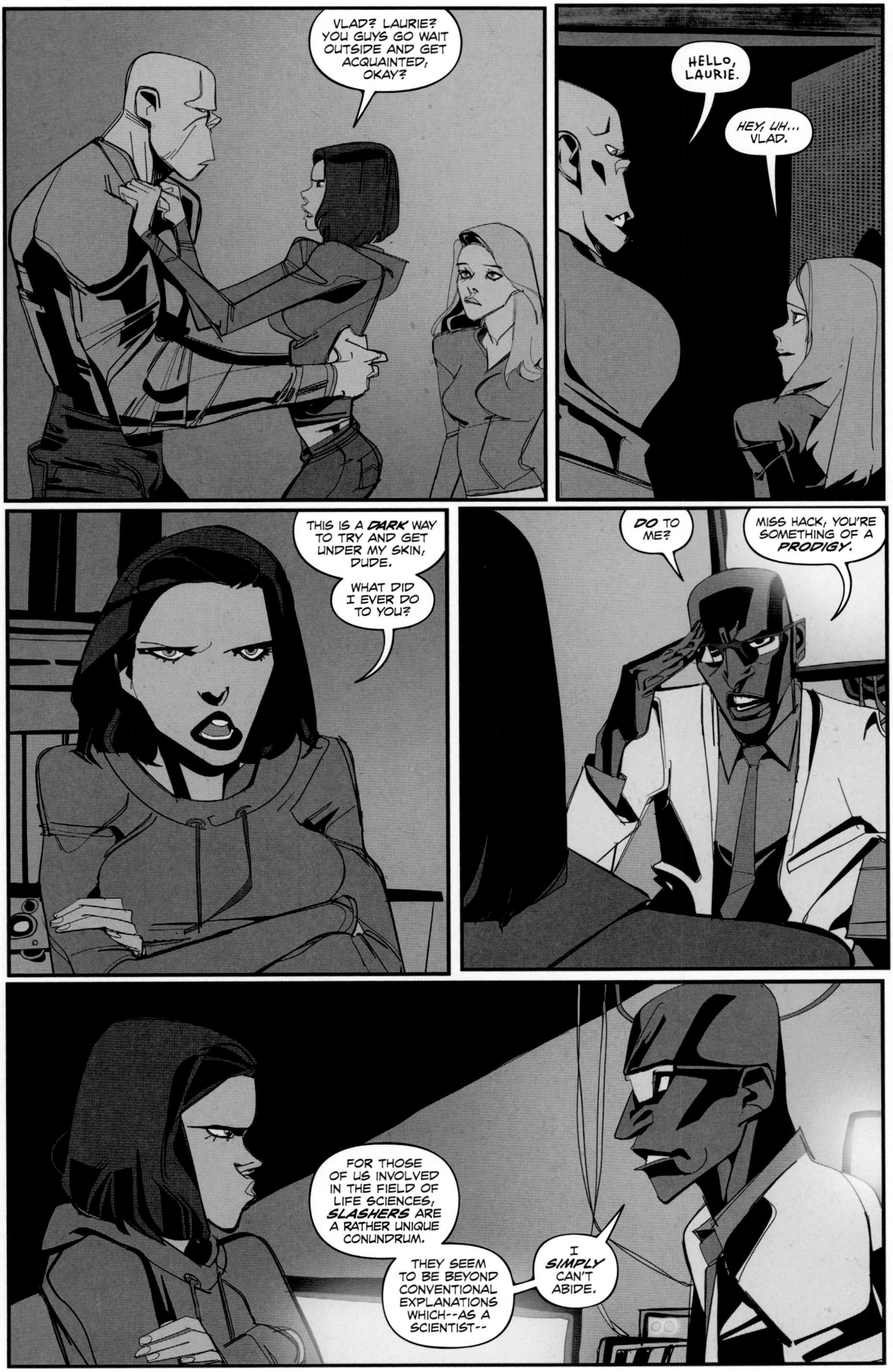
VLAD? LAURIE? YOU GUYS GO WAIT OUTSIDE AND GET ACQUAINTED, OKAY?
HELLO, LAURIE.
HEY, UH... VLAD.
THIS IS A **DARK** WAY TO TRY AND GET UNDER MY SKIN, DUDE.
WHAT DID I EVER DO TO YOU?
DO TO ME?
MISS HACK, YOU'RE SOMETHING OF A ***PRODIGY.***
FOR THOSE OF US INVOLVED IN THE FIELD OF LIFE SCIENCES, ***SLASHERS*** ARE A RATHER UNIQUE CONUNDRUM.
THEY SEEM TO BE BEYOND CONVENTIONAL EXPLANATIONS WHICH--AS A SCIENTIST--
I ***SIMPLY*** CAN'T ABIDE.

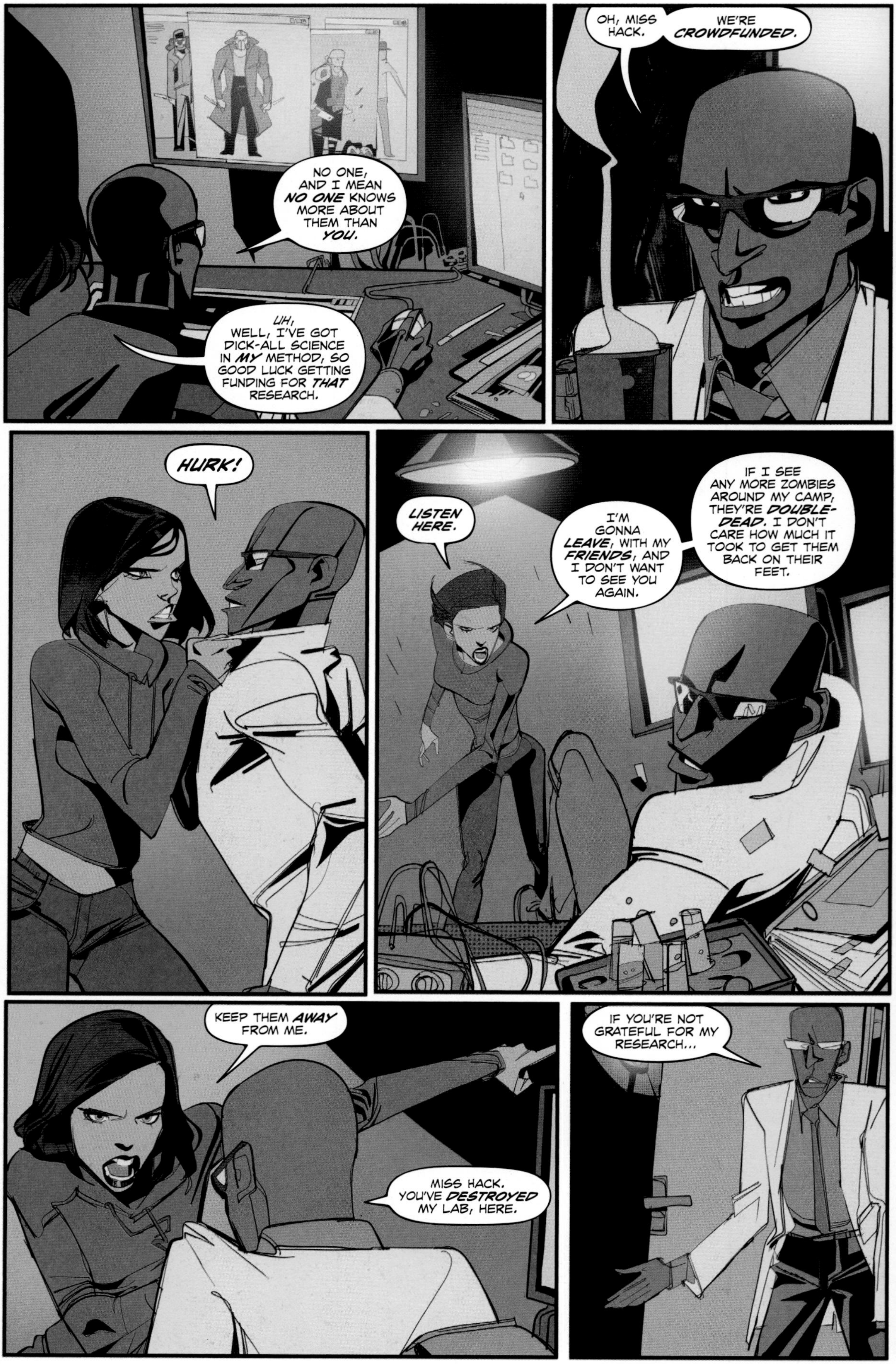
NO ONE, AND I MEAN NO ONE KNOWS MORE ABOUT THEM THAN YOU.
UH, WELL, I'VE GOT DICK-ALL SCIENCE IN MY METHOD, SO GOOD LUCK GETTING FUNDING FOR THAT RESEARCH.
OH, MISS HACK.
WE'RE CROWDFUNDED.
HURK!
LISTEN HERE.
I'M GONNA LEAVE, WITH MY FRIENDS, AND I DON'T WANT TO SEE YOU AGAIN.
IF I SEE ANY MORE ZOMBIES AROUND MY CAMP, THEY'RE DOUBLE-DEAD. I DON'T CARE HOW MUCH IT TOOK TO GET THEM BACK ON THEIR FEET.
KEEP THEM AWAY FROM ME.
MISS HACK. YOU'VE DESTROYED MY LAB, HERE.
IF YOU'RE NOT GRATEFUL FOR MY RESEARCH...

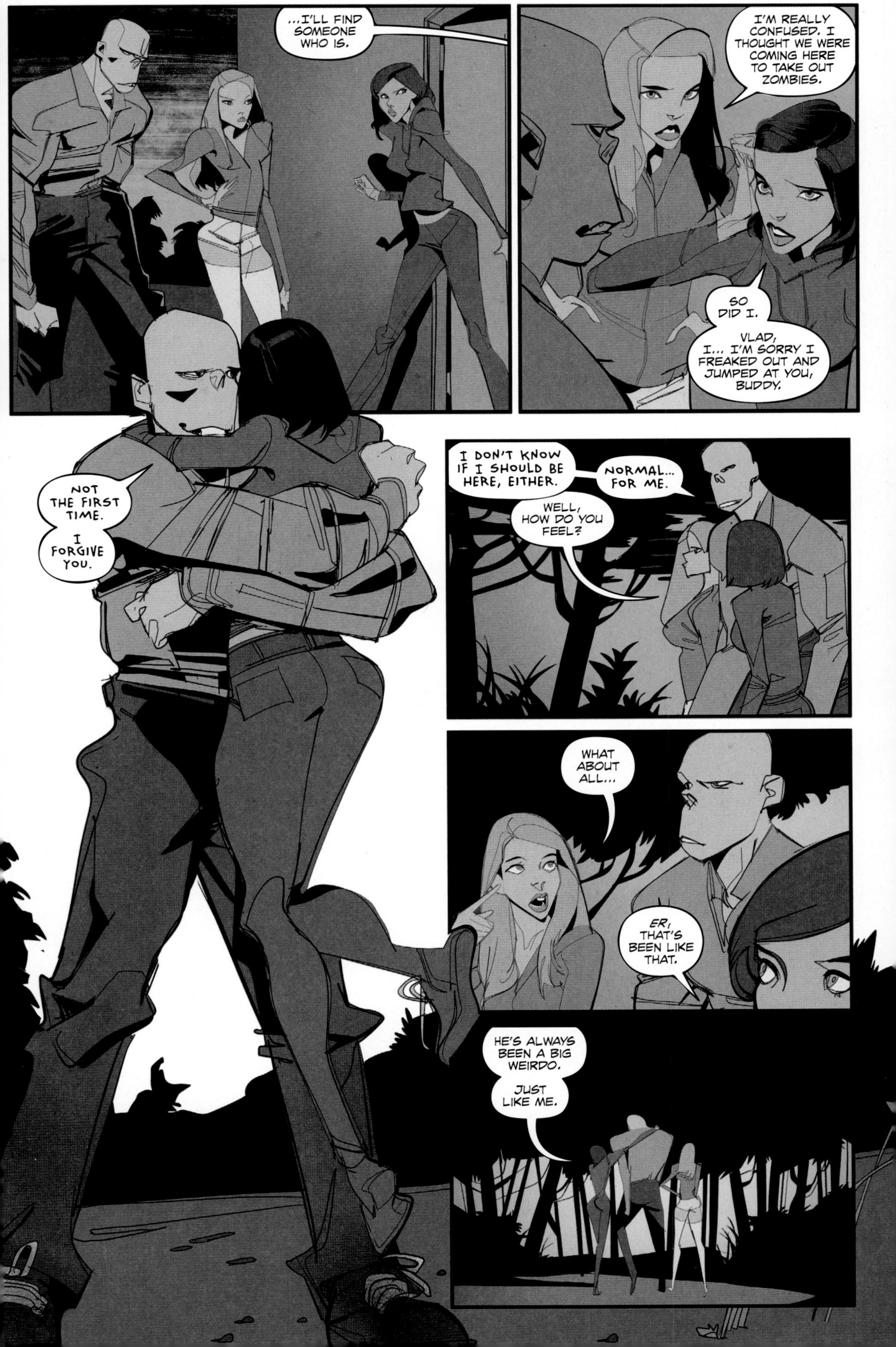
...I'LL FIND SOMEONE WHO IS.
I'M REALLY CONFUSED. I THOUGHT WE WERE COMING HERE TO TAKE OUT ZOMBIES.
SO DID I.
VLAD, I... I'M SORRY I FREAKED OUT AND JUMPED AT YOU, BUDDY.
NOT THE FIRST TIME.
I FORGIVE YOU.
I DON'T KNOW IF I SHOULD BE HERE, EITHER.
WELL, HOW DO YOU FEEL?
NORMAL... FOR ME.
WHAT ABOUT ALL...
ER, THAT'S BEEN LIKE THAT.
HE'S ALWAYS BEEN A BIG WEIRDO.
JUST LIKE ME.

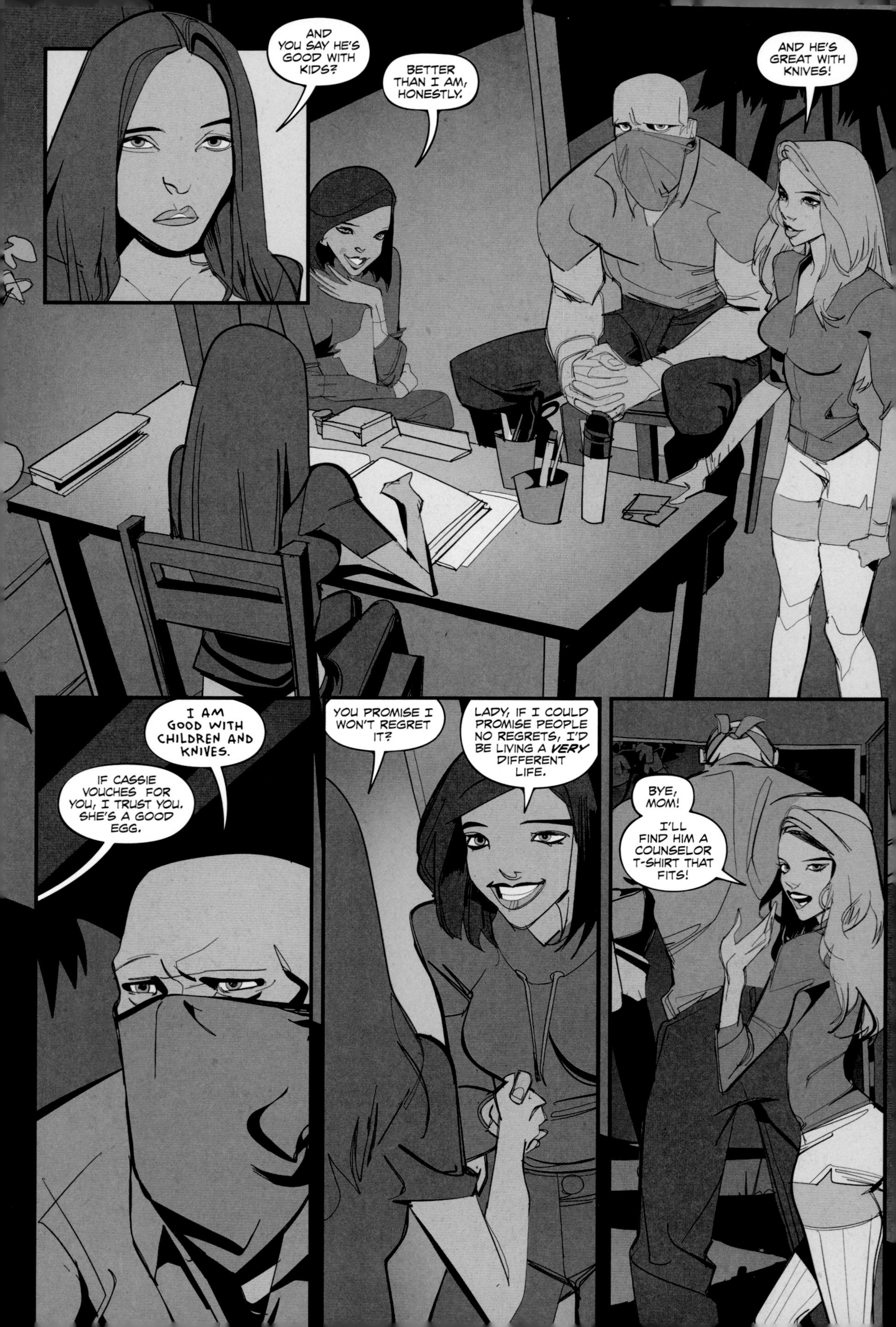
AND YOU SAY HE'S GOOD WITH KIDS?
BETTER THAN I AM, HONESTLY.
AND HE'S GREAT WITH KNIVES!
I AM GOOD WITH CHILDREN AND KNIVES.
IF CASSIE VOUCHES FOR YOU, I TRUST YOU. SHE'S A GOOD EGG.
YOU PROMISE I WON'T REGRET IT?
LADY, IF I COULD PROMISE PEOPLE NO REGRETS, I'D BE LIVING A VERY DIFFERENT LIFE.
BYE, MOM!
I'LL FIND HIM A COUNSELOR T-SHIRT THAT FITS!

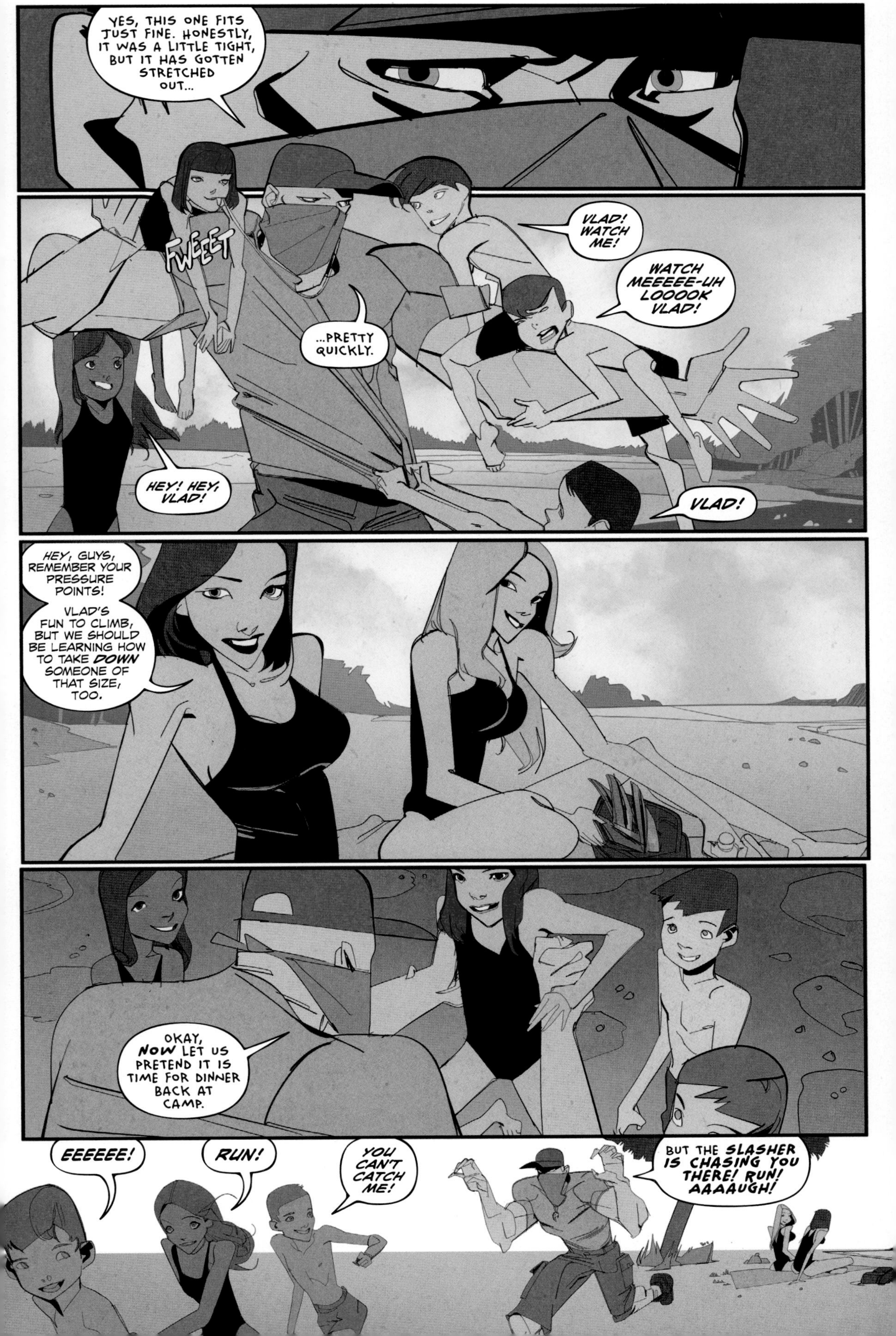
YES, THIS ONE FITS JUST FINE. HONESTLY, IT WAS A LITTLE TIGHT, BUT IT HAS GOTTEN STRETCHED OUT...
FWEEET
VLAD! WATCH ME!
WATCH MEEEEE-UH LOOOOK VLAD!
...PRETTY QUICKLY.
HEY! HEY, VLAD!
VLAD!
HEY, GUYS, REMEMBER YOUR PRESSURE POINTS!
VLAD'S FUN TO CLIMB, BUT WE SHOULD BE LEARNING HOW TO TAKE DOWN SOMEONE OF THAT SIZE, TOO.
OKAY, NOW LET US PRETEND IT IS TIME FOR DINNER BACK AT CAMP.
EEEEEE!
RUN!
YOU CAN'T CATCH ME!
BUT THE SLASHER IS CHASING YOU THERE! RUN! AAAAUGH!

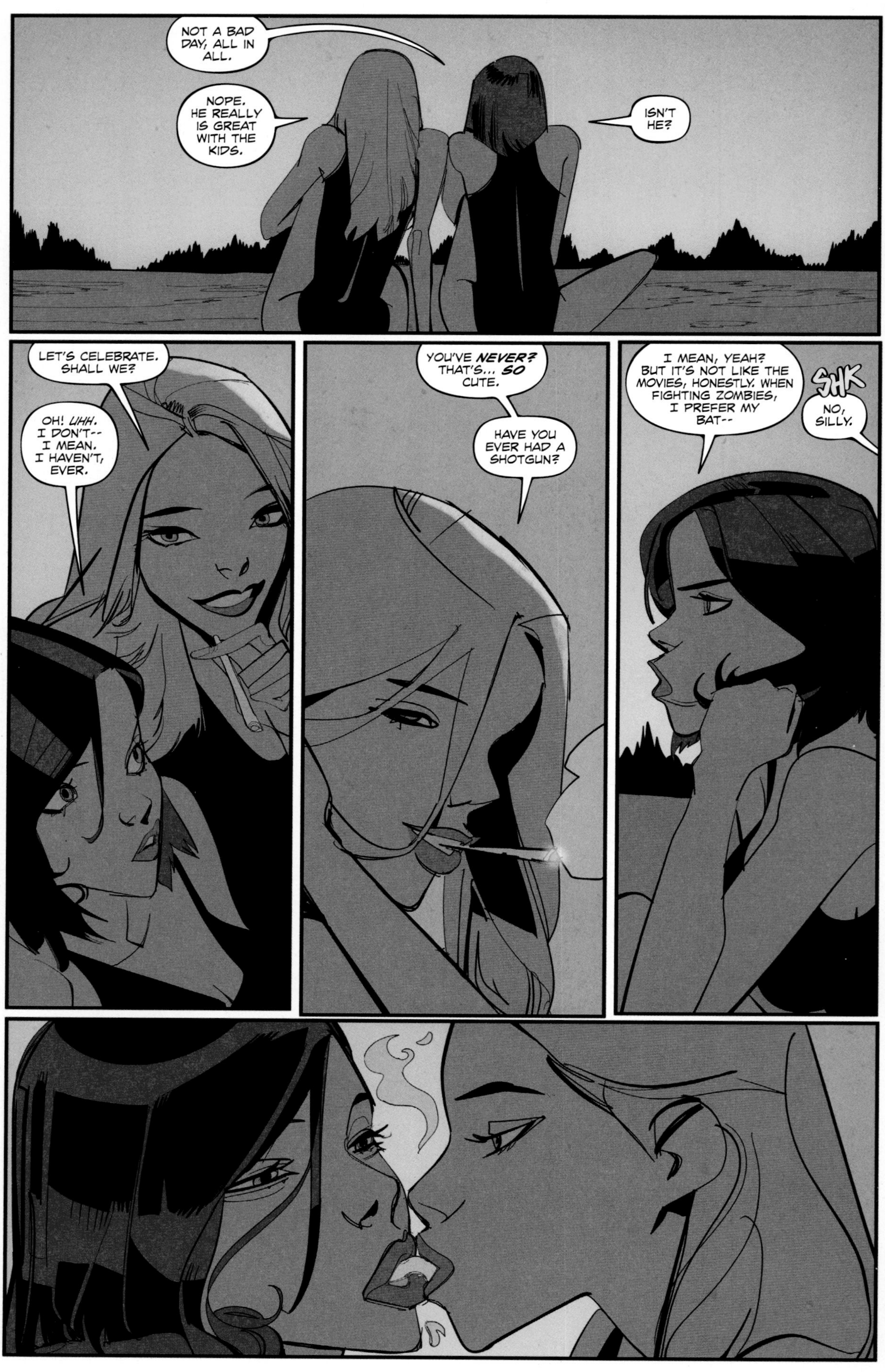
NOT A BAD DAY, ALL IN ALL.
NOPE. HE REALLY IS GREAT WITH THE KIDS.
ISN'T HE?
LET'S CELEBRATE. SHALL WE?
OH! UHH. I DON'T-- I MEAN. I HAVEN'T, EVER.
YOU'VE NEVER? THAT'S... SO CUTE.
HAVE YOU EVER HAD A SHOTGUN?
I MEAN, YEAH? BUT IT'S NOT LIKE THE MOVIES, HONESTLY. WHEN FIGHTING ZOMBIES, I PREFER MY BAT--
SHK
NO, SILLY.

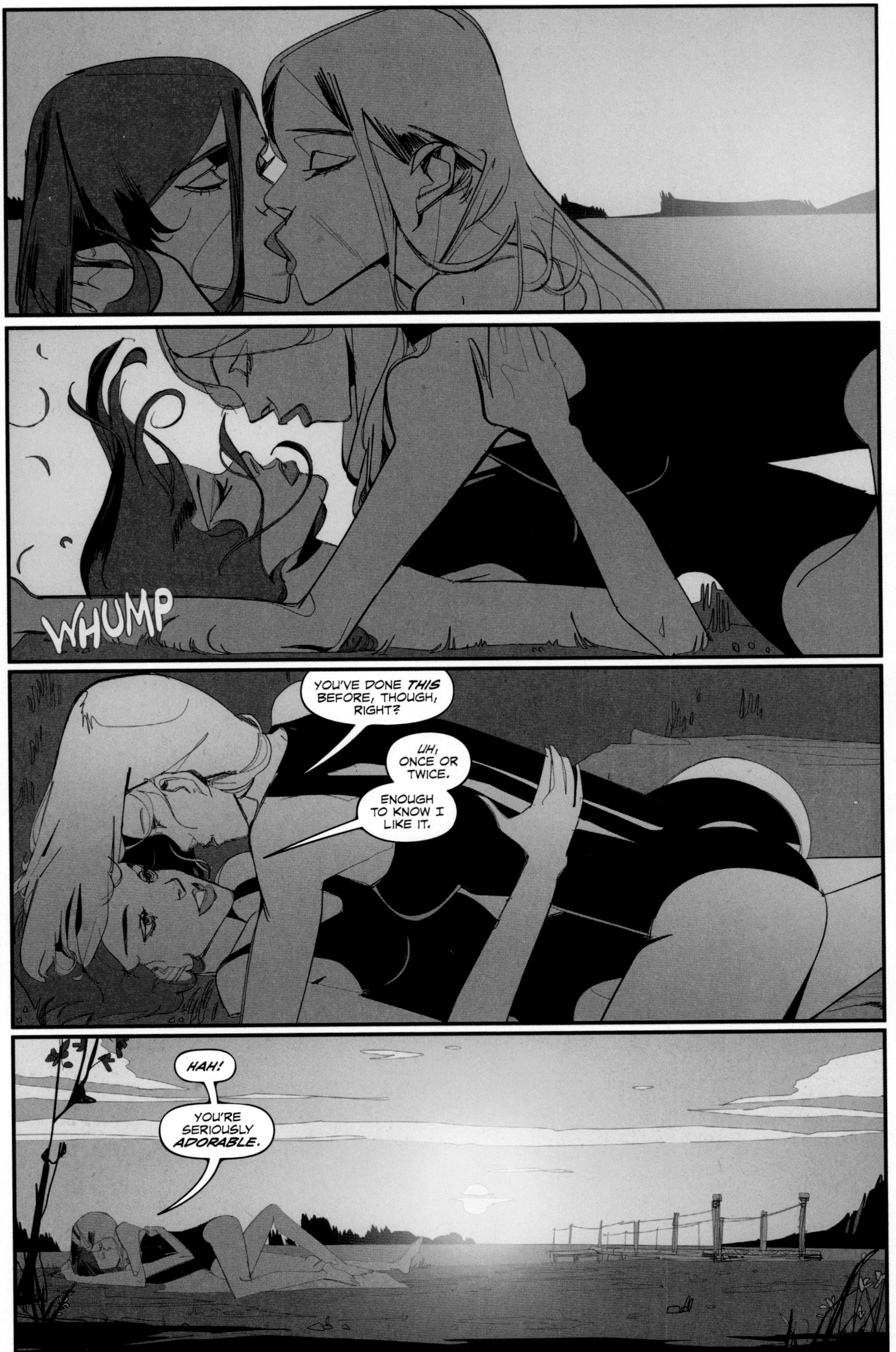
WHUMP
YOU'VE DONE THIS BEFORE, THOUGH, RIGHT?
UH, ONCE OR TWICE.
ENOUGH TO KNOW I LIKE IT.
HAH!
YOU'RE SERIOUSLY ADORABLE.

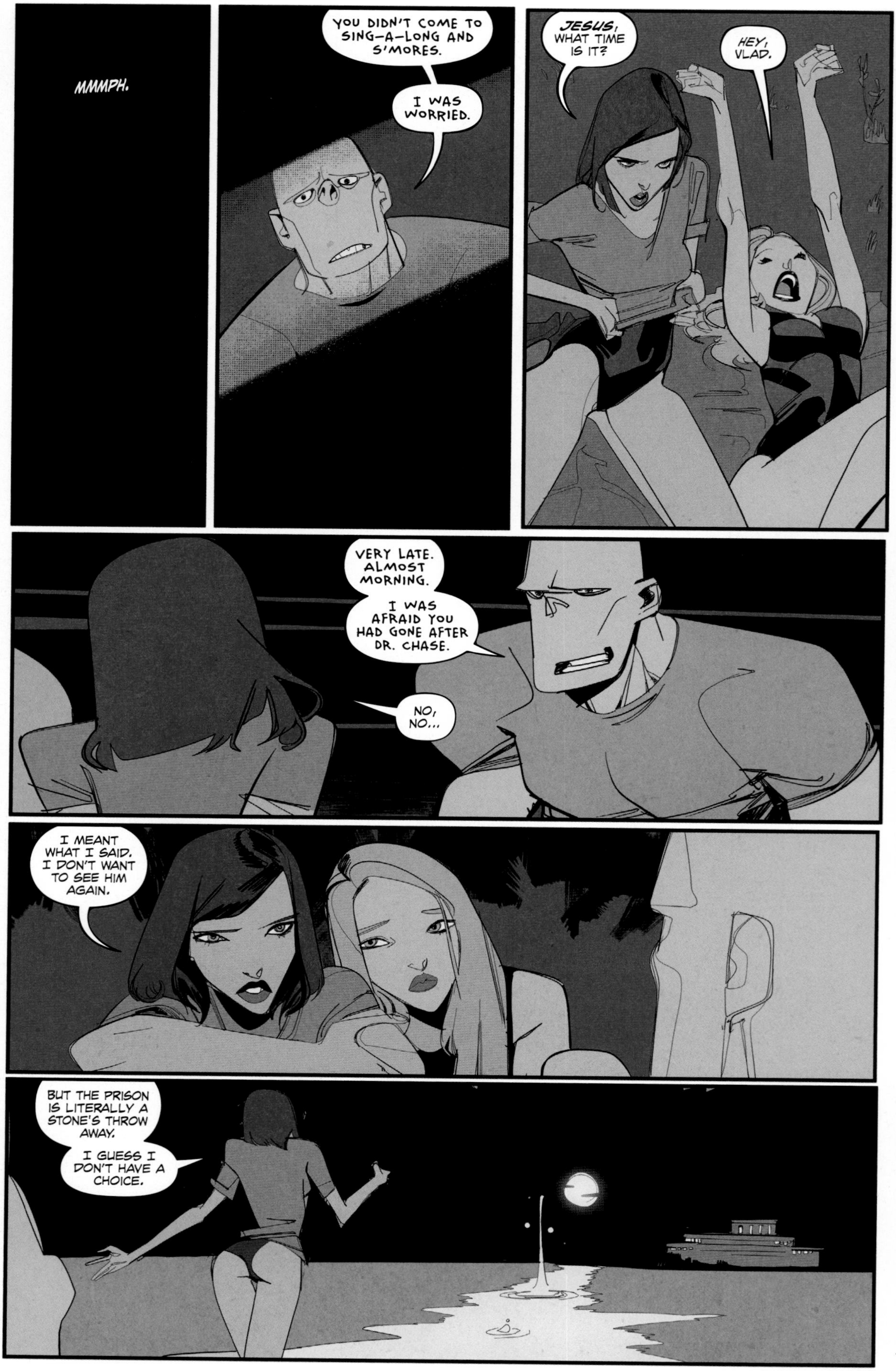
MMMPH.
YOU DIDN'T COME TO SING-A-LONG AND S'MORES.
I WAS WORRIED.
JESUS, WHAT TIME IS IT?
HEY, VLAD.
VERY LATE. ALMOST MORNING.
I WAS AFRAID YOU HAD GONE AFTER DR. CHASE.
NO, NO...
I MEANT WHAT I SAID. I DON'T WANT TO SEE HIM AGAIN.
BUT THE PRISON IS LITERALLY A STONE'S THROW AWAY.
I GUESS I DON'T HAVE A CHOICE.

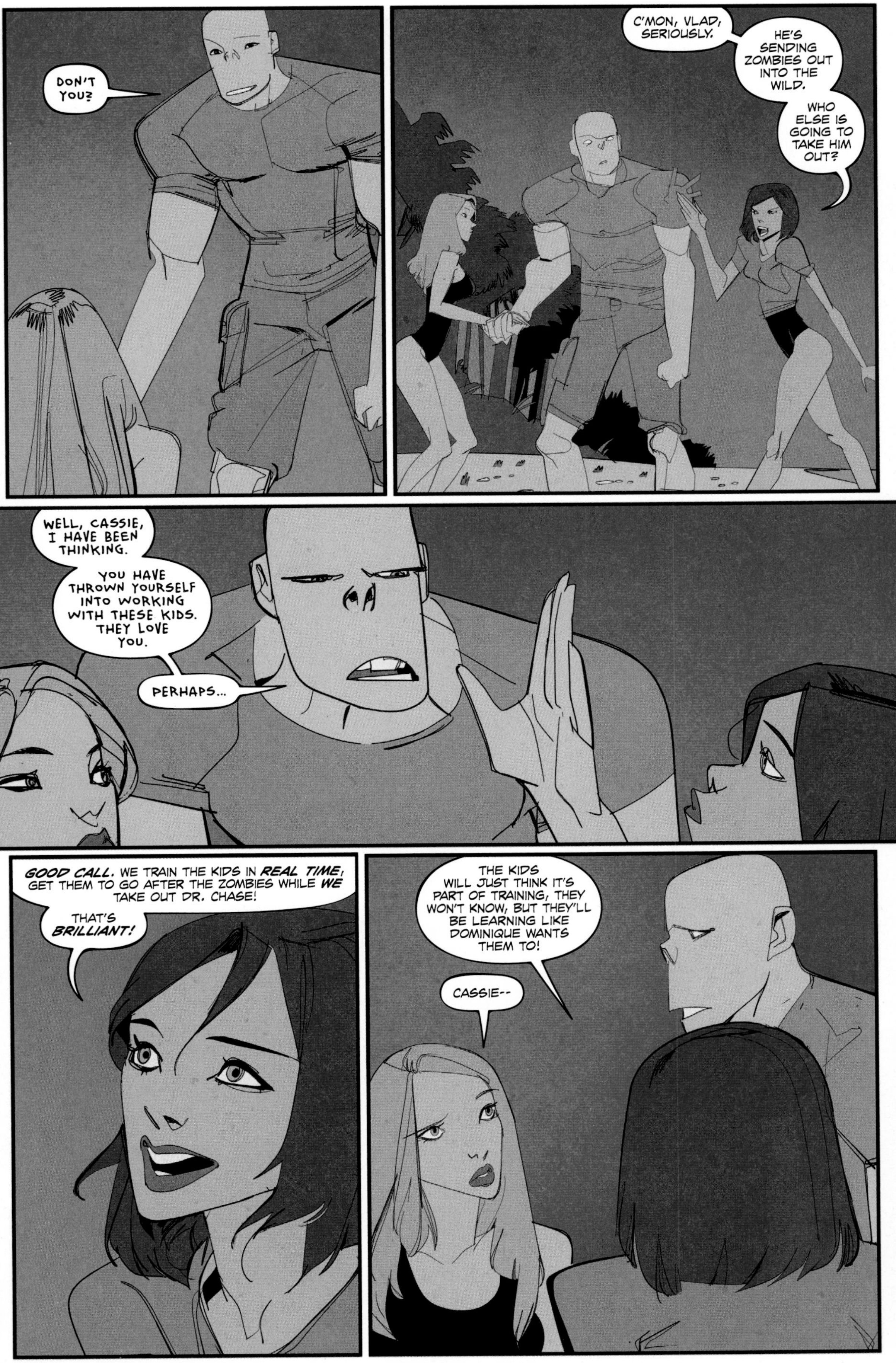
DON'T YOU?
C'MON, VLAD, SERIOUSLY.
HE'S SENDING ZOMBIES OUT INTO THE WILD.
WHO ELSE IS GOING TO TAKE HIM OUT?
WELL, CASSIE, I HAVE BEEN THINKING.
YOU HAVE THROWN YOURSELF INTO WORKING WITH THESE KIDS. THEY LOVE YOU.
PERHAPS...
GOOD CALL. WE TRAIN THE KIDS IN REAL TIME, GET THEM TO GO AFTER THE ZOMBIES WHILE WE TAKE OUT DR. CHASE!
THAT'S BRILLIANT!
THE KIDS WILL JUST THINK IT'S PART OF TRAINING, THEY WON'T KNOW, BUT THEY'LL BE LEARNING LIKE DOMINIQUE WANTS THEM TO!
CASSIE--

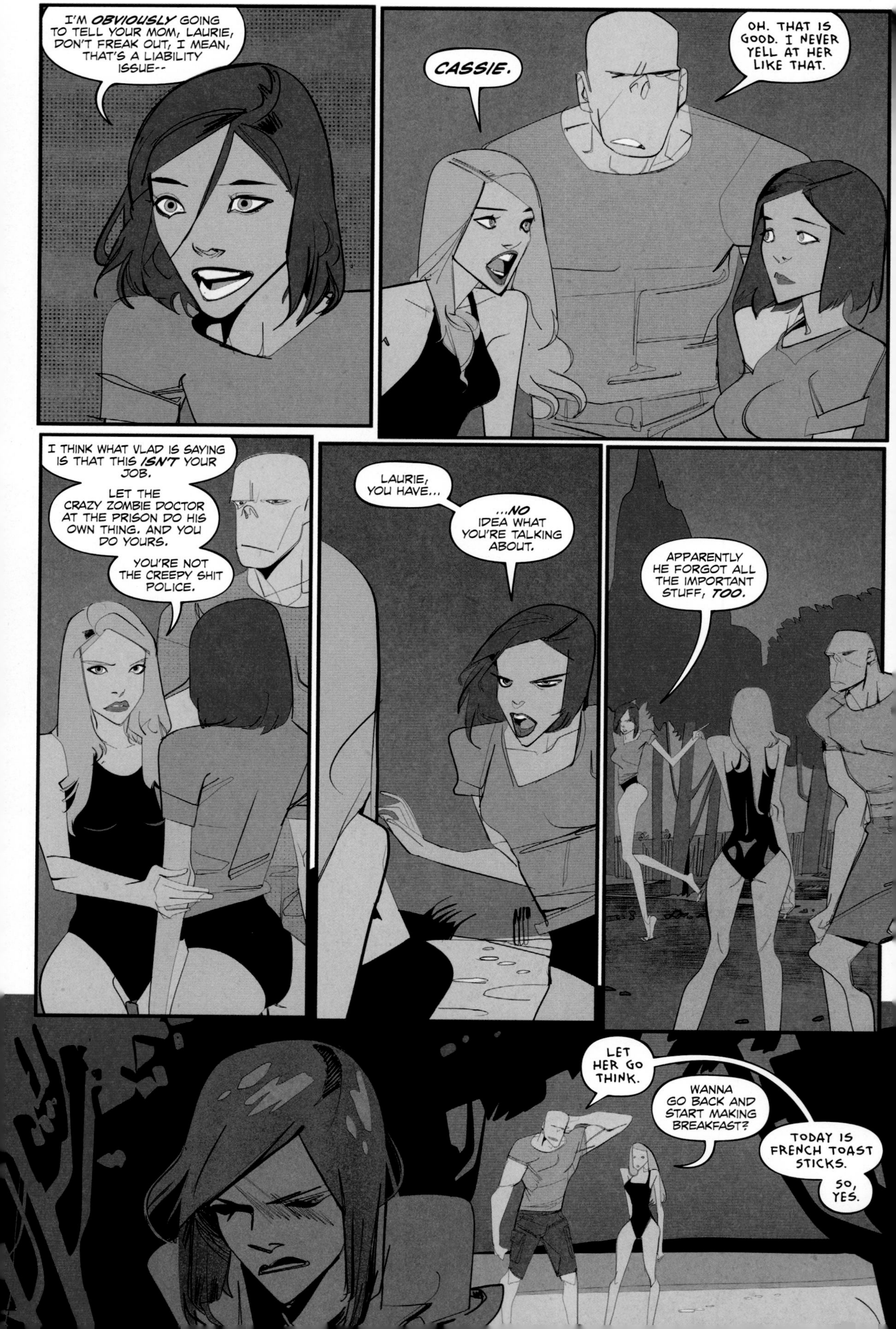

I'M OBVIOUSLY GOING TO TELL YOUR MOM, LAURIE, DON'T FREAK OUT, I MEAN, THAT'S A LIABILITY ISSUE--
CASSIE.
OH. THAT IS GOOD. I NEVER YELL AT HER LIKE THAT.
I THINK WHAT VLAD IS SAYING IS THAT THIS ISN'T YOUR JOB.
LET THE CRAZY ZOMBIE DOCTOR AT THE PRISON DO HIS OWN THING. AND YOU DO YOURS.
YOU'RE NOT THE CREEPY SHIT POLICE.
LAURIE, YOU HAVE...
...NO IDEA WHAT YOU'RE TALKING ABOUT.
APPARENTLY HE FORGOT ALL THE IMPORTANT STUFF, TOO.
LET HER GO THINK.
WANNA GO BACK AND START MAKING BREAKFAST?
TODAY IS FRENCH TOAST STICKS.
SO, YES.

THIS SEEMS REALLY DUMB, RIGHT?

GIRL GETS MAD AT FRIEND AND... GIRL... FRIEND?

STORMS OFF INTO ZOMBIE-FILLED WOODS, ALONE.

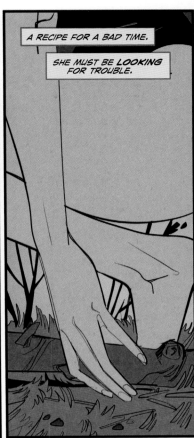

A RECIPE FOR A BAD TIME.

SHE MUST BE *LOOKING* FOR TROUBLE.

OH, SHE IS.

SHE'S GOT SOME *STEAM* TO BLOW OFF.

GROOOSH

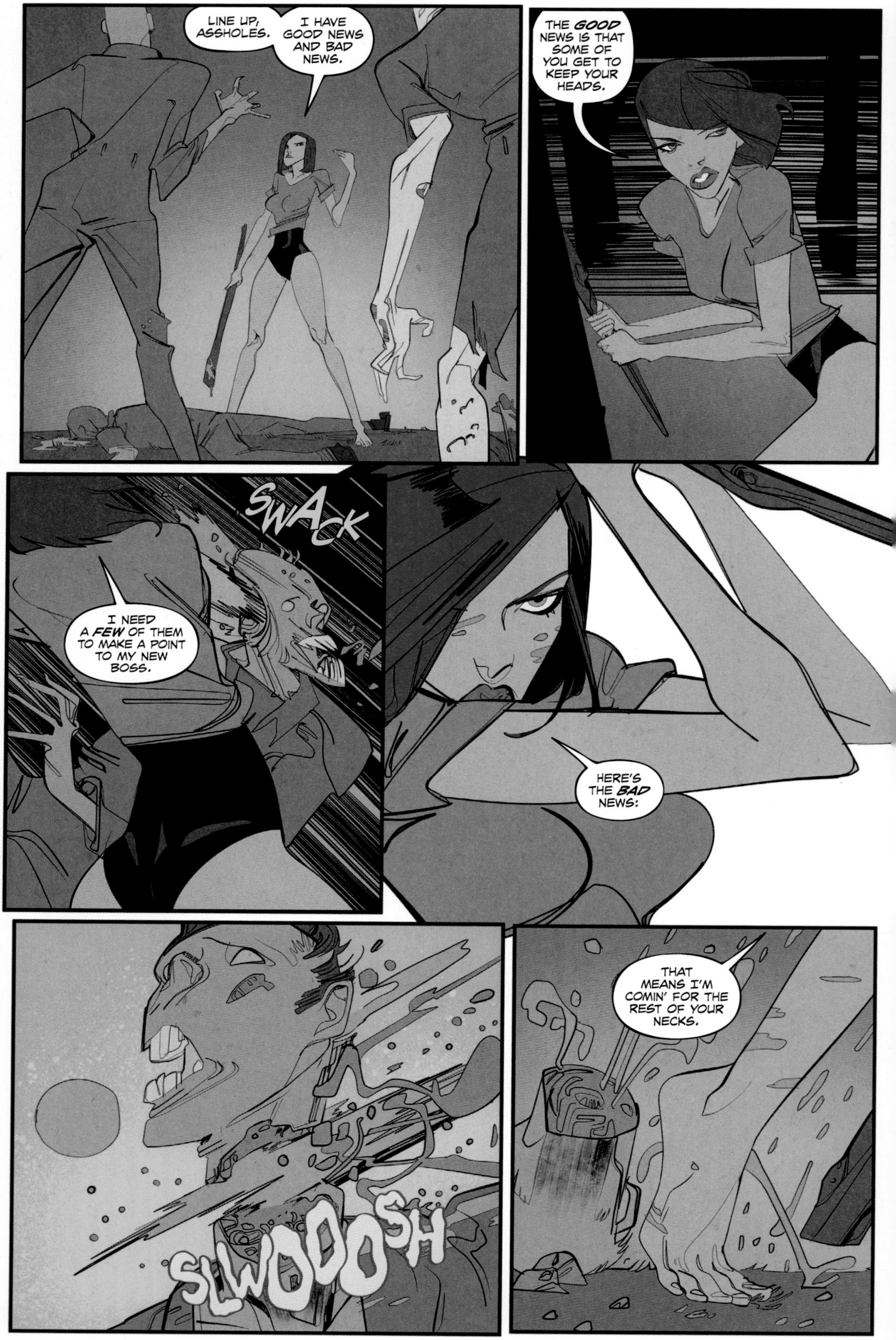
LINE UP, ASSHOLES.
I HAVE GOOD NEWS AND BAD NEWS.
THE GOOD NEWS IS THAT SOME OF YOU GET TO KEEP YOUR HEADS.
SWACK
I NEED A FEW OF THEM TO MAKE A POINT TO MY NEW BOSS.
HERE'S THE BAD NEWS:
SLWOOOSH
THAT MEANS I'M COMIN' FOR THE REST OF YOUR NECKS.

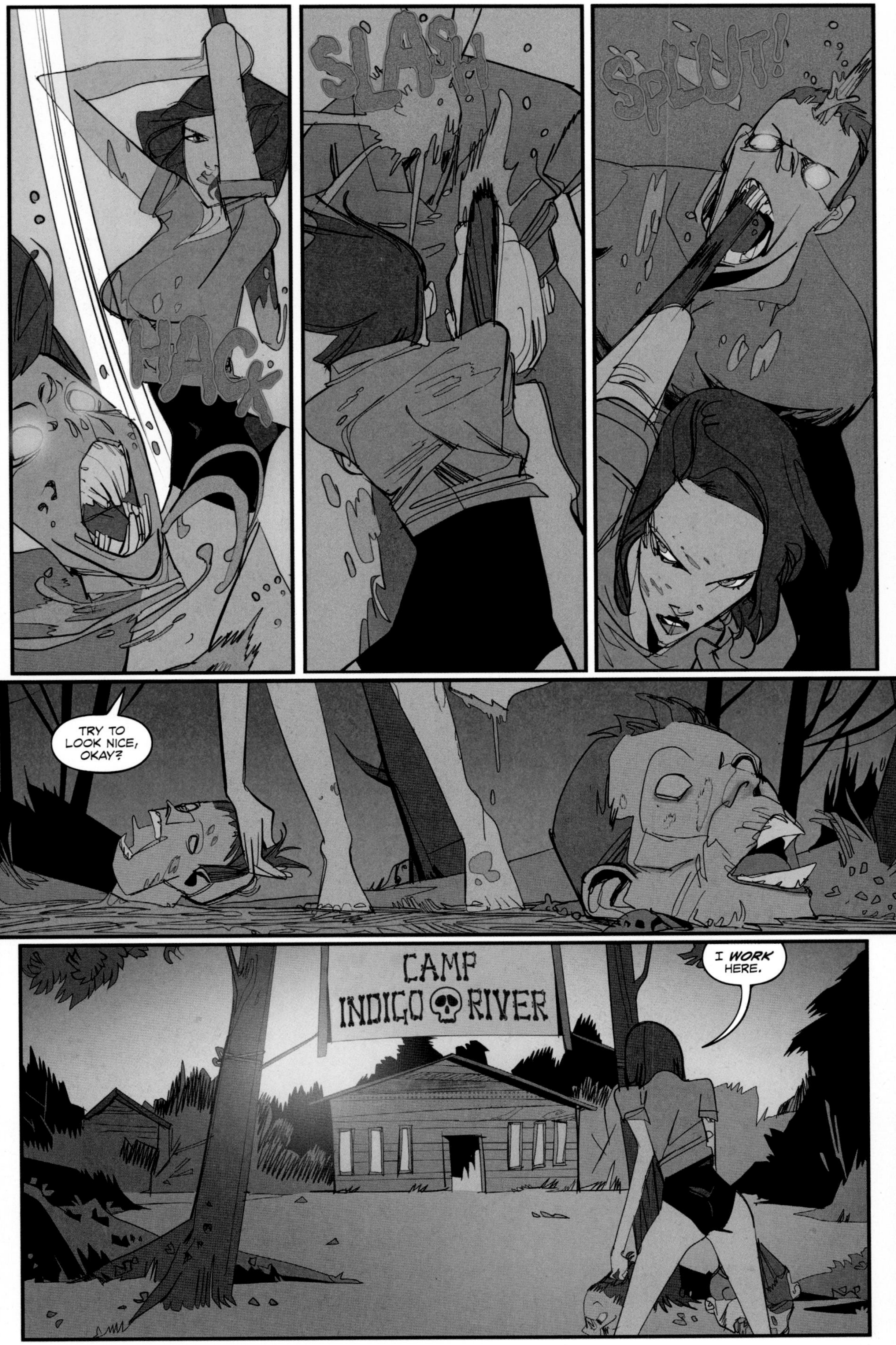
HACK
SLASH
SPLUT!
TRY TO LOOK NICE, OKAY?
CAMP INDIGO RIVER
I WORK HERE.

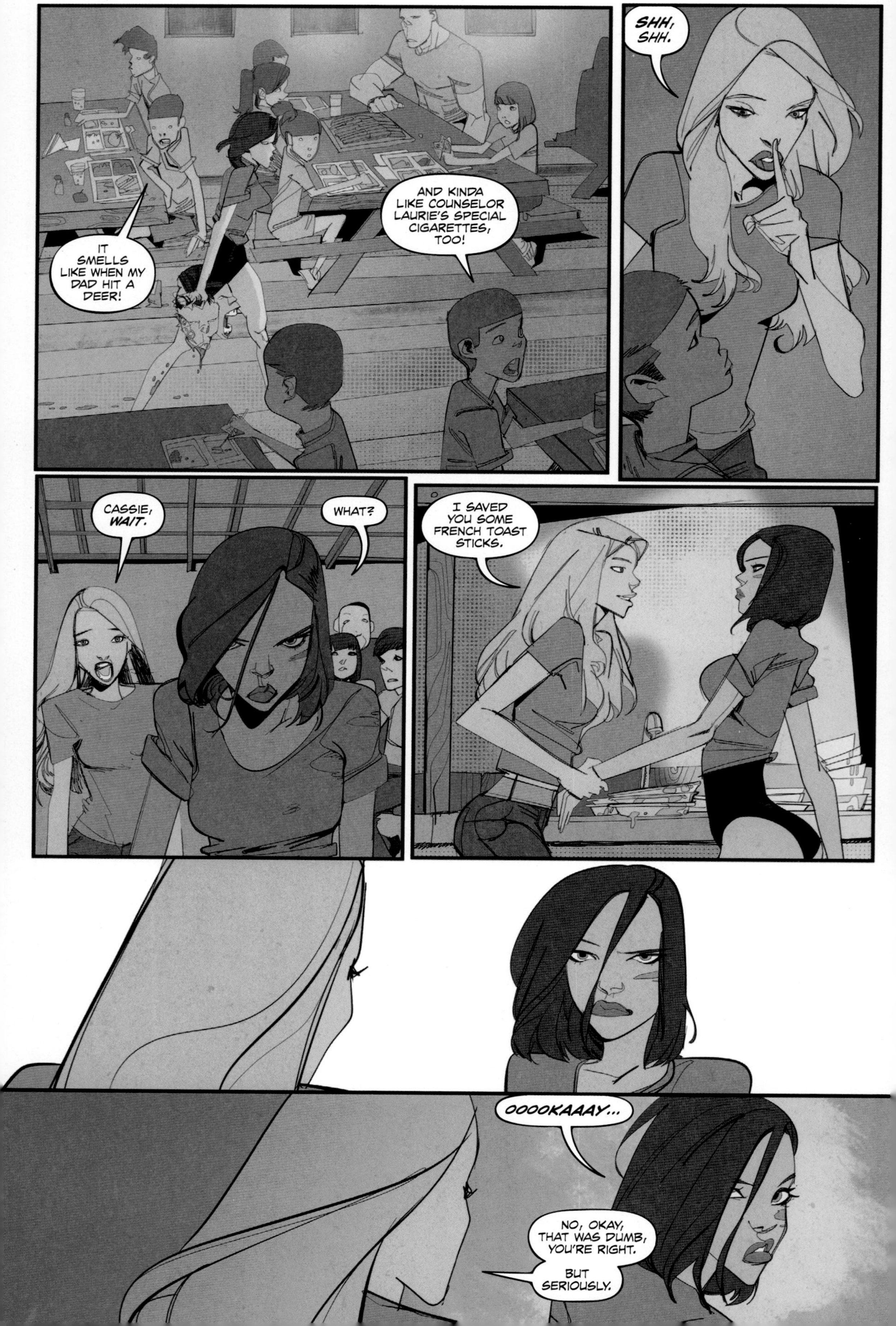
IT SMELLS LIKE WHEN MY DAD HIT A DEER!
AND KINDA LIKE COUNSELOR LAURIE'S SPECIAL CIGARETTES, TOO!
SHH, SHH.
CASSIE, *WAIT*.
WHAT?
I SAVED YOU SOME FRENCH TOAST STICKS.
OOOOKAAAY...
NO, OKAY, THAT WAS DUMB, YOU'RE RIGHT.
BUT SERIOUSLY.

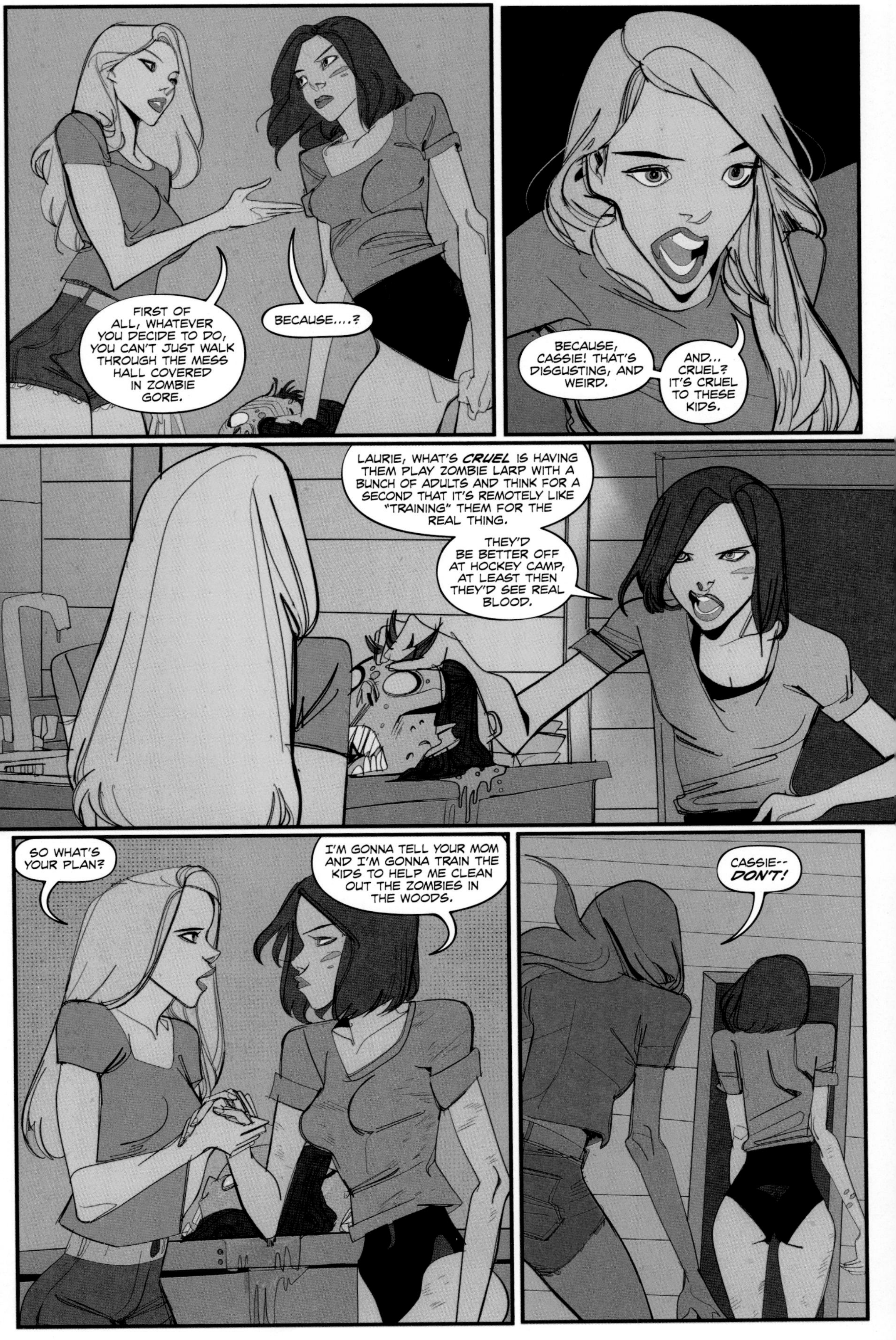
FIRST OF ALL, WHATEVER YOU DECIDE TO DO, YOU CAN'T JUST WALK THROUGH THE MESS HALL COVERED IN ZOMBIE GORE.
BECAUSE....?
BECAUSE, CASSIE! THAT'S DISGUSTING, AND WEIRD.
AND... CRUEL? IT'S CRUEL TO THESE KIDS.
LAURIE, WHAT'S CRUEL IS HAVING THEM PLAY ZOMBIE LARP WITH A BUNCH OF ADULTS AND THINK FOR A SECOND THAT IT'S REMOTELY LIKE "TRAINING" THEM FOR THE REAL THING.
THEY'D BE BETTER OFF AT HOCKEY CAMP, AT LEAST THEN THEY'D SEE REAL BLOOD.
SO WHAT'S YOUR PLAN?
I'M GONNA TELL YOUR MOM AND I'M GONNA TRAIN THE KIDS TO HELP ME CLEAN OUT THE ZOMBIES IN THE WOODS.
CASSIE-- DON'T!

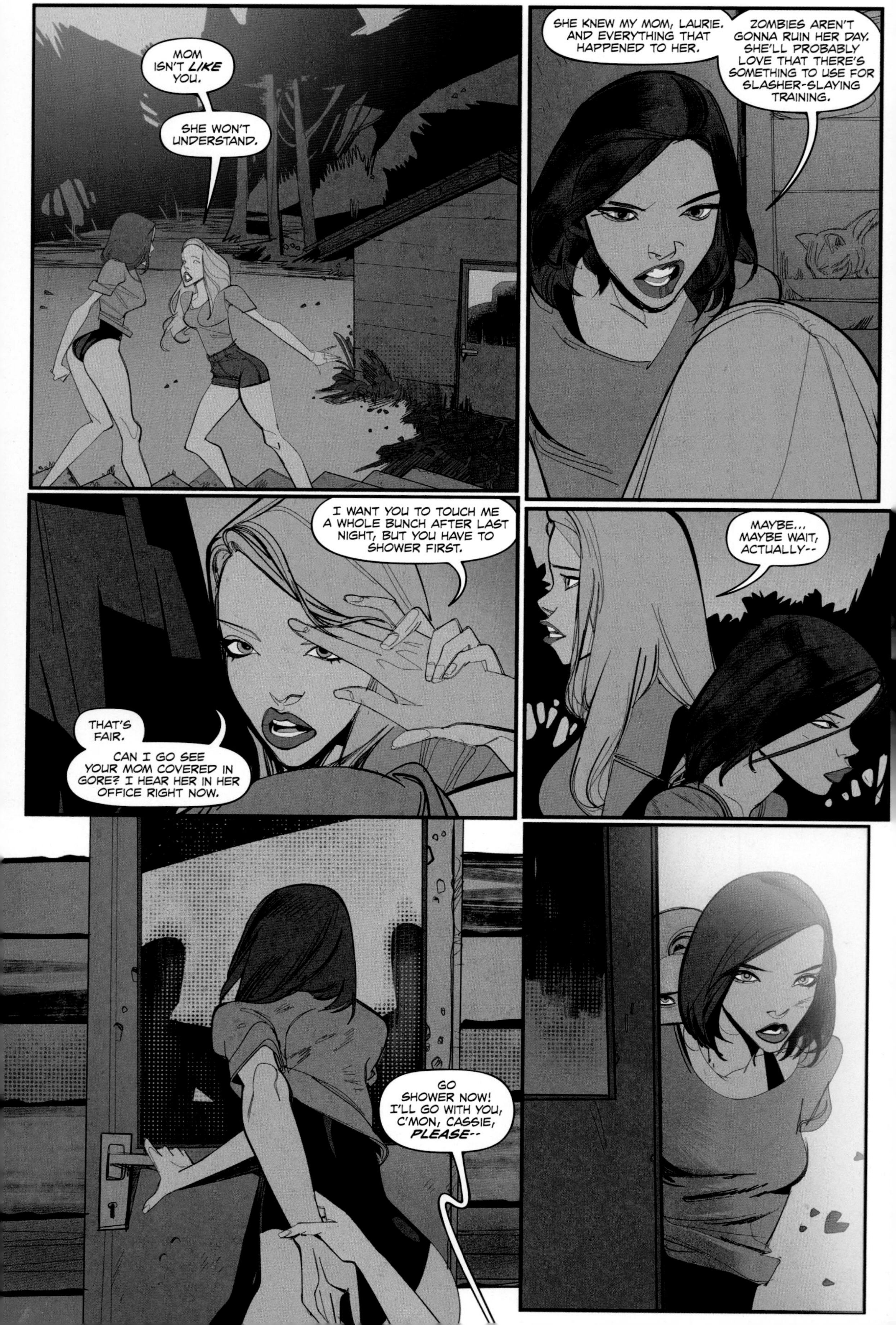
MOM ISN'T LIKE YOU.
SHE WON'T UNDERSTAND.
SHE KNEW MY MOM, LAURIE. AND EVERYTHING THAT HAPPENED TO HER.
ZOMBIES AREN'T GONNA RUIN HER DAY. SHE'LL PROBABLY LOVE THAT THERE'S SOMETHING TO USE FOR SLASHER-SLAYING TRAINING.
I WANT YOU TO TOUCH ME A WHOLE BUNCH AFTER LAST NIGHT, BUT YOU HAVE TO SHOWER FIRST.
THAT'S FAIR.
CAN I GO SEE YOUR MOM COVERED IN GORE? I HEAR HER IN HER OFFICE RIGHT NOW.
MAYBE... MAYBE WAIT, ACTUALLY--
GO SHOWER NOW! I'LL GO WITH YOU, C'MON, CASSIE, PLEASE--

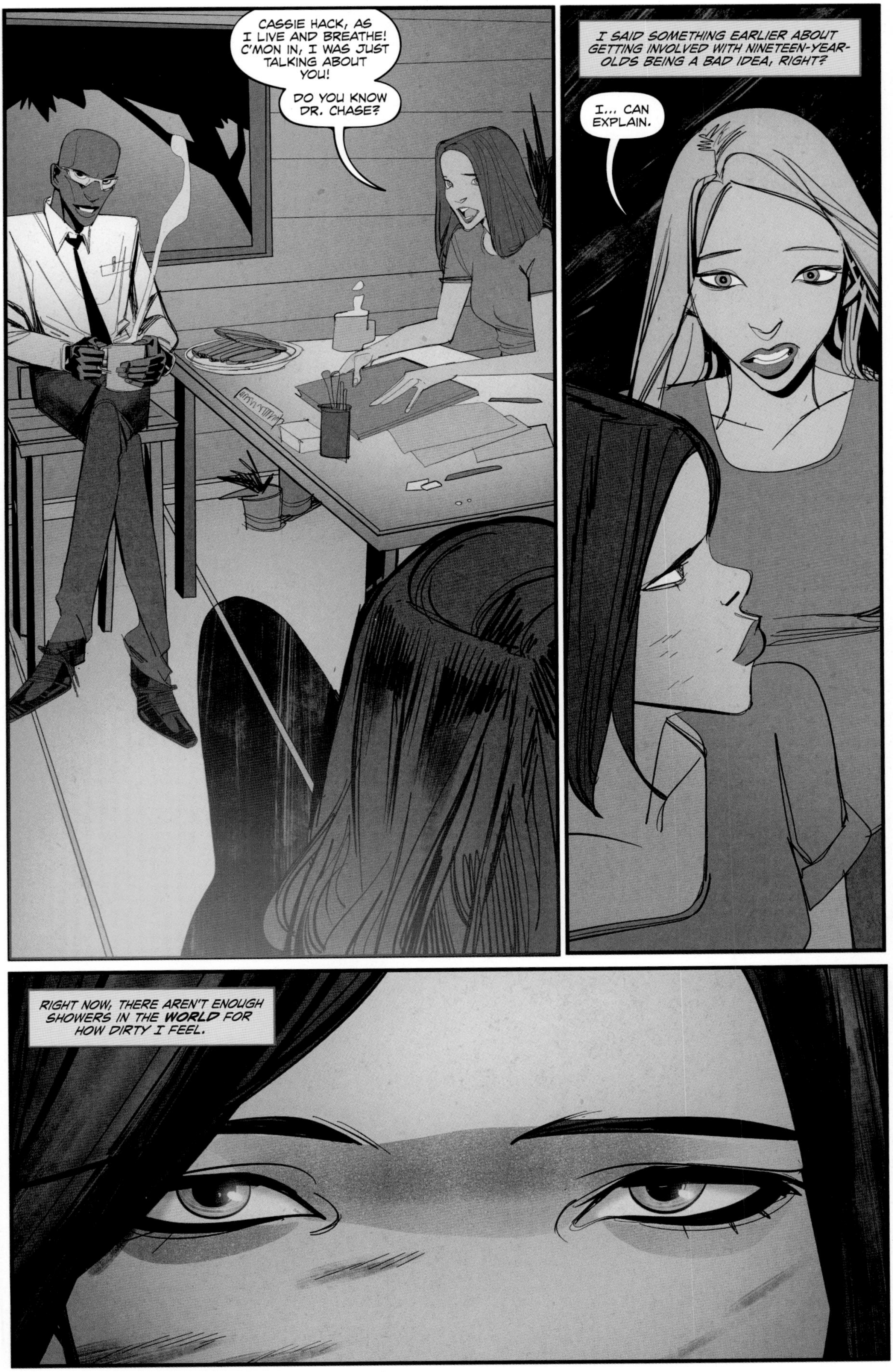
CASSIE HACK, AS I LIVE AND BREATHE! C'MON IN, I WAS JUST TALKING ABOUT YOU!
DO YOU KNOW DR. CHASE?
I SAID SOMETHING EARLIER ABOUT GETTING INVOLVED WITH NINETEEN-YEAR-OLDS BEING A BAD IDEA, RIGHT?
I... CAN EXPLAIN.
RIGHT NOW, THERE AREN'T ENOUGH SHOWERS IN THE WORLD FOR HOW DIRTY I FEEL.

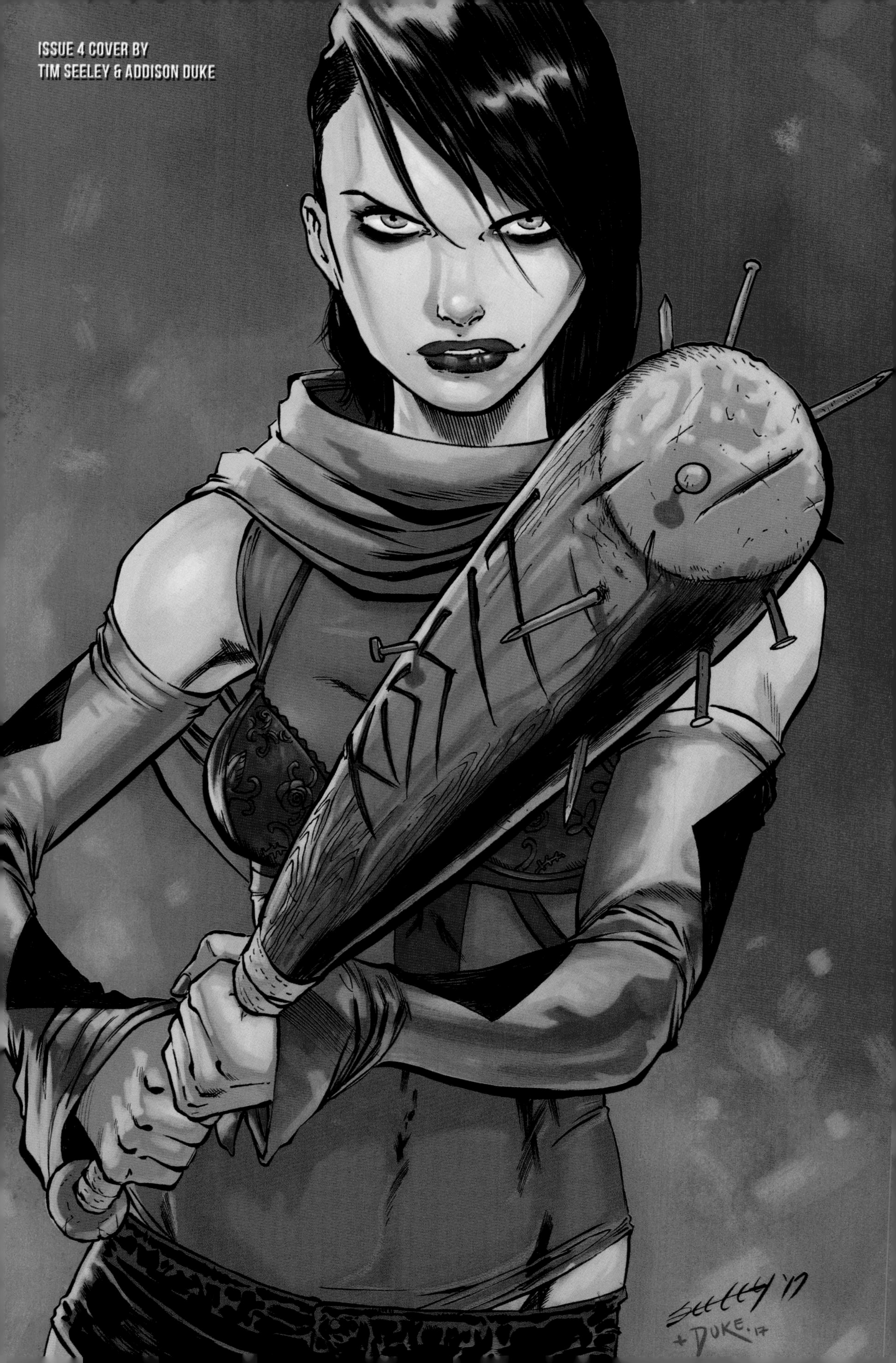
Seeley '17
+ DUKE. 17
ISSUE 4 COVER BY
TIM SEELEY & ADDISON DUKE

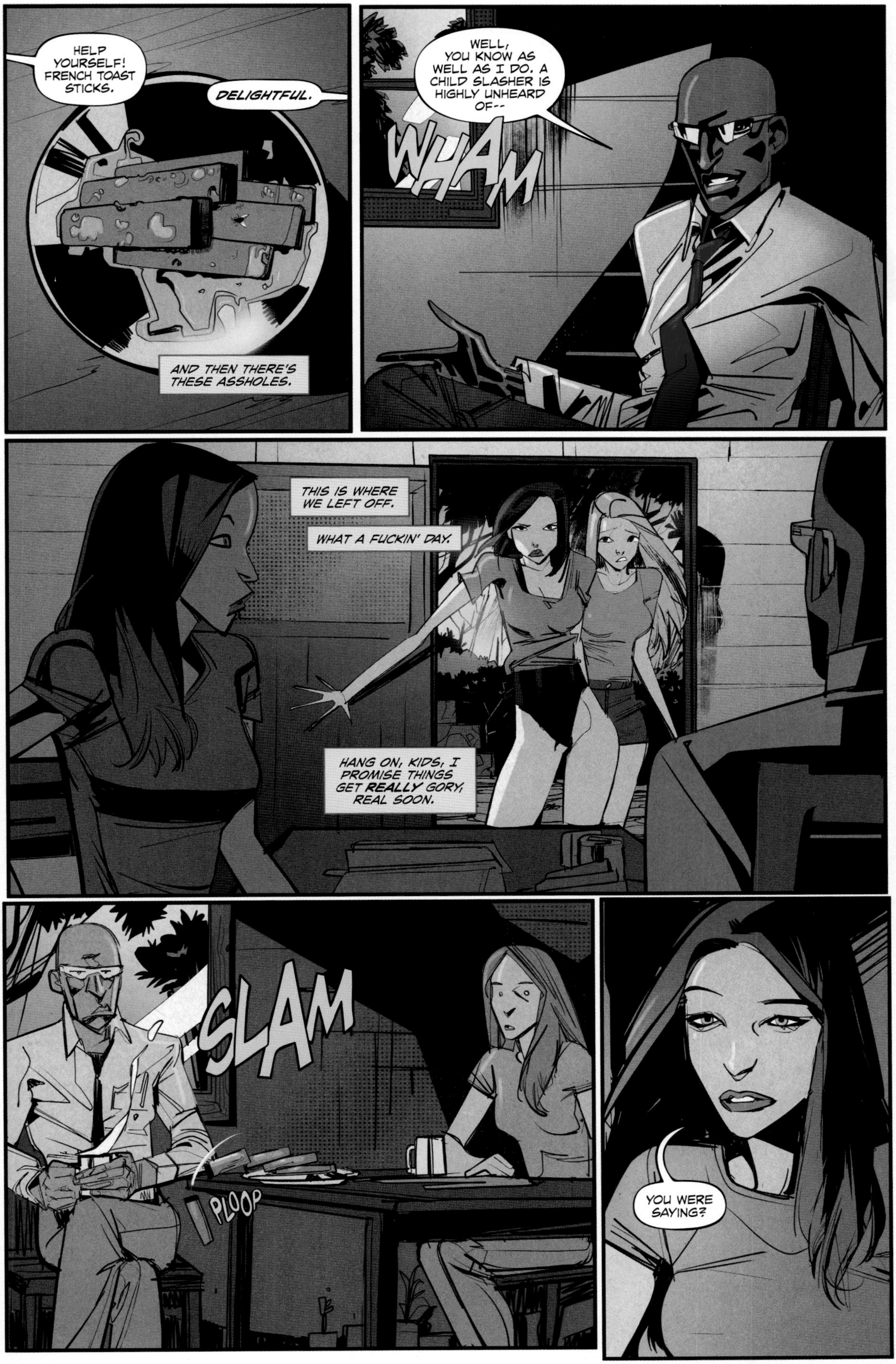
HELP YOURSELF! FRENCH TOAST STICKS.
DELIGHTFUL.
AND THEN THERE'S THESE ASSHOLES.
WELL, YOU KNOW AS WELL AS I DO. A CHILD SLASHER IS HIGHLY UNHEARD OF--
WHAM
THIS IS WHERE WE LEFT OFF.
WHAT A FUCKIN' DAY.
HANG ON, KIDS, I PROMISE THINGS GET REALLY GORY, REAL SOON.
SLAM
PLOOP
YOU WERE SAYING?

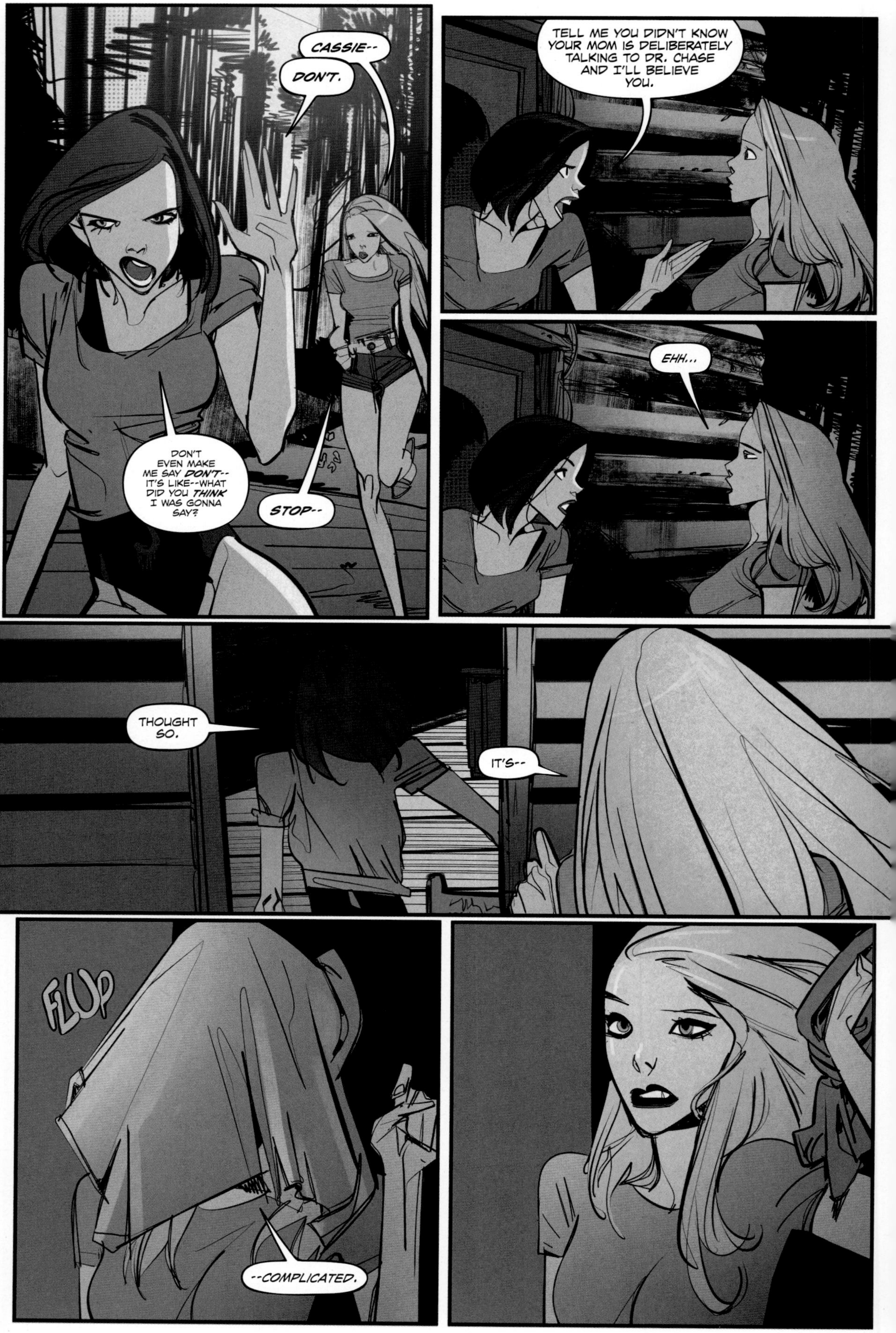
CASSIE--
DON'T.
DON'T EVEN MAKE ME SAY DON'T-- IT'S LIKE--WHAT DID YOU THINK I WAS GONNA SAY?
STOP--
TELL ME YOU DIDN'T KNOW YOUR MOM IS DELIBERATELY TALKING TO DR. CHASE AND I'LL BELIEVE YOU.
EHH...
THOUGHT SO.
IT'S--
FLUP
--COMPLICATED.

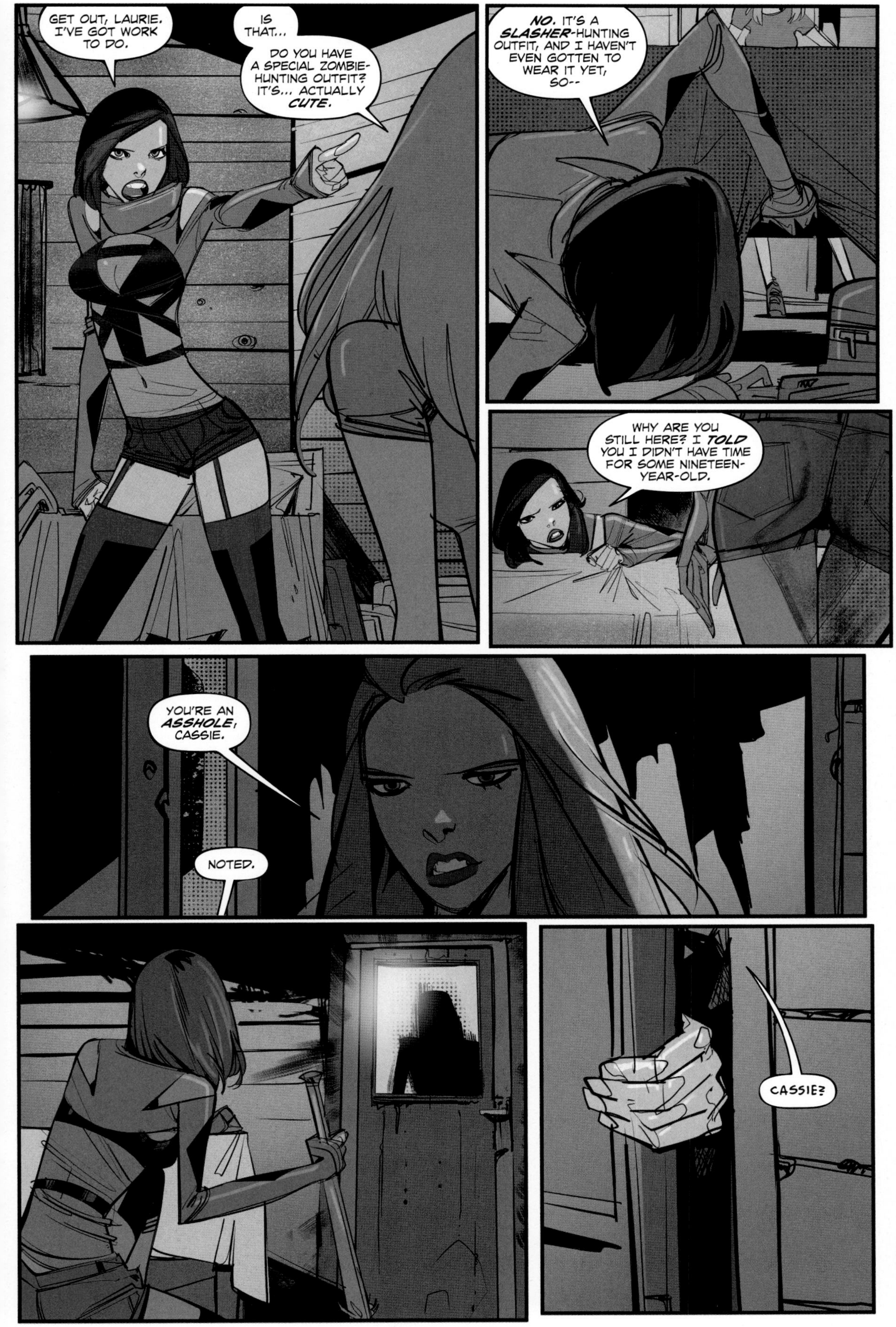
GET OUT, LAURIE. I'VE GOT WORK TO DO.
IS THAT...
DO YOU HAVE A SPECIAL ZOMBIE-HUNTING OUTFIT? IT'S... ACTUALLY CUTE.
NO. IT'S A SLASHER-HUNTING OUTFIT, AND I HAVEN'T EVEN GOTTEN TO WEAR IT YET, SO--
WHY ARE YOU STILL HERE? I TOLD YOU I DIDN'T HAVE TIME FOR SOME NINETEEN-YEAR-OLD.
YOU'RE AN ASSHOLE, CASSIE.
NOTED.
CASSIE?

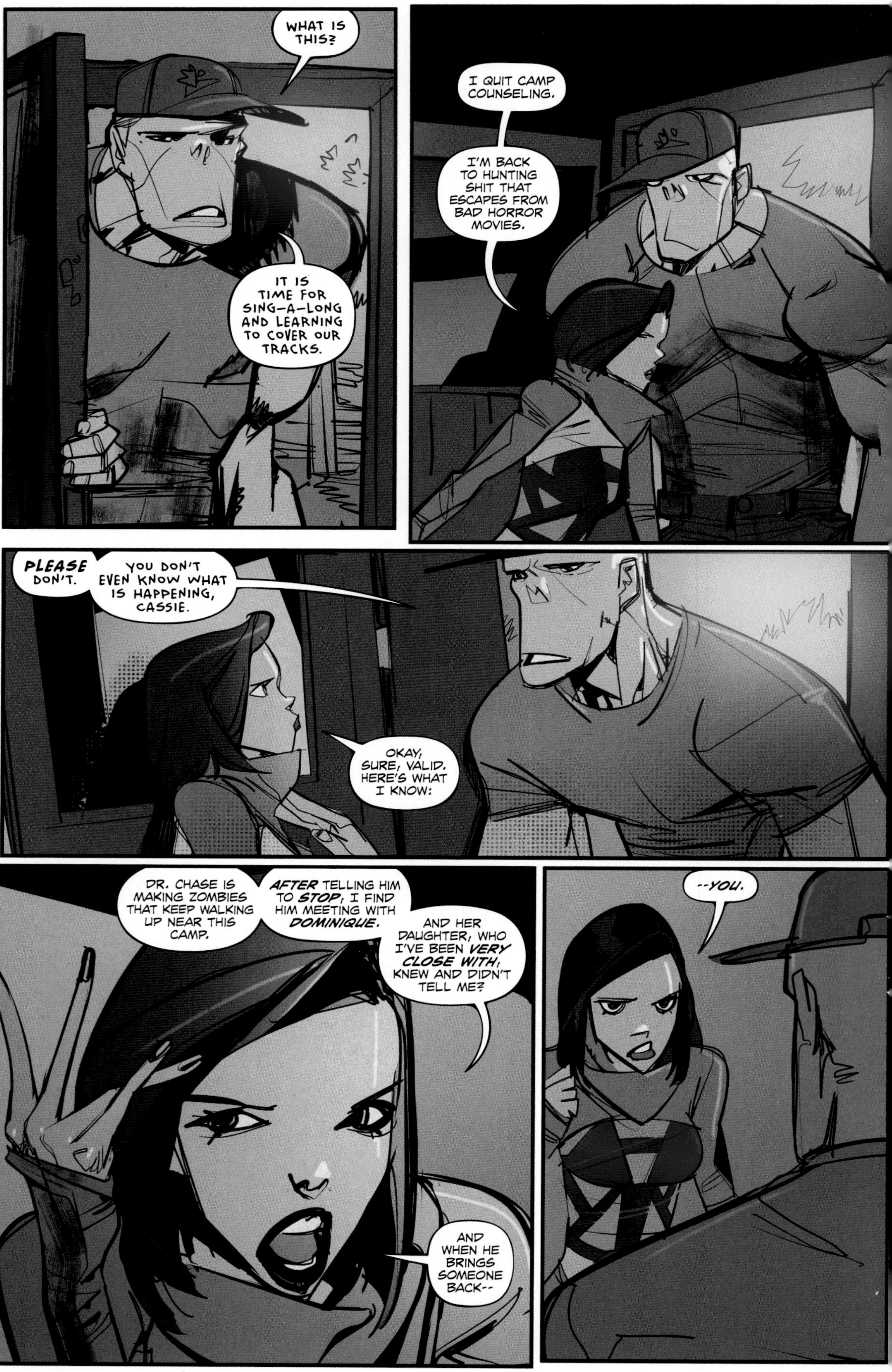
WHAT IS THIS?
IT IS TIME FOR SING-A-LONG AND LEARNING TO COVER OUR TRACKS.
I QUIT CAMP COUNSELING.
I'M BACK TO HUNTING SHIT THAT ESCAPES FROM BAD HORROR MOVIES.
PLEASE DON'T.
YOU DON'T EVEN KNOW WHAT IS HAPPENING, CASSIE.
OKAY, SURE, VALID. HERE'S WHAT I KNOW:
DR. CHASE IS MAKING ZOMBIES THAT KEEP WALKING UP NEAR THIS CAMP.
AFTER TELLING HIM TO STOP, I FIND HIM MEETING WITH DOMINIQUE.
AND HER DAUGHTER, WHO I'VE BEEN VERY CLOSE WITH, KNEW AND DIDN'T TELL ME?
AND WHEN HE BRINGS SOMEONE BACK--
--YOU.

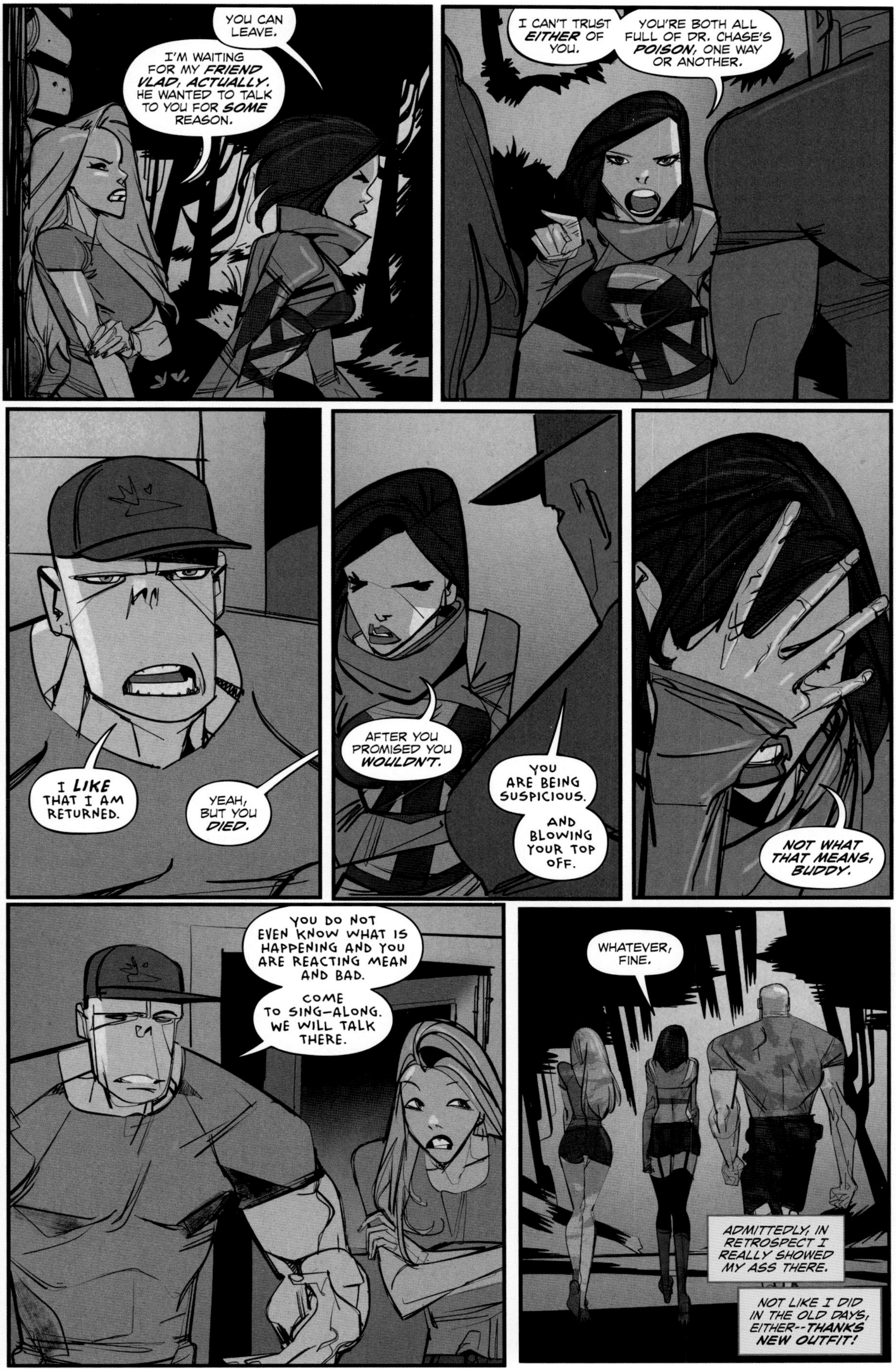
YOU CAN LEAVE.
I'M WAITING FOR MY FRIEND VLAD, ACTUALLY. HE WANTED TO TALK TO YOU FOR SOME REASON.
I CAN'T TRUST EITHER OF YOU.
YOU'RE BOTH ALL FULL OF DR. CHASE'S POISON, ONE WAY OR ANOTHER.
I LIKE THAT I AM RETURNED.
YEAH, BUT YOU DIED.
AFTER YOU PROMISED YOU WOULDN'T.
YOU ARE BEING SUSPICIOUS.
AND BLOWING YOUR TOP OFF.
NOT WHAT THAT MEANS, BUDDY.
YOU DO NOT EVEN KNOW WHAT IS HAPPENING AND YOU ARE REACTING MEAN AND BAD.
COME TO SING-ALONG. WE WILL TALK THERE.
WHATEVER, FINE.
ADMITTEDLY, IN RETROSPECT I REALLY SHOWED MY ASS THERE.
NOT LIKE I DID IN THE OLD DAYS, EITHER--THANKS NEW OUTFIT!

HERE'S THE PLAN--FIRST OF ALL, I DON'T TRUST DR. CHASE FOR A *SECOND*.

OH MY GOD, WE DON'T *TRUST* HIM *EITHER*--

♪ BLAAAAAACK SOCKS! ♪ THEY NEVER GET DIRTY

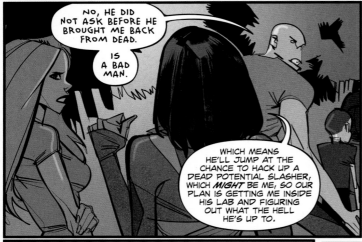

NO, HE DID NOT ASK BEFORE HE BROUGHT ME BACK FROM DEAD.

IS A BAD MAN.

WHICH MEANS HE'LL JUMP AT THE CHANCE TO HACK UP A DEAD POTENTIAL SLASHER, WHICH *MIGHT* BE ME, SO OUR PLAN IS GETTING ME INSIDE HIS LAB AND FIGURING OUT WHAT THE HELL HE'S UP TO.

♪ THE LONGER YOU WEAR THEM ♪ THE BLACKER THEY GET!

UH?

SLASHERS. LIKE MY MOM. LIKE I TOLD YOU?*

I MIGHT BE ONE?

KIND OF? IT'S COMPLICATED.

*EDITOR TIM'S NOTE: OH, WOW, HAHA, CHECK THE RE-CAP PAGE, KIDS!

OW!

YANK

YOU ARE NOT *DYING* SO THIS *WEIRDO* LEAVES A SUMMER CAMP ALONE.

NO--JESUS, THAT HURT.

M'NOT *DYING*. I HAVE A PLAN. I SAW IT ON *FORENSIC FILES*. FIRST WE NEED A SYRINGE AND BLOOD.

PREFERABLY NOT *PEOPLE* BLOOD.

BUT REAL BLOOD.

LIKE FROM A--

♪ DO! A DEER! ♪ A FEMALE DEER! ♪

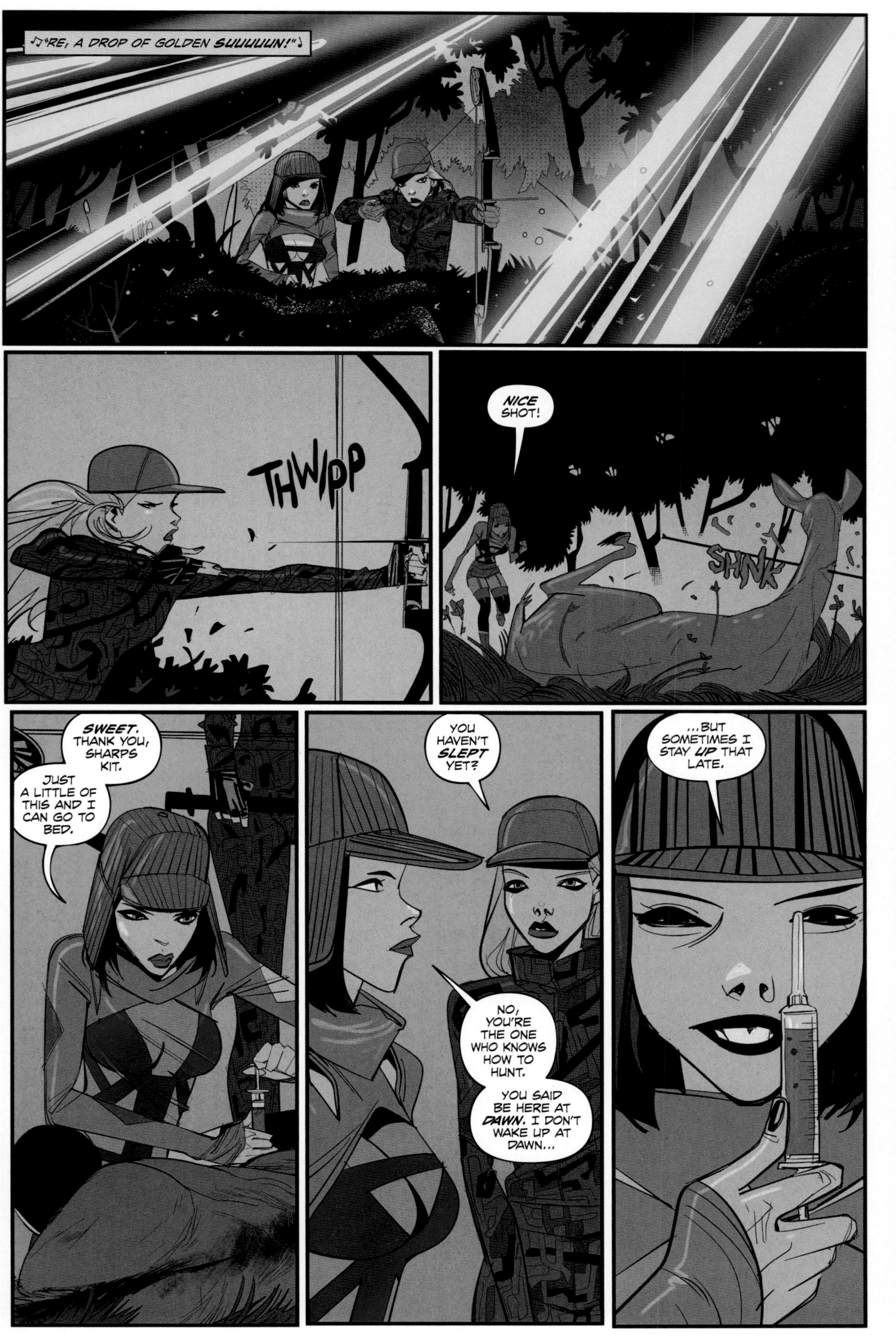
♫"RE, A DROP OF GOLDEN SUUUUUN!"♪
THWIPP
NICE SHOT!
SHNK
SWEET. THANK YOU, SHARPS KIT.
JUST A LITTLE OF THIS AND I CAN GO TO BED.
YOU HAVEN'T SLEPT YET?
NO, YOU'RE THE ONE WHO KNOWS HOW TO HUNT.
YOU SAID BE HERE AT DAWN. I DON'T WAKE UP AT DAWN...
...BUT SOMETIMES I STAY UP THAT LATE.

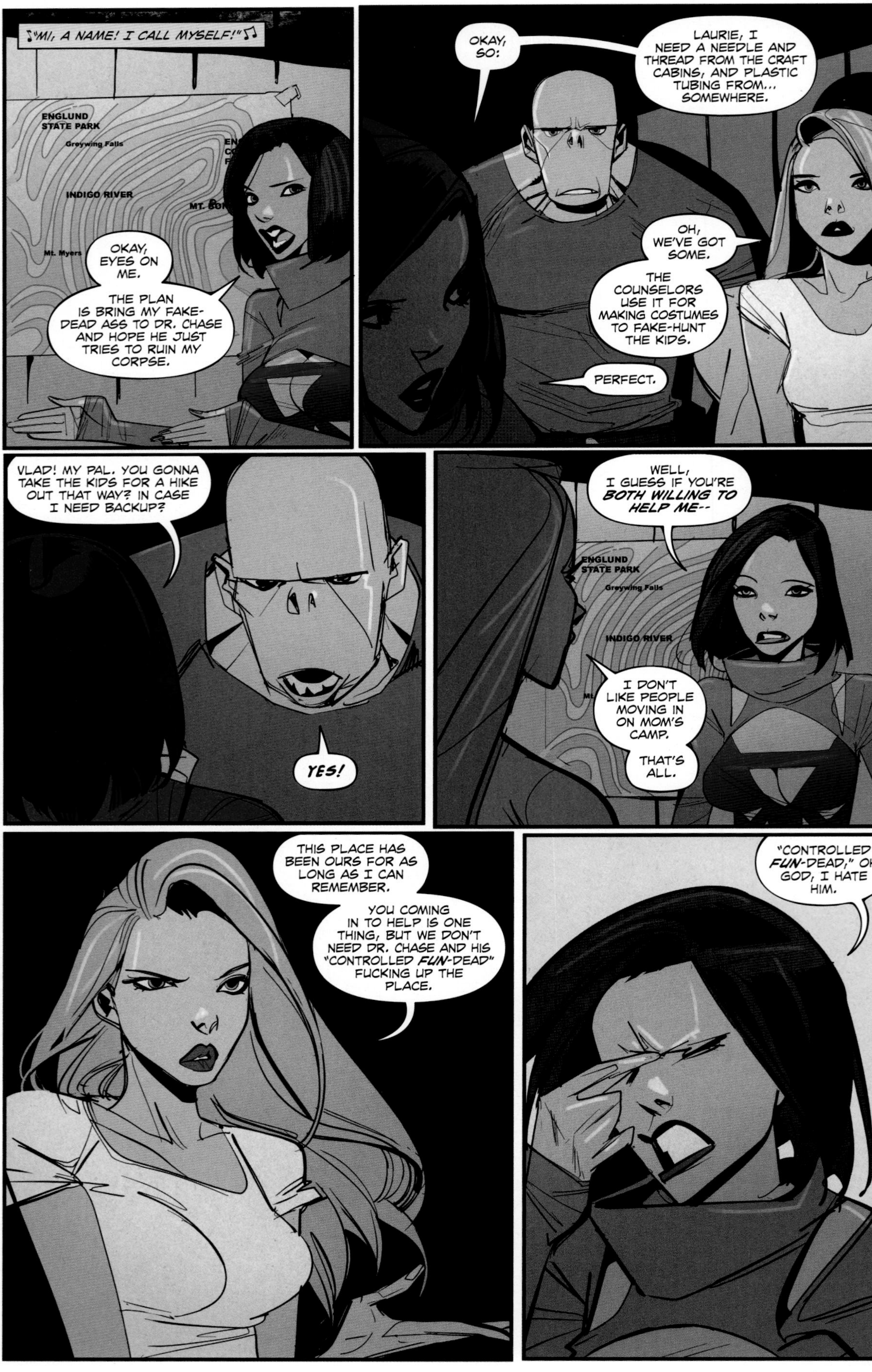
♪"MI, A NAME! I CALL MYSELF!"♫
ENGLUND STATE PARK
Greywing Falls
INDIGO RIVER
Mt. Myers
OKAY, EYES ON ME.
THE PLAN IS BRING MY FAKE-DEAD ASS TO DR. CHASE AND HOPE HE JUST TRIES TO RUIN MY CORPSE.
OKAY, SO:
LAURIE, I NEED A NEEDLE AND THREAD FROM THE CRAFT CABINS, AND PLASTIC TUBING FROM... SOMEWHERE.
OH, WE'VE GOT SOME.
THE COUNSELORS USE IT FOR MAKING COSTUMES TO FAKE-HUNT THE KIDS.
PERFECT.
VLAD! MY PAL. YOU GONNA TAKE THE KIDS FOR A HIKE OUT THAT WAY? IN CASE I NEED BACKUP?
YES!
WELL, I GUESS IF YOU'RE BOTH WILLING TO HELP ME--
ENGLUND STATE PARK
Greywing Falls
INDIGO RIVER
I DON'T LIKE PEOPLE MOVING IN ON MOM'S CAMP.
THAT'S ALL.
THIS PLACE HAS BEEN OURS FOR AS LONG AS I CAN REMEMBER.
YOU COMING IN TO HELP IS ONE THING, BUT WE DON'T NEED DR. CHASE AND HIS "CONTROLLED FUN-DEAD" FUCKING UP THE PLACE.
"CONTROLLED FUN-DEAD," OH GOD, I HATE HIM.

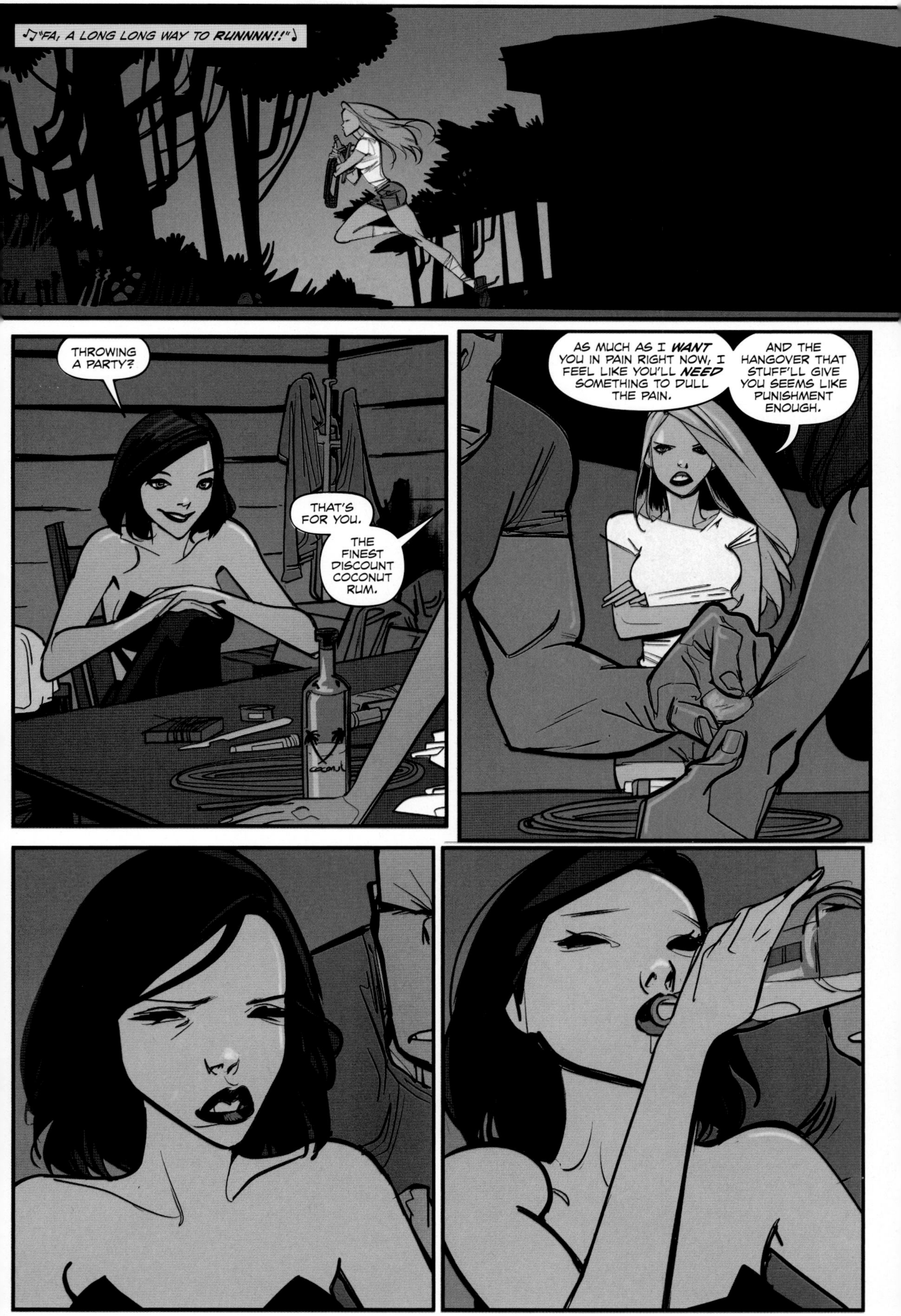

♪♫"FA, A LONG LONG WAY TO RUNNNN!!"♪
THROWING A PARTY?
THAT'S FOR YOU.
THE FINEST DISCOUNT COCONUT RUM.
coconut
AS MUCH AS I WANT YOU IN PAIN RIGHT NOW, I FEEL LIKE YOU'LL NEED SOMETHING TO DULL THE PAIN.
AND THE HANGOVER THAT STUFF'LL GIVE YOU SEEMS LIKE PUNISHMENT ENOUGH.

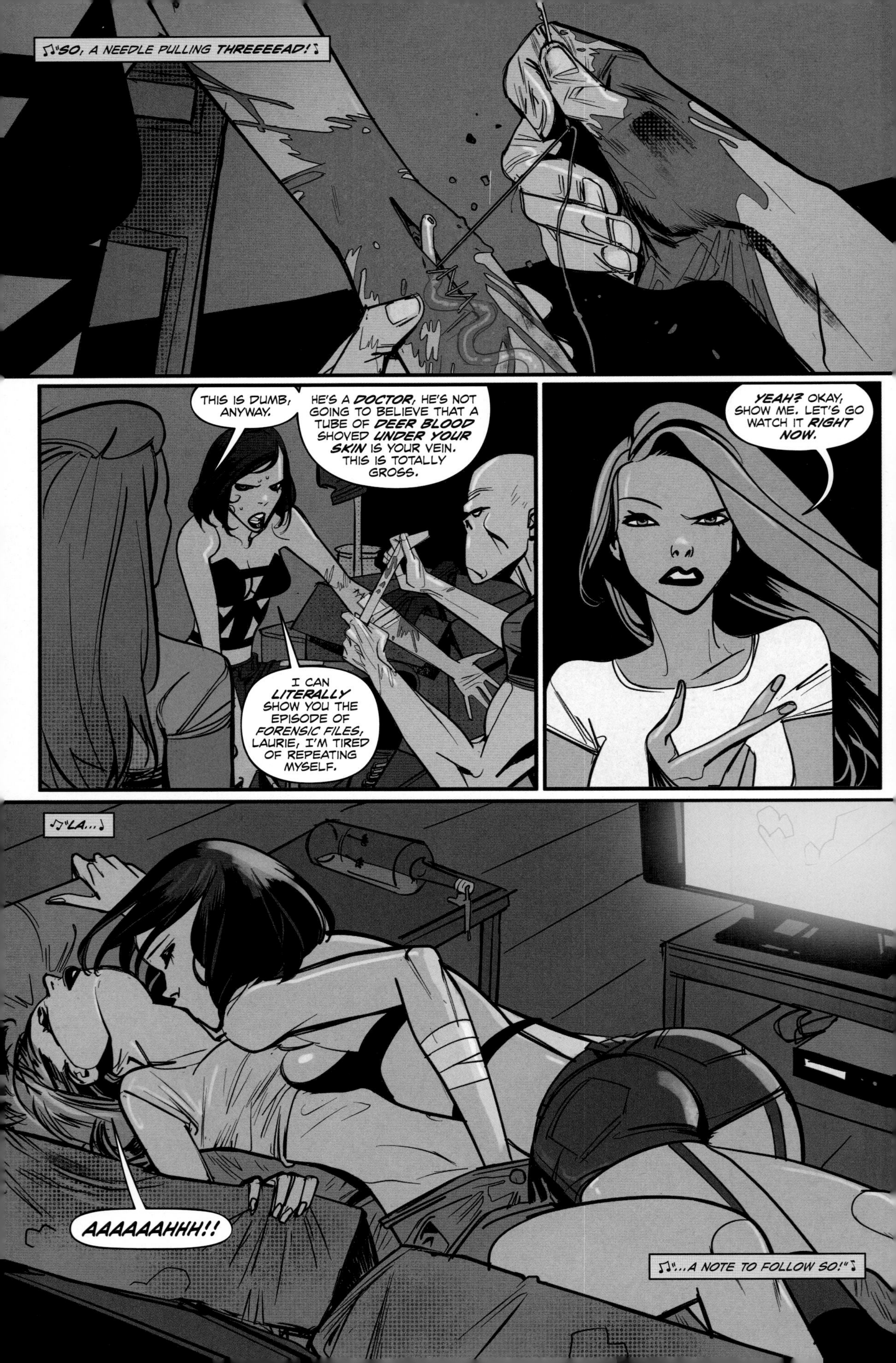
♫"SO, A NEEDLE PULLING THREEEEAD!♪
THIS IS DUMB, ANYWAY.
HE'S A DOCTOR, HE'S NOT GOING TO BELIEVE THAT A TUBE OF DEER BLOOD SHOVED UNDER YOUR SKIN IS YOUR VEIN. THIS IS TOTALLY GROSS.
I CAN LITERALLY SHOW YOU THE EPISODE OF FORENSIC FILES, LAURIE, I'M TIRED OF REPEATING MYSELF.
YEAH? OKAY, SHOW ME. LET'S GO WATCH IT RIGHT NOW.
♫"LA...♪
AAAAAAHHH!!
♫"...A NOTE TO FOLLOW SO!"♪

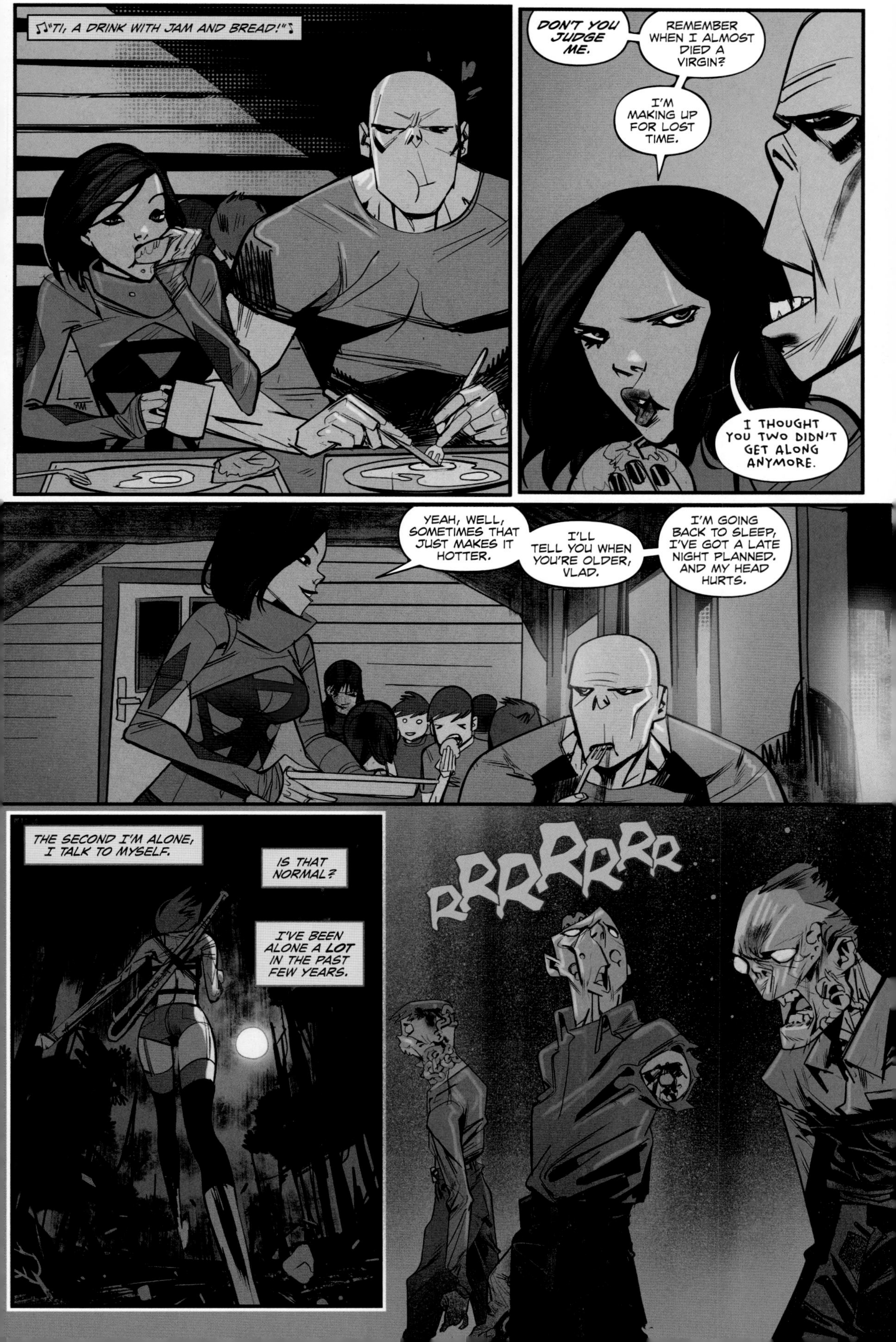
♫"TI, A DRINK WITH JAM AND BREAD!"♪
DON'T YOU JUDGE ME.
REMEMBER WHEN I ALMOST DIED A VIRGIN?
I'M MAKING UP FOR LOST TIME.
I THOUGHT YOU TWO DIDN'T GET ALONG ANYMORE.
YEAH, WELL, SOMETIMES THAT JUST MAKES IT HOTTER.
I'LL TELL YOU WHEN YOU'RE OLDER, VLAD.
I'M GOING BACK TO SLEEP, I'VE GOT A LATE NIGHT PLANNED. AND MY HEAD HURTS.
THE SECOND I'M ALONE, I TALK TO MYSELF.
IS THAT NORMAL?
I'VE BEEN ALONE A LOT IN THE PAST FEW YEARS.
RRRRRRR

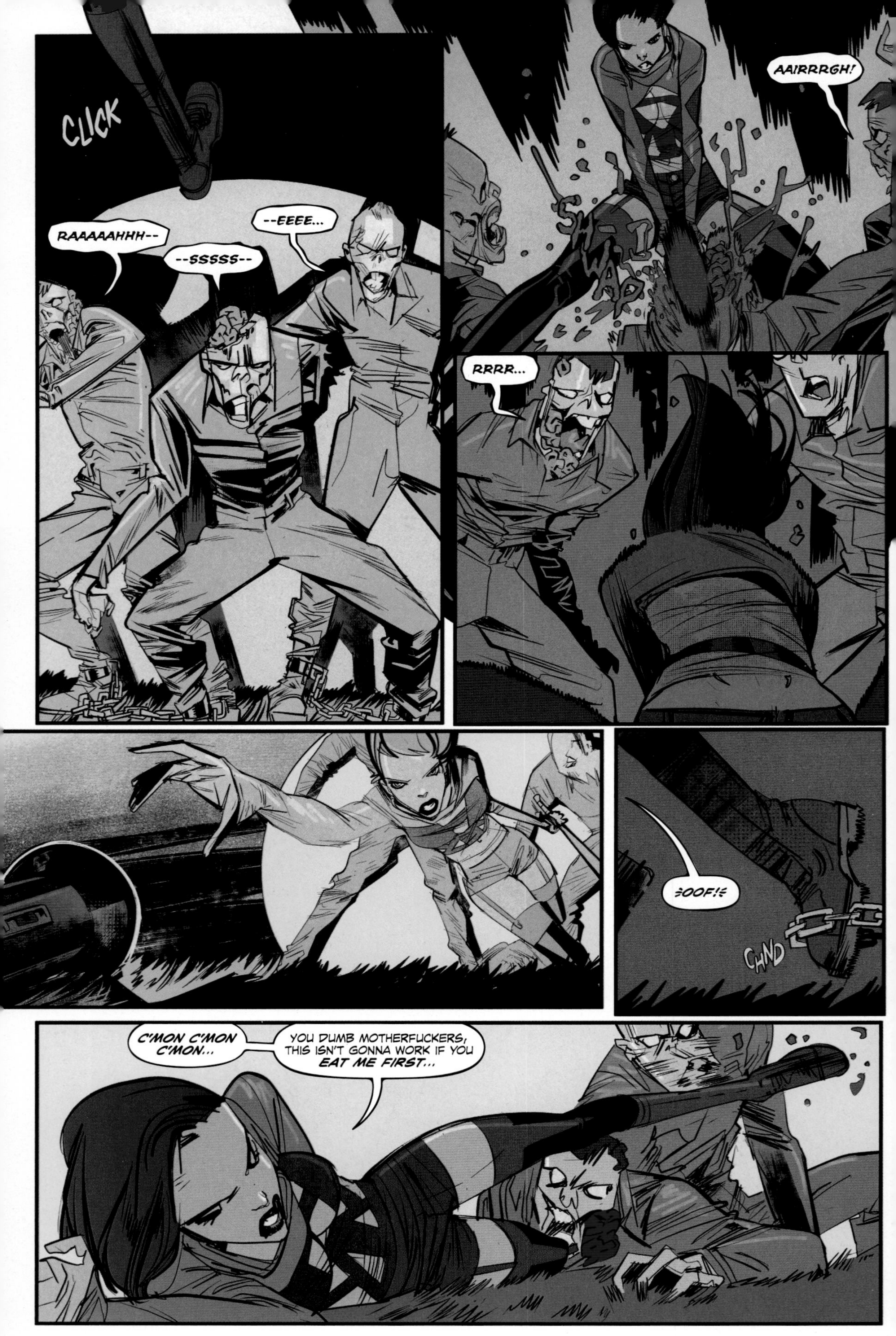
CLICK
RAAAAAHHH--
--SSSSS--
--EEEE...
AAIRRRGH!
RRRR...
OOF!
CHND
C'MON C'MON C'MON...
YOU DUMB MOTHERFUCKERS, THIS ISN'T GONNA WORK IF YOU EAT ME FIRST...

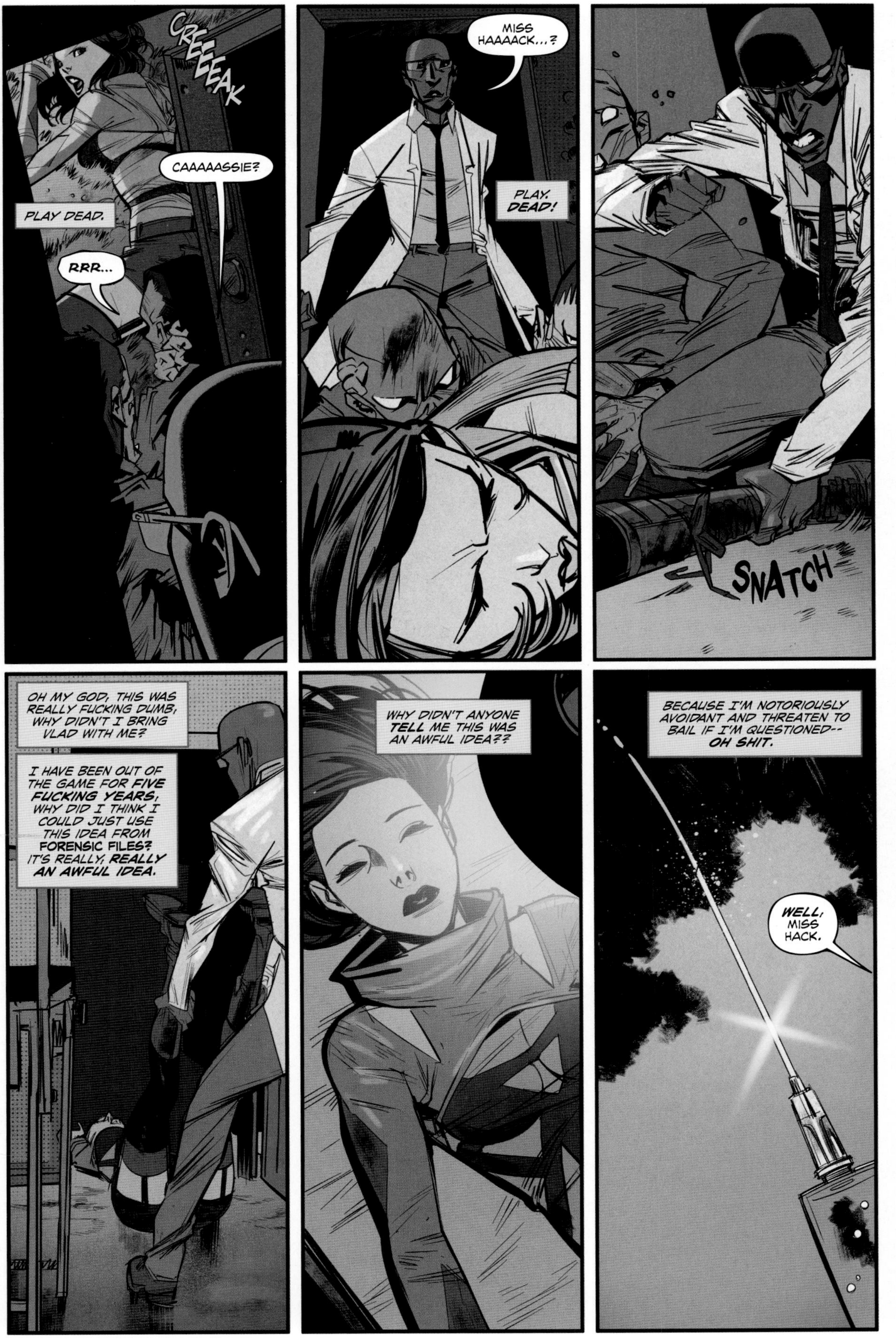
CREEEEAK
CAAAAAASSIE?
PLAY DEAD.
RRR...
MISS HAAAACK...?
PLAY. DEAD!
SNATCH
OH MY GOD, THIS WAS REALLY FUCKING DUMB, WHY DIDN'T I BRING VLAD WITH ME?
I HAVE BEEN OUT OF THE GAME FOR FIVE FUCKING YEARS, WHY DID I THINK I COULD JUST USE THIS IDEA FROM FORENSIC FILES? IT'S REALLY, REALLY AN AWFUL IDEA.
WHY DIDN'T ANYONE TELL ME THIS WAS AN AWFUL IDEA??
BECAUSE I'M NOTORIOUSLY AVOIDANT AND THREATEN TO BAIL IF I'M QUESTIONED-- OH SHIT.
WELL, MISS HACK.

ISN'T IT FUNNY THAT WE ALCOHOL PREP THE ARM OF SOMEONE WE'RE ABOUT TO KILL?

GALLOWS HUMOR, I SUPPOSE.

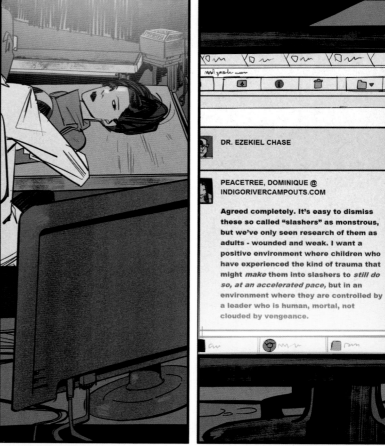

DR. EZEKIEL CHASE

PEACETREE, DOMINIQUE @ INDIGORIVERCAMPOUTS.COM

Agreed completely. It's easy to dismiss these so called "slashers" as monstrous, but we've only seen research of them as adults - wounded and weak. I want a positive environment where children who have experienced the kind of trauma that might *make* them into slashers to *still do so, at an accelerated pace,* but in an environment where they are controlled by a leader who is human, mortal, not clouded by vengeance.

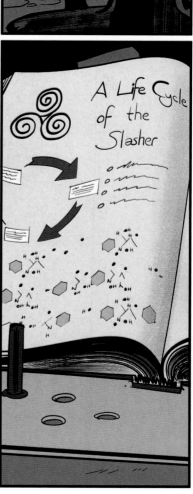

A Life Cycle of the Slasher

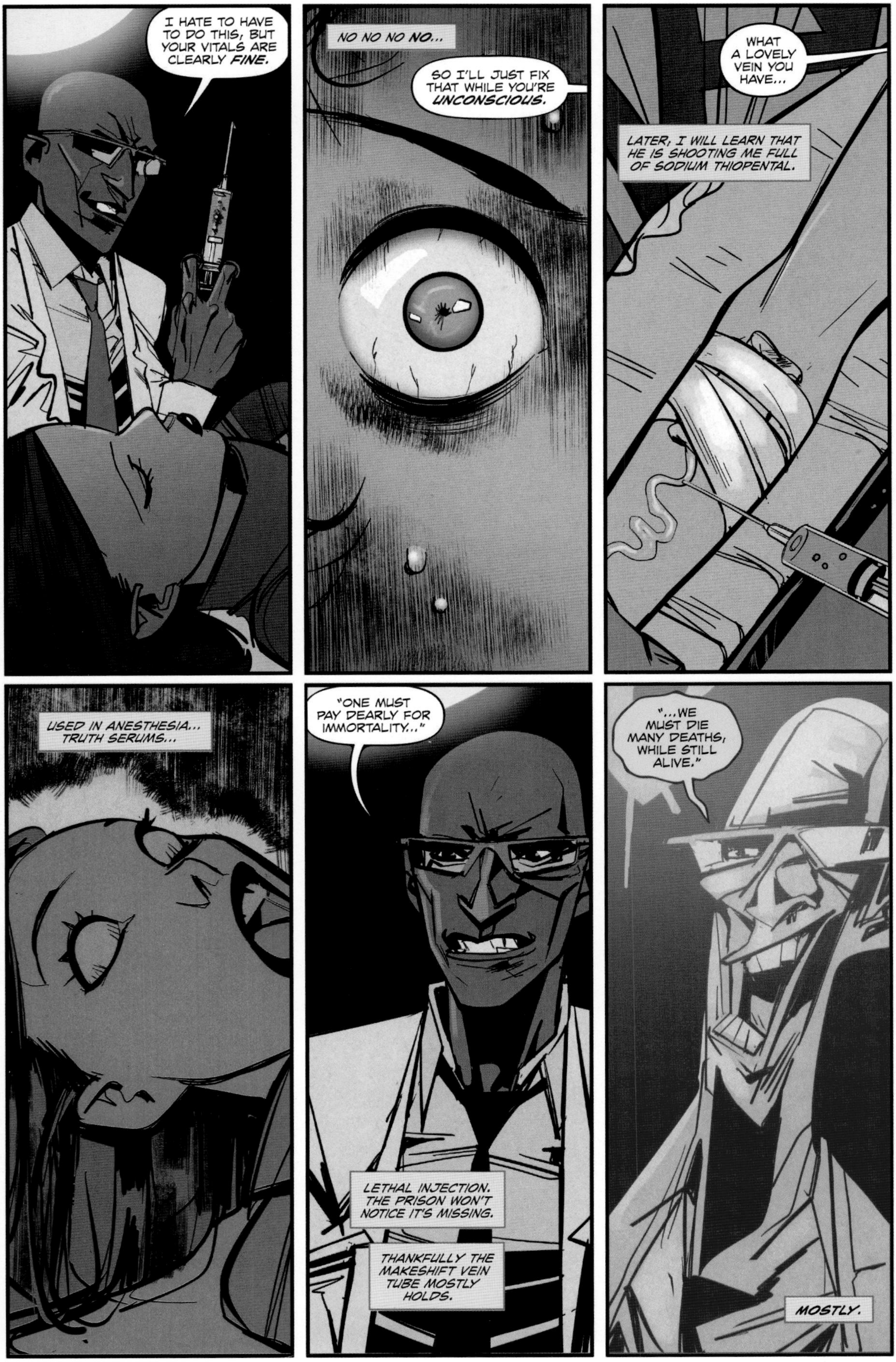
I HATE TO HAVE TO DO THIS, BUT YOUR VITALS ARE CLEARLY *FINE.*
NO NO NO *NO...*
SO I'LL JUST FIX THAT WHILE YOU'RE *UNCONSCIOUS.*
WHAT A LOVELY VEIN YOU HAVE...
LATER, I WILL LEARN THAT HE IS SHOOTING ME FULL OF SODIUM THIOPENTAL.
USED IN ANESTHESIA... TRUTH SERUMS...
"ONE MUST PAY DEARLY FOR IMMORTALITY..."
LETHAL INJECTION. THE PRISON WON'T NOTICE IT'S MISSING.
THANKFULLY THE MAKESHIFT VEIN TUBE MOSTLY HOLDS.
"...WE MUST DIE MANY DEATHS, WHILE STILL ALIVE."
MOSTLY.

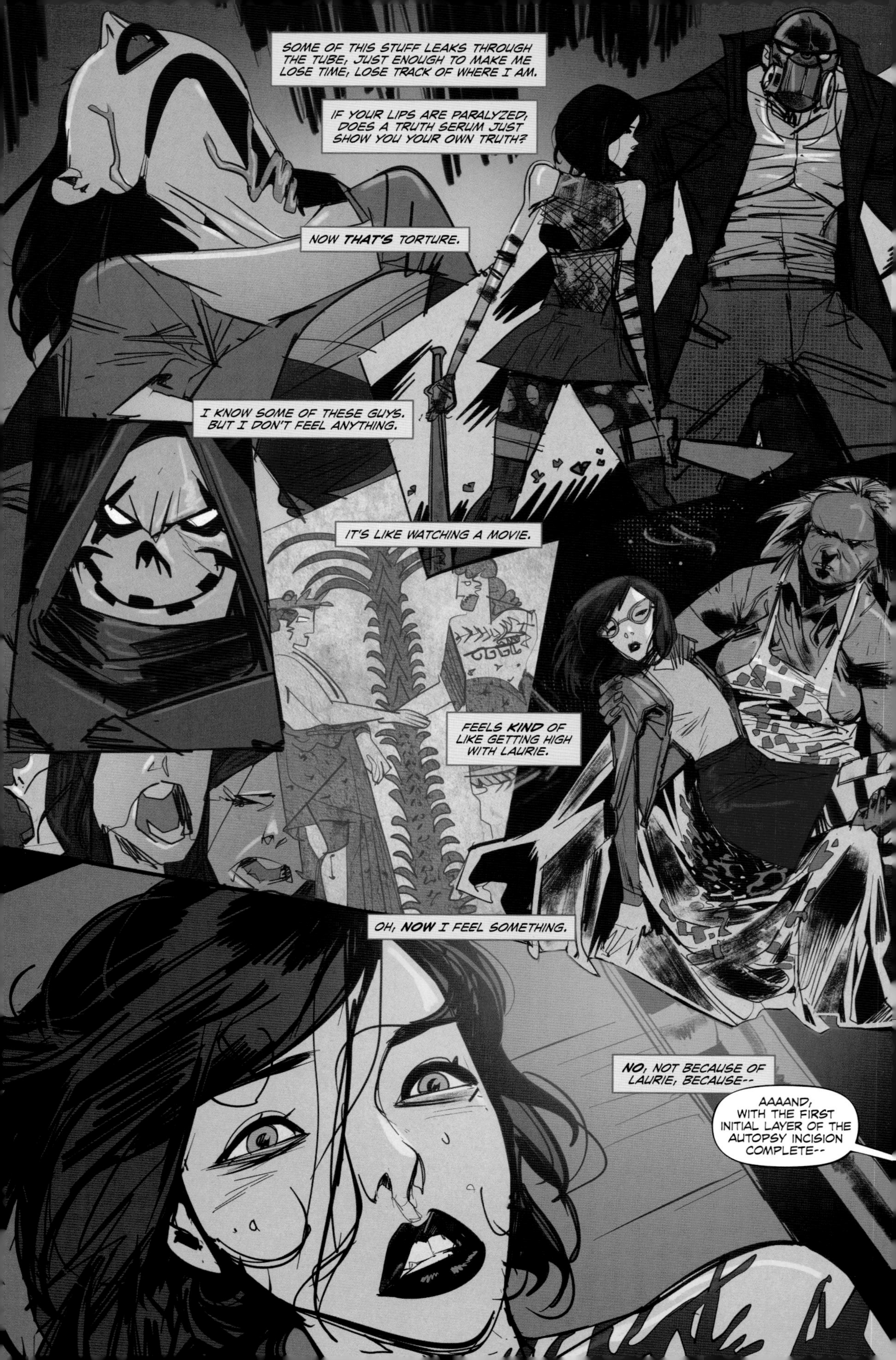
SOME OF THIS STUFF LEAKS THROUGH THE TUBE, JUST ENOUGH TO MAKE ME LOSE TIME, LOSE TRACK OF WHERE I AM.
IF YOUR LIPS ARE PARALYZED, DOES A TRUTH SERUM JUST SHOW YOU YOUR OWN TRUTH?
NOW **THAT'S** TORTURE.
I KNOW SOME OF THESE GUYS. BUT I DON'T FEEL ANYTHING.
IT'S LIKE WATCHING A MOVIE.
FEELS **KIND** OF LIKE GETTING HIGH WITH LAURIE.
OH, **NOW** I FEEL SOMETHING.
NO, NOT BECAUSE OF LAURIE, BECAUSE--
AAAAND, WITH THE FIRST INITIAL LAYER OF THE AUTOPSY INCISION COMPLETE--

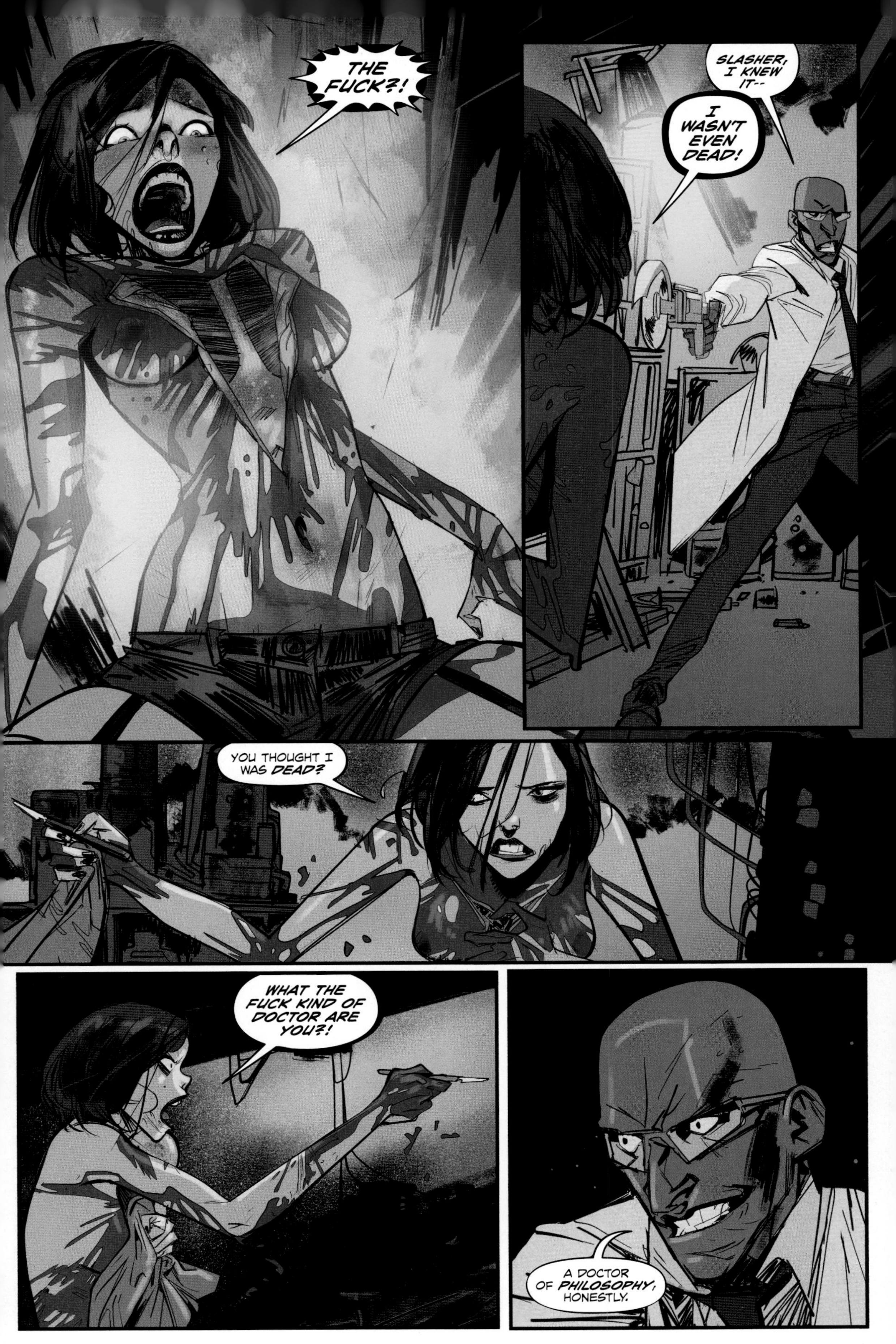
THE FUCK?!
SLASHER, I KNEW IT--
I WASN'T EVEN DEAD!
YOU THOUGHT I WAS DEAD?
WHAT THE FUCK KIND OF DOCTOR ARE YOU?!
A DOCTOR OF PHILOSOPHY, HONESTLY.

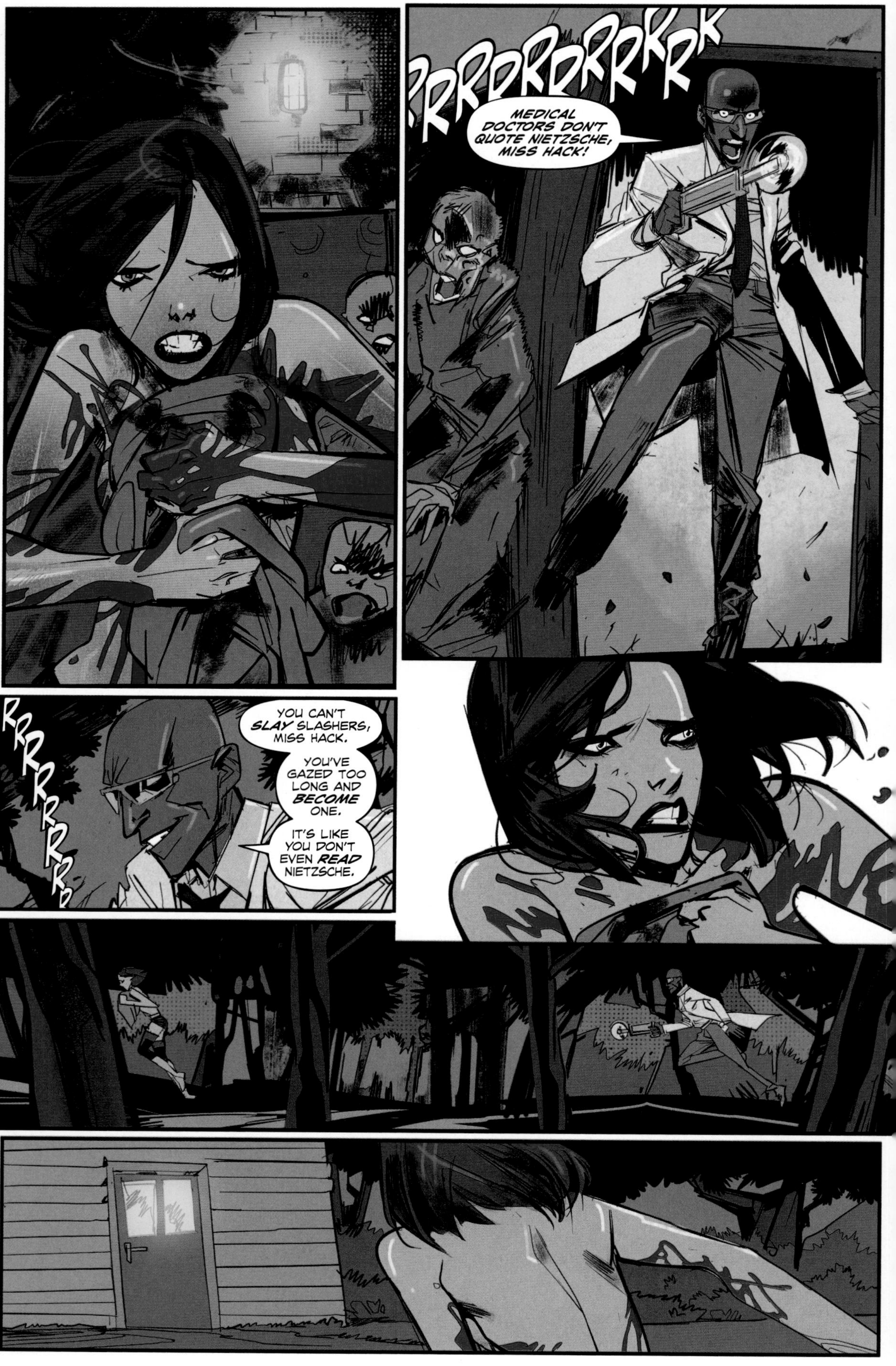
RRRDRDRRRRRK
MEDICAL DOCTORS DON'T QUOTE NIETZSCHE, MISS HACK!
RRRRRRRRD
YOU CAN'T SLAY SLASHERS, MISS HACK.
YOU'VE GAZED TOO LONG AND BECOME ONE.
IT'S LIKE YOU DON'T EVEN READ NIETZSCHE.

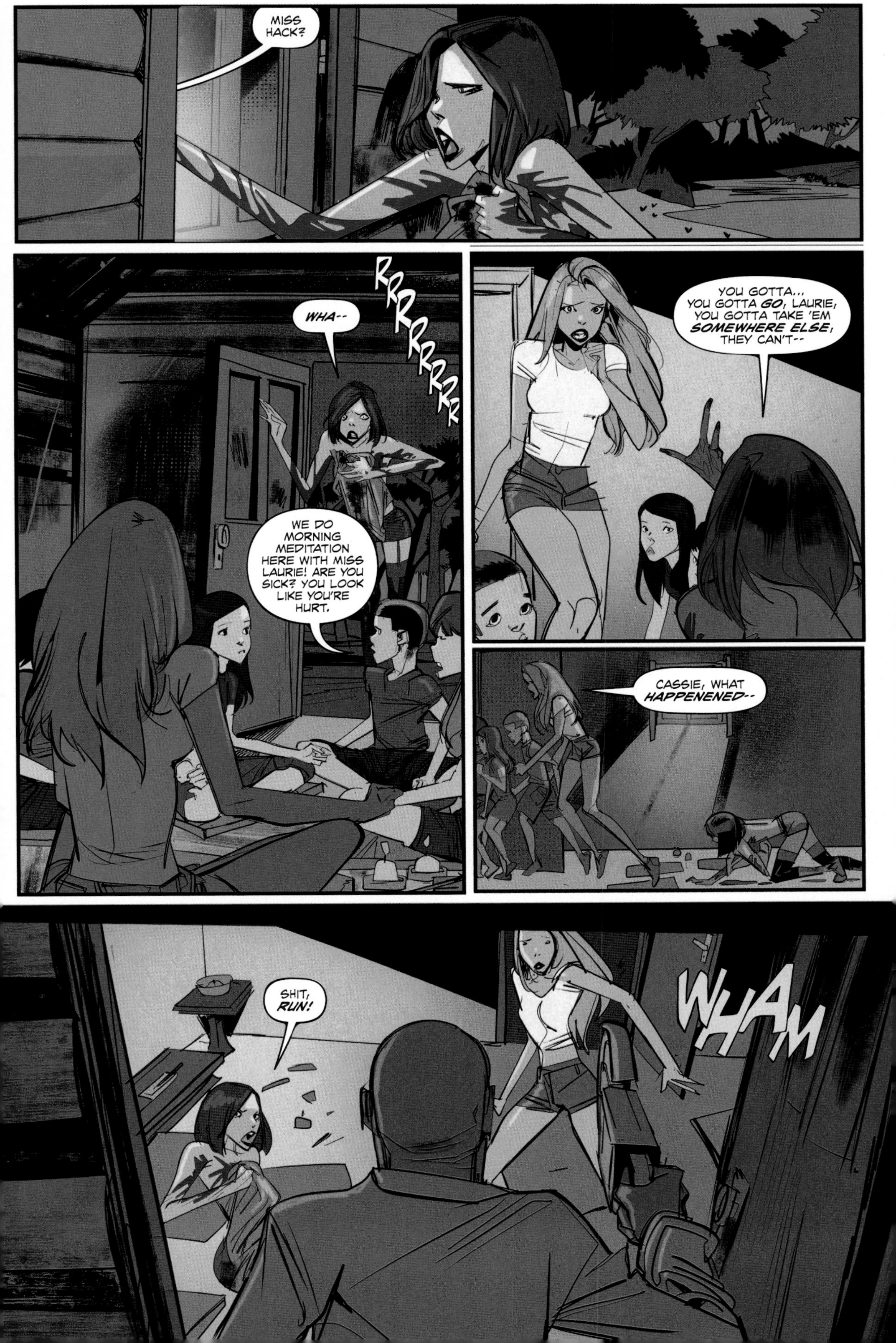

MISS HACK?
RRRRRRRRRRR
WHA--
WE DO MORNING MEDITATION HERE WITH MISS LAURIE! ARE YOU SICK? YOU LOOK LIKE YOU'RE HURT.
YOU GOTTA... YOU GOTTA *GO*, LAURIE, YOU GOTTA TAKE 'EM *SOMEWHERE ELSE*; THEY CAN'T--
CASSIE, WHAT *HAPPENED*--
SHIT, *RUN!*
WHAM

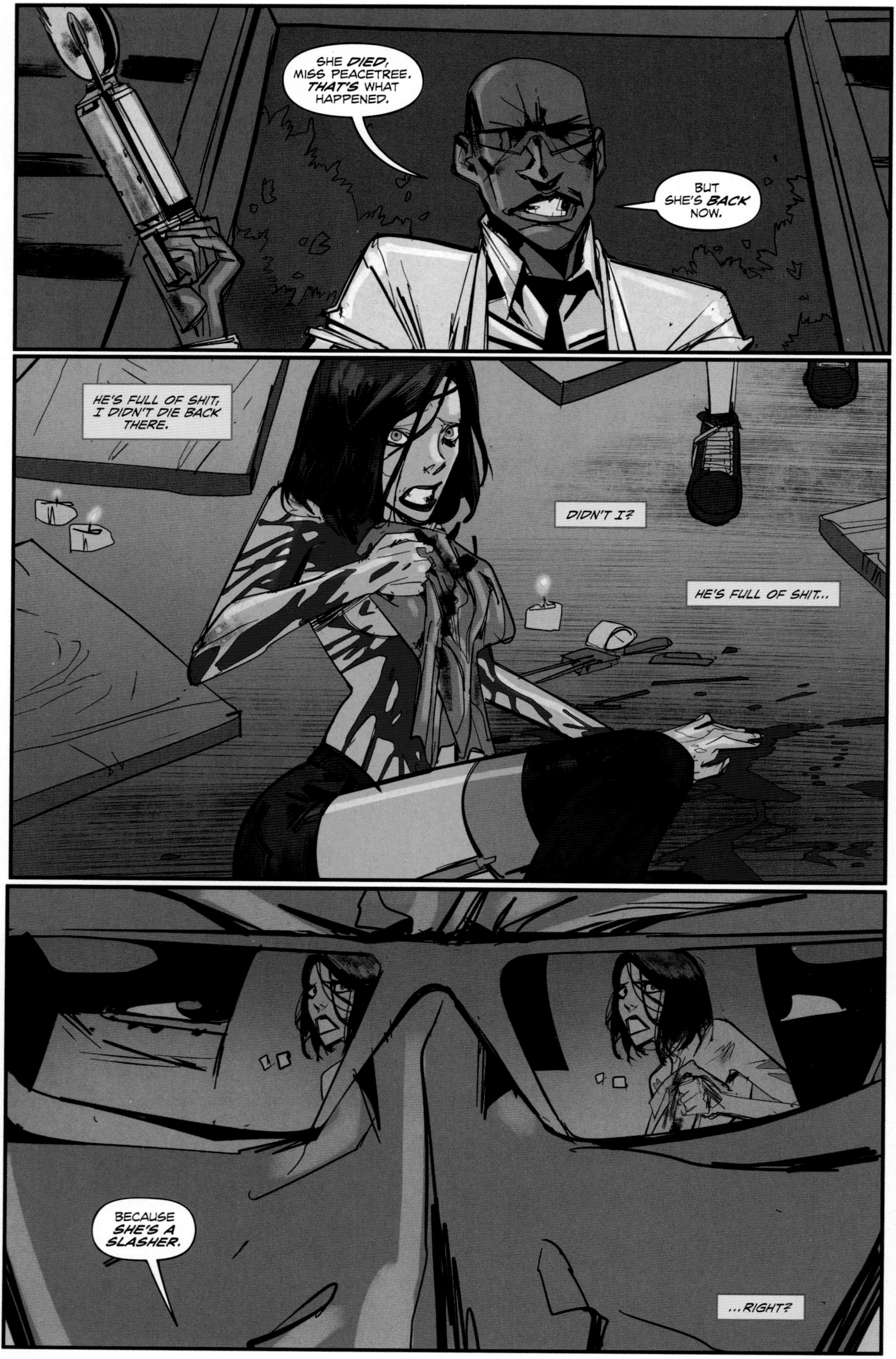
SHE *DIED*, MISS PEACETREE. *THAT'S* WHAT HAPPENED.
BUT SHE'S *BACK* NOW.
HE'S FULL OF SHIT, I DIDN'T DIE BACK THERE.
DIDN'T I?
HE'S FULL OF SHIT...
BECAUSE *SHE'S A SLASHER.*
...RIGHT?

ISSUE 5 COVER BY
TIM SEELEY & ADDISON DUKE

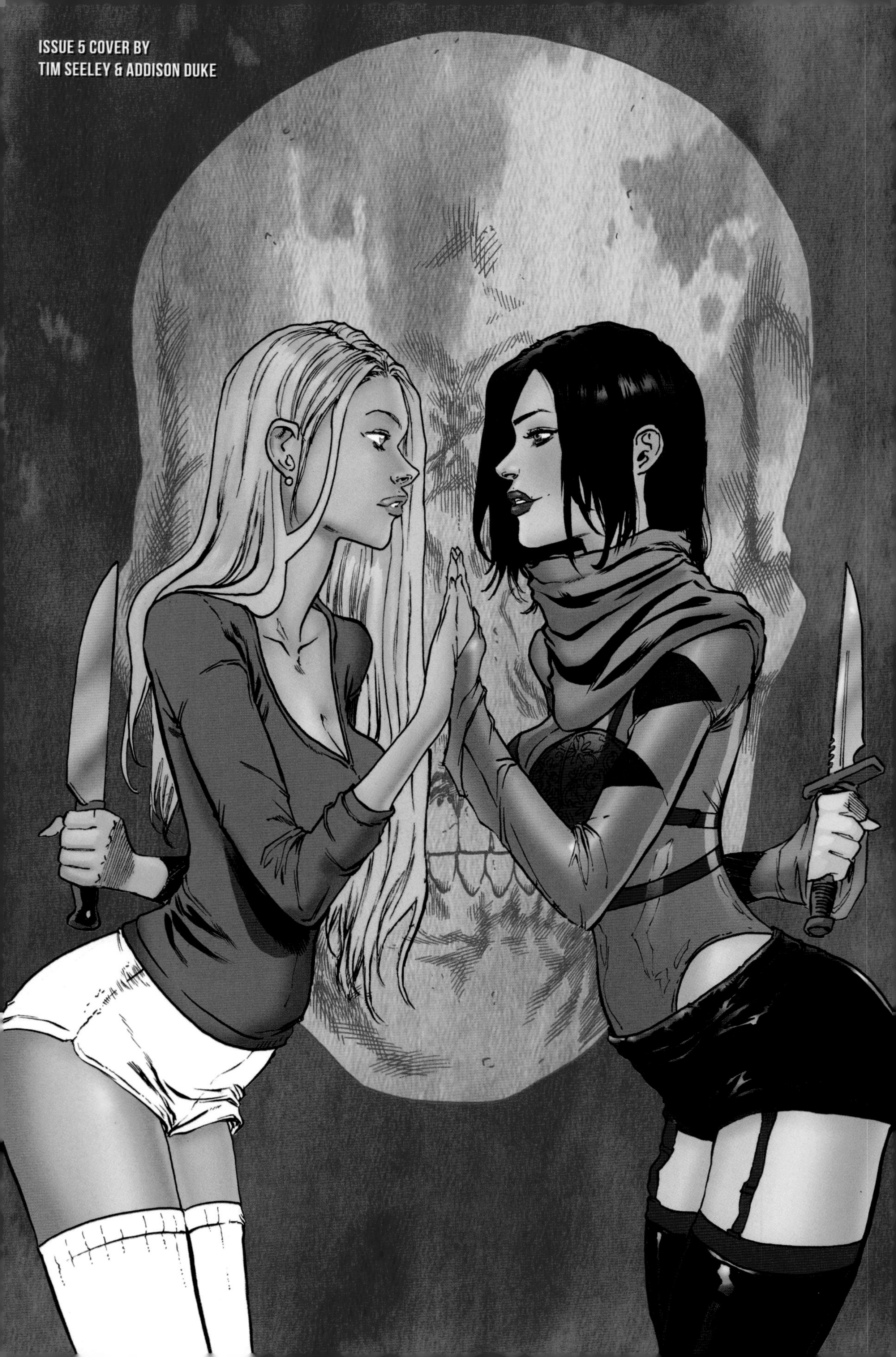

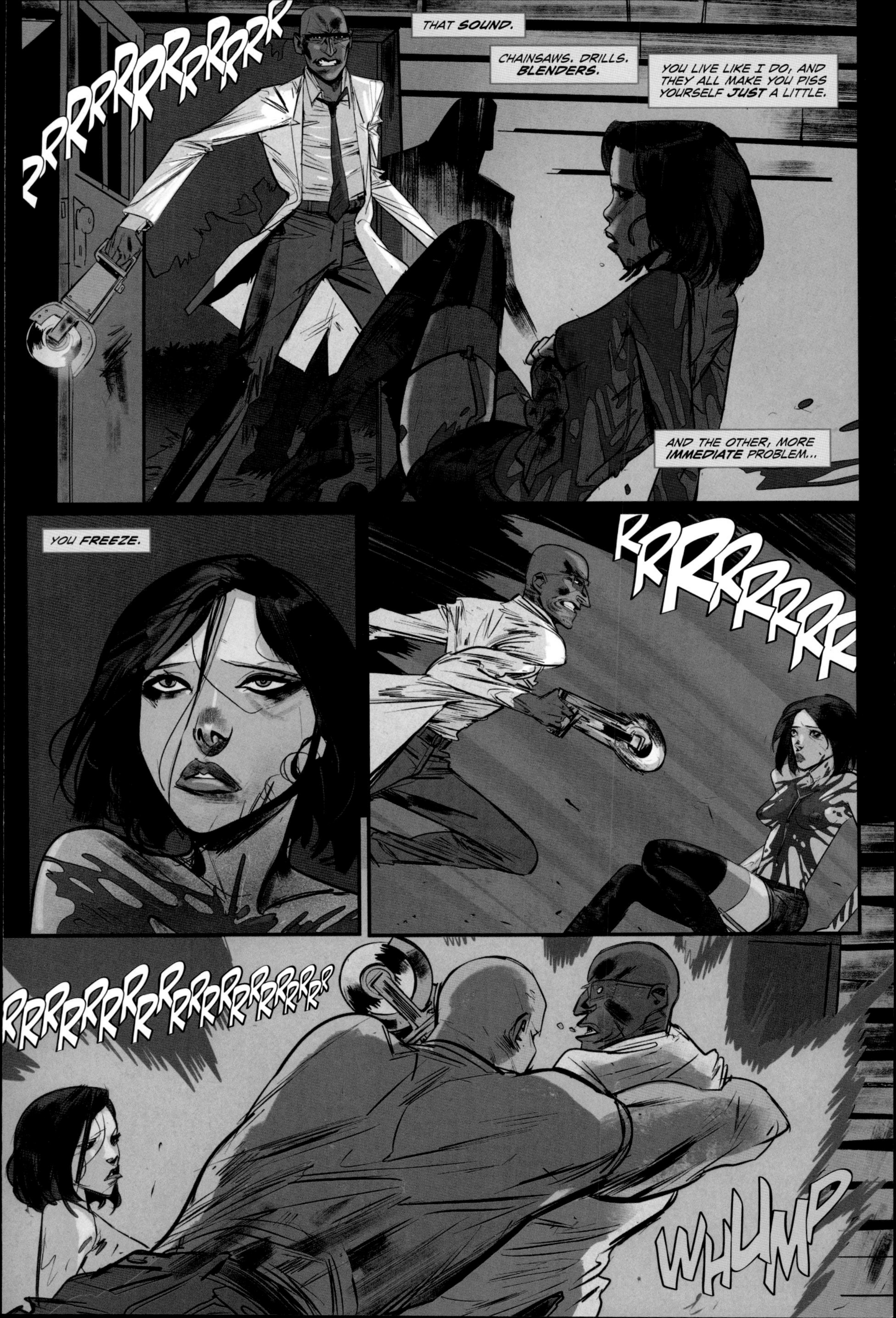
RRRRRRRRRRRRRRRRR
THAT SOUND.
CHAINSAWS. DRILLS. BLENDERS.
YOU LIVE LIKE I DO, AND THEY ALL MAKE YOU PISS YOURSELF JUST A LITTLE.
AND THE OTHER, MORE IMMEDIATE PROBLEM...
YOU FREEZE.
RRRRRRRRRR
RRRRRRRRRRRRRRRRRR
WHUMP

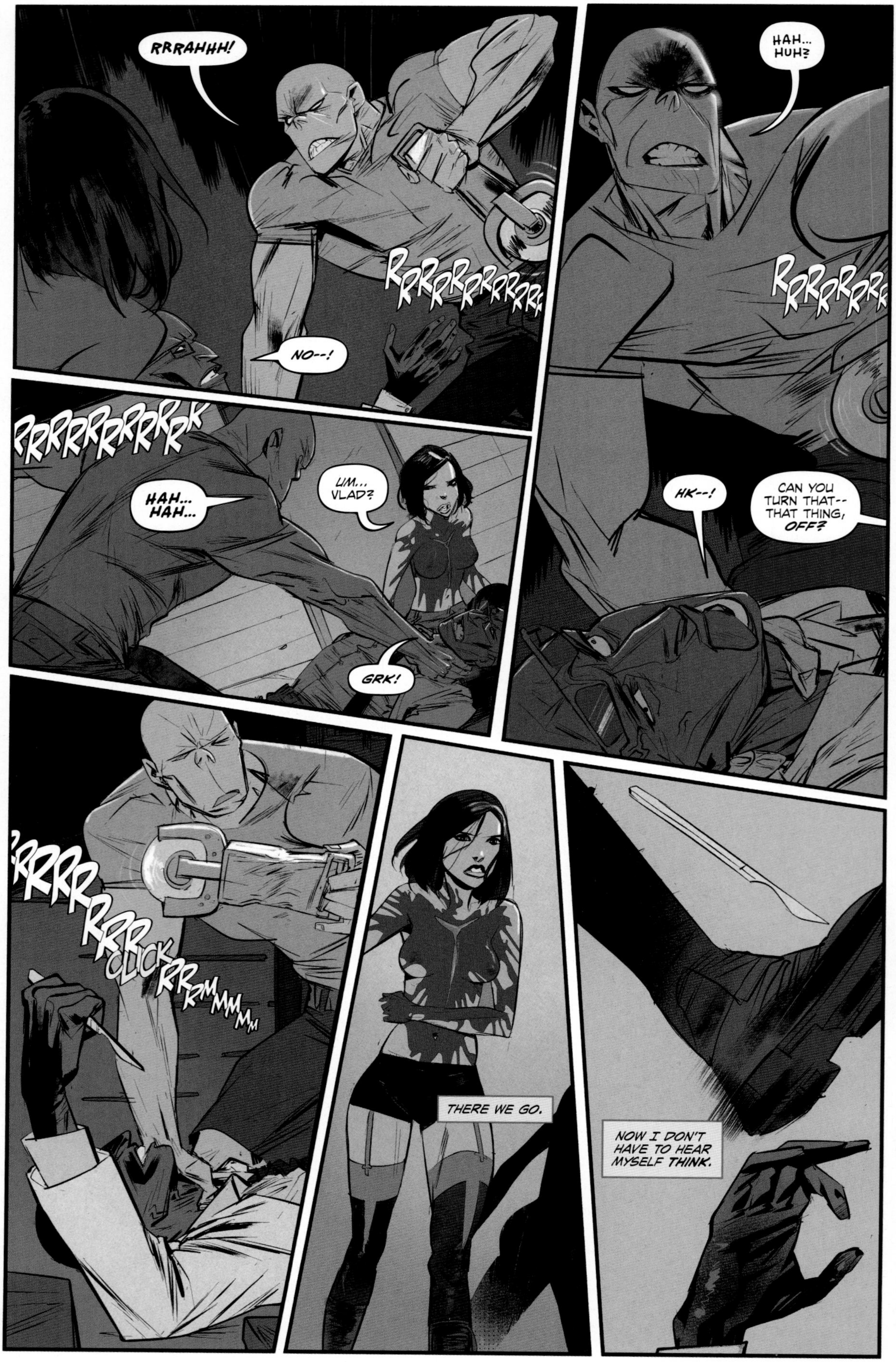
RRRAHHH!
RRRRRRRRRRRRK
NO--!
HAH... HUH?
RRRRRRK
RRRRRRRRRRK
HAH... HAH...
UM... VLAD?
GRK!
HK--!
CAN YOU TURN THAT-- THAT THING, OFF?
RRRRRRRR
CLICK
RRMMMMM
THERE WE GO.
NOW I DON'T HAVE TO HEAR MYSELF THINK.

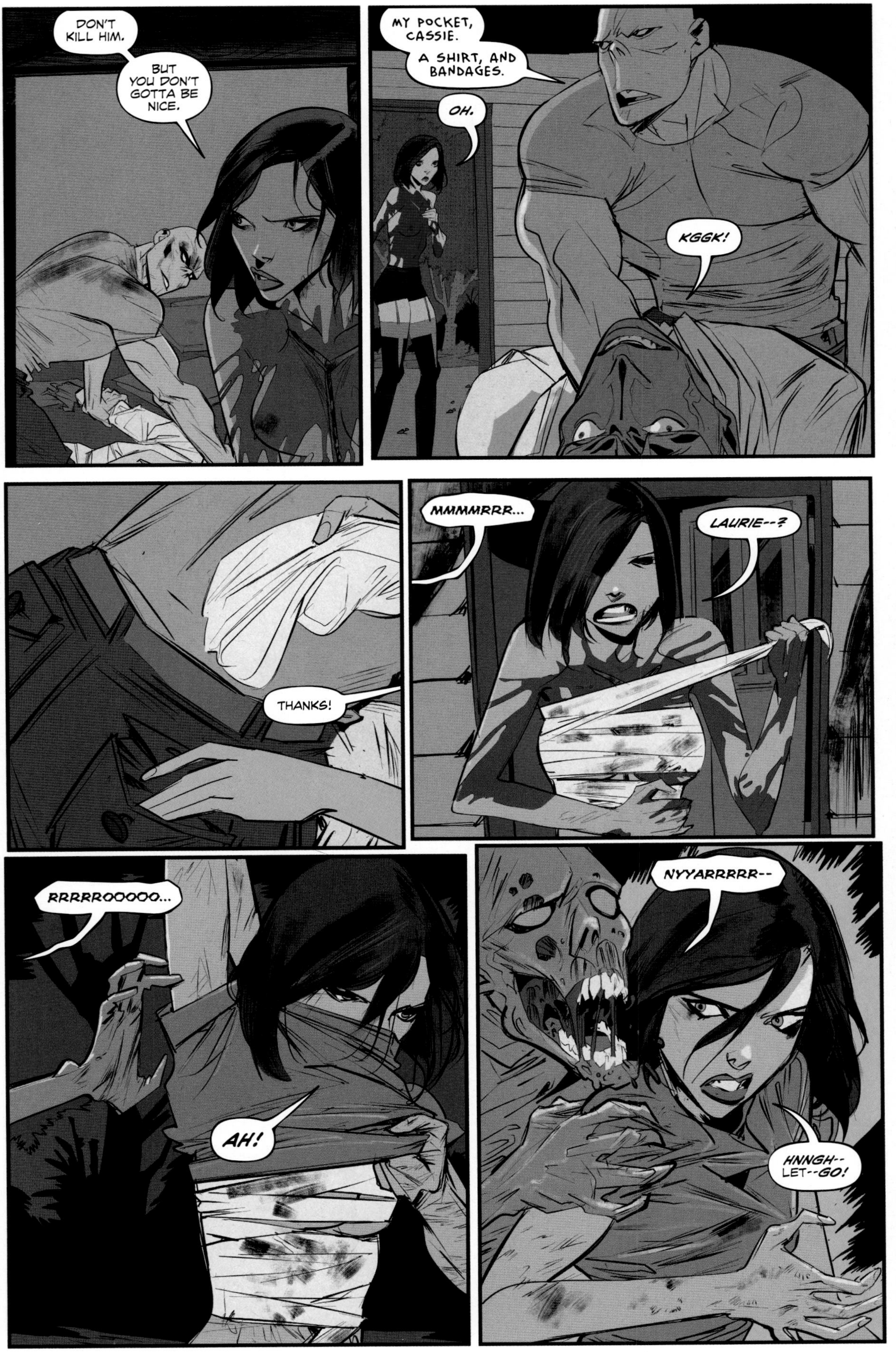
DON'T KILL HIM.
BUT YOU DON'T GOTTA BE NICE.
MY POCKET, CASSIE.
A SHIRT, AND BANDAGES.
OH.
KGGK!
THANKS!
MMMMRRR...
LAURIE--?
RRRRROOOOO...
AH!
NYYARRRRR--
HNNGH-- LET--GO!

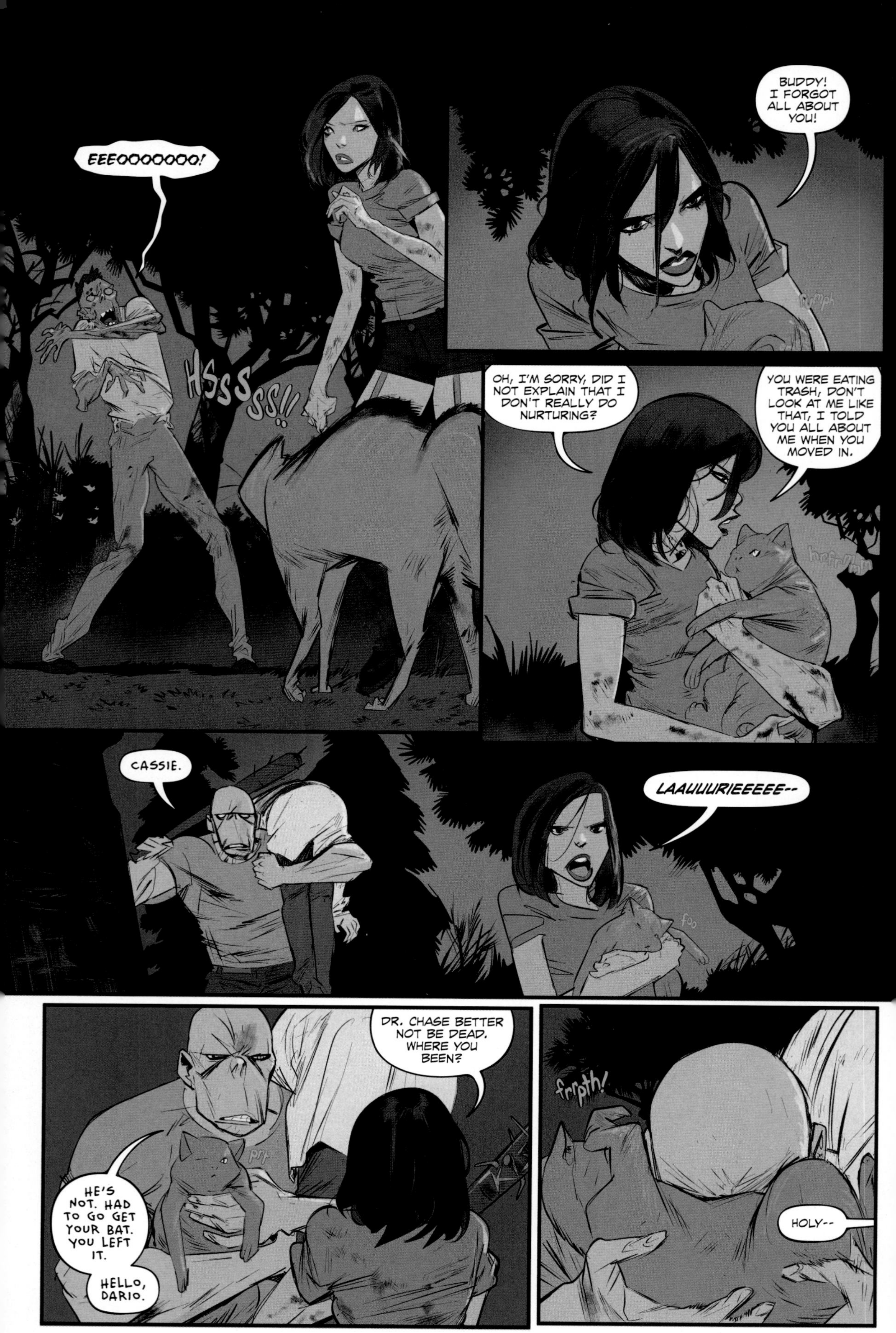

EEEOOOOOOOO!
HSSSSS!!
BUDDY! I FORGOT ALL ABOUT YOU!
hrumph
OH, I'M SORRY, DID I NOT EXPLAIN THAT I DON'T REALLY DO NURTURING?
YOU WERE EATING TRASH, DON'T LOOK AT ME LIKE THAT, I TOLD YOU ALL ABOUT ME WHEN YOU MOVED IN.
CASSIE.
LAAUUURIEEEEE--
foo
DR. CHASE BETTER NOT BE DEAD. WHERE YOU BEEN?
prt
HE'S NOT. HAD TO GO GET YOUR BAT. YOU LEFT IT.
HELLO, DARIO.
frrpth!
HOLY--

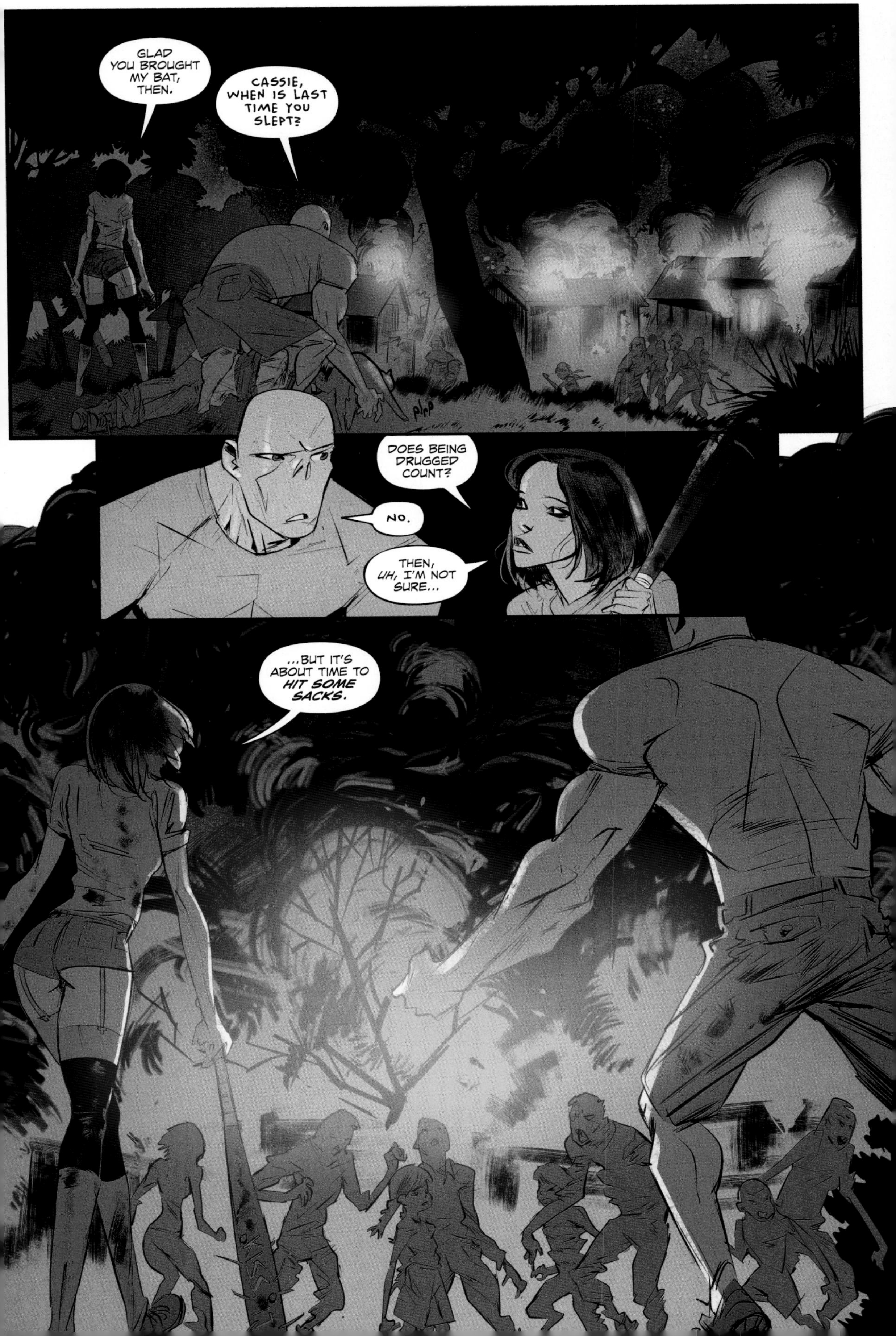
GLAD YOU BROUGHT MY BAT, THEN.
CASSIE, WHEN IS LAST TIME YOU SLEPT?
plop
DOES BEING DRUGGED COUNT?
NO.
THEN, UH, I'M NOT SURE...
...BUT IT'S ABOUT TIME TO HIT SOME SACKS.

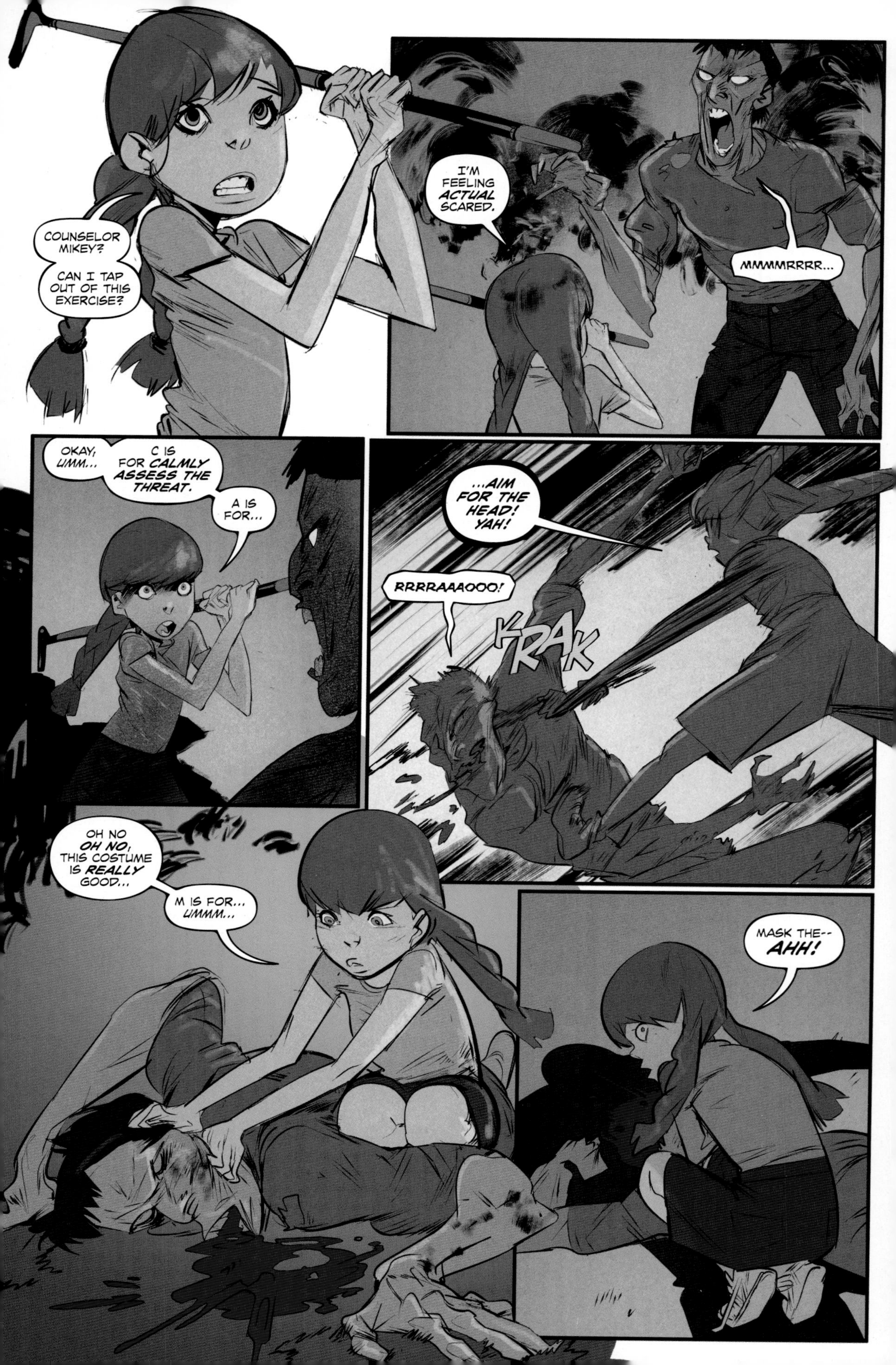
COUNSELOR MIKEY?
CAN I TAP OUT OF THIS EXERCISE?
I'M FEELING *ACTUAL* SCARED.
MMMMRRRR...
OKAY, *UMM...*
C IS FOR *CALMLY ASSESS THE THREAT.*
A IS FOR...
...*AIM FOR THE HEAD! YAH!*
RRRRAAAOOO!
KRAK
OH NO *OH NO,* THIS COSTUME IS *REALLY* GOOD...
M IS FOR... *UMMM...*
MASK THE-- *AHH!*

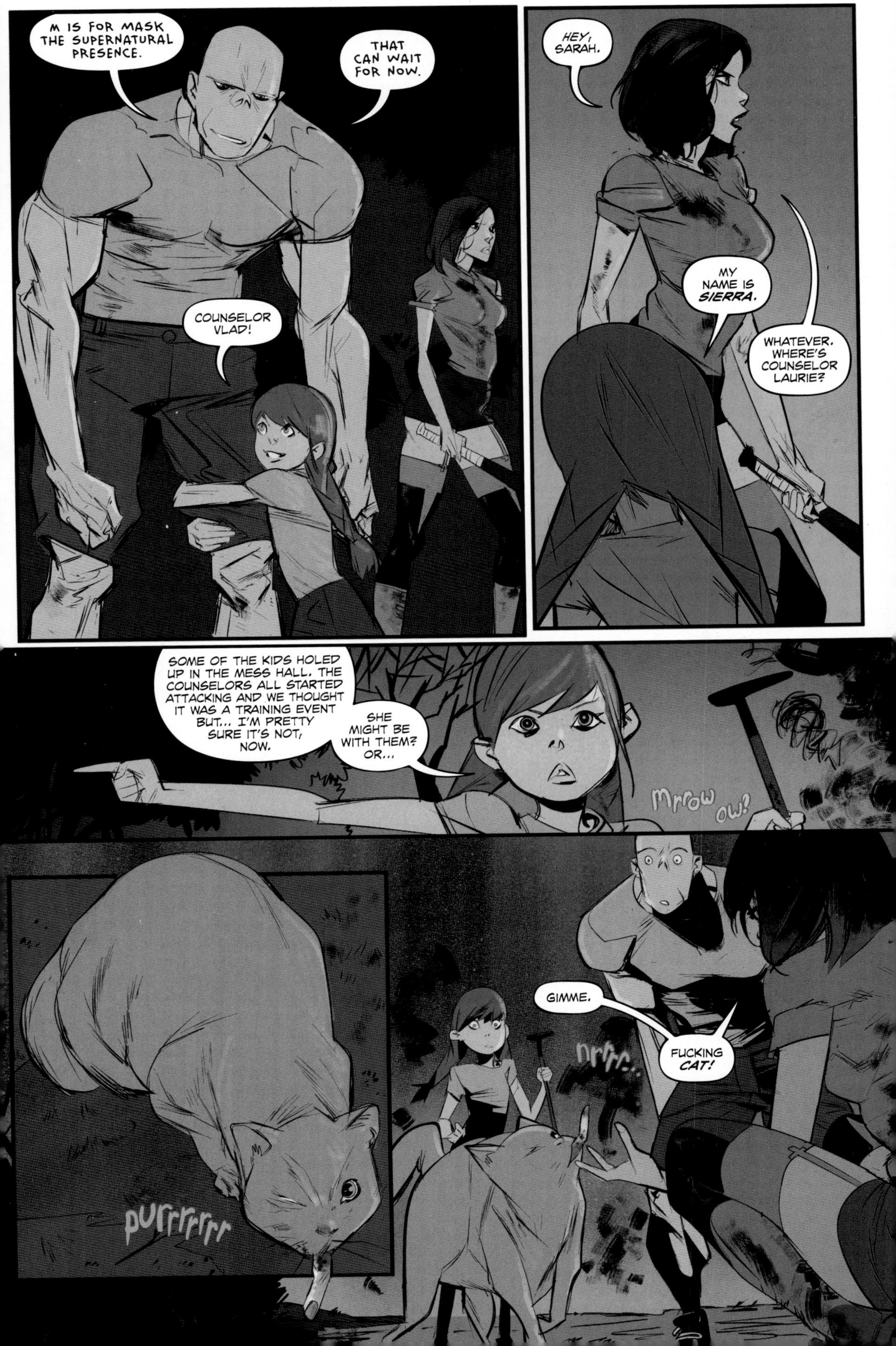
M IS FOR MASK THE SUPERNATURAL PRESENCE.
THAT CAN WAIT FOR NOW.
COUNSELOR VLAD!
HEY, SARAH.
MY NAME IS SIERRA.
WHATEVER. WHERE'S COUNSELOR LAURIE?
SOME OF THE KIDS HOLED UP IN THE MESS HALL. THE COUNSELORS ALL STARTED ATTACKING AND WE THOUGHT IT WAS A TRAINING EVENT BUT... I'M PRETTY SURE IT'S NOT, NOW.
SHE MIGHT BE WITH THEM? OR...
Mrrow ow?
purrrrrrr
GIMME.
FUCKING CAT!
nrrrr..

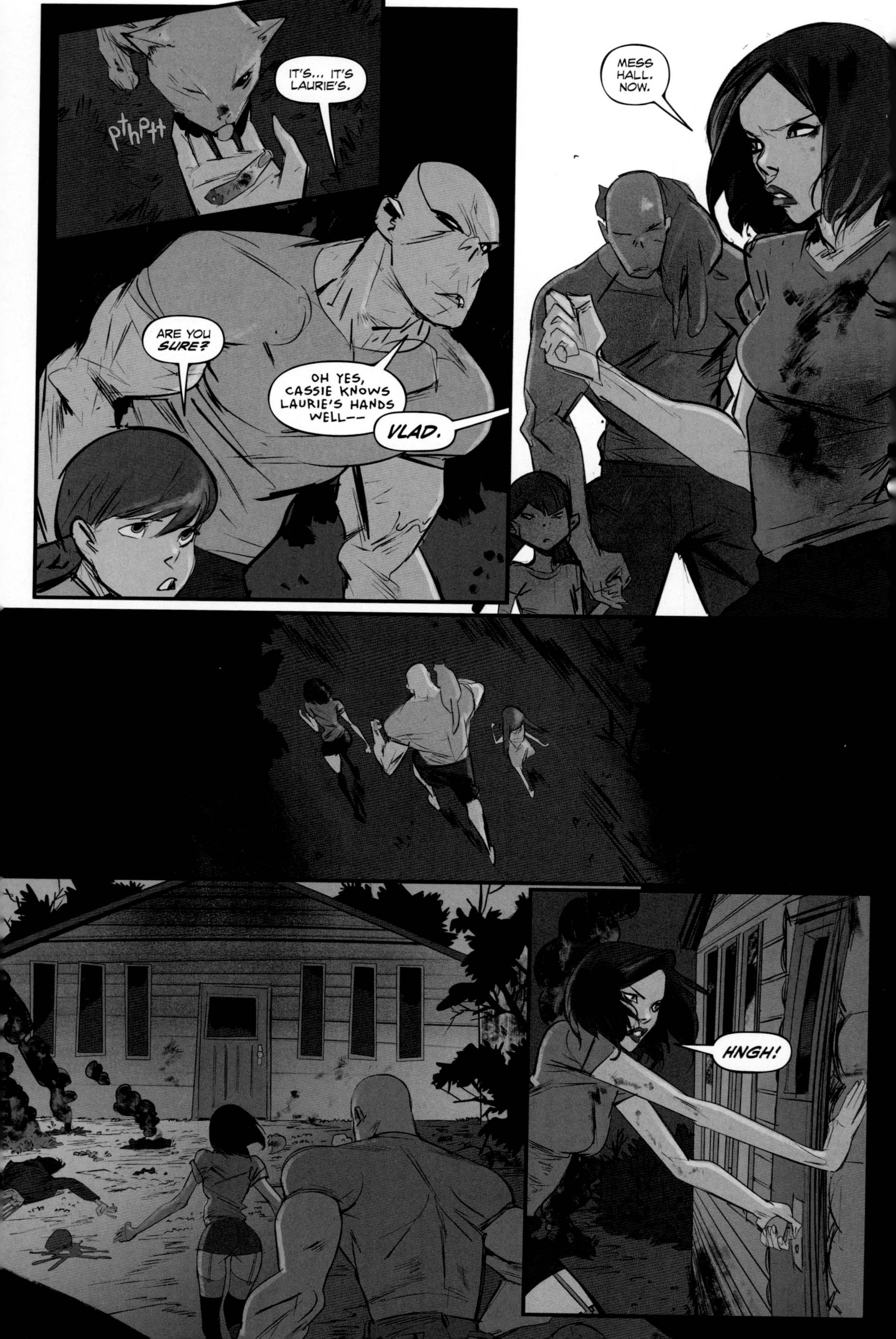
ptHptt
IT'S... IT'S LAURIE'S.
ARE YOU *SURE?*
OH YES, CASSIE KNOWS LAURIE'S HANDS WELL--
VLAD.
MESS HALL. NOW.
HNGH!

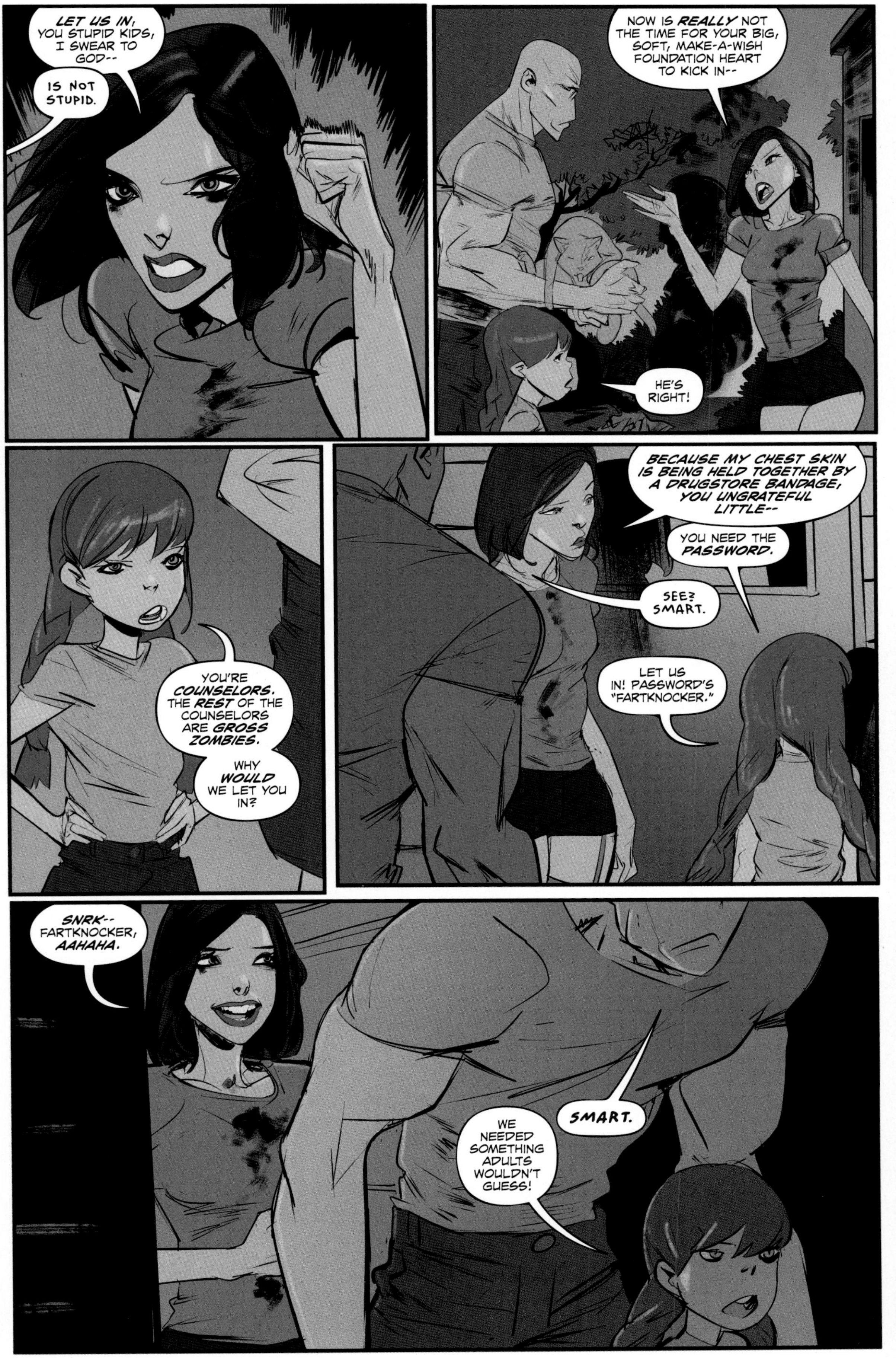
LET US IN, YOU STUPID KIDS, I SWEAR TO GOD--
IS NOT STUPID.
NOW IS REALLY NOT THE TIME FOR YOUR BIG, SOFT, MAKE-A-WISH FOUNDATION HEART TO KICK IN--
HE'S RIGHT!
YOU'RE COUNSELORS. THE REST OF THE COUNSELORS ARE GROSS ZOMBIES.
WHY WOULD WE LET YOU IN?
BECAUSE MY CHEST SKIN IS BEING HELD TOGETHER BY A DRUGSTORE BANDAGE, YOU UNGRATEFUL LITTLE--
YOU NEED THE PASSWORD.
SEE? SMART.
LET US IN! PASSWORD'S "FARTKNOCKER."
SNRK-- FARTKNOCKER, AAHAHA.
SMART.
WE NEEDED SOMETHING ADULTS WOULDN'T GUESS!

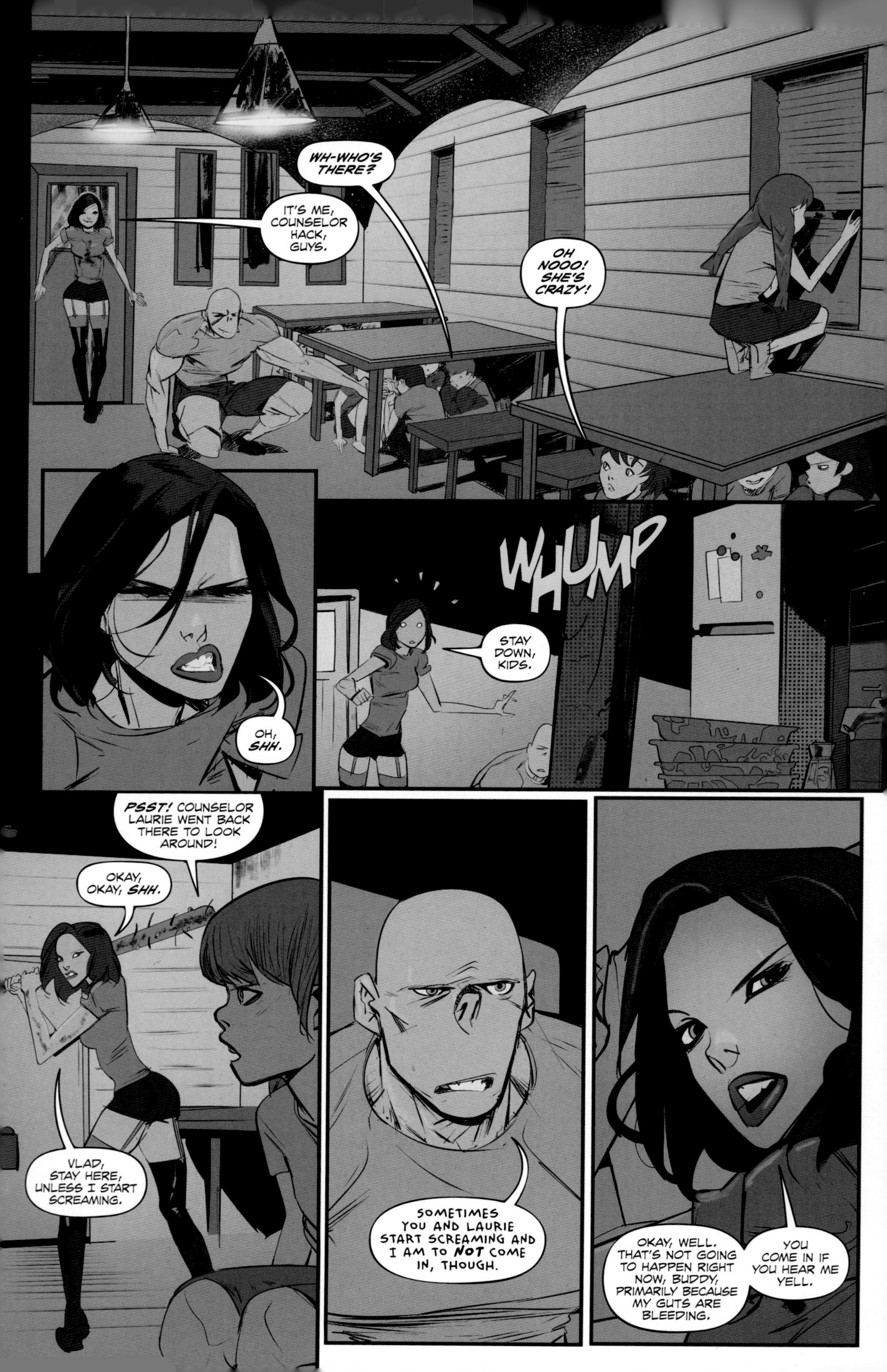
WH-WHO'S THERE?
IT'S ME, COUNSELOR HACK, GUYS.
OH NOOO! SHE'S CRAZY!
OH, SHH.
WHUMP
STAY DOWN, KIDS.
PSST! COUNSELOR LAURIE WENT BACK THERE TO LOOK AROUND!
OKAY, OKAY, SHH.
VLAD, STAY HERE, UNLESS I START SCREAMING.
SOMETIMES YOU AND LAURIE START SCREAMING AND I AM TO NOT COME IN, THOUGH.
OKAY, WELL. THAT'S NOT GOING TO HAPPEN RIGHT NOW, BUDDY, PRIMARILY BECAUSE MY GUTS ARE BLEEDING.
YOU COME IN IF YOU HEAR ME YELL.

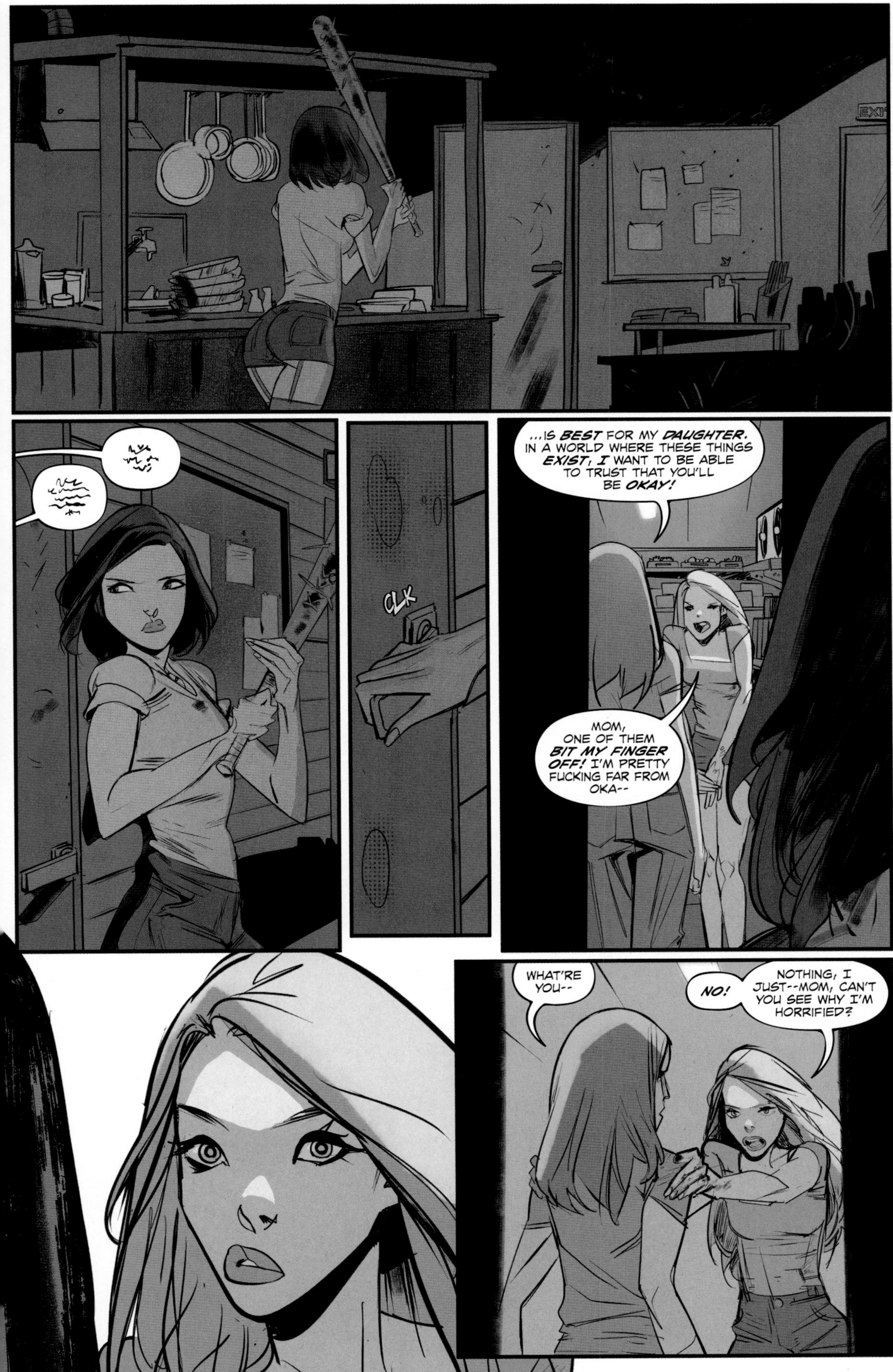
...IS BEST FOR MY DAUGHTER. IN A WORLD WHERE THESE THINGS EXIST, I WANT TO BE ABLE TO TRUST THAT YOU'LL BE OKAY!
CLK
MOM, ONE OF THEM BIT MY FINGER OFF! I'M PRETTY FUCKING FAR FROM OKA--
WHAT'RE YOU--
NO!
NOTHING, I JUST--MOM, CAN'T YOU SEE WHY I'M HORRIFIED?

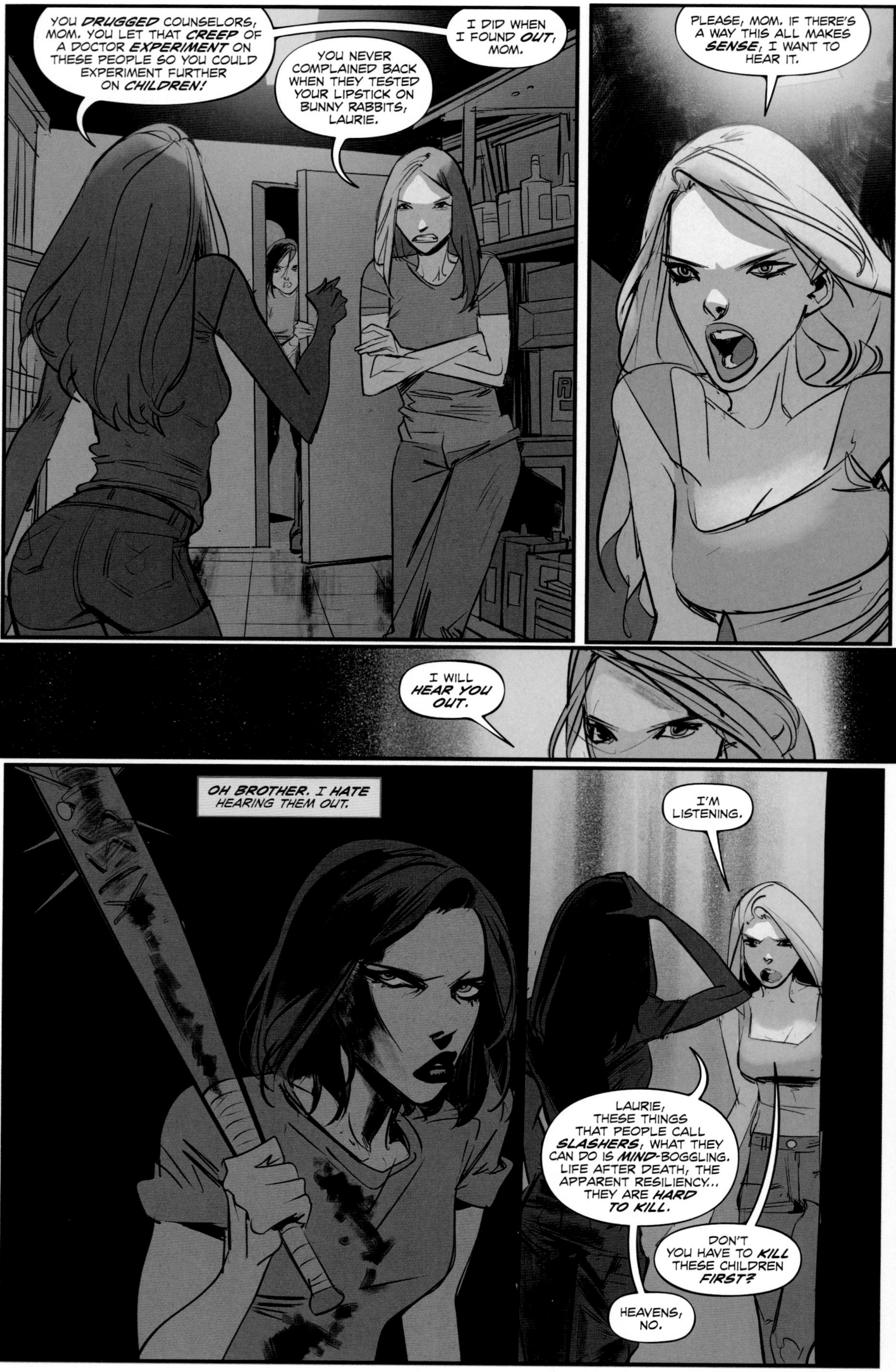
YOU DRUGGED COUNSELORS, MOM. YOU LET THAT CREEP OF A DOCTOR EXPERIMENT ON THESE PEOPLE SO YOU COULD EXPERIMENT FURTHER ON CHILDREN!
YOU NEVER COMPLAINED BACK WHEN THEY TESTED YOUR LIPSTICK ON BUNNY RABBITS, LAURIE.
I DID WHEN I FOUND OUT, MOM.
PLEASE, MOM. IF THERE'S A WAY THIS ALL MAKES SENSE, I WANT TO HEAR IT.
I WILL HEAR YOU OUT.
OH BROTHER. I HATE HEARING THEM OUT.
I'M LISTENING.
LAURIE, THESE THINGS THAT PEOPLE CALL SLASHERS, WHAT THEY CAN DO IS MIND-BOGGLING. LIFE AFTER DEATH, THE APPARENT RESILIENCY... THEY ARE HARD TO KILL.
DON'T YOU HAVE TO KILL THESE CHILDREN FIRST?
HEAVENS, NO.

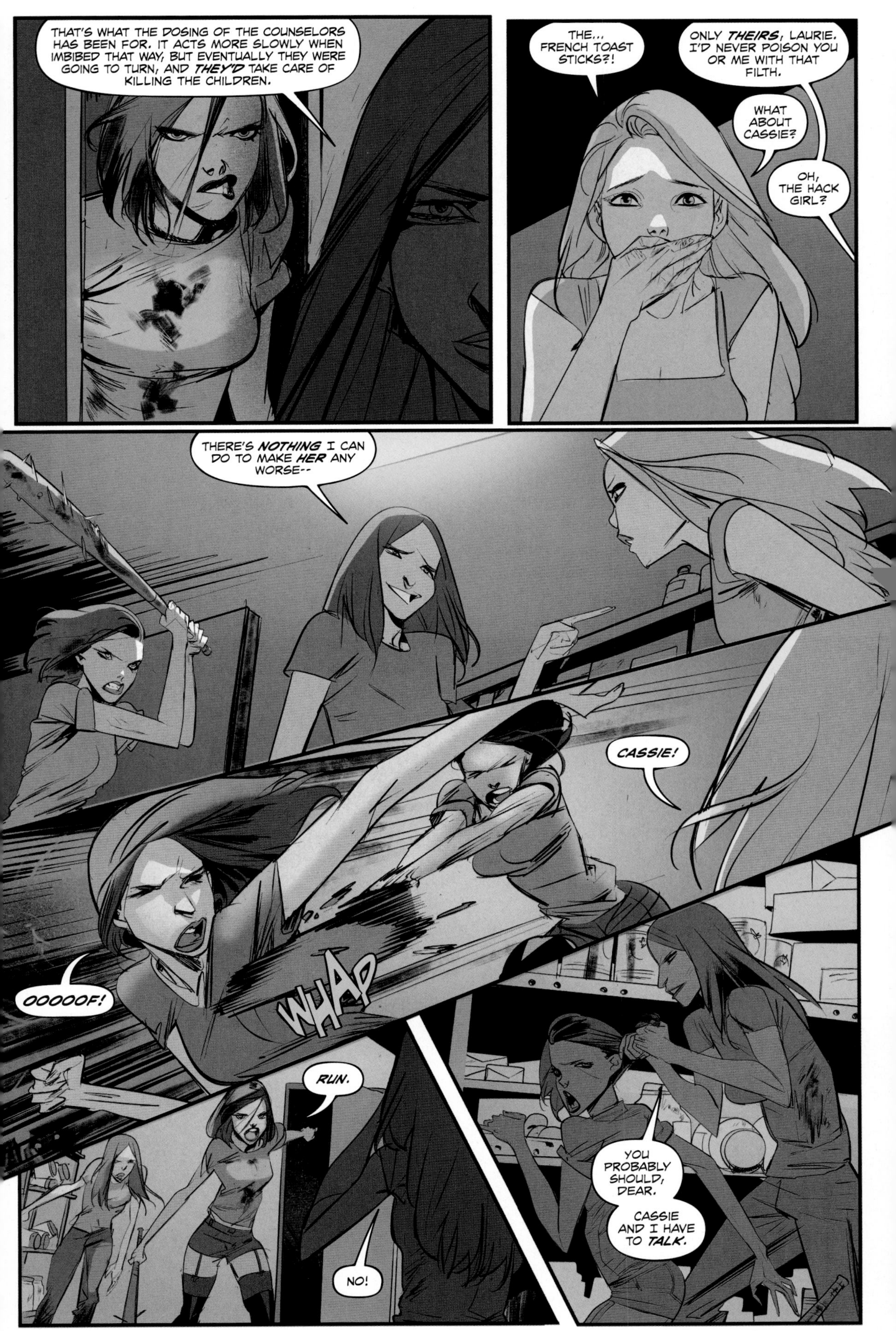

THAT'S WHAT THE DOSING OF THE COUNSELORS HAS BEEN FOR. IT ACTS MORE SLOWLY WHEN IMBIBED THAT WAY, BUT EVENTUALLY THEY WERE GOING TO TURN, AND THEY'D TAKE CARE OF KILLING THE CHILDREN.
THE... FRENCH TOAST STICKS?!
ONLY THEIRS, LAURIE. I'D NEVER POISON YOU OR ME WITH THAT FILTH.
WHAT ABOUT CASSIE?
OH, THE HACK GIRL?
THERE'S NOTHING I CAN DO TO MAKE HER ANY WORSE--
CASSIE!
OOOOOF!
WHAP
RUN.
NO!
YOU PROBABLY SHOULD, DEAR.
CASSIE AND I HAVE TO TALK.

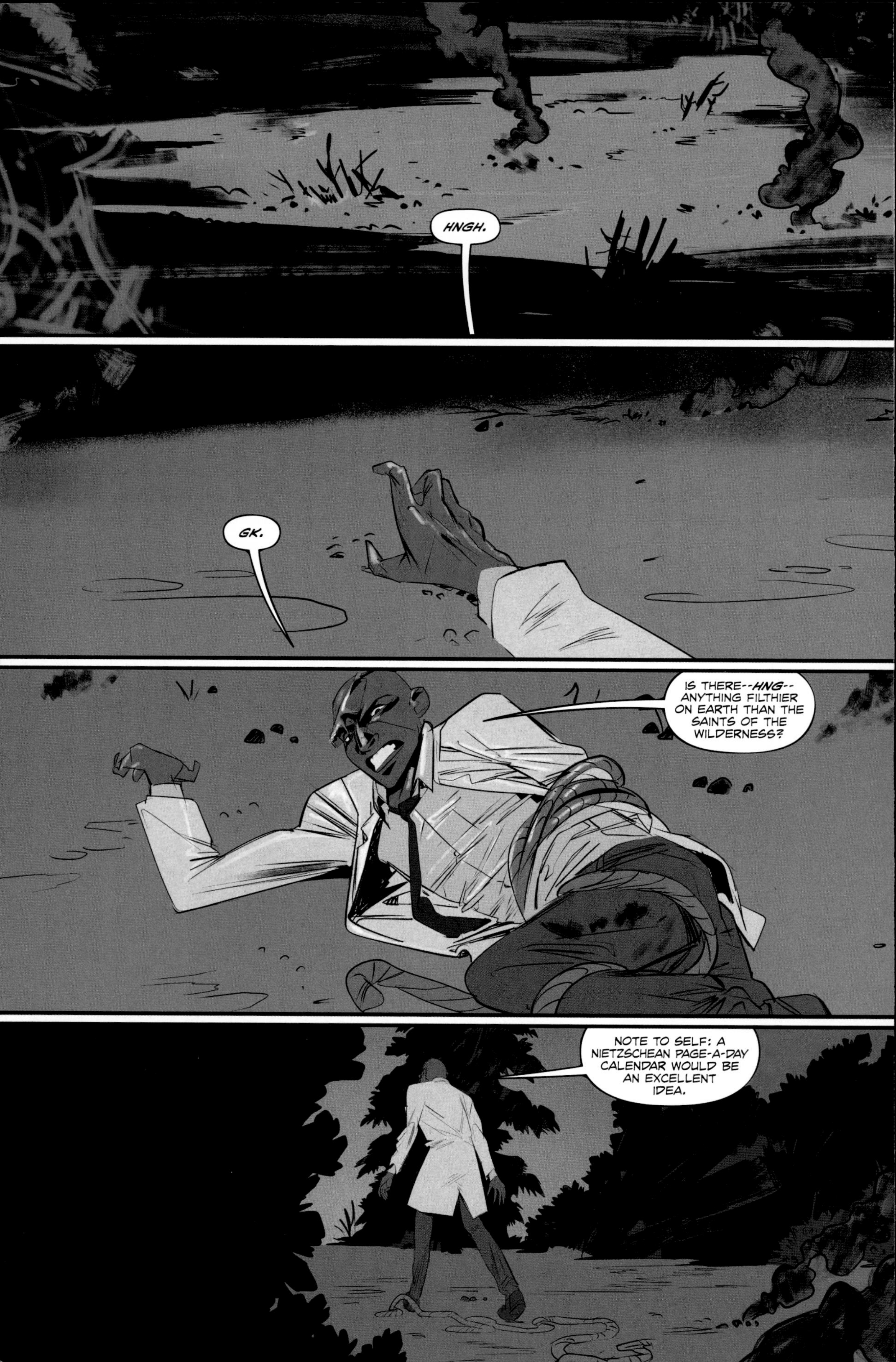
HNGH.
GK.
IS THERE--HNG--ANYTHING FILTHIER ON EARTH THAN THE SAINTS OF THE WILDERNESS?
NOTE TO SELF: A NIETZSCHEAN PAGE-A-DAY CALENDAR WOULD BE AN EXCELLENT IDEA.

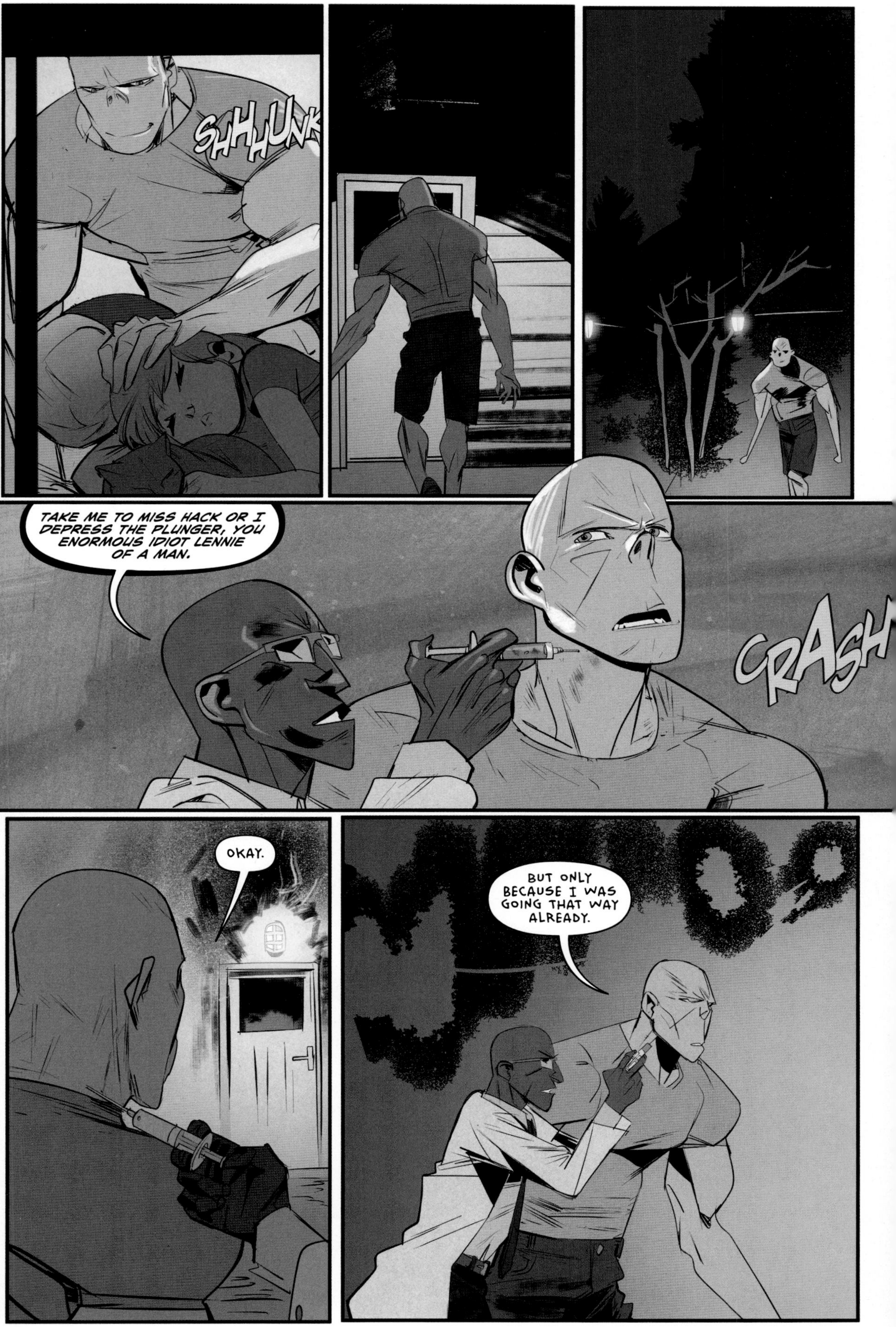
SHHHUNK
TAKE ME TO MISS HACK OR I DEPRESS THE PLUNGER, YOU ENORMOUS IDIOT LENNIE OF A MAN.
CRASH
OKAY.
BUT ONLY BECAUSE I WAS GOING THAT WAY ALREADY.

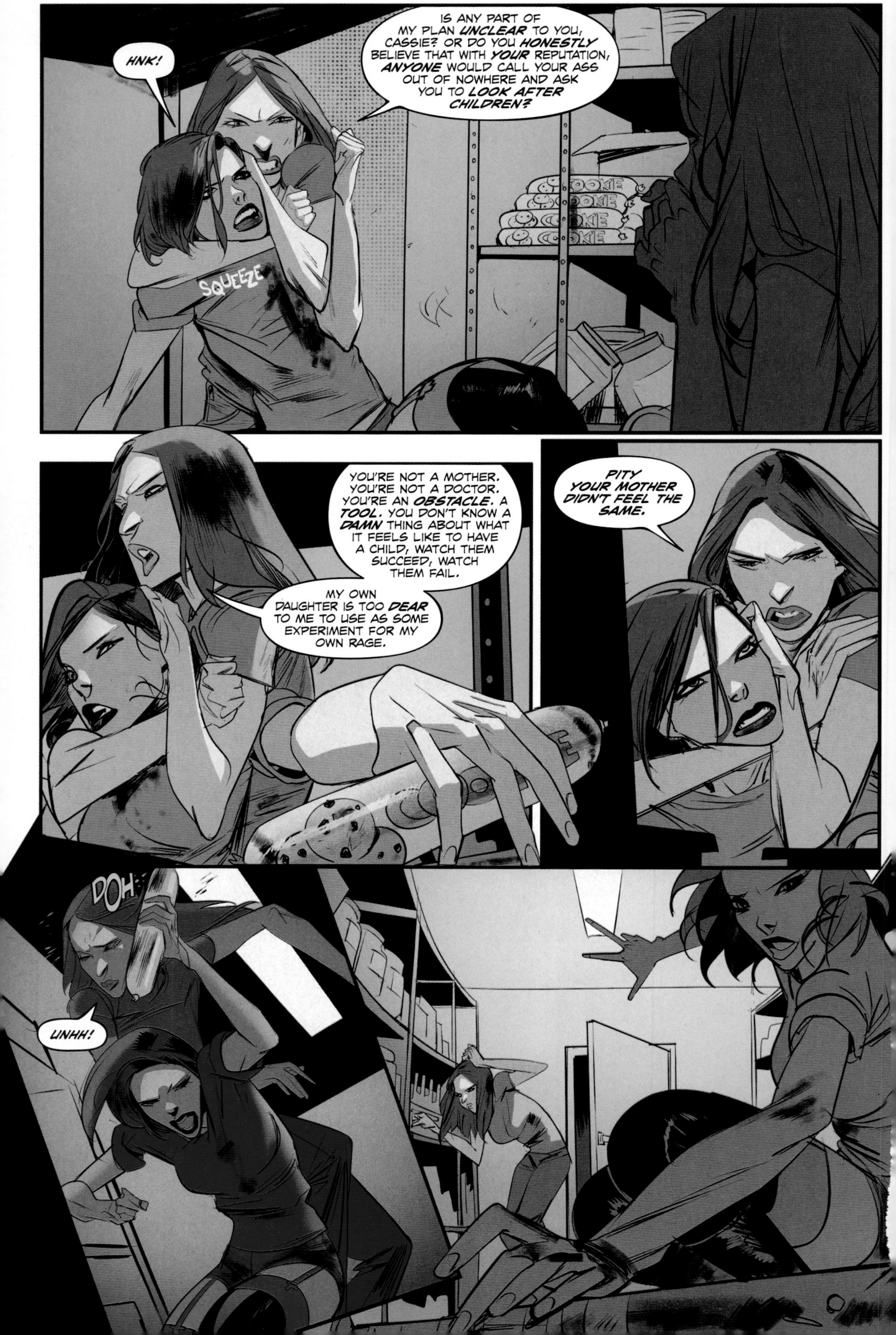
HNK!
IS ANY PART OF MY PLAN UNCLEAR TO YOU, CASSIE? OR DO YOU HONESTLY BELIEVE THAT WITH YOUR REPUTATION, ANYONE WOULD CALL YOUR ASS OUT OF NOWHERE AND ASK YOU TO LOOK AFTER CHILDREN?
SQUEEZE
COOKIE
YOU'RE NOT A MOTHER. YOU'RE NOT A DOCTOR. YOU'RE AN OBSTACLE. A TOOL. YOU DON'T KNOW A DAMN THING ABOUT WHAT IT FEELS LIKE TO HAVE A CHILD, WATCH THEM SUCCEED, WATCH THEM FAIL.
MY OWN DAUGHTER IS TOO DEAR TO ME TO USE AS SOME EXPERIMENT FOR MY OWN RAGE.
PITY YOUR MOTHER DIDN'T FEEL THE SAME.
DOH
UNHH!

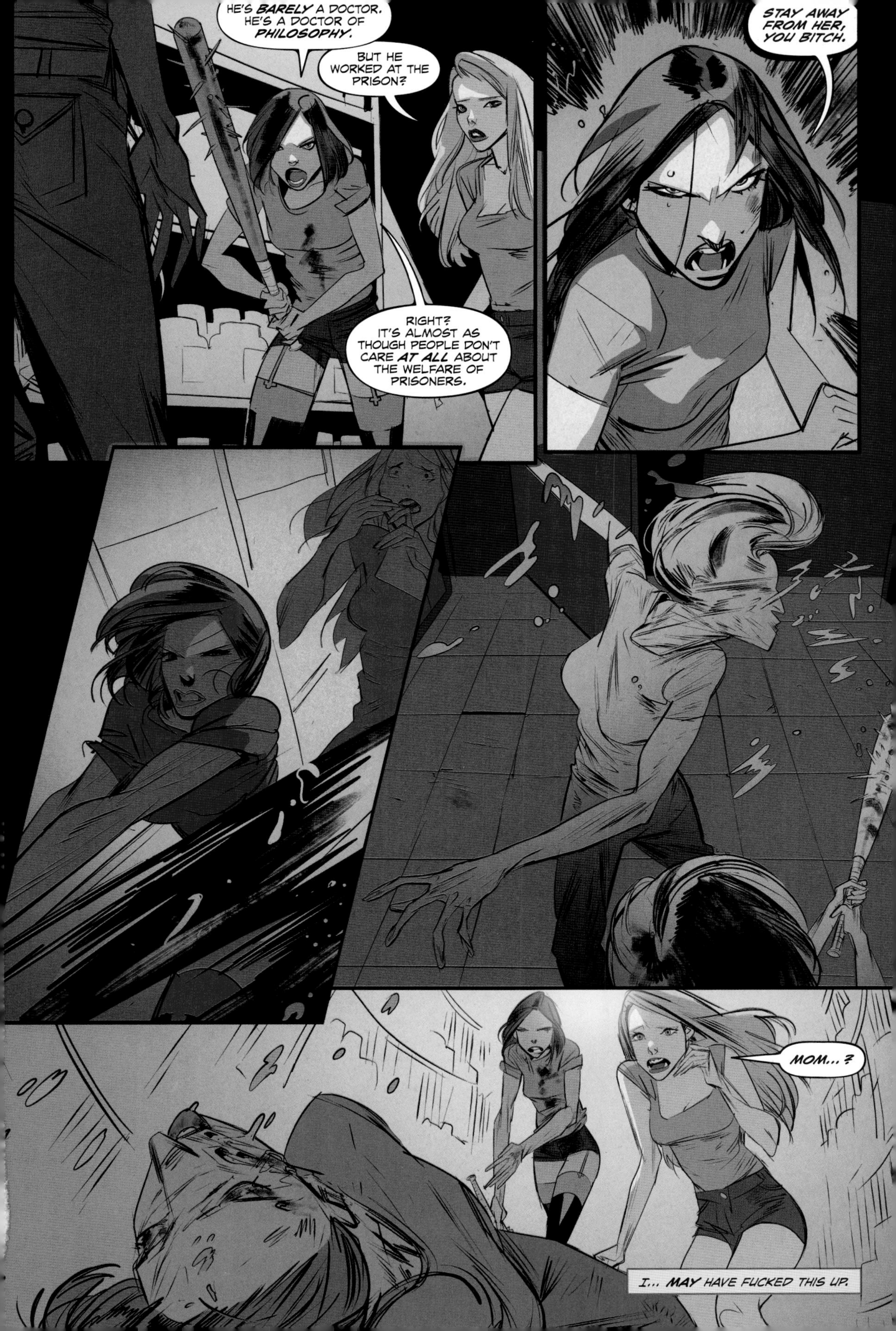

HE'S BARELY A DOCTOR. HE'S A DOCTOR OF PHILOSOPHY.
BUT HE WORKED AT THE PRISON?
RIGHT? IT'S ALMOST AS THOUGH PEOPLE DON'T CARE AT ALL ABOUT THE WELFARE OF PRISONERS.
STAY AWAY FROM HER, YOU BITCH.
MOM...?
I... MAY HAVE FUCKED THIS UP.

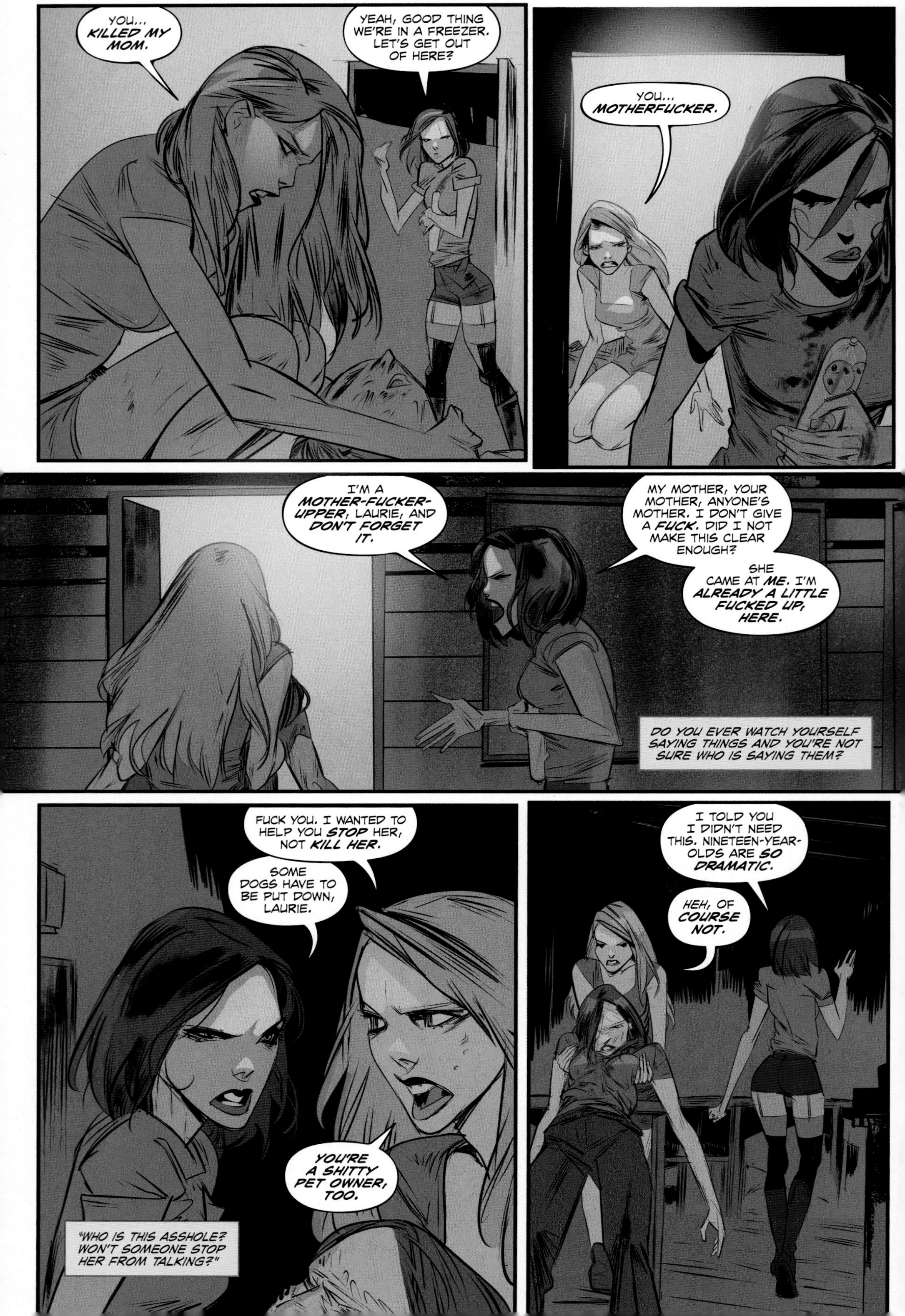
YOU... KILLED MY MOM.
YEAH, GOOD THING WE'RE IN A FREEZER. LET'S GET OUT OF HERE?
YOU... MOTHERFUCKER.
I'M A MOTHER-FUCKER-UPPER, LAURIE, AND DON'T FORGET IT.
MY MOTHER, YOUR MOTHER, ANYONE'S MOTHER. I DON'T GIVE A FUCK. DID I NOT MAKE THIS CLEAR ENOUGH?
SHE CAME AT ME. I'M ALREADY A LITTLE FUCKED UP, HERE.
DO YOU EVER WATCH YOURSELF SAYING THINGS AND YOU'RE NOT SURE WHO IS SAYING THEM?
FUCK YOU. I WANTED TO HELP YOU STOP HER, NOT KILL HER.
SOME DOGS HAVE TO BE PUT DOWN, LAURIE.
YOU'RE A SHITTY PET OWNER, TOO.
"WHO IS THIS ASSHOLE? WON'T SOMEONE STOP HER FROM TALKING?"
I TOLD YOU I DIDN'T NEED THIS. NINETEEN-YEAR-OLDS ARE SO DRAMATIC.
HEH, OF COURSE NOT.

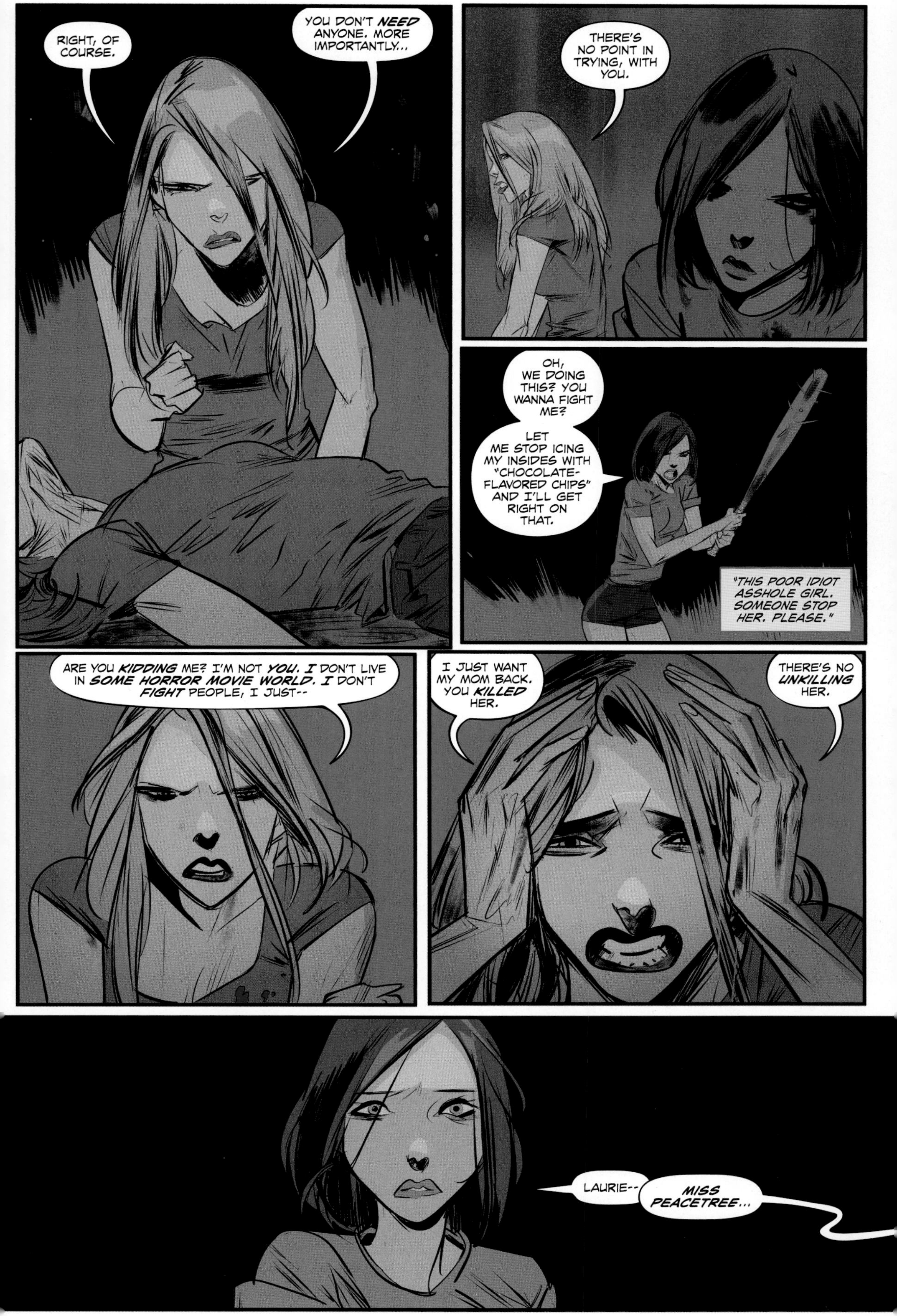
RIGHT, OF COURSE.
YOU DON'T NEED ANYONE. MORE IMPORTANTLY...
THERE'S NO POINT IN TRYING, WITH YOU.
OH, WE DOING THIS? YOU WANNA FIGHT ME?
LET ME STOP ICING MY INSIDES WITH "CHOCOLATE-FLAVORED CHIPS" AND I'LL GET RIGHT ON THAT.
"THIS POOR IDIOT ASSHOLE GIRL. SOMEONE STOP HER. PLEASE."
ARE YOU KIDDING ME? I'M NOT YOU. I DON'T LIVE IN SOME HORROR MOVIE WORLD. I DON'T FIGHT PEOPLE, I JUST--
I JUST WANT MY MOM BACK. YOU KILLED HER.
THERE'S NO UNKILLING HER.
LAURIE--
MISS PEACETREE...

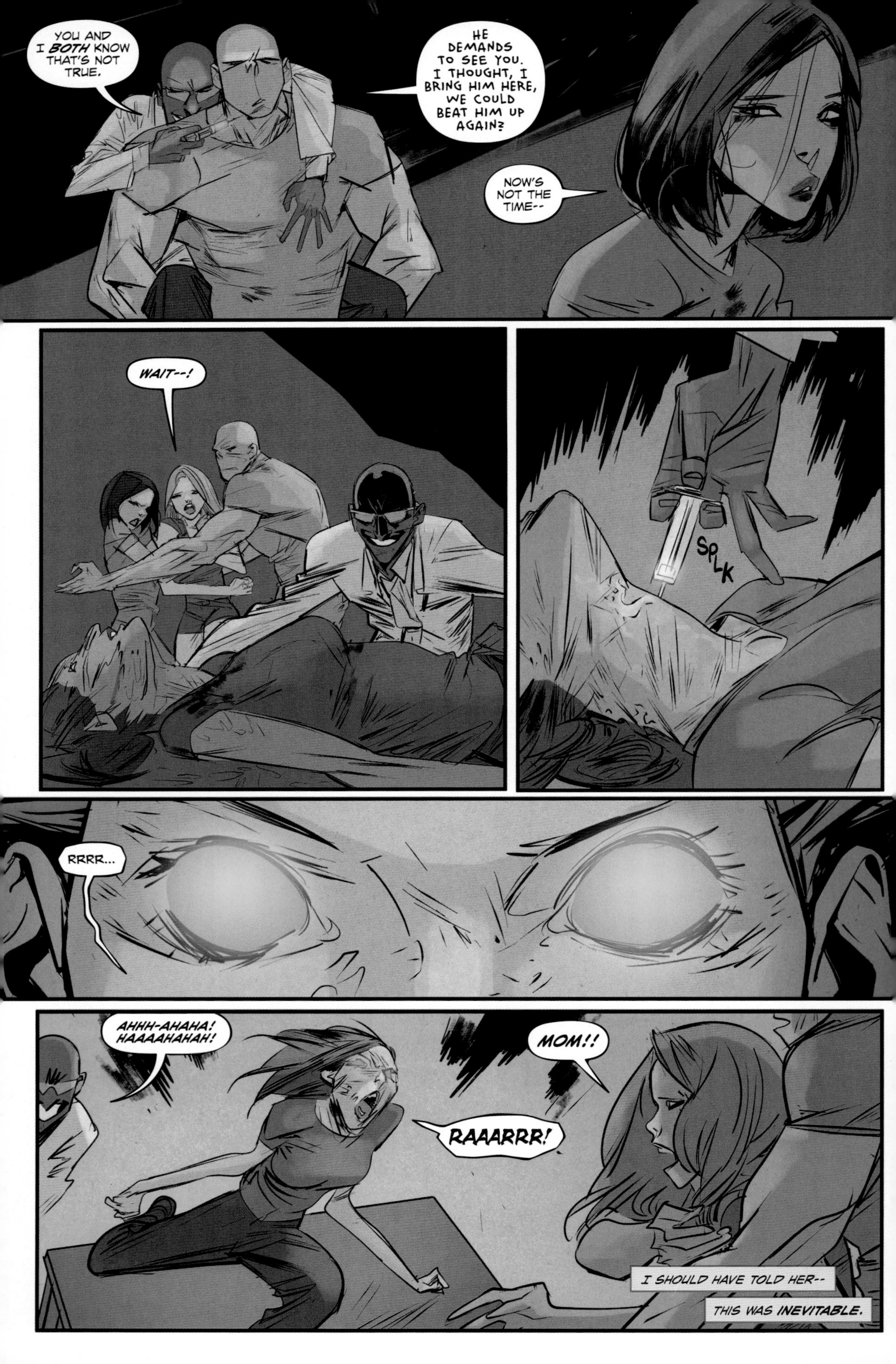
YOU AND I BOTH KNOW THAT'S NOT TRUE.
HE DEMANDS TO SEE YOU. I THOUGHT, I BRING HIM HERE, WE COULD BEAT HIM UP AGAIN?
NOW'S NOT THE TIME--
WAIT--!
SPLK
RRRR...
AHHH-AHAHA! HAAAAHAHAH!
MOM!!
RAAARRR!
I SHOULD HAVE TOLD HER--
THIS WAS INEVITABLE.

ISSUE 6 COVER BY
TIM SEELEY & CARLOS BADILLA

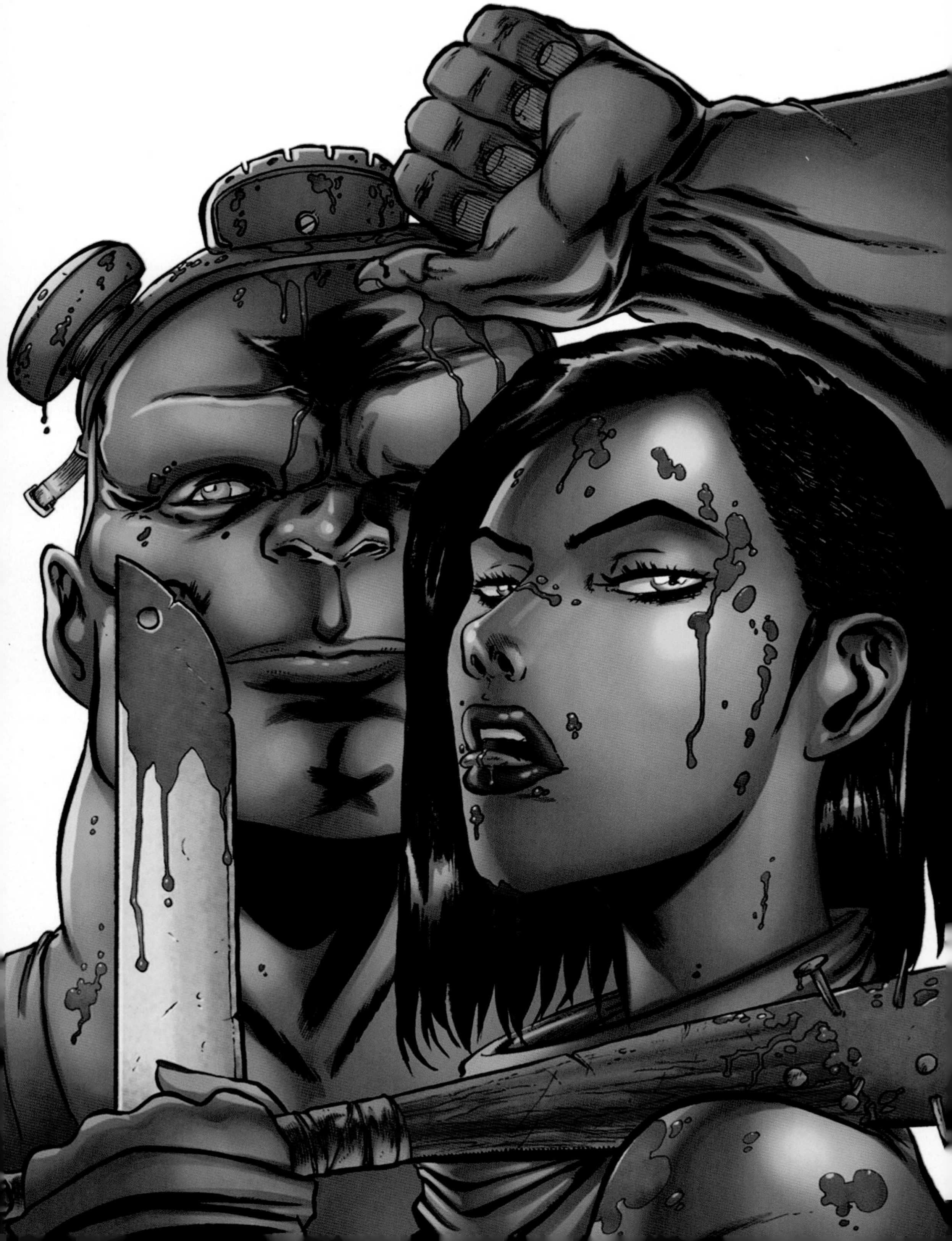

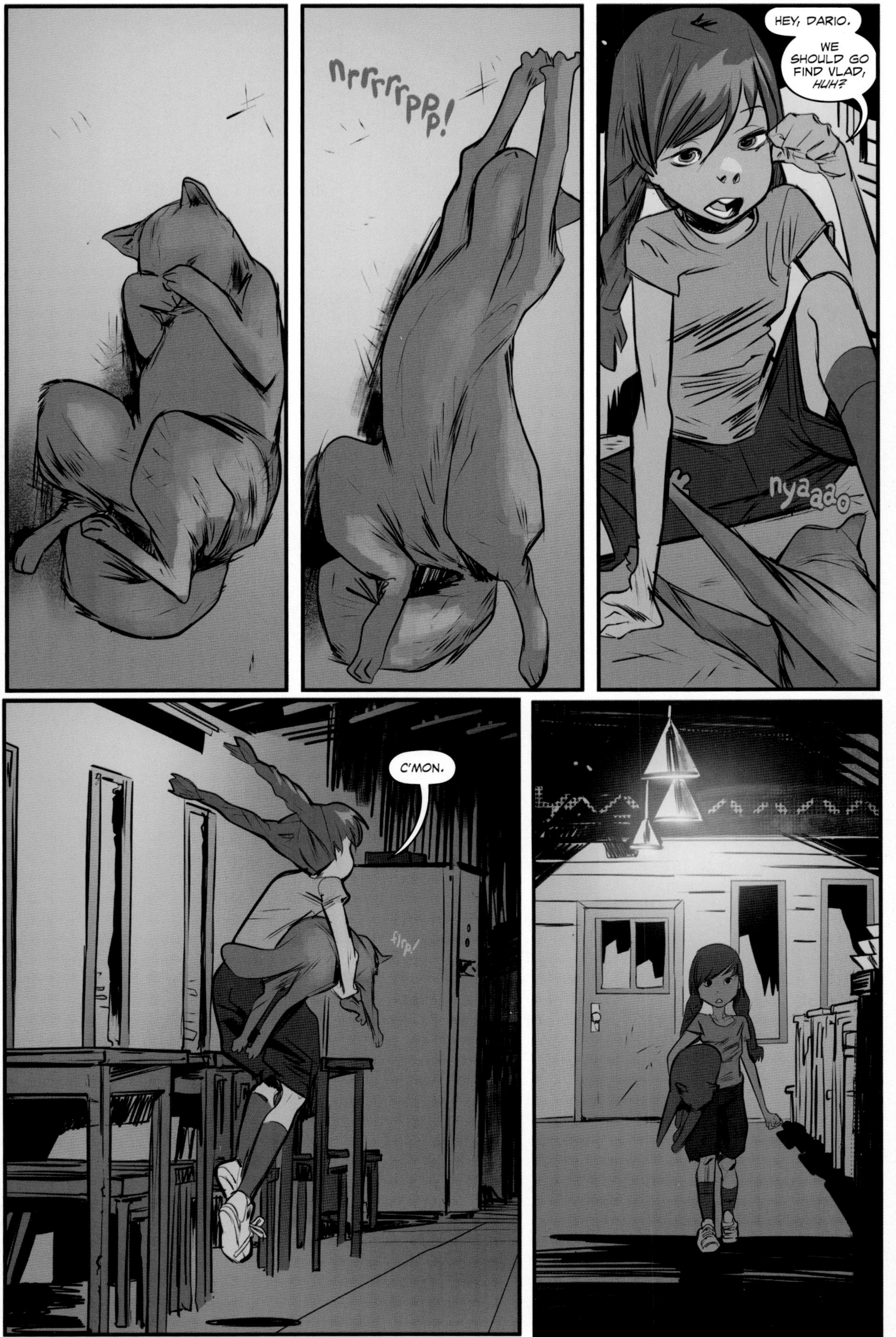
nrrrrrppp!
HEY, DARIO.
WE SHOULD GO FIND VLAD, HUH?
nyaaao
C'MON.
flrp!

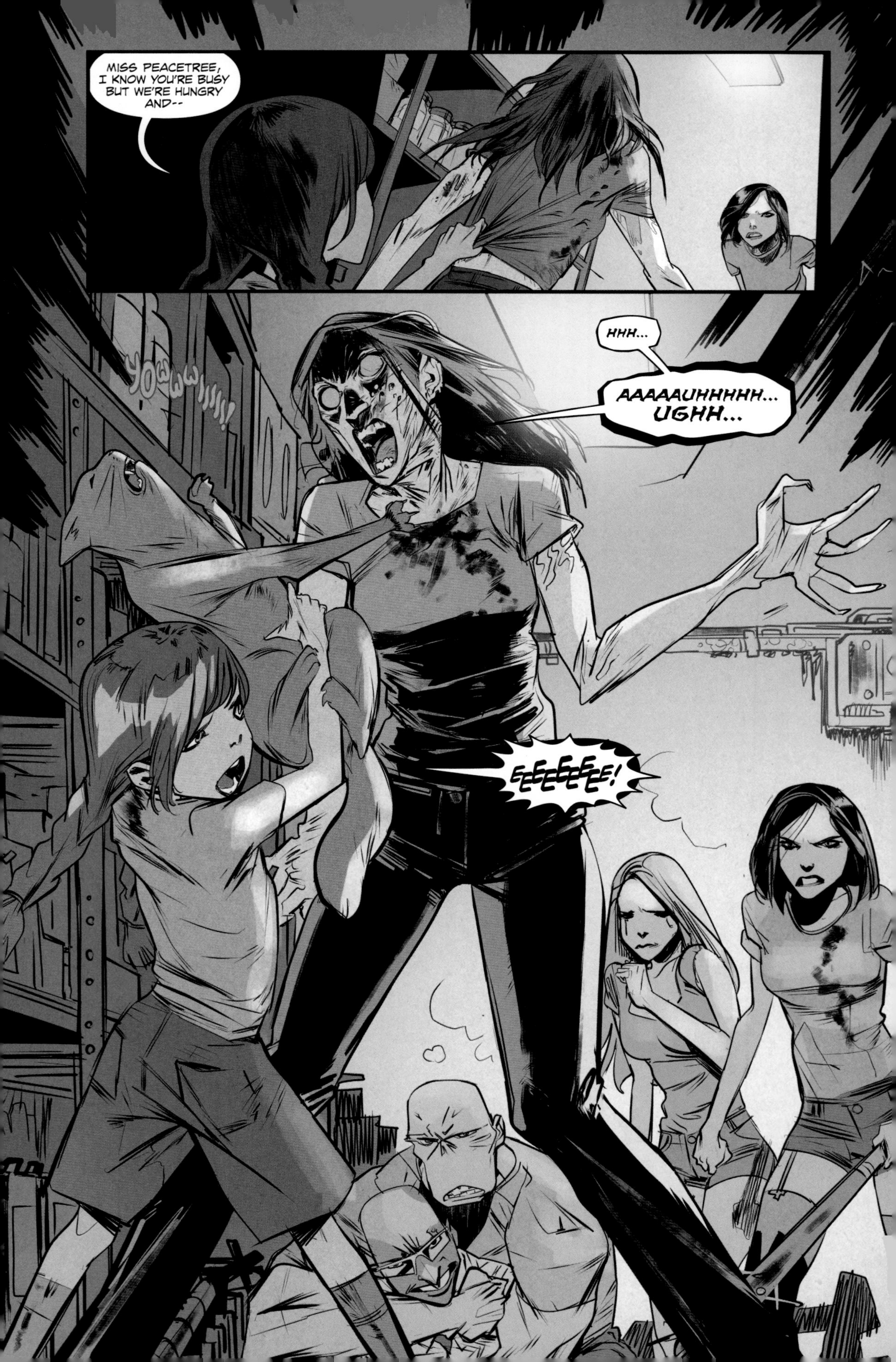
MISS PEACETREE, I KNOW YOU'RE BUSY BUT WE'RE HUNGRY AND--
YOWWWIIII!!
HHH...
AAAAAUHHHHH... UGHH...
EEEEEEEEE!

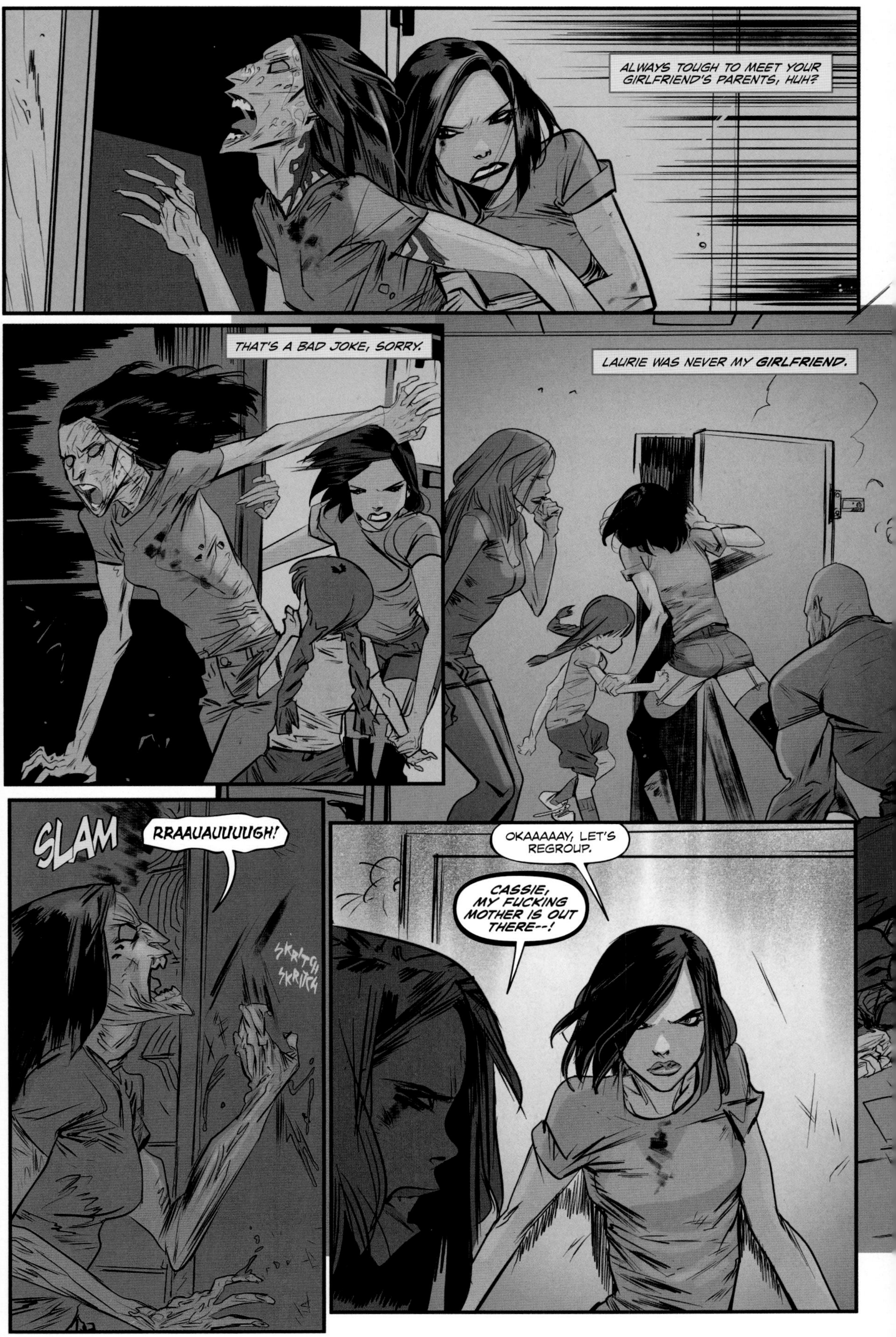
ALWAYS TOUGH TO MEET YOUR GIRLFRIEND'S PARENTS, HUH?
THAT'S A BAD JOKE, SORRY.
LAURIE WAS NEVER MY GIRLFRIEND.
SLAM
RRAAUAUUUUGH!
SKRITCH SKRITCH
OKAAAAAY, LET'S REGROUP.
CASSIE, MY FUCKING MOTHER IS OUT THERE--!

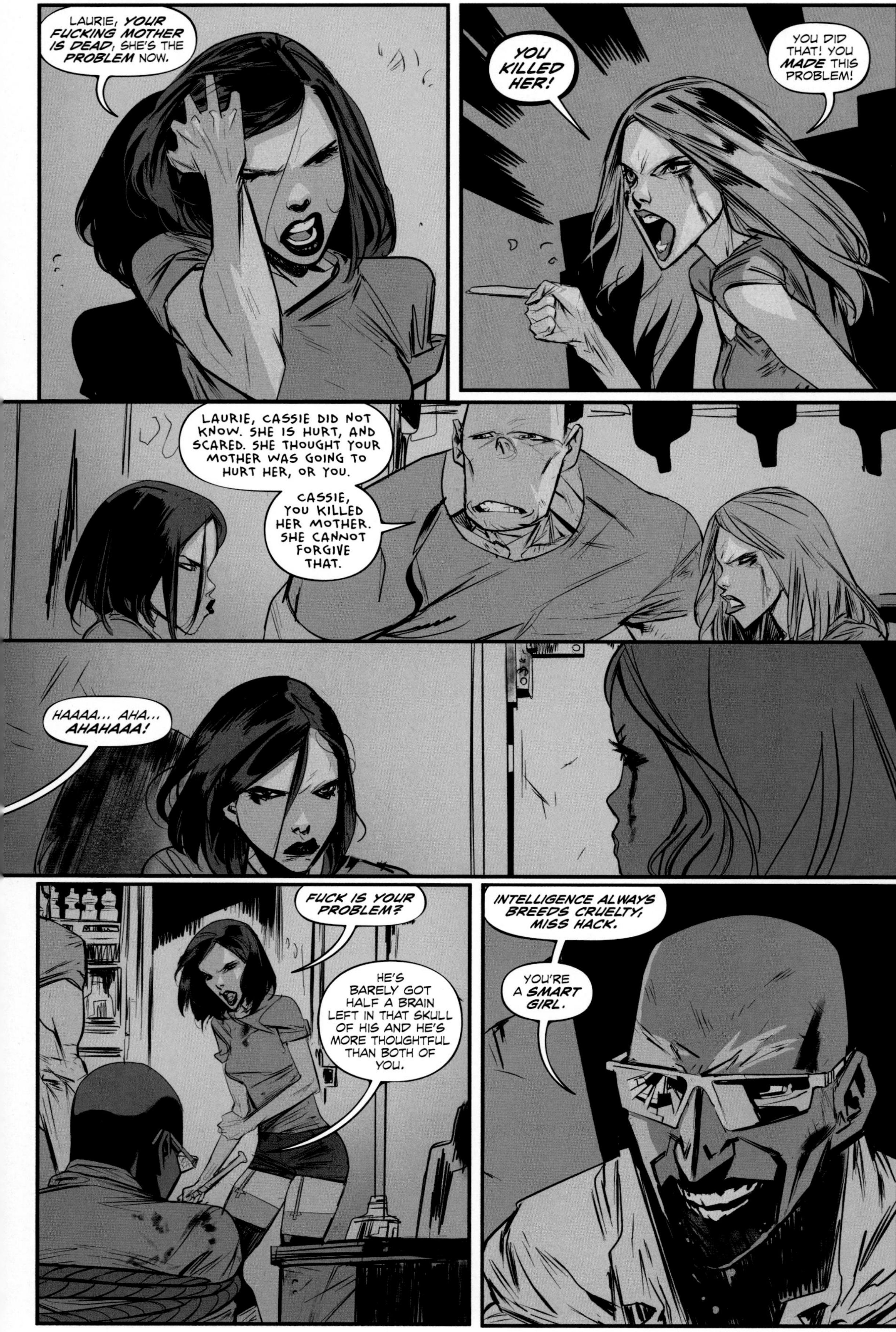
LAURIE, YOUR FUCKING MOTHER IS DEAD, SHE'S THE PROBLEM NOW.
YOU KILLED HER!
YOU DID THAT! YOU MADE THIS PROBLEM!
LAURIE, CASSIE DID NOT KNOW. SHE IS HURT, AND SCARED. SHE THOUGHT YOUR MOTHER WAS GOING TO HURT HER, OR YOU.
CASSIE, YOU KILLED HER MOTHER. SHE CANNOT FORGIVE THAT.
HAAAA... AHA... AHAHAAA!
FUCK IS YOUR PROBLEM?
HE'S BARELY GOT HALF A BRAIN LEFT IN THAT SKULL OF HIS AND HE'S MORE THOUGHTFUL THAN BOTH OF YOU.
INTELLIGENCE ALWAYS BREEDS CRUELTY, MISS HACK.
YOU'RE A SMART GIRL.

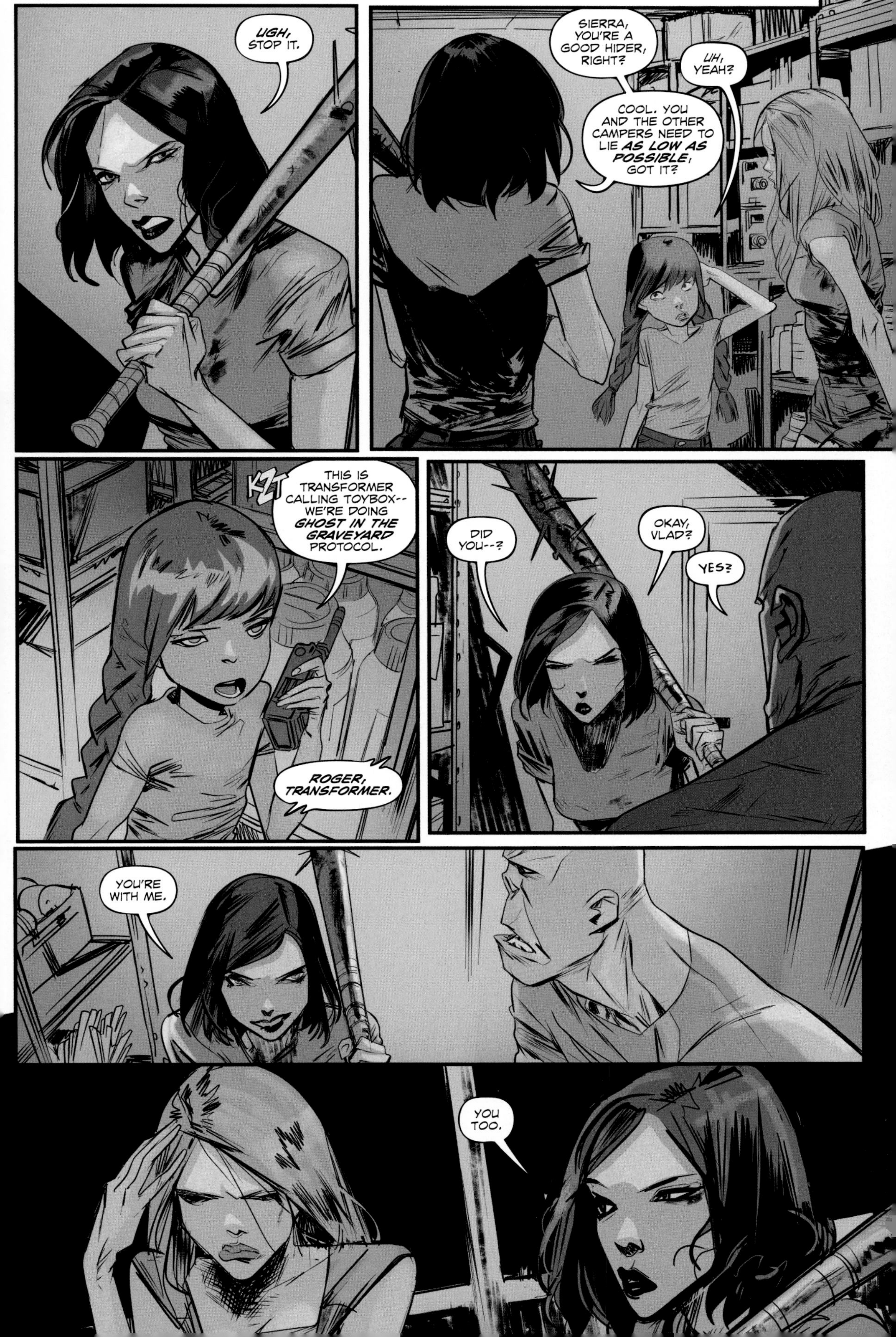
UGH, STOP IT.
SIERRA, YOU'RE A GOOD HIDER, RIGHT?
UH, YEAH?
COOL. YOU AND THE OTHER CAMPERS NEED TO LIE AS LOW AS POSSIBLE, GOT IT?
KZT
THIS IS TRANSFORMER CALLING TOYBOX-- WE'RE DOING GHOST IN THE GRAVEYARD PROTOCOL.
ROGER, TRANSFORMER.
DID YOU--?
OKAY, VLAD?
YES?
YOU'RE WITH ME.
YOU TOO.

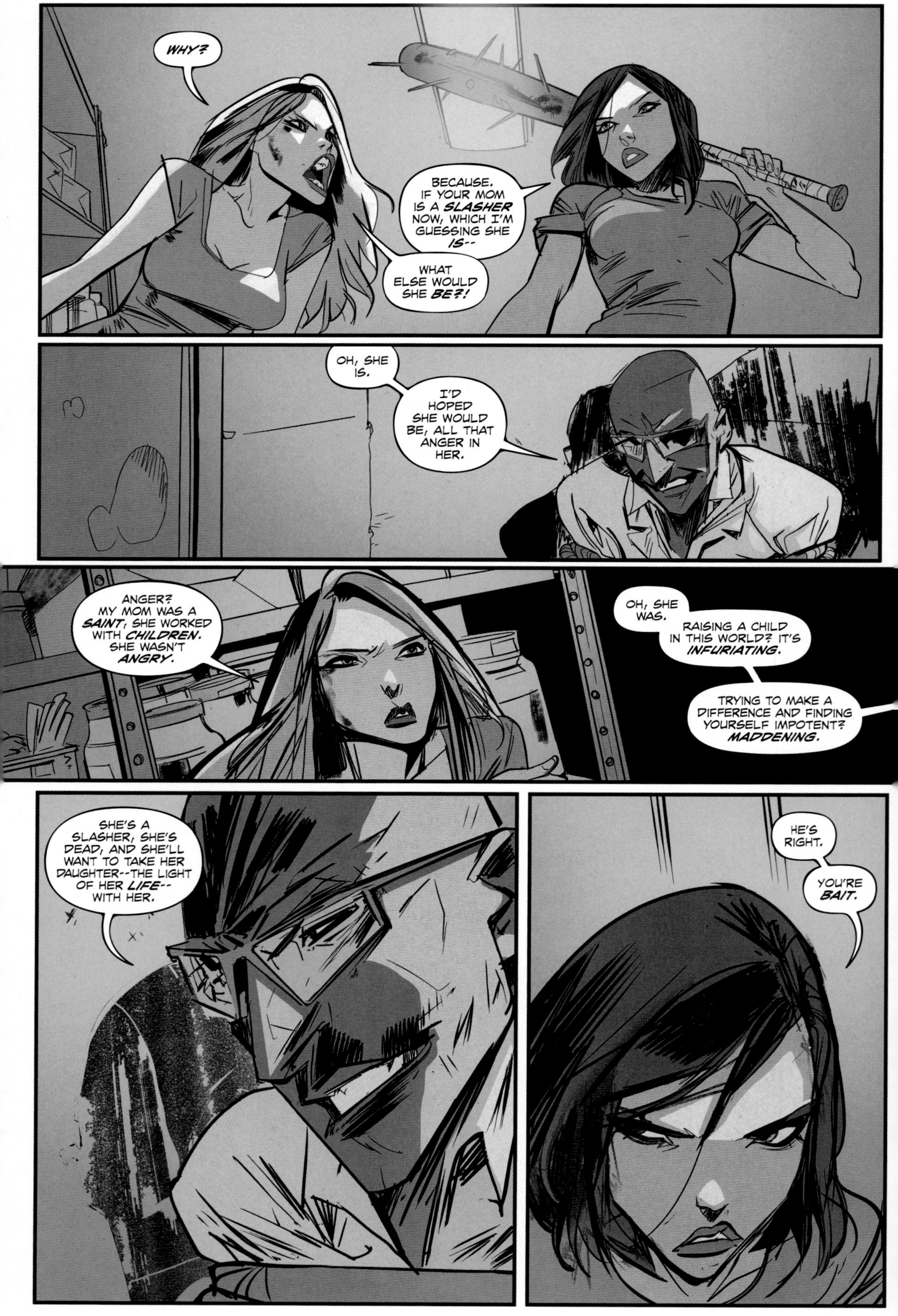
WHY?
BECAUSE. IF YOUR MOM IS A SLASHER NOW, WHICH I'M GUESSING SHE IS--
WHAT ELSE WOULD SHE BE?!
OH, SHE IS.
I'D HOPED SHE WOULD BE, ALL THAT ANGER IN HER.
ANGER? MY MOM WAS A SAINT, SHE WORKED WITH CHILDREN. SHE WASN'T ANGRY.
OH, SHE WAS.
RAISING A CHILD IN THIS WORLD? IT'S INFURIATING.
TRYING TO MAKE A DIFFERENCE AND FINDING YOURSELF IMPOTENT? MADDENING.
SHE'S A SLASHER, SHE'S DEAD, AND SHE'LL WANT TO TAKE HER DAUGHTER--THE LIGHT OF HER LIFE--WITH HER.
HE'S RIGHT.
YOU'RE BAIT.

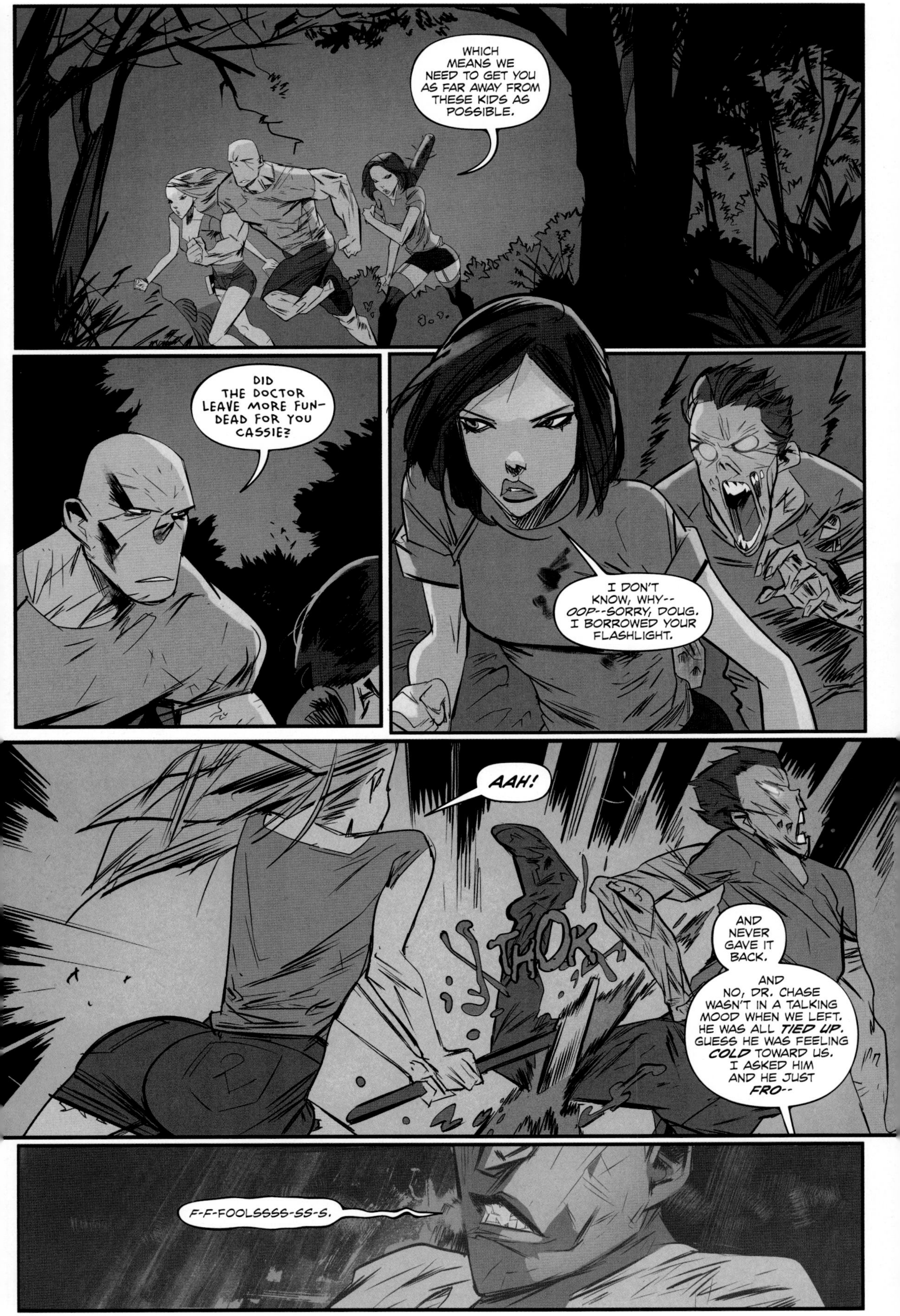
WHICH MEANS WE NEED TO GET YOU AS FAR AWAY FROM THESE KIDS AS POSSIBLE.
DID THE DOCTOR LEAVE MORE FUN-DEAD FOR YOU CASSIE?
I DON'T KNOW, WHY-- OOP--SORRY, DOUG. I BORROWED YOUR FLASHLIGHT.
AAH!
THOK
AND NEVER GAVE IT BACK.
AND NO, DR. CHASE WASN'T IN A TALKING MOOD WHEN WE LEFT. HE WAS ALL TIED UP. GUESS HE WAS FEELING COLD TOWARD US. I ASKED HIM AND HE JUST FRO--
F-F-FOOLSSSS-SS-S.

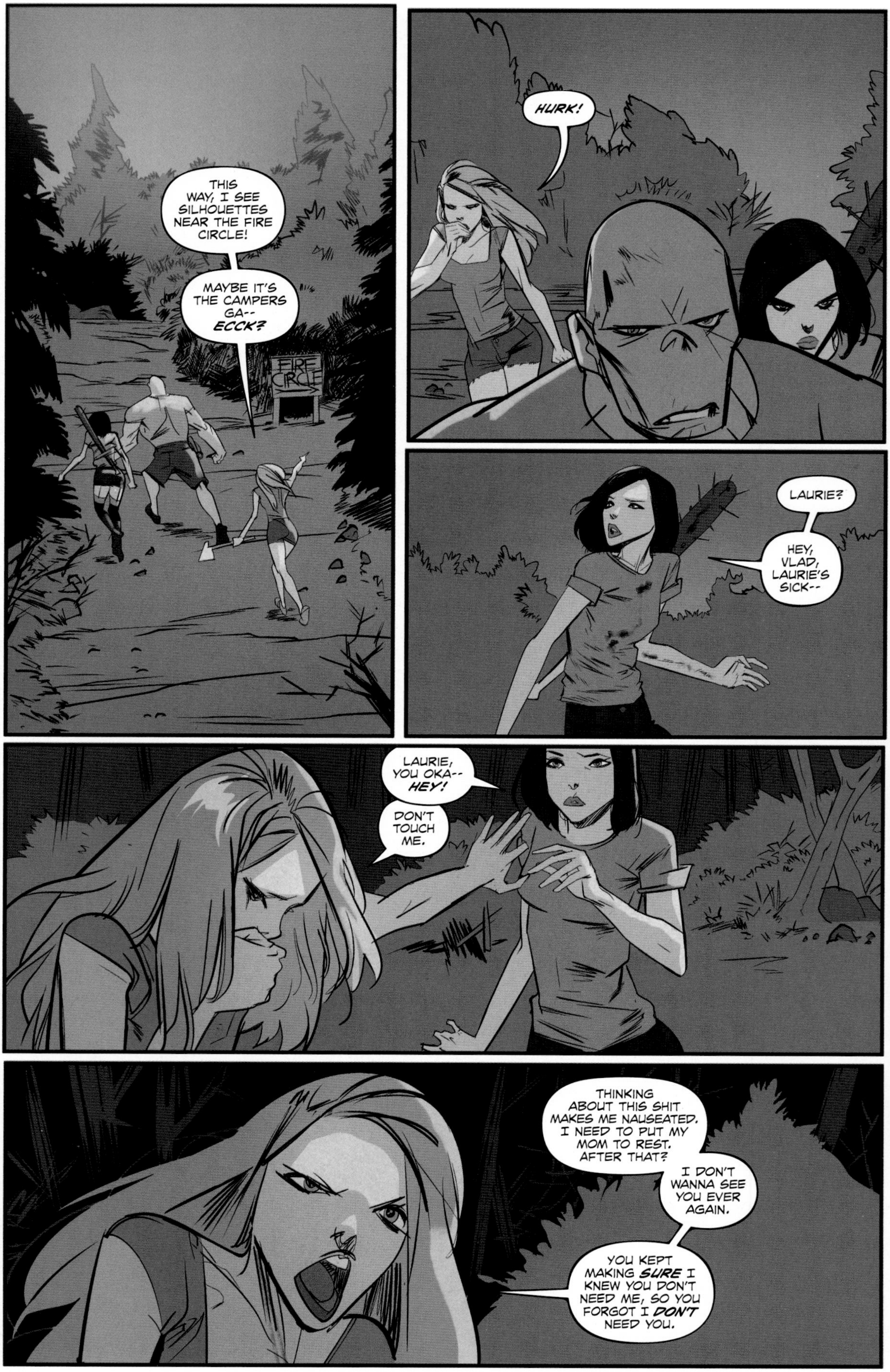

THIS WAY, I SEE SILHOUETTES NEAR THE FIRE CIRCLE!
MAYBE IT'S THE CAMPERS GA-- ECCK?
FIRE CIRCLE
HURK!
LAURIE?
HEY, VLAD, LAURIE'S SICK--
LAURIE, YOU OKA-- HEY!
DON'T TOUCH ME.
THINKING ABOUT THIS SHIT MAKES ME NAUSEATED. I NEED TO PUT MY MOM TO REST. AFTER THAT?
I DON'T WANNA SEE YOU EVER AGAIN.
YOU KEPT MAKING SURE I KNEW YOU DON'T NEED ME, SO YOU FORGOT I DON'T NEED YOU.

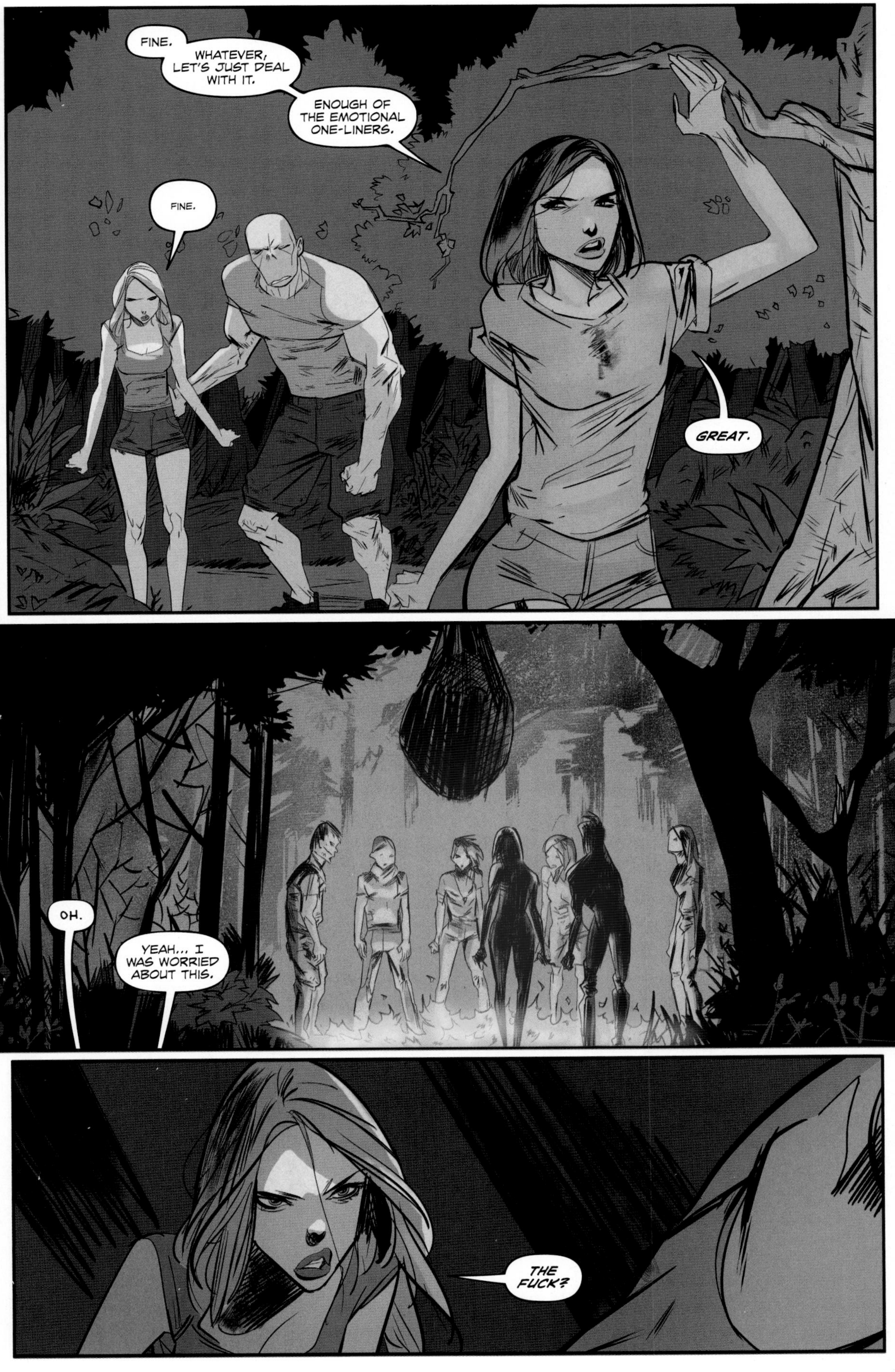
FINE.
WHATEVER, LET'S JUST DEAL WITH IT.
ENOUGH OF THE EMOTIONAL ONE-LINERS.
FINE.
GREAT.
OH.
YEAH... I WAS WORRIED ABOUT THIS.
THE FUCK?

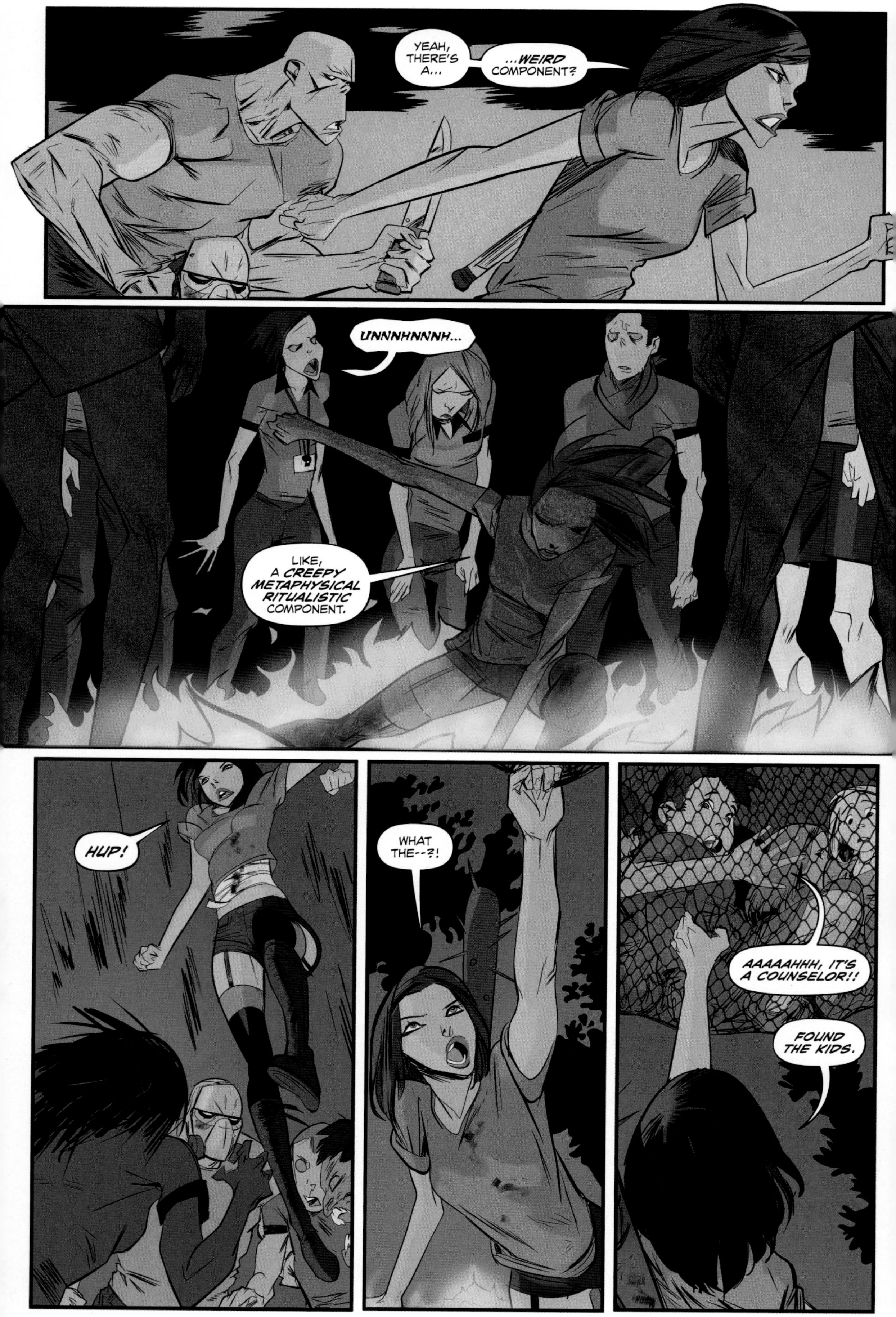
YEAH, THERE'S A...
...WEIRD COMPONENT?
UNNNHNNNH...
LIKE, A CREEPY METAPHYSICAL RITUALISTIC COMPONENT.
HUP!
WHAT THE--?!
AAAAAHHH, IT'S A COUNSELOR!!
FOUND THE KIDS.

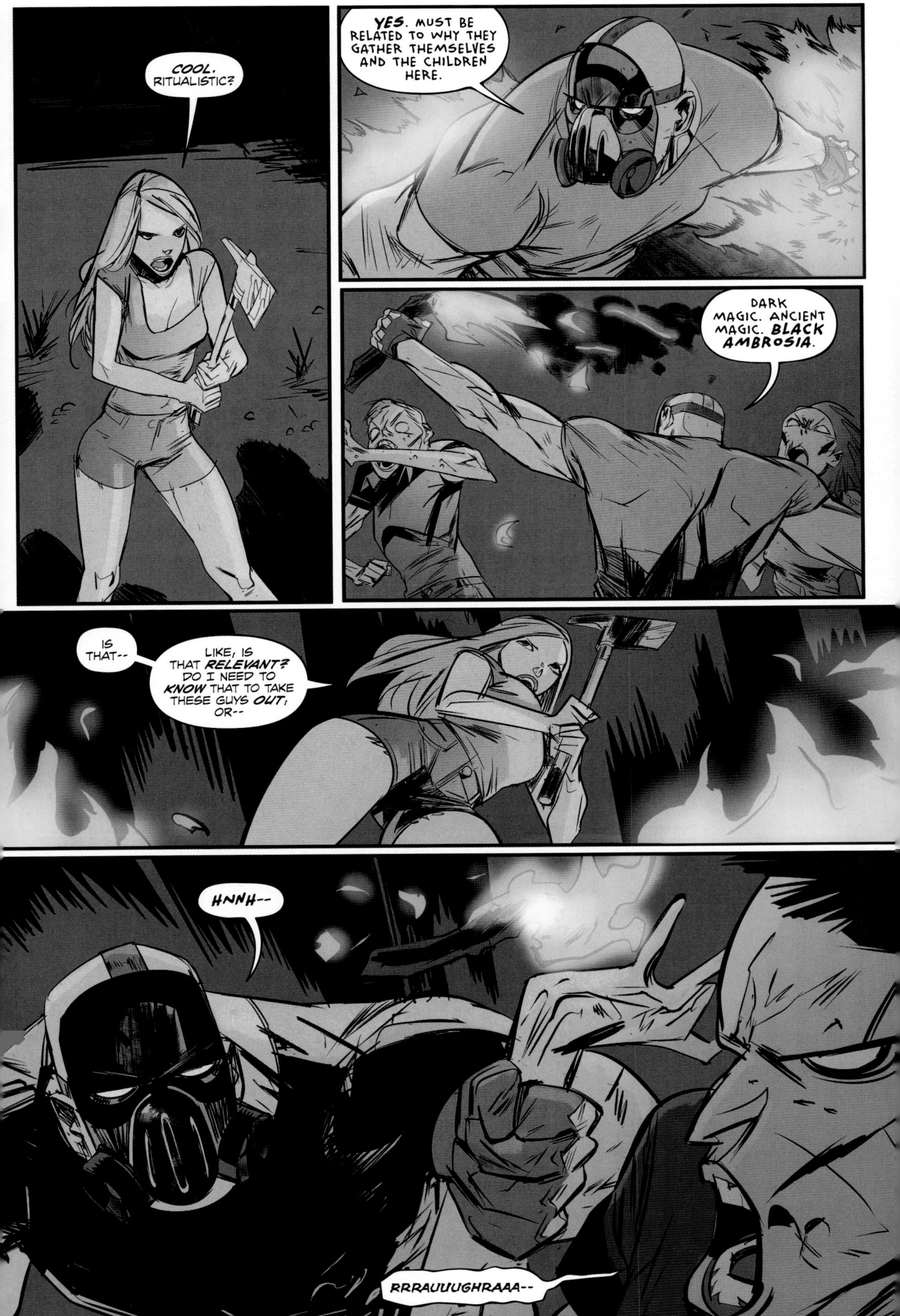
COOL. RITUALISTIC?
YES. MUST BE RELATED TO WHY THEY GATHER THEMSELVES AND THE CHILDREN HERE.
DARK MAGIC. ANCIENT MAGIC. BLACK AMBROSIA.
IS THAT--
LIKE, IS THAT RELEVANT? DO I NEED TO KNOW THAT TO TAKE THESE GUYS OUT, OR--
HNNH--
RRRAUUUGHRAAA--

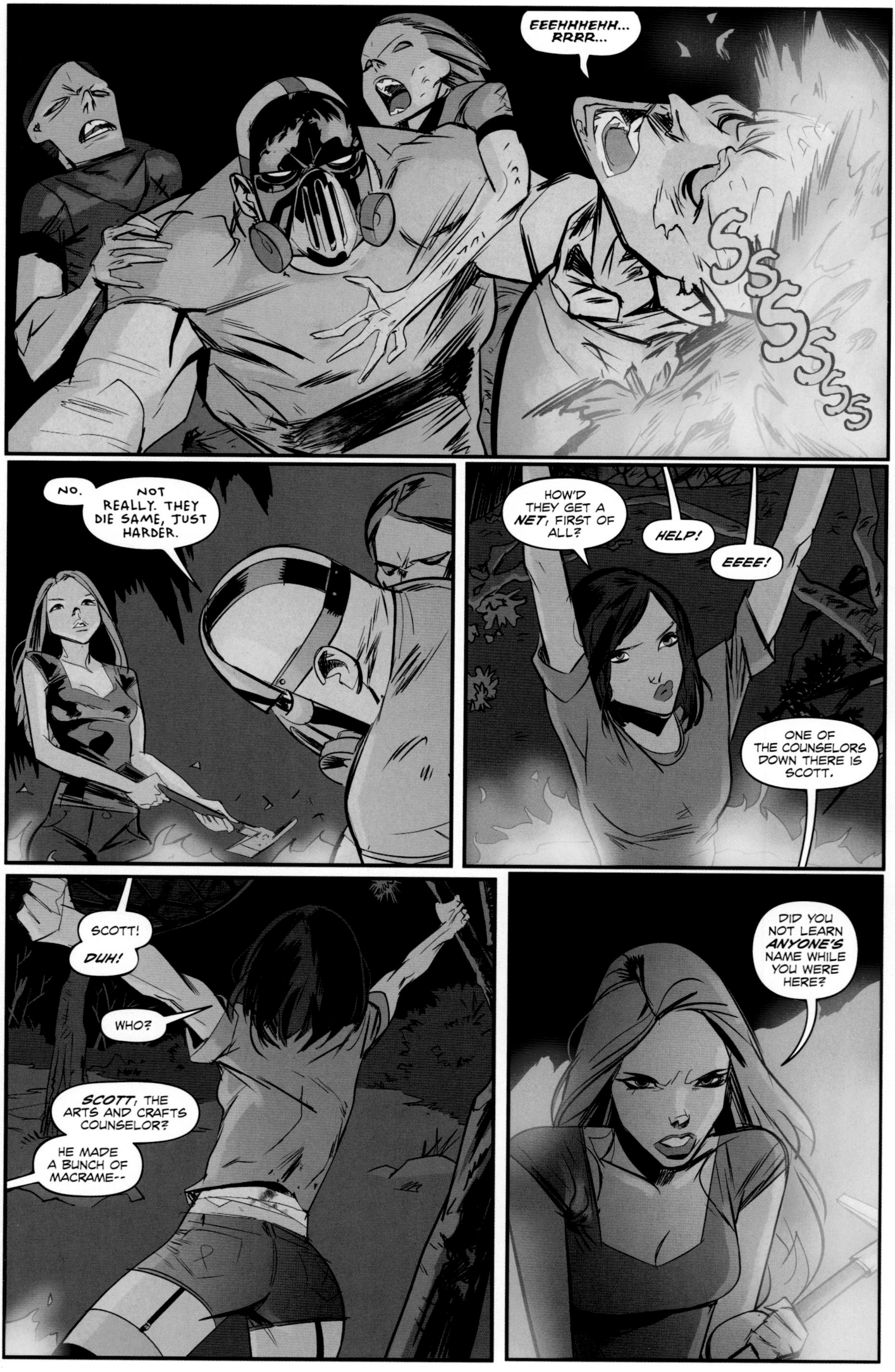
EEEHHHEHH... RRRR...
SSSSSSS
NO.
NOT REALLY. THEY DIE SAME, JUST HARDER.
HOW'D THEY GET A *NET*, FIRST OF ALL?
HELP!
EEEE!
ONE OF THE COUNSELORS DOWN THERE IS SCOTT.
SCOTT! *DUH!*
WHO?
SCOTT, THE ARTS AND CRAFTS COUNSELOR?
HE MADE A BUNCH OF MACRAME--
DID YOU NOT LEARN *ANYONE'S* NAME WHILE YOU WERE HERE?

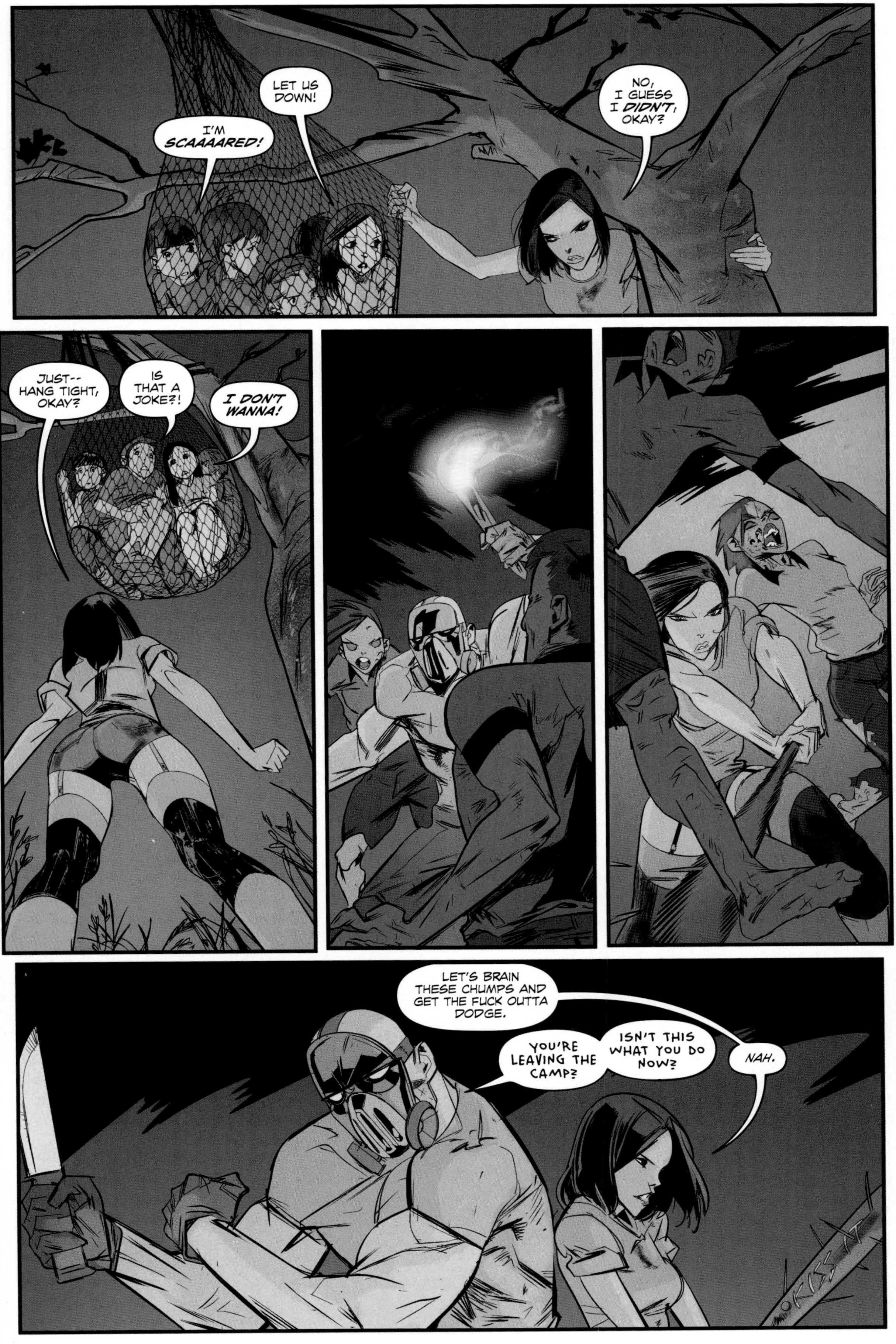
I'M *SCAAAARED!*
LET US DOWN!
NO, I GUESS I *DIDN'T*, OKAY?
JUST-- HANG TIGHT, OKAY?
IS THAT A JOKE?!
I DON'T WANNA!
LET'S BRAIN THESE CHUMPS AND GET THE FUCK OUTTA DODGE.
YOU'RE LEAVING THE CAMP?
ISN'T THIS WHAT YOU DO NOW?
NAH.

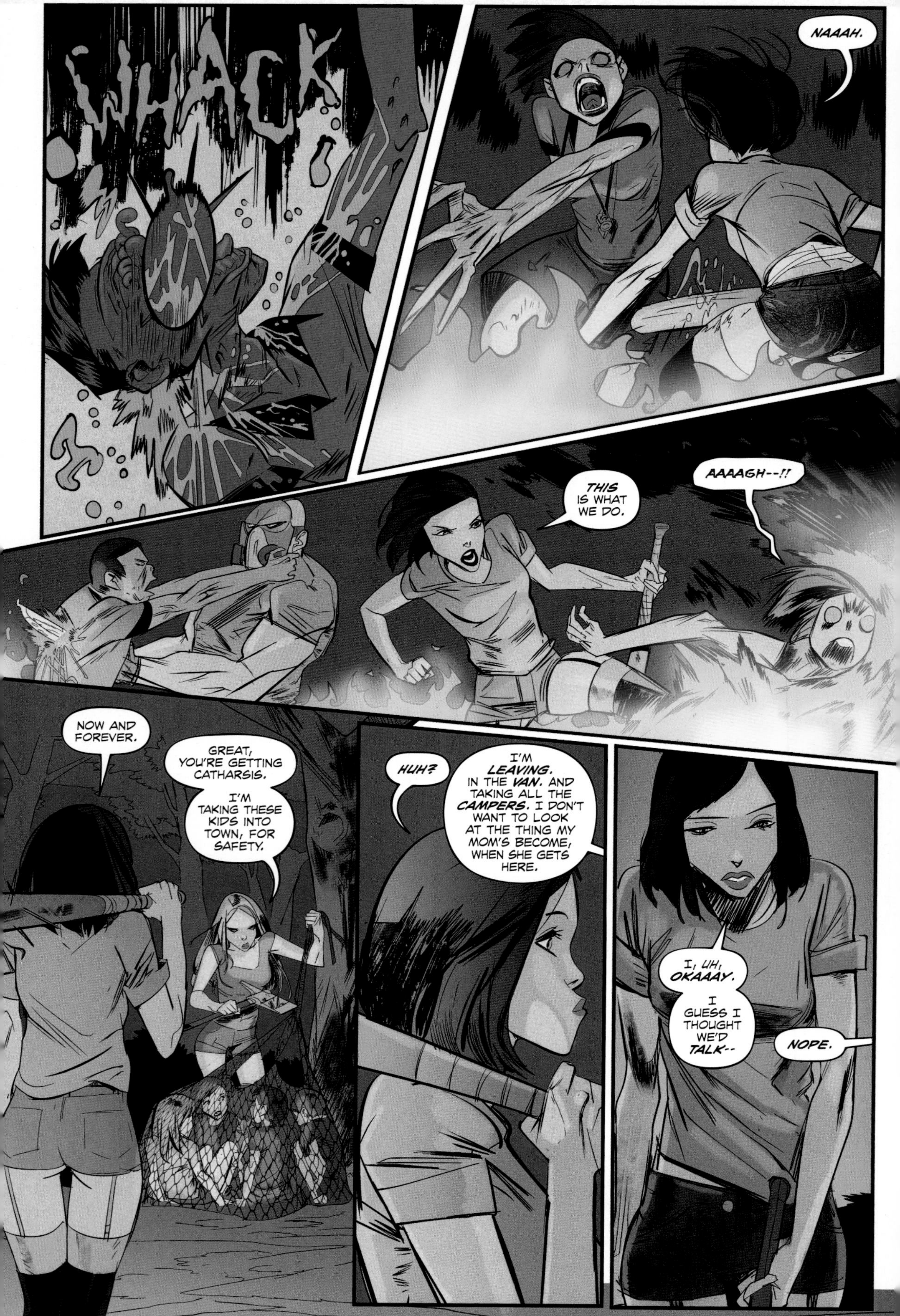
WHACK
NAAAH.
THIS IS WHAT WE DO.
AAAAGH--!!
NOW AND FOREVER.
GREAT, YOU'RE GETTING CATHARSIS.
I'M TAKING THESE KIDS INTO TOWN, FOR SAFETY.
HUH?
I'M LEAVING. IN THE VAN. AND TAKING ALL THE CAMPERS. I DON'T WANT TO LOOK AT THE THING MY MOM'S BECOME, WHEN SHE GETS HERE.
I, UH, OKAAAY.
I GUESS I THOUGHT WE'D TALK--
NOPE.

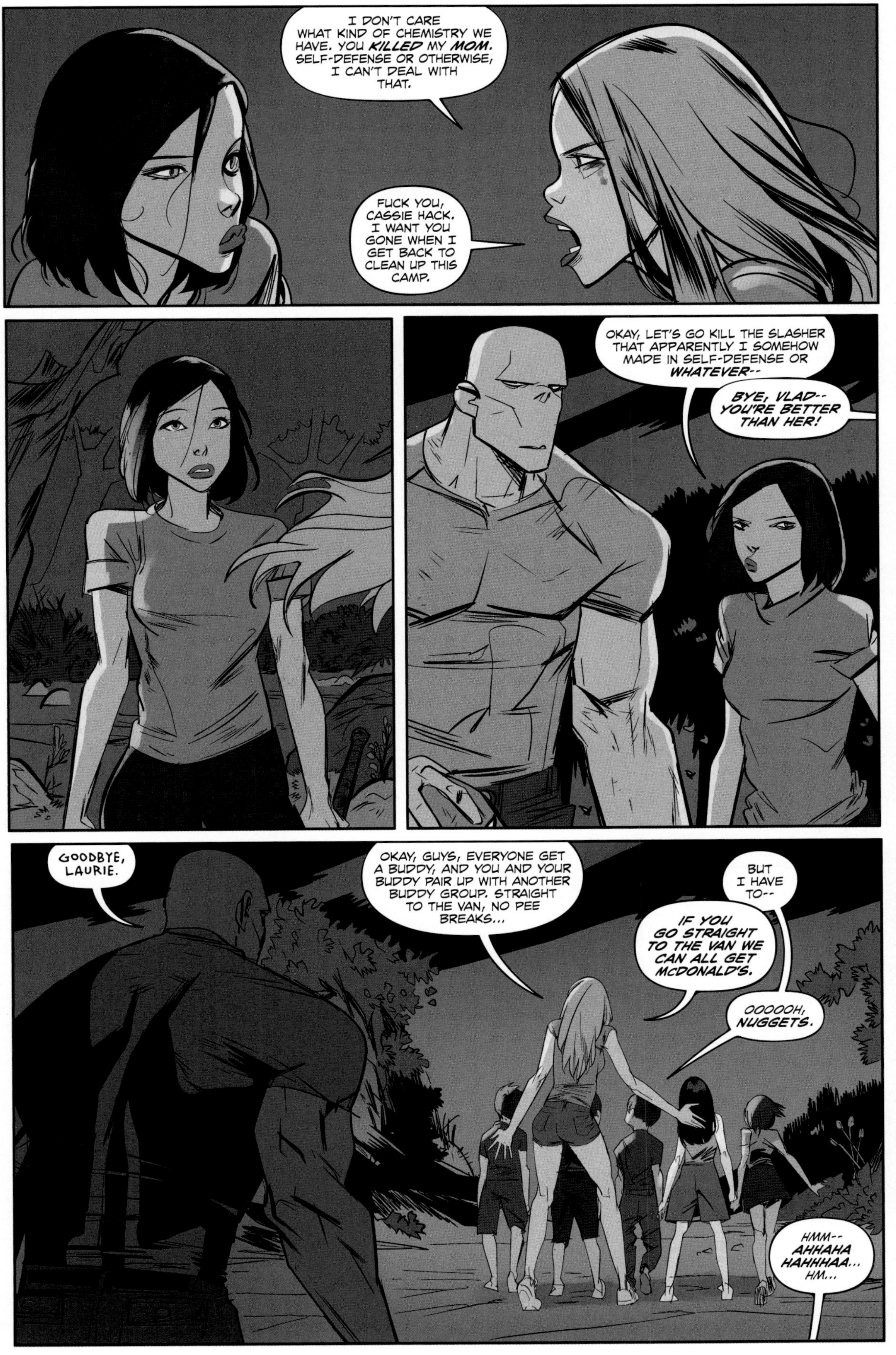
I DON'T CARE WHAT KIND OF CHEMISTRY WE HAVE. YOU KILLED MY MOM. SELF-DEFENSE OR OTHERWISE, I CAN'T DEAL WITH THAT.
FUCK YOU, CASSIE HACK. I WANT YOU GONE WHEN I GET BACK TO CLEAN UP THIS CAMP.
OKAY, LET'S GO KILL THE SLASHER THAT APPARENTLY I SOMEHOW MADE IN SELF-DEFENSE OR WHATEVER--
BYE, VLAD-- YOU'RE BETTER THAN HER!
GOODBYE, LAURIE.
OKAY, GUYS, EVERYONE GET A BUDDY, AND YOU AND YOUR BUDDY PAIR UP WITH ANOTHER BUDDY GROUP. STRAIGHT TO THE VAN, NO PEE BREAKS...
BUT I HAVE TO--
IF YOU GO STRAIGHT TO THE VAN WE CAN ALL GET McDONALD'S.
OOOOOH, NUGGETS.
HMM-- AHHAHA HAHHHAA... HM...

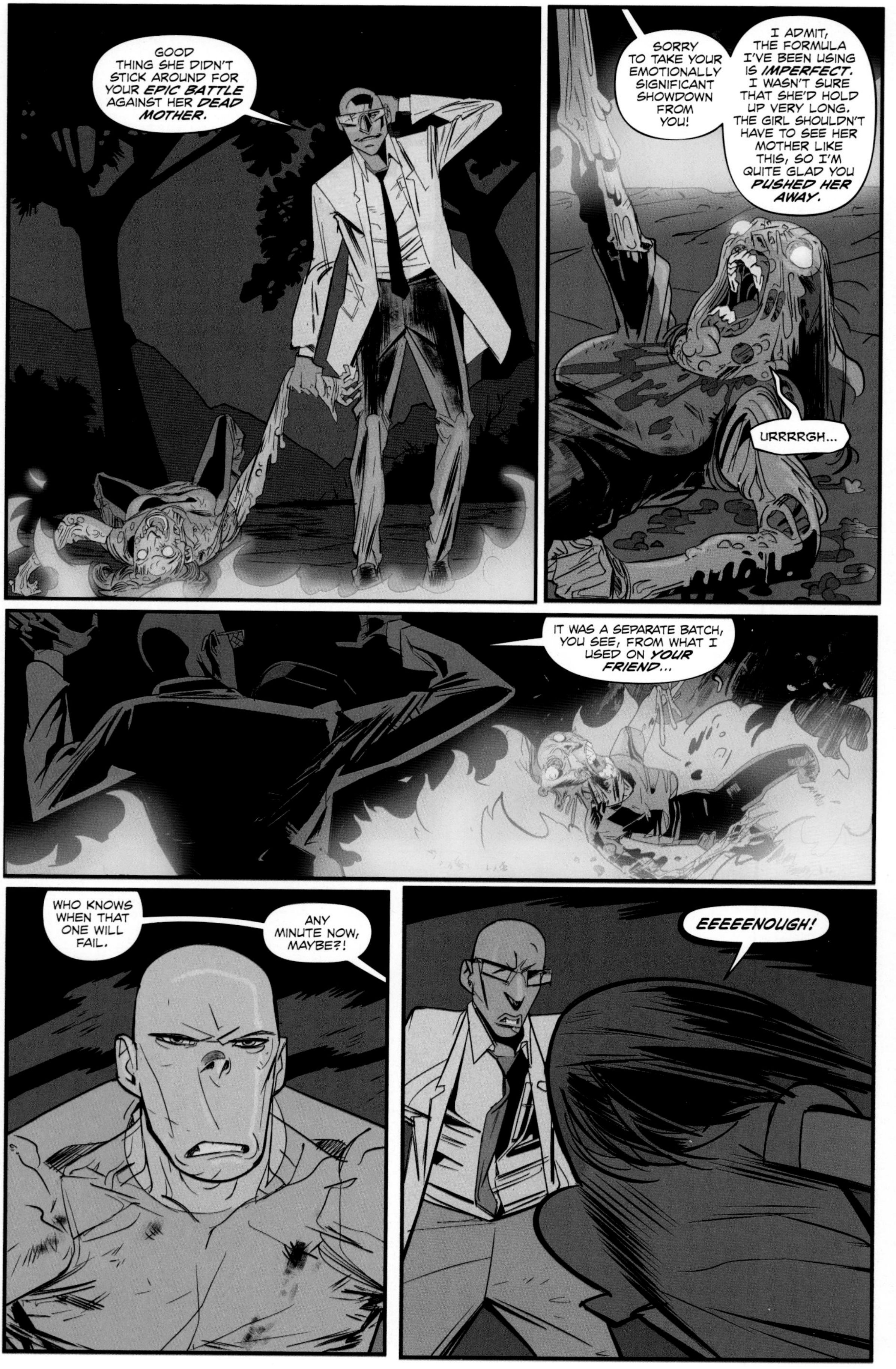

GOOD THING SHE DIDN'T STICK AROUND FOR YOUR EPIC BATTLE AGAINST HER DEAD MOTHER.
SORRY TO TAKE YOUR EMOTIONALLY SIGNIFICANT SHOWDOWN FROM YOU!
I ADMIT, THE FORMULA I'VE BEEN USING IS IMPERFECT. I WASN'T SURE THAT SHE'D HOLD UP VERY LONG. THE GIRL SHOULDN'T HAVE TO SEE HER MOTHER LIKE THIS, SO I'M QUITE GLAD YOU PUSHED HER AWAY.
URRRRGH...
IT WAS A SEPARATE BATCH, YOU SEE, FROM WHAT I USED ON YOUR FRIEND...
WHO KNOWS WHEN THAT ONE WILL FAIL.
ANY MINUTE NOW, MAYBE?!
EEEEENOUGH!

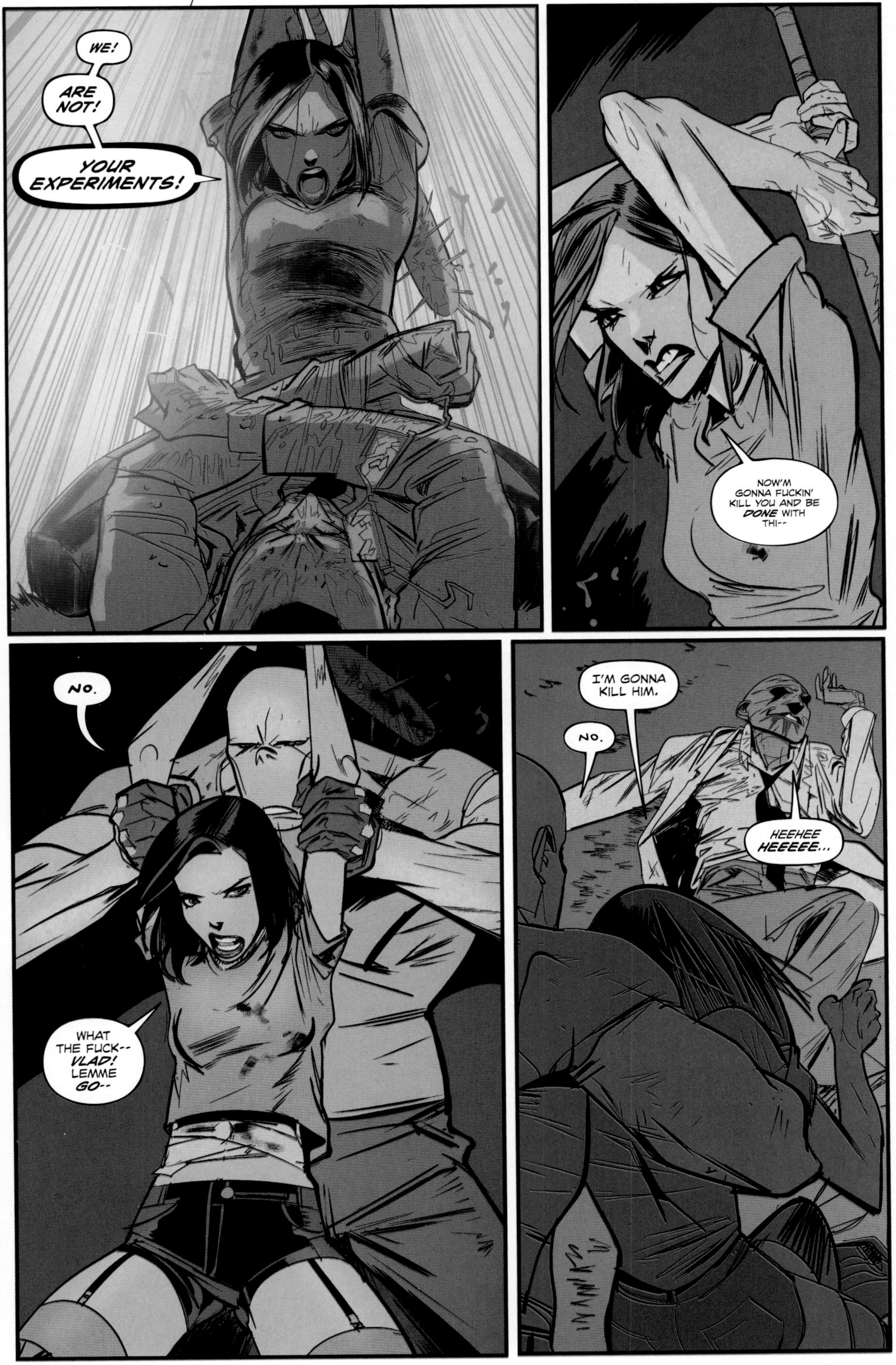
WE!
ARE NOT!
YOUR EXPERIMENTS!
NOW'M GONNA FUCKIN' KILL YOU AND BE DONE WITH THI--
NO.
WHAT THE FUCK-- VLAD! LEMME GO--
I'M GONNA KILL HIM.
NO.
HEEHEE HEEEEE...

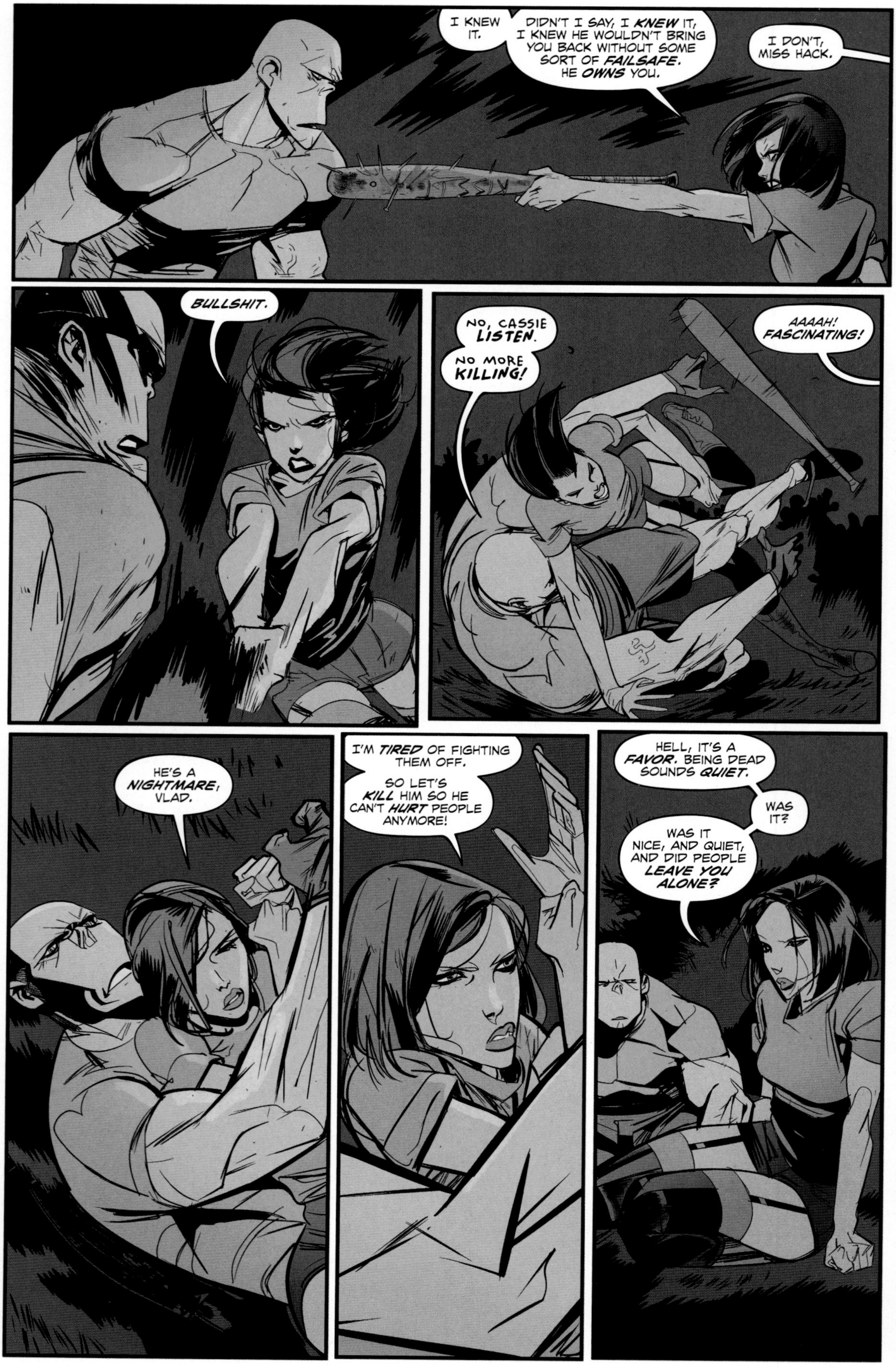

I KNEW IT.
DIDN'T I SAY, I KNEW IT, I KNEW HE WOULDN'T BRING YOU BACK WITHOUT SOME SORT OF FAILSAFE. HE OWNS YOU.
I DON'T, MISS HACK.
BULLSHIT.
NO, CASSIE LISTEN.
NO MORE KILLING!
AAAAH! FASCINATING!
HE'S A NIGHTMARE, VLAD.
I'M TIRED OF FIGHTING THEM OFF.
SO LET'S KILL HIM SO HE CAN'T HURT PEOPLE ANYMORE!
HELL, IT'S A FAVOR. BEING DEAD SOUNDS QUIET.
WAS IT?
WAS IT NICE, AND QUIET, AND DID PEOPLE LEAVE YOU ALONE?

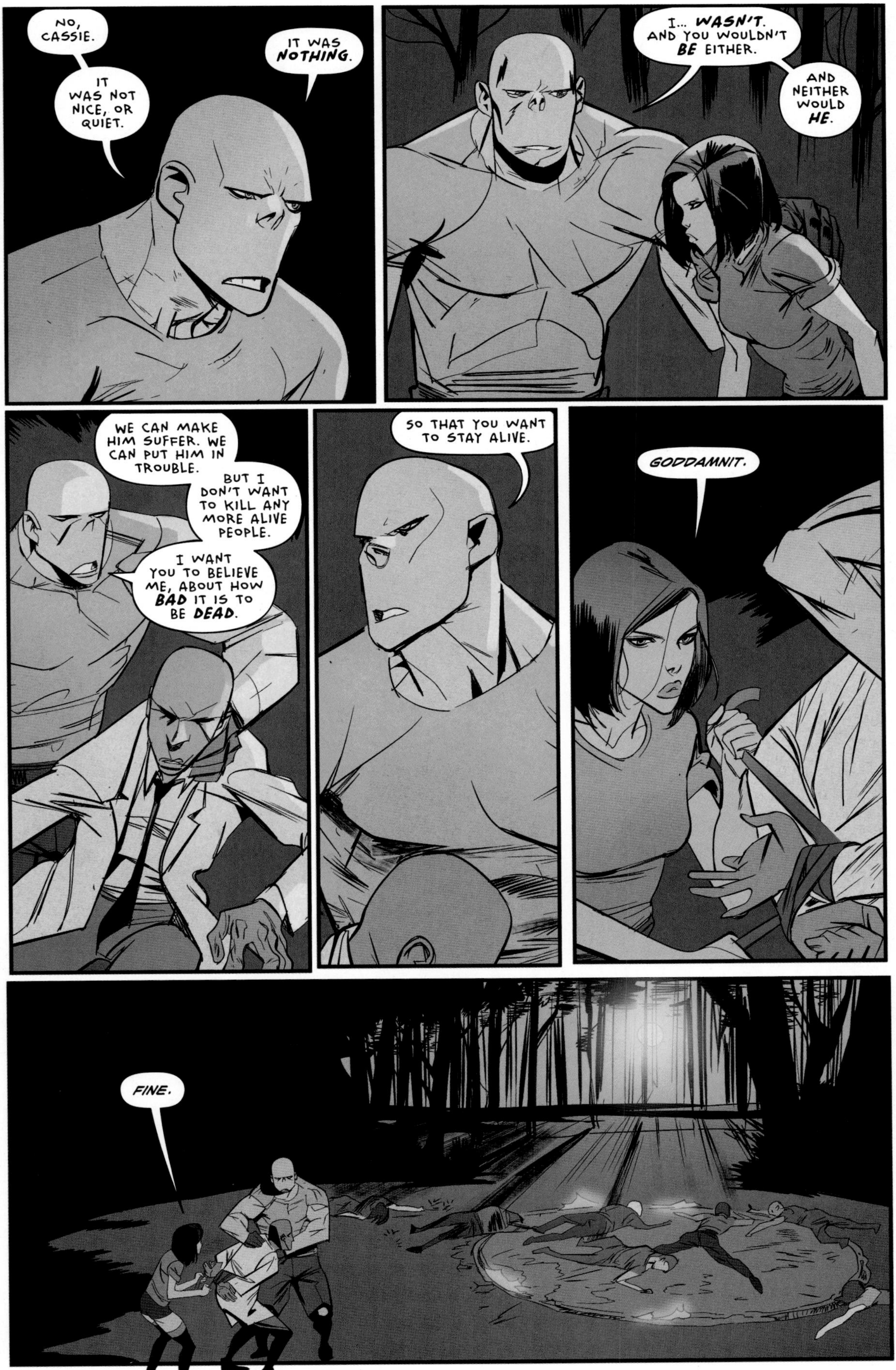
NO, CASSIE.
IT WAS NOT NICE, OR QUIET.
IT WAS NOTHING.
I... WASN'T. AND YOU WOULDN'T BE EITHER.
AND NEITHER WOULD HE.
WE CAN MAKE HIM SUFFER. WE CAN PUT HIM IN TROUBLE.
BUT I DON'T WANT TO KILL ANY MORE ALIVE PEOPLE.
I WANT YOU TO BELIEVE ME, ABOUT HOW BAD IT IS TO BE DEAD.
SO THAT YOU WANT TO STAY ALIVE.
GODDAMNIT.
FINE.

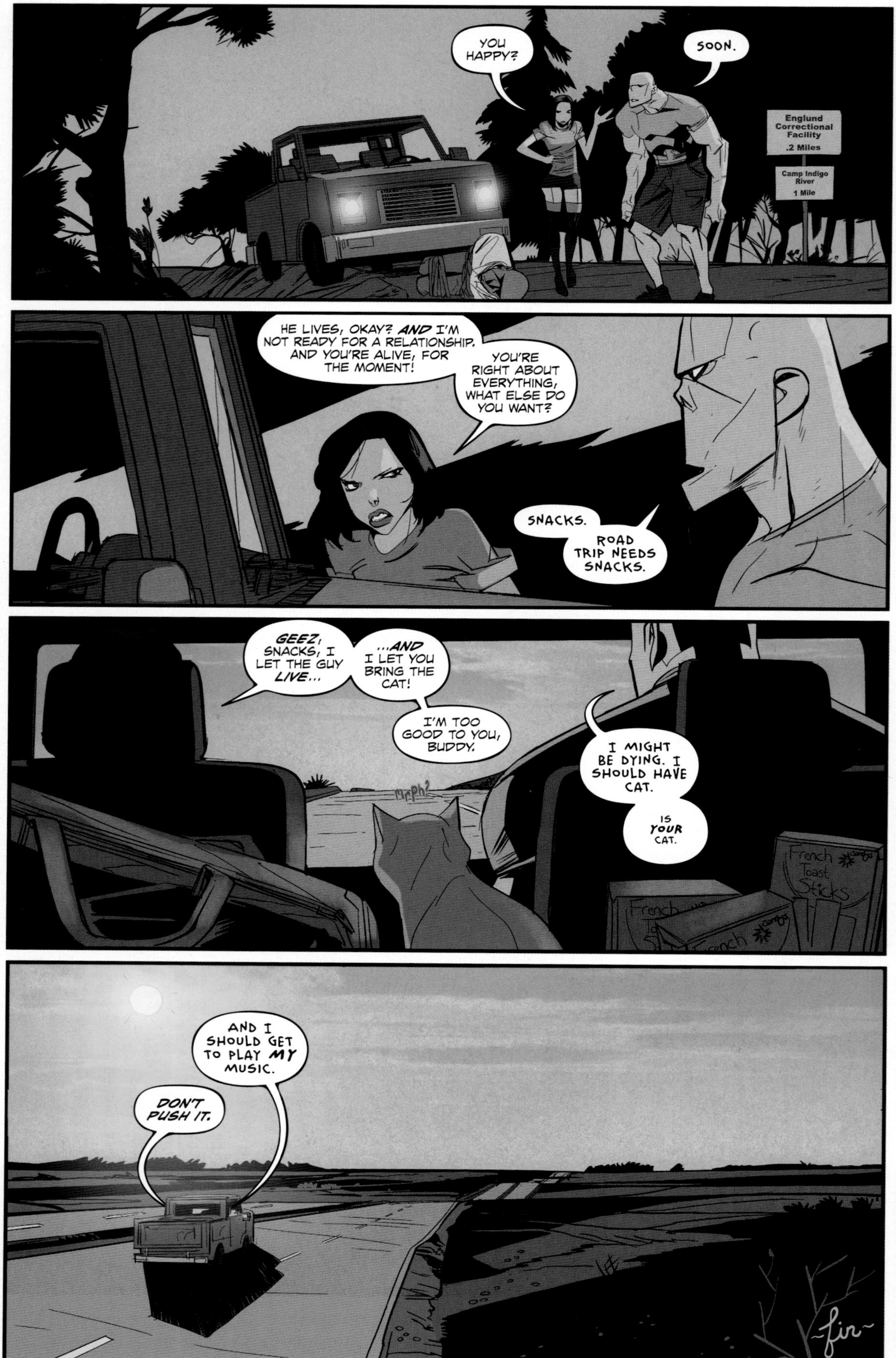
YOU HAPPY?
SOON.
Englund Correctional Facility .2 Miles
Camp Indigo River 1 Mile
HE LIVES, OKAY? AND I'M NOT READY FOR A RELATIONSHIP. AND YOU'RE ALIVE, FOR THE MOMENT!
YOU'RE RIGHT ABOUT EVERYTHING, WHAT ELSE DO YOU WANT?
SNACKS.
ROAD TRIP NEEDS SNACKS.
GEEZ, SNACKS, I LET THE GUY LIVE...
...AND I LET YOU BRING THE CAT!
I'M TOO GOOD TO YOU, BUDDY.
mrph?
I MIGHT BE DYING. I SHOULD HAVE CAT.
IS YOUR CAT.
French Toast Sticks
AND I SHOULD GET TO PLAY MY MUSIC.
DON'T PUSH IT.
~fin~

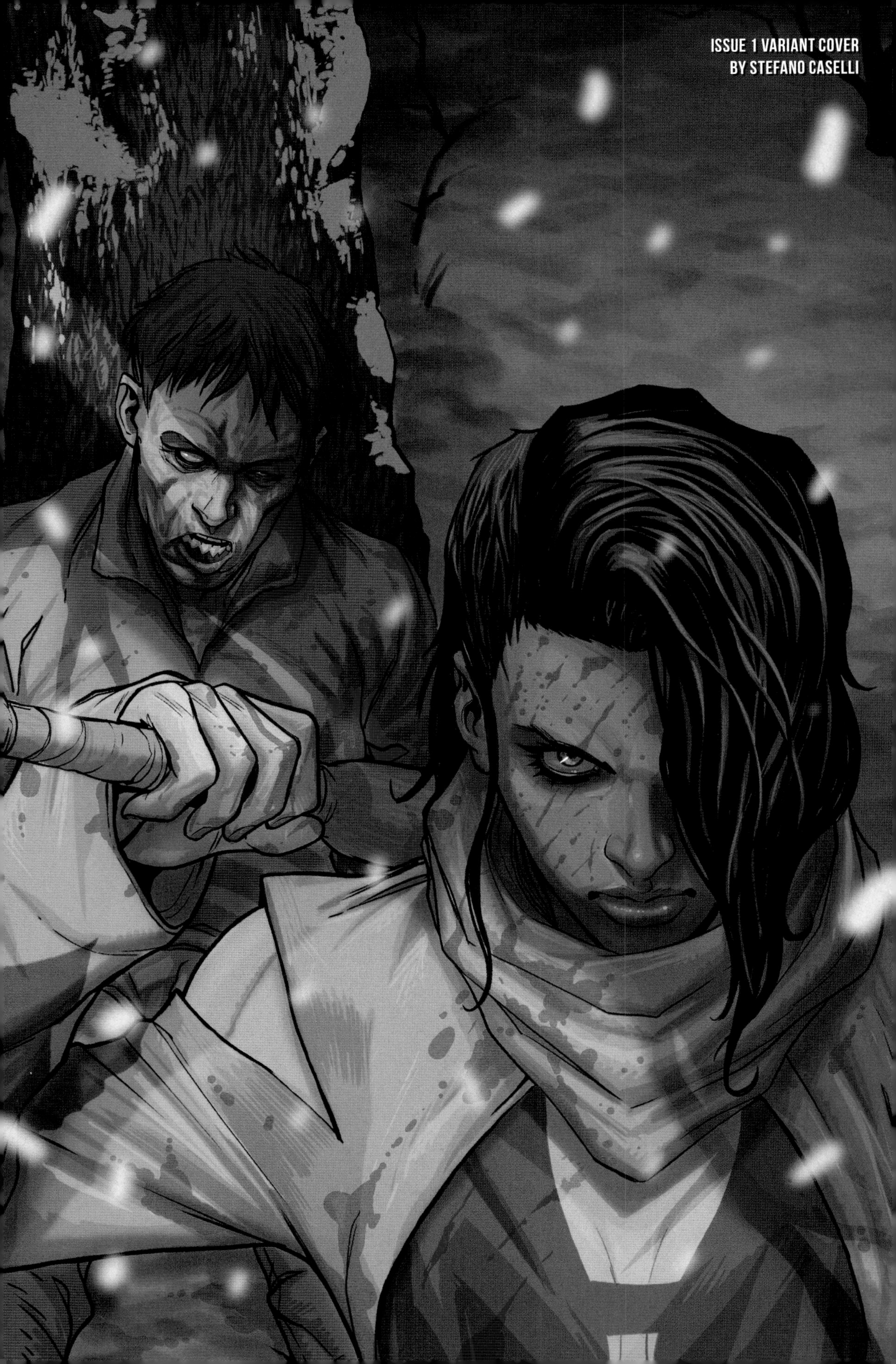

ISSUE 1 VARIANT COVER
BY STEFANO CASELLI

ISSUE 1 VARIANT COVER
BY JIM RUGG

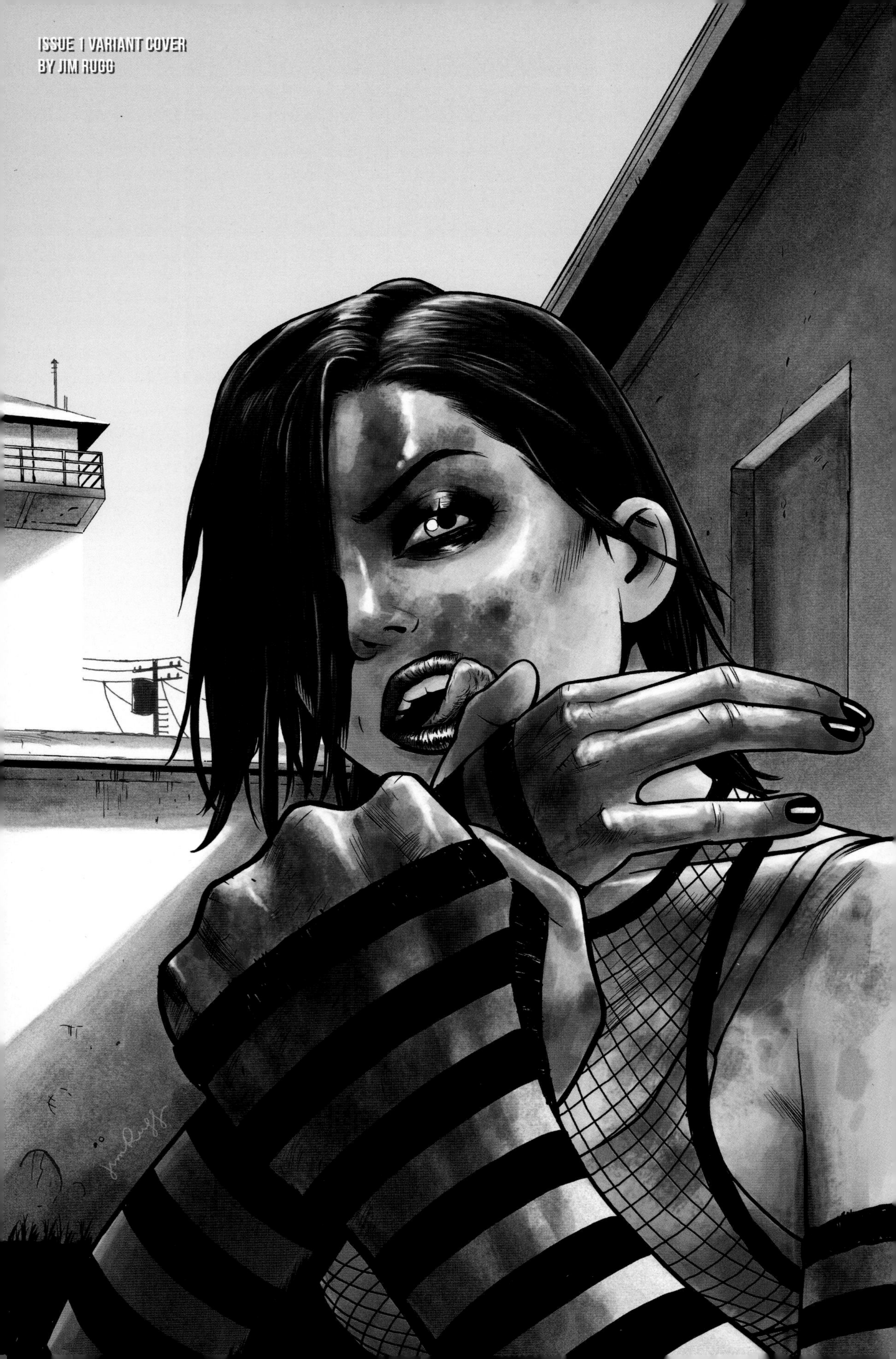

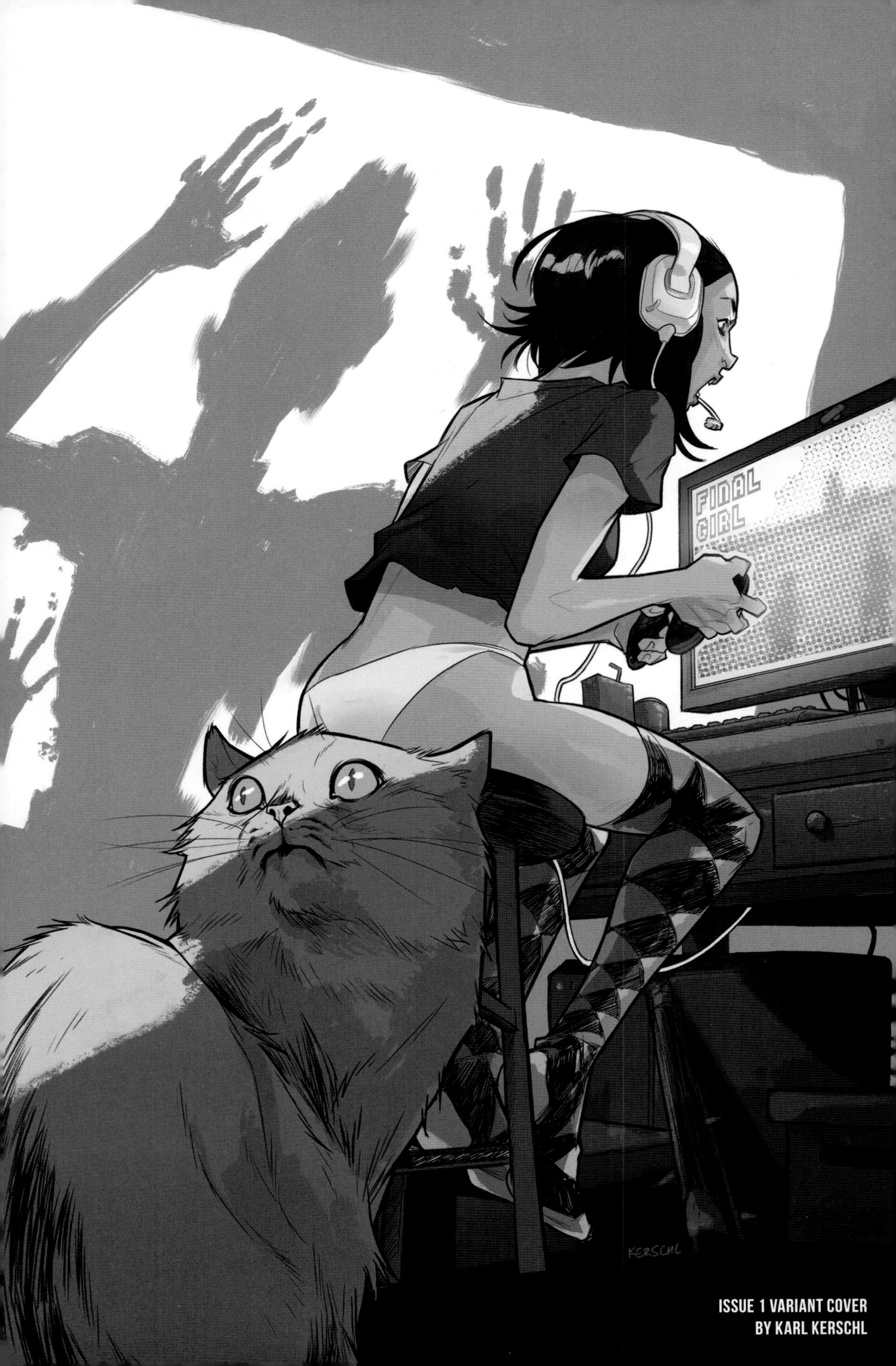
FINAL
GIRL
KERSCHL

ISSUE 1 VARIANT COVER
BY KARL KERSCHL

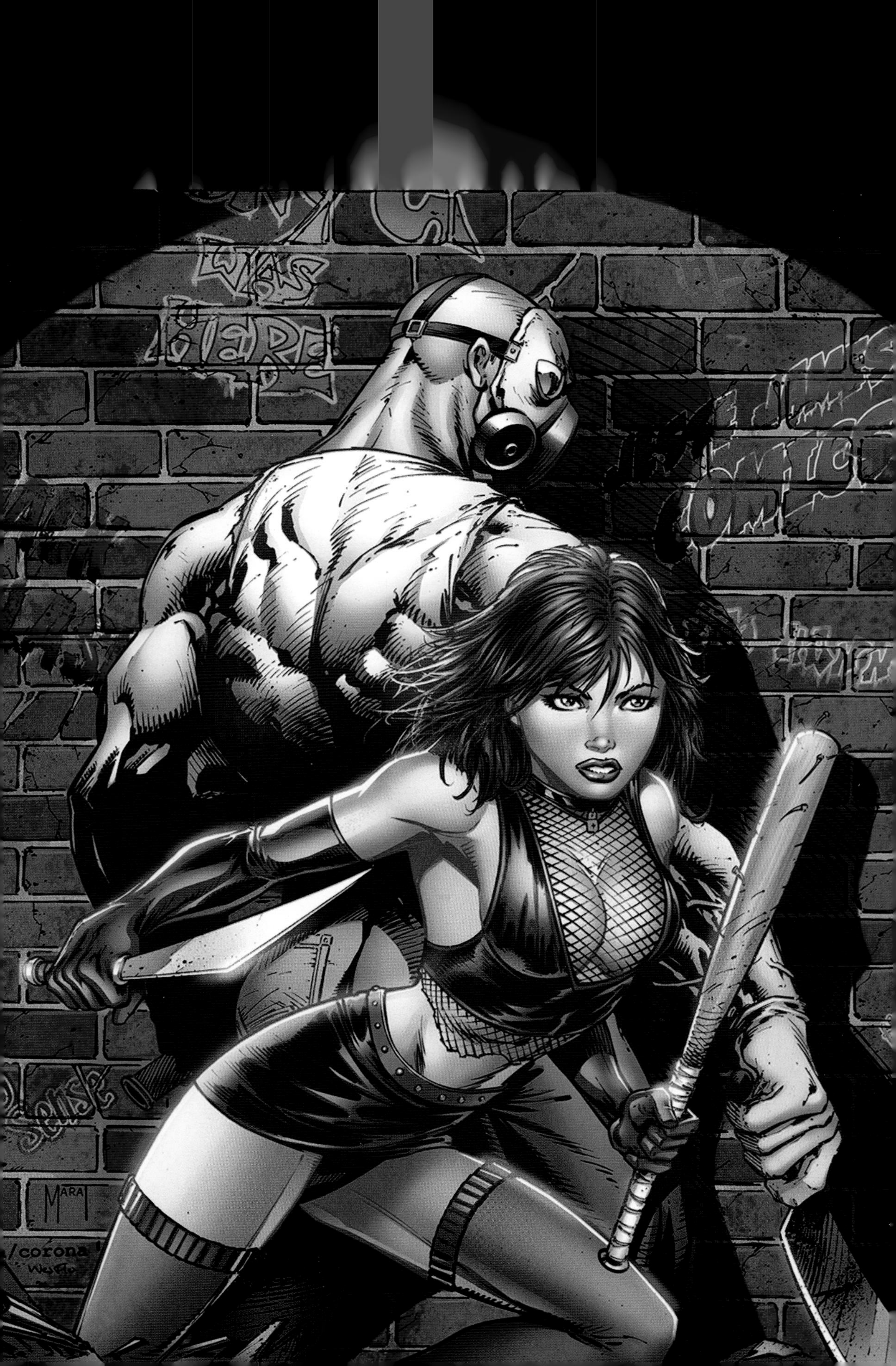
MARA
/corona

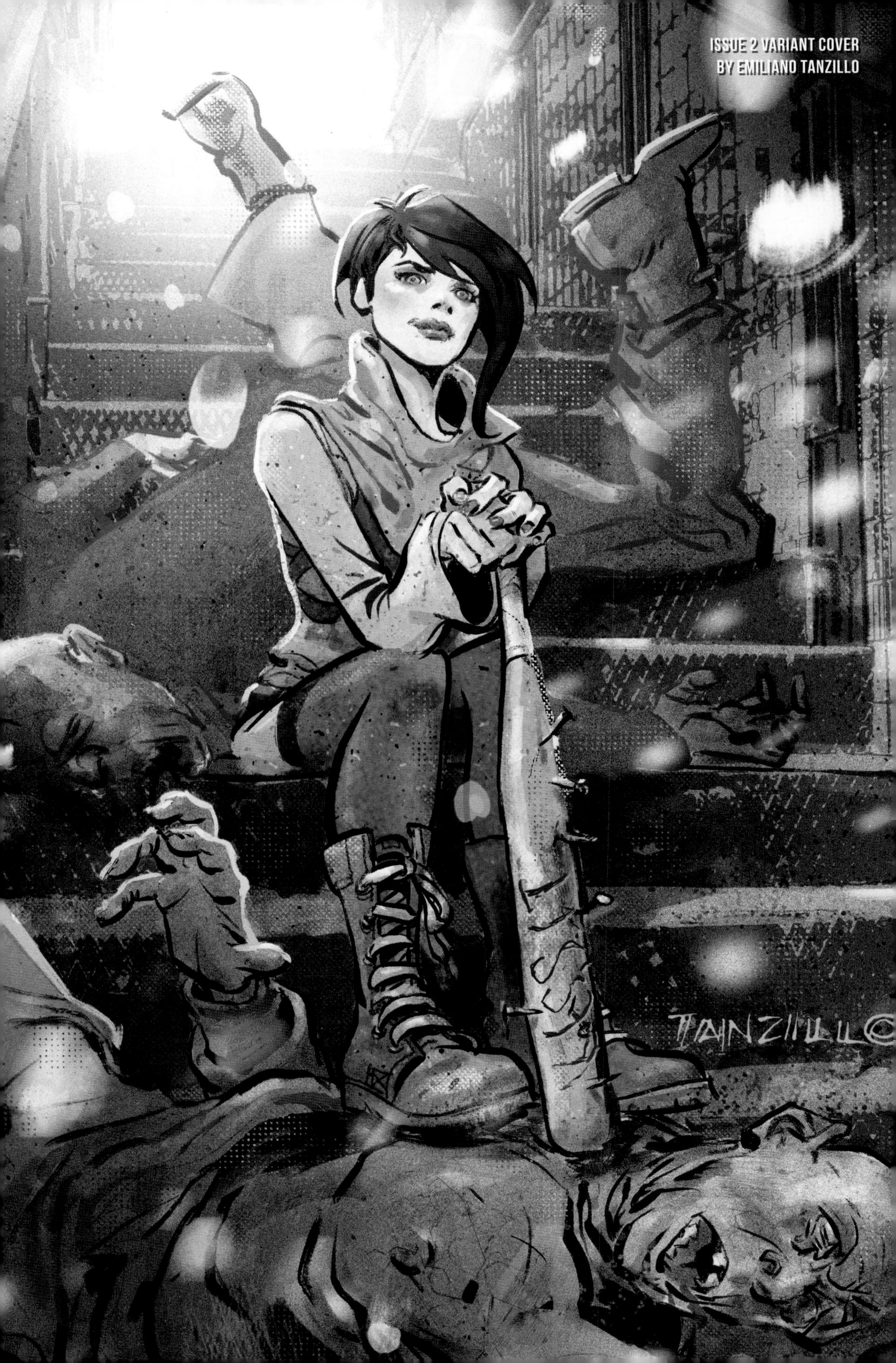
TANZILLO

ISSUE 2 VARIANT COVER
BY EMILIANO TANZILLO

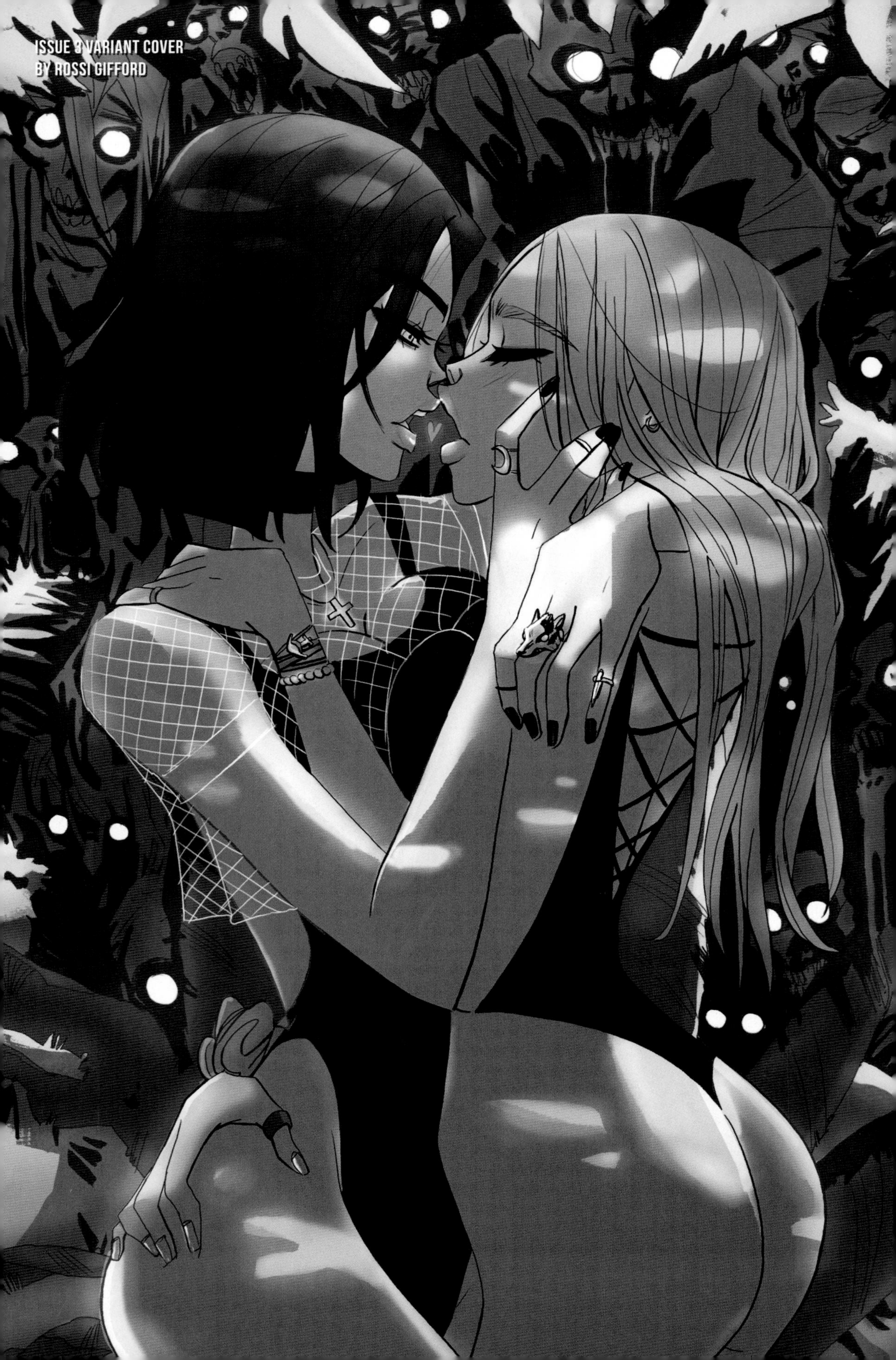

ISSUE 3 VARIANT COVER
BY ROSSI GIFFORD

ISSUE 4 VARIANT COVER
BY EMILIANO TANZILLO

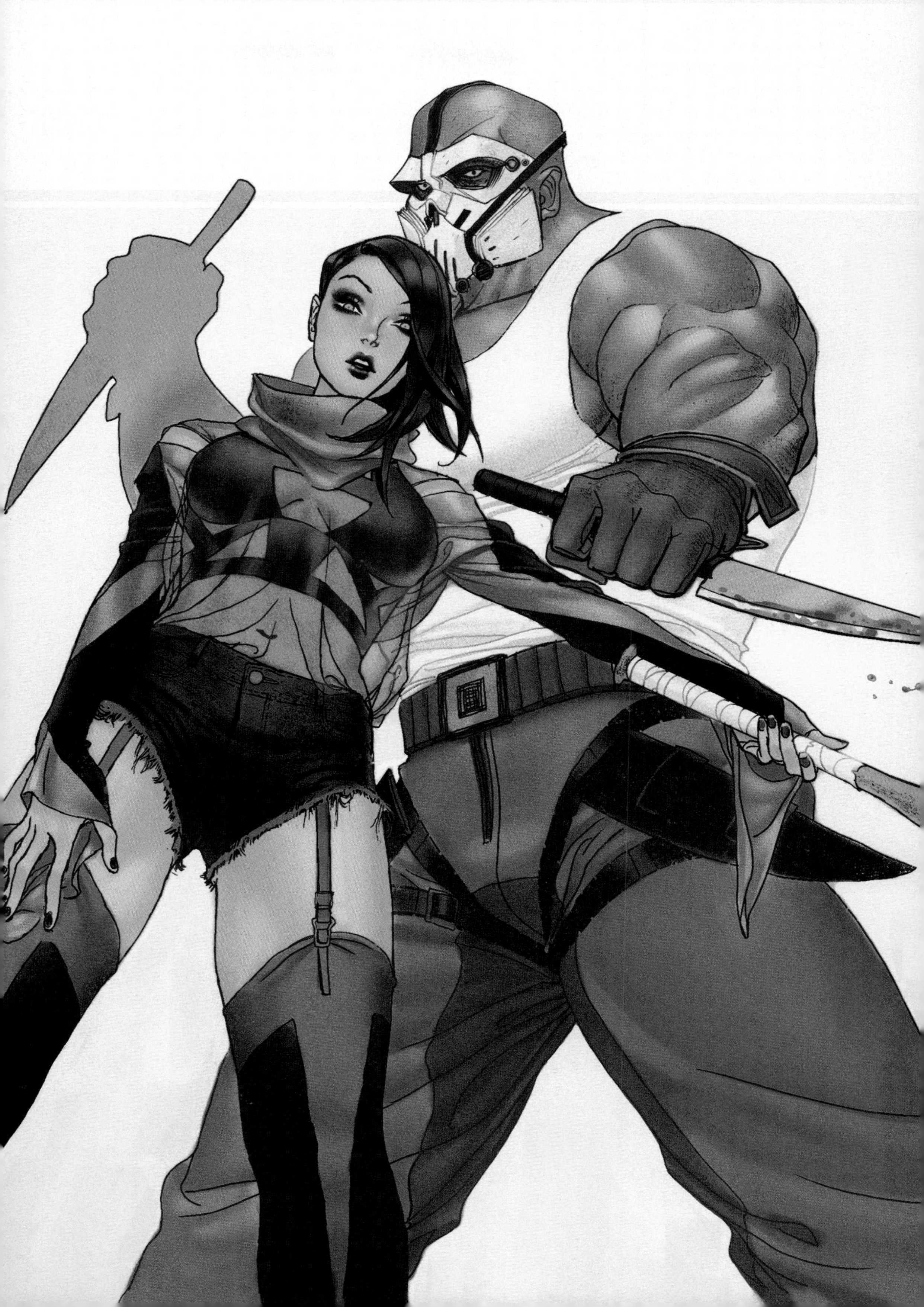

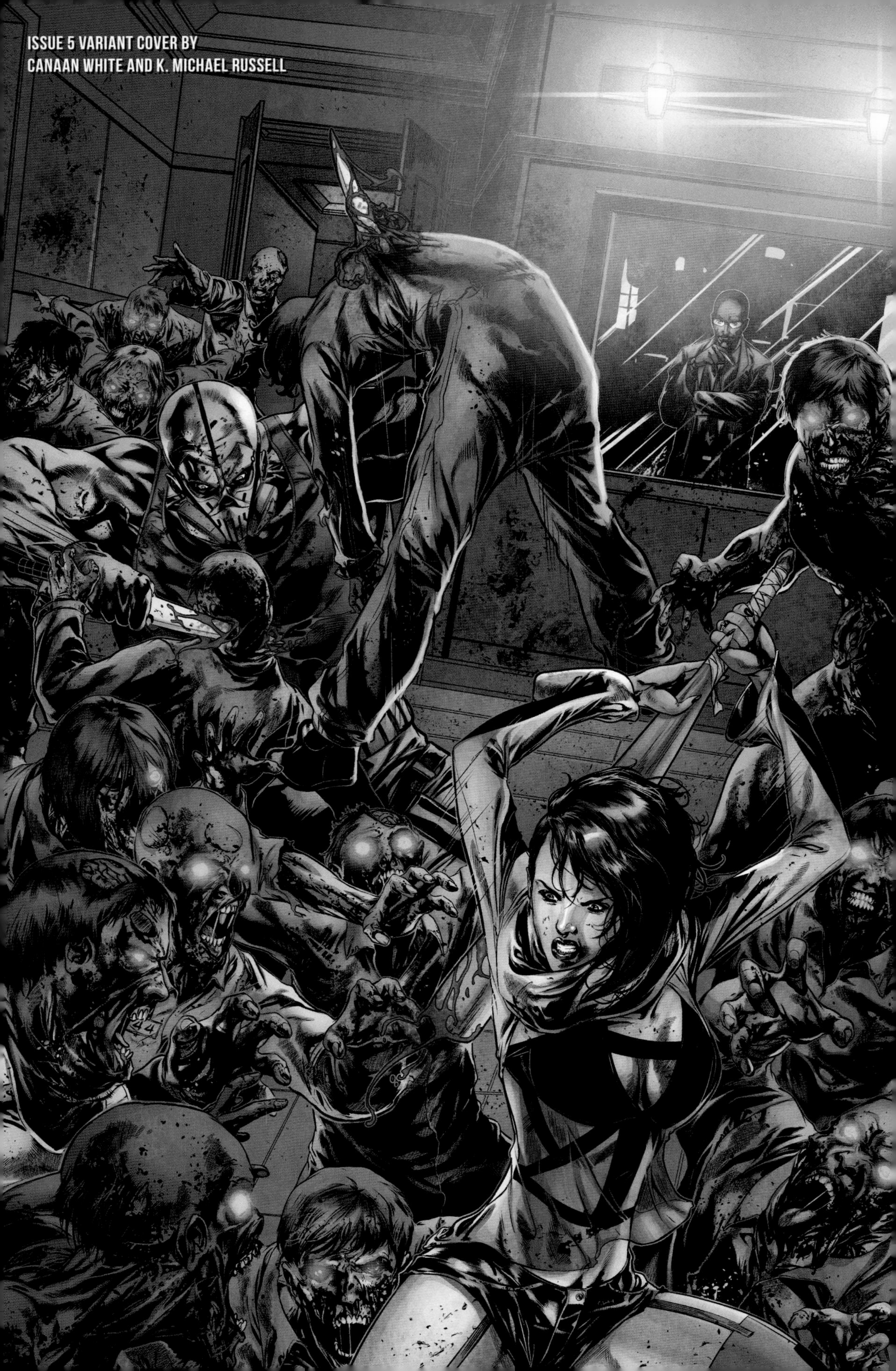

ISSUE 5 VARIANT COVER BY
CANAAN WHITE AND K. MICHAEL RUSSELL

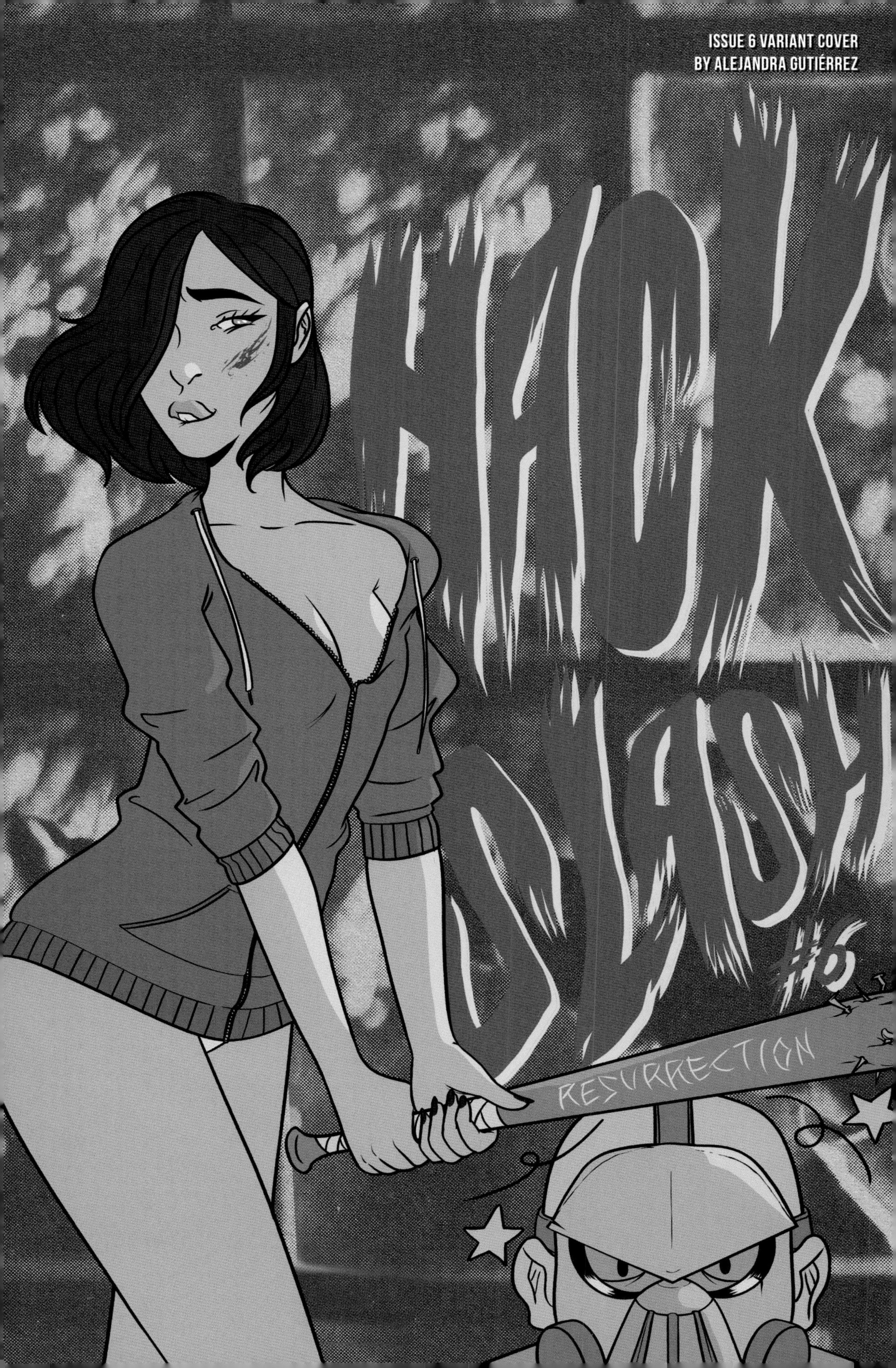
HACK
SLASH
#6
RESURRECTION
ISSUE 6 VARIANT COVER
BY ALEJANDRA GUTIÉRREZ

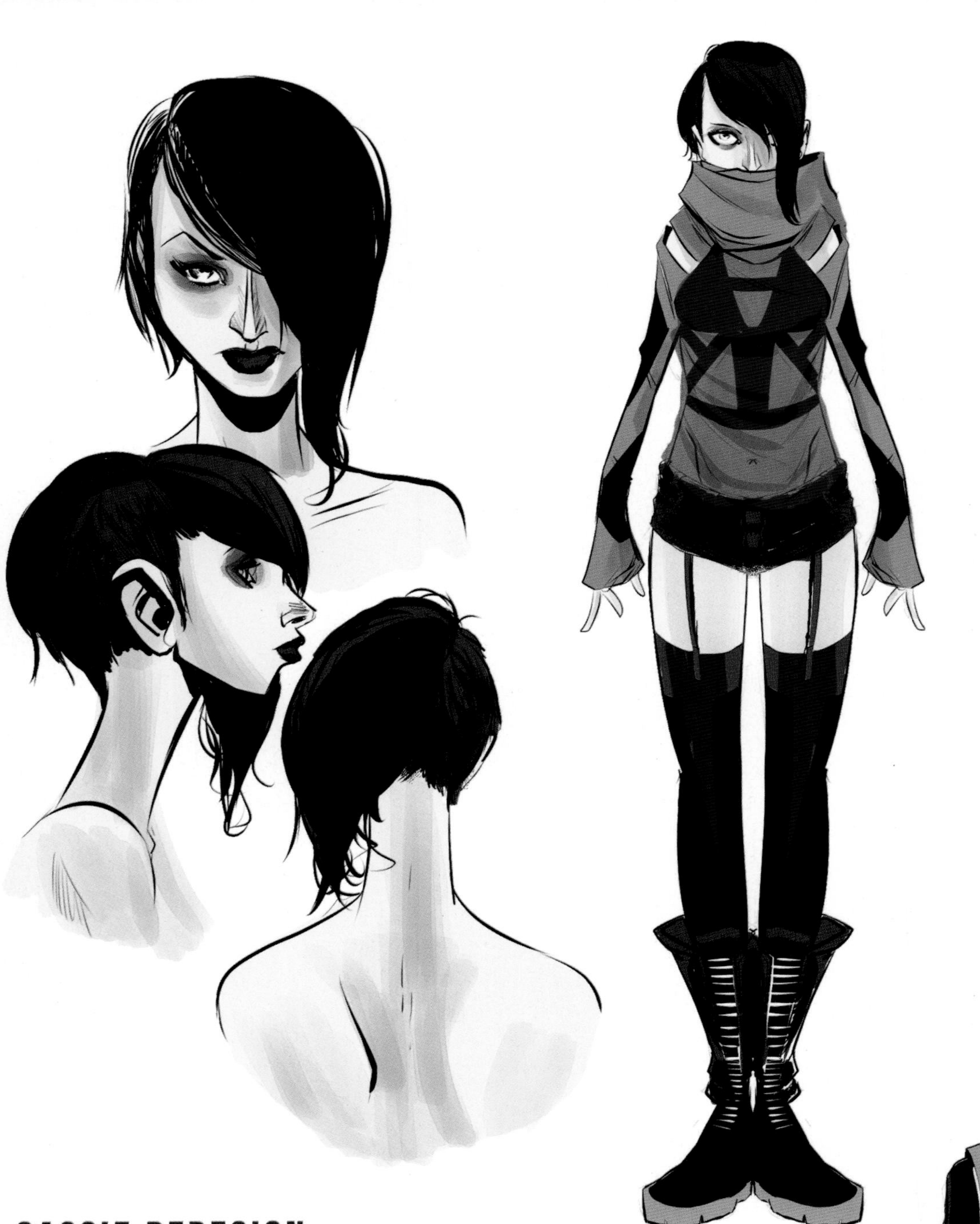

CASSIE REDESIGN

BY ROBBI RODRIGUEZ

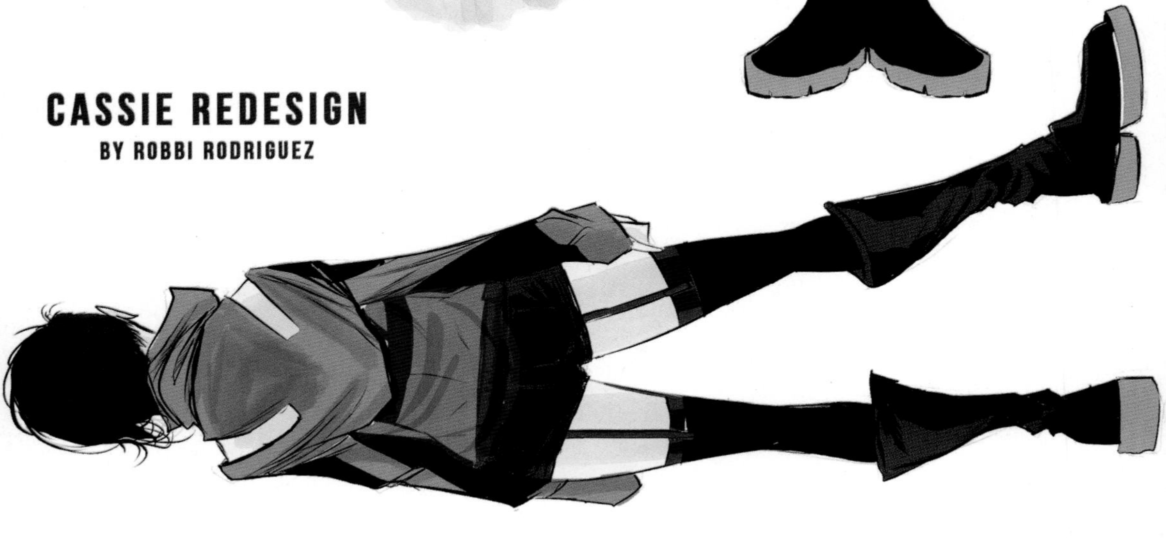

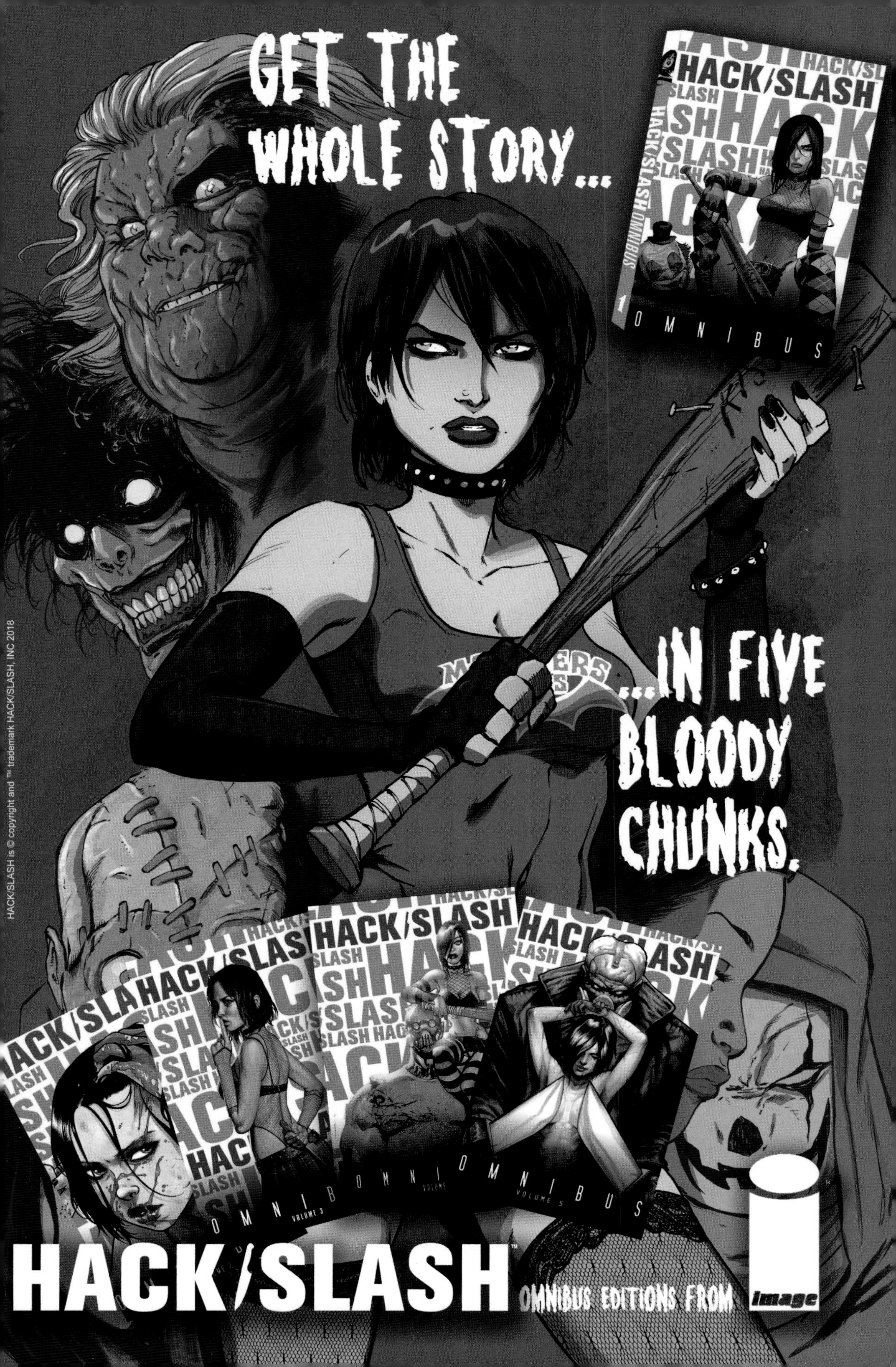
GET THE
WHOLE STORY...
...IN FIVE
BLOODY
CHUNKS.
HACK/SLASH™
OMNIBUS EDITIONS FROM
image
HACK/SLASH is © copyright and ™ trademark HACK/SLASH, INC 2018

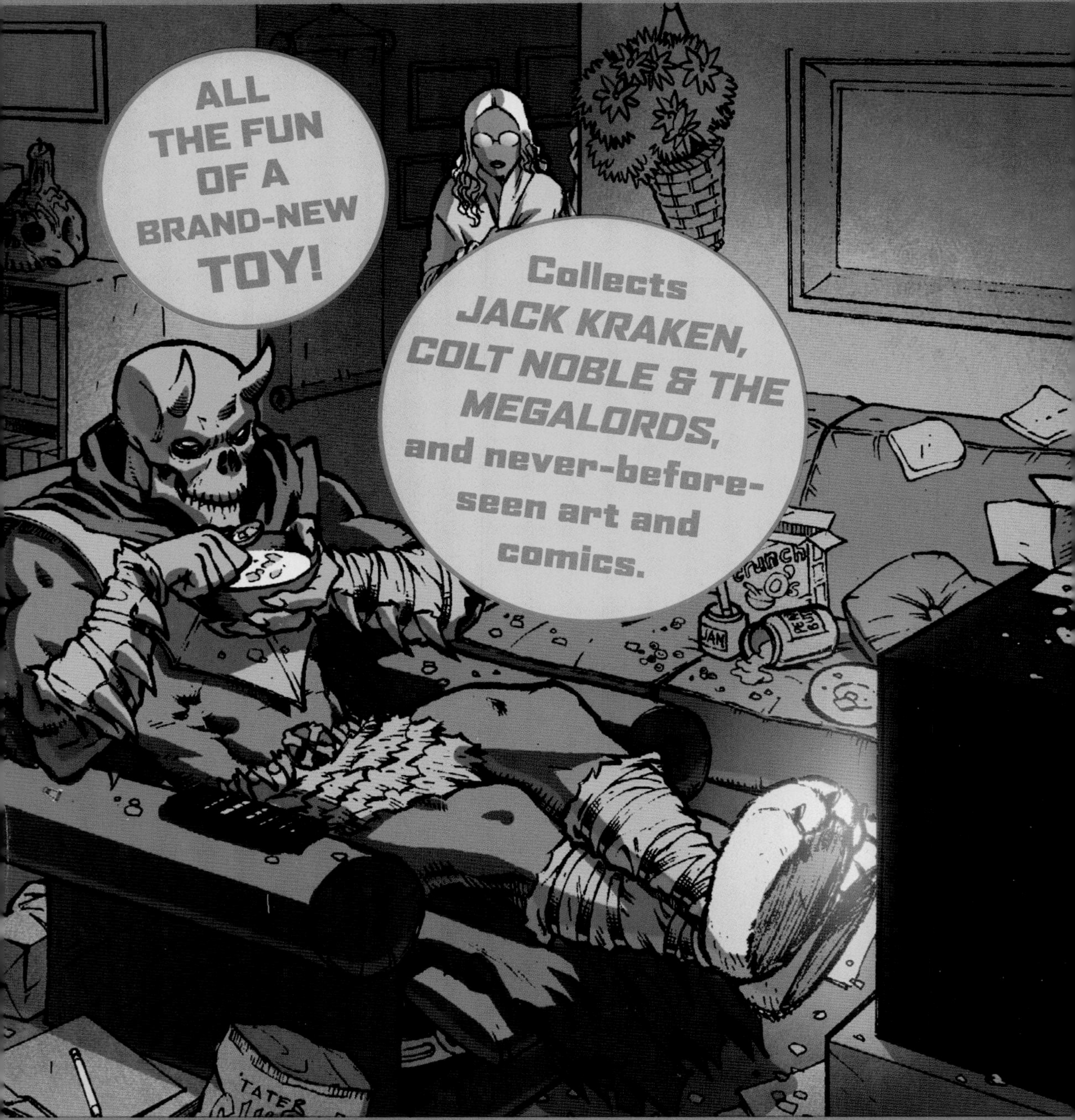
ALL THE FUN OF A BRAND-NEW TOY!
Collects JACK KRAKEN, COLT NOBLE & THE MEGALORDS, and never-before-seen art and comics.
crunch
JAN
TATER

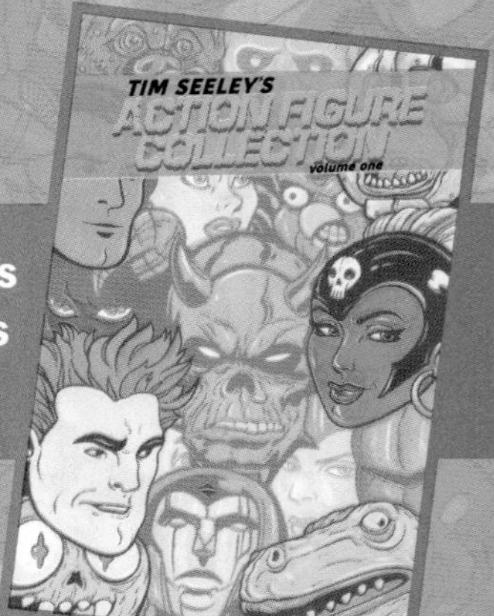
TIM SEELEY'S
ACTION FIGURE COLLECTION
volume one